The Forgotten Room

The Forgotten Room

Karen
White

Beatriz
Williams

Lauren
Willig

 NEW AMERICAN LIBRARY

NEW AMERICAN LIBRARY
Published by New American Library,
an imprint of Penguin Random House LLC
375 Hudson Street, New York, New York 10014

This book is an original publication of New American Library.

First Printing, January 2016

For more information about Penguin Random House, visit penguin.com.

LIBRARY OF CONGRESS CATALOGING-IN-PUBLICATION DATA:

White, Karen (Karen S.)
The forgotten room / Karen White, Beatriz Williams, Lauren Willig.
pages cm
ISBN 978-0-451-47462-9 (hardcover)
1. Women physicians—Fiction.   2. Mothers and daughters—Fiction.   3. Family secrets—Fiction.
I. Williams, Beatriz, author.   II. Willig, Lauren, author.   III. Title.
PS3623.H5776F67 2016
813'.6—dc23   2015032901

Printed in the United States of America
10 9 8 7 6 5 4 3 2 1

Designed by Laura K. Corless

To red wine, good friends, and old houses

Acknowledgments

This book could not have happened without the support of our fearless editor, Cindy Hwang, and the terrific team at NAL, who believed in this unconventional book since its inception.

Thanks also to Alice's Tea Cup—the marvelous Manhattan tearoom that saw the three of us huddled over tea and delicious scones while we hashed out the story outline. A big nod goes to the Inn at Palmetto Bluff for our plotting time, caffeine, and stronger beverages while we were in the throes of deadline dementia. And, of course, a huge thank-you to the Hospital for Special Surgery for letting us roam around, take pictures, and populate their space with imaginary people. To Anne O'Connor—thank you for all your memories of New York City during World War II and for all the time you spent looking up extraneous details. You are the perfect research assistant.

Last but not least, thank you to our husbands, children, and assorted pets for their patience and understanding while we spent time with all those people who existed only in our imaginations until we could get them on the page.

The Forgotten Room

One

⟨ornament⟩

Kate

The patter of rain against the blacked-out stained glass dome above where I sat numbed me like a hypnotist's gold watch. Neither the hard marble step beneath me nor the delicately carved staircase spindle pressed against my forehead was enough to override the lullaby effect of the raindrops. I tried to focus on the ornate staircase of the old mansion, to study the fine architectural details of the structure that even the conversion into a hospital couldn't mask.

I recalled the walks I took as a child down Sixty-ninth Street with my mother, walks that weren't convenient to our neighborhood but instead appeared to be a destination rather than a happenstance. We'd cross the road and pause, looking up at the seven-story stone mansion, the elongated windows staring blankly out at us, seemingly as curious as I was about why we were there. My mother had once told me that she'd lived there briefly when the building had been a boardinghouse for respectable women. But she'd never mentioned why she felt compelled to return to the spot across the street again and again, until her death three years before. It had seemed almost serendipitous when I had accepted the position at Stornaway Hospital following medical school, almost as if my mother had planned it all along.

My gaze settled on the far wall, on a bas-relief depicting a recurring motif of Saint George slaying the dragon, which I'd noticed throughout the building since I'd begun working at the hospital nearly a year before. My eyelids fluttered closed for a moment, watching the scene against the dark backdrop of my lids, imagining I could see the saint and the dragon stepping from the wall and writhing on the tiled floor in their perpetual battle.

I forced my eyes open, if only to assure myself that the stone adversaries were still stationary. Holding on to the banister, I pulled myself to stand. I was so very, very tired. It was my second double shift in a row, and I doubted it would be my last. The city's hospitals were being flooded with the arrival of wounded soldiers from the recent invasion of the French coast. With our ranks already spread thin by doctors enlisting and heading overseas, those remaining were working hours rarely seen past medical school.

The blare of an approaching siren helped me to stand up straighter, to compose myself before any of the nurses could find me in such mental disarray. As the only female doctor on staff, it was hard enough maintaining the persona of a woman with no feelings or personal needs in front of the male doctors. It was nearly impossible in front of the nurses. If they'd asked me why I'd become a doctor, I would have told them. But they didn't ask. They seemed to be of like minds when it came to me—I was a doctor because I thought I was too good to be a nurse.

There were a few who were deferential to my status of doctor regardless of my gender, but the rest were too traditional, having worked hard to come up the ranks in nursing, to consider me to be any more than an upstart.

I almost laughed at the thought, recalling all the bedpans I'd changed and sutures I'd sewn due to the abysmal shortage of healthcare workers. But the laugh died in my throat when I realized the siren was getting louder, as if it was headed in my direction. I inwardly cursed the blackout curtains and painted windows that obscured all views from inside the hospital with the same effectiveness as blacking out the city's skyline from potential attackers.

Fully awake now, I ran down the spiral staircase, past elegant rooms retrofitted into surgical theaters, a laboratory, and a convalescents' dormitory brimming at full capacity, my white coat flapping against my bare legs. It had been years since I'd had a good pair of nylons, but I'd seen too much of war to mourn their absence.

I was the first one to reach the foyer, grabbing a flashlight on the hall table and flipping it on. The inner doors to the vestibule were temporarily affixed to the wall, requiring only a swift pull on the outer doors to access the outside. A strong gust of rain knocked into me, effectively soaking me and plastering my coat and dress to my body.

I ran down the slippery stone steps toward the ambulance as it pulled to the curb, its headlights with the tops half painted black, its flashing lights extinguished. The driver, a large man with sad eyes peering out from beneath the brim of his dripping hat, stepped out of the ambulance.

"Wait," I said, blocking his path, having to shout to be heard over the din of the rain as it hammered the ambulance and streets. "We have no more room. We even have patients on cots in the dining room. We are beyond capacity."

"Just following orders, ma'am. We got an officer here right off the boat who's in pretty bad shape. They told me to bring him here."

"But . . ."

The man walked past me as if I were a small yipping dog just as Dr. Howard Greeley walked calmly down the stairs with an umbrella and approached the back of the ambulance. His bug eyes raked over me, taking in my sodden appearance and clothes, which had melded to my body. He didn't offer shelter under his umbrella.

With a quick shake of disapproval, he turned to the driver. "What do we have here?"

"Officer, sir. He's in bad shape."

"We'll find room for him." Dr. Greeley sent me a withering look.

Both men continued to ignore me as the ambulance doors were thrown open by an orderly, allowing us to peer inside to where a form lay huddled beneath a blanket. Despite the June heat, the body twitched as if seized by chills.

As the orderlies began to prepare the patient, Dr. Greeley was handed a folder that I assumed was the patient's medical records. No longer willing to be a bystander, I grabbed the folder, then moved to stand under the doctor's umbrella. Ignoring his scowl, I said, "Good idea. You hold the umbrella while I look at this."

Trying not to drip onto the pages, I skimmed the notes inside, paraphrasing for Dr. Greeley. "He sustained a bullet wound to his leg at Cherbourg—damage to the bone. Field doctor wanted to amputate, but"—my gaze drifted to the top of the page, where the soldier's name was printed—"Captain Ravenel talked them out of it. They debrided the wound and applied a topical sulfanilamide, but lack of time prohibited delaying primary closure." I felt my lips tighten over my teeth, understanding now how the wound had become infected. "The apparent effectiveness of the sulfanilamide led them to the conclusion that he was well enough to be stitched up and put on a ship home, seeing as how his leg, assuming it recovers, won't be much use to an infantryman."

I held the flashlight higher as I scanned down to the last paragraph, written in another hand and presumably by the ship's surgeon. "A piece of bone fragment or another foreign body must still be lodged in the leg, causing the infection, but because of a scarcity of penicillin on the ship, the captain said he'd wait for surgery until he got stateside." I closed the folder. *Fool*, I thought, but with a tinge of admiration. "You're a real hero, Captain Ravenel," I said softly.

The orderlies began removing the stretcher from the ambulance, eliciting a groan from its inhabitant. The exposed part of the blanket quickly darkened to a muddy brown from the rain, and, rather than wrest the umbrella from Dr. Greeley, I thrust the folder and flashlight at him before shedding my white coat, determined to shield the soldier from any further harm.

As the orderlies carried the stretcher up the steps toward the door, I did my best to block the patient from the teeming rain, succeeding only marginally due to the saturated nature of my coat. I couldn't see his face, but I leaned down to where it would be positioned on the stretcher and spoke to him. "Captain Ravenel, I am Dr. Kate Schuyler and you're at Stornaway Hospital in New York City. We are going to take very good care of you."

It was my standard refrain to each and every patient who came through the elegant brass and wrought-iron doors, but for some reason it seemed this soldier needed to hear those words more than most.

Two nurses held the doors as the orderlies brought in the stretcher, then looked at Dr. Greeley for instructions. "Take him to surgical theater one. It's the only remaining bed we have. We'll need to examine him first, of course, but my bet is we're going to have to take off his leg."

"No."

We looked at each other in surprise, wondering where the seemingly disembodied voice had come from.

"No," the voice came again, yet this time it was accompanied by a firm grip on my wrist, the fingers strong and warm.

For the first time, I looked down into the face of Captain Ravenel, and the air between us stilled. He was the most beautiful man I'd ever seen, with eyes the color of winter grass illuminated under fine dark brows and straight black hair. His skin, though drawn and pale around his mouth, was deeply tanned.

But it wasn't even his looks that made it impossible for me to glance away. It was the way he was looking at me. As if he knew me.

"Don't let them take my leg," he said, speaking only to me. Sweat beaded his forehead and the chills continued, yet his plea did not seem to come from delirium. "Please," he added softly, his eyes boring into mine. Then his grip slipped from my wrist until his arm lay useless at his side, his eyes closed.

"Operating room one, please," Dr. Greeley repeated as if he hadn't heard the man's plea.

A nurse led the way toward the small elevator.

"No," I said, as surprised as everyone else that I'd said the word aloud. I faced Dr. Greeley. "We should clear up any infection before we can operate, and that can take days. He can have my room."

Because of my long hours at the hospital, I'd been given an attic room on the seventh floor of the building. It had been meant to be temporary, but when my apartment lease had come due, I'd allowed it to expire, realizing that I was wasting rent money by sleeping there only rarely. I had no remaining family, and it seemed almost natural to move into the top room, where I could pretend, if just for a little while, that this was my home and that I had family in the rooms below.

The room itself was currently used as a storeroom. But with its domed skylight and rows of tall, fanned windows, I imagined that the room had once had a much more glamorous existence.

"That's hardly appropriate," Dr. Greeley said, looking affronted, as if he'd never made inappropriate suggestions to me.

"I'll move into the overnight nurses' room. Even if I have to sleep on blankets on the floor—it's just for a little while."

He frowned. "I can't be running up and down those stairs all day to see to him. He'll be much better off in the operating room."

"Then I will," I said, sensing the restlessness of the stretcher-bearers as they waited. I wasn't sure why I was fighting so hard for this man I didn't even know. But I remembered his eyes, and the feel of his fingers on my bare skin. Remembered the way he seemed to recognize me.

"After we examine him and begin treatment, we will set him up in my room and I will be responsible for his care. And if I cannot clear up the infection and his leg needs to be amputated, then you will have my full support."

Slightly mollified and delighted to have the opportunity to watch me fail, Dr. Greeley gave a curt nod. "Fine. Let's take him to the operating room to examine him, and if all looks well we'll move him to the top of the building. Just know that he is your full responsibility along with all of your other duties. It would be a shame if his condition worsens because you are not up to the task."

"I won't shirk my duties," I said, wondering at my vehemence. I looked down at the officer again, surprised to find his eyes open. But they were glazed, and even though he was looking at me, I wasn't sure he was seeing me.

"Victorine," he said softly before his eyelids slowly fluttered closed.

I watched as the stretcher disappeared into the elevator, feeling suddenly bereft.

Two

DECEMBER 1892

Olive

On the night Olive Van Alan discovered what lay at the top of the mansion on East Sixty-ninth Street, she was planning a different kind of mischief altogether. But that was how these things happened, wasn't it? You were always too busy looking in the wrong direction.

So there Olive lay in her narrow bed, turning over her plans, as blind as a mole in the darkened room. If she felt any foreboding at all, it was focused on the housekeeper, who was making her usual final inspection down the corridor—petticoats rustling starchily against her rumored legs, knuckles rapping against the doors, each crisp *Good night, Mona* and *Good night, Ellen* followed by the automatic *Good night, Mrs. Keane*—before she locked the vestibule behind her.

The lock, Olive had been told, was for her own protection. Mrs. Keane came from England—apparently it was a prestigious thing, in these circles, to have an English housekeeper—and she had explained, in her voice like the cracking of eggs, that the girls were not being locked *in*, goodness no, but rather the outside world and particularly its base male appetites locked *out*.

Olive, as she went about her daily business, encountering males in every corner, had wondered where these base appetites were hidden, and why their owners could not be expected to control them without the support of a stout Yale dead bolt lock—apparently these were nocturnal appetites, as well as base—but she hadn't dared to ask Mrs. Keane outright. *Don't be cheeky,* Mrs. Keane would say, cheekiness being classified among the most subversive and therefore the most dangerous crimes among a domestic staff run along strict English lines.

Mrs. Keane would then crinkle her brow in suspicion and take perhaps a closer look at Olive's well-tended face and soft hands, her careful voice and quick eyes, and that was the last thing Olive needed.

So the lock remained on its guard, and the row of identical little rooms on the sixth floor of the Pratt mansion on Sixty-ninth Street remained about as pregnable to the base male appetite as Miss Ellis's Academy for Young Ladies, where Olive had been sent for her education in a lifetime lived long ago. Then as now, Olive spent those dark hours between lockdown and sleep plotting her escape, like a cat brooding in a window. She counted the minutes that passed since the careful click of Mrs. Keane's shoes had receded down the stairs and out of hearing. She listened to the creak of bedsprings as her fellow housemaids tossed themselves to sleep. She fought the inevitable tide of languor that stole over her like a kind of drunkenness—yes, that was it!—she was plain stone *drunk* on the long day's labor, scrubbing and polishing and making beds and fetching, fetching, fetching, on the double, up and down the enormous marble staircase that wound past seven floors to the stained glass dome at the top of the mansion. The temptation of sleep was like the temptation of oxygen.

So tempting, in fact, that she had given in the previous four nights.

She had woken up bemused and defeated to the unlocking of the vestibule door and the brisk summons from Mrs. Keane.

Olive slid one hand across her body, under the blanket, and pinched her opposite arm, from shoulder to elbow, until the tears started out from her eyes and her mind sprang into a fragile alertness.

The bedsprings were quiet now. The house was quiet, too, so quiet Olive could now pick out the few outside noises: the hum of a gentle rain against the glass dome, a distant argument in someone's garden. The Pratt mansion stood in a residential street, far from the hurly-burly of downtown, but there seemed to be more noise every day, more commerce, and if Olive lay absolutely still, she could feel the creep of the metropolis reaching the Pratt doorstep, reaching rapaciously all the way to the tip of Manhattan island and beyond. New York was a boomtown, New York was where everybody lived or wanted to live, and its lust for fashionable new buildings—unlike the base male appetites—couldn't be contained by any old lock on a vestibule door. Already more superb houses were rising around the Pratt mansion, which itself was only a year old, and which stood on land that had formed part of James Lenox's farm only a decade or so before that. Poor Mr. Lenox: Even before he sold his land in building lots, it had appeared on maps with the proposed grid of streets overlaid eagerly on its hilly fields, a foregone conclusion, the ambitious blueprint for a Manhattan paved over in orderly rectangles of houses and shops.

It was a good time to be a builder in Manhattan. It was a good time to be an architect, or so Olive's father had believed, in that lifetime ago. A year ago.

Many minutes had now passed since the last bedspring had squeaked, since the last pipe had trickled and groaned. The floorboards were still too new to creak. Olive pinched herself again, waited another five minutes, and rose so carefully from her bed that she didn't disturb a single coil.

Her flannel dressing gown lay over the wooden chair. She slid her feet into her slippers and eased the robe over her shoulders and arms.

Mrs. Keane was right: The Pratt family housemaids weren't locked in. Olive's own father had, toward the dusty end of construction, insisted that the newly hung vestibule door should operate a dead bolt from the inside, because—my God!—think of the plight of the poor housemaids if, heaven forbid, a fire should tear through the house in the middle of the night! The scandal would be enormous, the headlines thick and torrid and accusatory. They would brand Mr. Henry August Pratt a heartless slayer of the innocent lower classes, a Dickensian villain of the worst sort: in short, a real prat. Possibly he might face criminal charges. So, thanks to her father's indignant intervention, the dead bolt lifted and the new brass knob turned easily under Olive's hand, and before she closed the door again she slid her Bible into the crack between portal and frame, a trick she'd learned at Miss Ellis's.

Outside the housemaids' corridor, the air was almost fresh. The grand staircase, winding like a great marble ribbon up the center of the house, had been built not so much for ornamentation, Olive's father had told her, running his finger along the neat architectural drawings before them, though ornamentation—eye-watering, breath-snatching, jaw-weakening—drove Mr. Pratt's approval of the design. That thick vertical column of empty space, soaring into the dome, created a vital circulation of healthful air. No cramped and stuffy corridors, no atmosphere allowed to fester in place. In the summer, when the vents were opened and the rising hot molecules were allowed to escape harmlessly into the Manhattan sky, why, you might almost call it bearable. You might not even want to flee to your cottage in Newport or East Hampton or Rumson.

But that, reflected Olive, as she turned the corner and found the back staircase with her foot, just in time to avoid tumbling down it, had been her father's problem all along. He hadn't understood that, to men like Mr. Pratt, the healthful aspects of his beautiful soaring staircase didn't matter.

It didn't matter that Mr. Pratt and his wife and children *could* stay in Manhattan in the summer, instead of spending money on an entirely different mansion in an entirely different town. The point was to show off, to demonstrate to your wealthy friends that—oh, yes—*you* could afford the finest, too. Even if you couldn't, really, or wouldn't. Even if you refused payment to your architect, after taking up two years of his undivided professional time, just because you could. Just because you'd been clever enough to seal your contract on a handshake and nothing else. A gentleman's agreement.

Now, that was a laugh, Olive thought. Mr. Henry August Pratt, a gentleman.

The lights were out, and Olive didn't dare light the candle she held in her left hand as she navigated the narrow little staircase, the poor cousin of the one so impressively occupying the center of the house. No, this was Olive's staircase, the service stairs, plain and honest, her new lot in life, and anyway it got her where she wanted to go, didn't it? Utility, that was the point. She could slip through quite unnoticed this way, without making any noise, without stirring the tremendous column of healthful air that fed into all the principal rooms of the Pratt mansion. She could enter Mr. Henry August Pratt's august library without anyone knowing at all.

Still, her pulse slammed against her throat as she pushed open the heavy door. She felt like a thief, even though she knew she was right. She was only correcting a great wrong; she was fighting for her father's justice, since he could no longer fight for himself. The *real* thief, she told herself, as her shaking fingers found the small box of safety matches in the pocket of her dressing gown, as she tried and failed to strike one alight against the edge of the box, was Mr. Pratt.

At last the tip of the match burst into light. The crisp sound of the flare, the acrid saltpeter scent, struck Olive's senses so forcibly that she nearly gasped, certain that everyone in the house would hear and smell them, too. Her blood felt like ice as it pumped along the arteries of her body, down her limbs, up to her head, making her dizzy. My God, she was actually *here*. Actually standing here in Mr. Pratt's library, five feet away from his massive desk, holding a guilty candle in the middle of the night.

She had better get to it, hadn't she?

But where did one begin to find written evidence of a professional relationship that had never been properly formalized? *Just send me the bill,* Mr. Pratt had said indulgently, and her father had sent the bill, and it hadn't been paid. Had Mr. Pratt saved that bill? And if he had, was it proof enough that her father had been cheated of his rightful fees?

That Mr. Pratt had, by cheating her father, effectively destroyed his career, because who would employ an architect who gave such unsatisfactory service that his client wouldn't pay the bill? And who would employ an architect who dared to make any trouble about those unpaid bills?

That Mr. Pratt had, by destroying his career, effectively destroyed his life, because if her father wasn't an architect, he was nothing, a negation, an invisible column of empty space for whom no one was willing to pay?

Olive realized she was trembling, that the match had nearly gone out. She whipped the candle under the flame. The wick caught instantly, and she dropped the match onto the rug just as it singed her fingers.

She held still for a moment, while the taper flickered uncertainly in her hand. The room looked different by night, forbidding, almost Gothic in the ominous dim wavering of the candle flame. There were the bookcases she had polished so industriously that afternoon; there were the deep armchairs and the leather Chesterfield sofa near the fireplace. There was the liquor cabinet, the enormous sash windows now enclosed by damask curtains, the paneled walls, and the long-necked brass floor lamps, one poised next to each armchair.

And the desk.

Of course, the huge brown desk, supported by curved legs and feet in the shape of lions' paws, covered by a red baize blotter and a small

Chinese lamp and a sleek black enamel fountain pen perched in its sleek black enamel holder at the very top and center.

Olive picked up the spent match, placed it in the pocket of her dressing gown, and stepped carefully across the rug and around the corner of the desk, where the drawers lined up on either side of an immense leather chair. (Mr. Pratt was a large man to begin with, six feet tall and framed like a Cossack, and he had allowed a layer of prosperous fat to gather and thicken over that frame, steeped with smoke from the finest imported cigars, so that Olive imagined if he were slaughtered and brought to market, he would taste exactly like a well-cured side of bacon.) The chair was too large to fit between the drawers, so Olive had to pull it away. The wheels squeaked softly, and she froze for an instant, horrified, waiting for doors to bang and footsteps to drum along the stairs. Sleepwalk? She would pretend to be sleepwalking. It might work; you never knew.

But the house remained still. Olive counted the gentle ticks of the clock above the mantel, until her heartbeat slowed to match them. A curious dark spot appeared before the curtains, and another, and she realized she had stopped breathing. A silly thing to do.

She released her lungs and bent down to address the first drawer on the right.

It was locked.

Of course it was locked. My God. What had she been thinking? Even her father had locked up all his papers, and her father's papers consisted of nothing more than drawings and bills and technical correspondence. She rattled the drawer gently, hoping the lock might somehow wake up and take pity on her, the way one took pity on the beggar children who inhabited the street corners downtown. But of course it didn't. How stupid. How disastrously stupid, to think she could just steal into Henry Pratt's library and find incriminating papers, hey presto, lying about unguarded. When even the housemaids' virtue was kept under lock and key in the Pratt mansion.

Still she went on staring at the desk drawer, unable to accept her defeat. Just to give up and go back to her bed, after all that effort. To admit that, perhaps, the entire project was beyond her: Olive, reader of books, dreamer of dreams, middle-class daughter of a failed middle-class architect. Absurd, to think that she could carry off a deception like this, a plot for revenge (*justice*, not revenge, she reminded herself), a clandestine midnight search for papers that, if they did exist, would be hidden well beyond the reach of a common housemaid, even a clever one.

Olive's hand fell away from the handle of the drawer.

The climb back upstairs was cold and weary. The library lay on the third floor, along with the billiards room at the back (the masculine floor, she called it in her mind); the next floor held Mr. and Mrs. Pratt's stately bedrooms, and the next held the children's bedrooms. Well, not children, really. The youngest was Prunella, who was eighteen years old and newly engaged to a wealthy idiot, a widower with a young child; Olive couldn't remember his name. Then there were the twin boys, August and Harry, who had just returned home from Harvard for the Christmas holiday. It was their last year of university, and everybody was speculating what they would do next: the family home or bachelor apartments? Professional ambitions? Wedding bells? Olive hadn't listened much. One of them was supposed to be quite wild and artistic; the other was supposed to be simply wild. They had gotten into daily scrapes when they were younger, said one of the maids, who had been with the Pratts at their old house on Fifty-seventh Street. One of them had gotten some poor woman with child—so it was rumored, anyway—some earlier housemaid; Mr. Pratt had dealt with the matter himself, so Mrs. Pratt wouldn't be bothered.

Olive paused with her foot on the final step at the sixth-floor landing. Now, that might serve Mr. Pratt right. *If* the story was true, of course, and *if* it reached the newspapers . . .

A soft sound reached her ears.

Olive glanced down the stairwell and saw a faint triangle of light on the floor below.

She bolted without thinking, right past the entry to the sixth floor and up the last narrow flight to the seventh floor. A storeroom, wasn't it? She'd never been there. But she couldn't go to her room; the intruder would hear her opening the vestibule door, would hear her creeping down the corridor to her cramped little chamber.

But no one would be going as high as the seventh-floor stairs.

She waited in the shadows of the landing. There was no door here; the stairs opened right out to a short hallway. A small round window let in a hint of moonlight, illuminating a narrow portal at the end of the hall, six or seven feet away.

A voice called out in a low, rumbling whisper.

"Is someone there?"

Olive took a single step back, toward the door.

"Hello?" the voice whispered again. Not a threatening whisper at all; only curious. Curious and quite male, she thought. There was no doubt of that. The whisper had *resonance*; it had timbre; it matched, somehow, the expansive, backslapping voices she'd overheard a few hours ago, when the boys had arrived home together in a cab from the station.

He's sneaking out, she thought. Sneaking out to see a shopgirl, perhaps, or to meet his friends for God knew what mischief.

Olive stood quietly, hardly breathing, while her heart smacked and smacked against the wall of her chest.

Then footsteps, careful and quiet and heavy. Making their way not down toward the first floor, Olive realized in horror, as the tread became louder, but *up*. Up toward the seventh floor, and Olive's helpless and guilty body on the landing.

She took another silent step back, and another. The door was at her shoulders now.

A shadow lifted itself up the final steps and came to rest on the landing. Olive could see a large hand on the newel post, a large frame blocking the moonlight from the small round window.

"Hello there," said the voice, surprisingly gentle. "Who the devil are you?"

"I'm Olive," she whispered. "The new housemaid. I—I couldn't sleep."

"Ah, of course. I couldn't sleep, either."

Olive fingered her dressing gown.

A hand extended toward her. "I'm Harry Pratt. The younger son, by about twelve minutes."

Olive, not knowing what else to do, reached out and took the offered hand and gave it a too-brisk shake. His palm was warm and dry and quite large, swallowing hers in a single gulp, and he smelled very faintly of tobacco. She whispered, without thinking, "Are you the wild one or the artistic one?"

The outline of his face adjusted, as if he were smiling. "Both, I expect."

"Well. It's—It's a pleasure to meet you, Mr. Pratt."

"Just Harry. Have you been having a look in there?" He nodded to the door behind her.

She hesitated. What else could she say? "Yes."

"What do you think?"

"Of what?"

"Of my paintings, of course."

"I—I don't know. I couldn't see much." She turned the last word upward, like a question.

"You didn't switch the light on?"

"No."

The young man took a single step forward, and good Lord, just like that, the moonlight from the window poured in around them, and Olive lost her breath.

Harry Pratt was the handsomest man she had ever seen.

She thrust her hand behind her back and braced it against the door.

"Don't be afraid," he said softly. "I'm not going to tell anyone."

"Y—you're not?" She was stammering like a schoolgirl, utterly unnerved by the angle of his cheekbones, drenched in moonlight. It was unfair, she thought, the effect of unexpected beauty on a sensible mind. (Olive had always prided herself on her sensible mind.) He was Henry Pratt's son; he was probably a reprobate, a complete ass, undeserving in every way, no doubt just *chock*-full of those base male appetites that had to be locked up every night by Mrs. Keane. And yet Olive stammered for him. That was biology for you.

Harry Pratt was tilting his head as he stared at her. "No," he said, a little absent, and Olive had to think back and remember what question he was answering. He tilted his head the other way, and then he moved to her side and peered, eyes narrowed, muttering to himself, as if she were a specimen brought up for his inspection.

"What's wrong?" Olive whispered.

"I need you," said Harry Pratt, and he snatched her hand, threw open the narrow door, and pulled her inside.

Three

JULY 1920

Lucy

"There'll be no gentleman callers in the rooms." Matron looked at Lucy sternly over the rims of her spectacles, spectacles that appeared to be there for no purpose other than overlooking potentially problematic young female persons. "A gentleman in one of the rooms is a cause for immediate expulsion."

Did they throw the errant sinner on the street with all her goods and chattels?

Not that it mattered. Lucy wasn't in Manhattan for romantic entanglements.

"That won't be a problem," said Lucy coolly, wishing she had spectacles of her own. It was difficult, at twenty-six, to look suitably forbidding, especially when one had been blessed—or cursed—with long, curling lashes that gave a false promise of pleasures to come. "I don't expect to have any gentlemen callers."

"I wouldn't be quite so sure about that, my dear." Matron's eyes, an unexpected cornflower blue, crinkled slightly at the corners. Before

Lucy could relax, Matron asked, with a studied casualness that fooled neither of them, "What brings you to the city?"

"I have a job at Cromwell, Polk and Moore," said Lucy quickly. Surely, Matron couldn't find fault with that. It even had the benefit of being true. "The law offices."

"Yes, I have heard of them." Lucy did her best not to squirm beneath Matron's level gaze. "But wouldn't you be served better by lodgings farther downtown? There's the Townsend or the Gladstone . . ."

"It would be so tedious to live too near where you work, don't you think?" said Lucy glibly. "And, besides, it's not really so far. It's just a quick ride on the Third Avenue El. And the air is fresher up here near the park."

Lucy sniffed enthusiastically, getting a noseful of cleaning fluid and someone's stockings left out to dry.

Matron looked long at Lucy, but what she saw there must have convinced her, because she said, in her brisk way, "You will find all the rules posted in the lobby. Gentlemen guests are welcome in the back parlor on the third floor between the hours of four and six Wednesday through Saturday. The front door is locked at midnight and will remain locked until six the following morning. Baths are taken by rota—"

The list went on and on, in Matron's calm voice. Hot baths allotted at the rate of one every other day, no more than ten minutes apiece; towels and sheets to be laundered on alternate Mondays . . .

Was breathing rationed, too? No more than ten exhalations per tenant per minute, except on Easter Sunday and Christmas, when they might have extra for a treat?

Lucy began to wonder just what she was letting herself in for. In the July sunshine, the attic room was stifling. She could feel the sweat trickling beneath the collar of her suit jacket; her blouse clung damply to her back. The only window was high and small, nailed shut. Through a film of decades of coal smoke, the sunshine swam dimly, painting the walls of the room with dingy shadows.

She found herself seized with a longing for her room in Brooklyn, with the bookcases her father had built for her with his own hands and the mural on the wall that her mother had painted when she was quite small, a mural of spreading trees and wandering lanes, of castle towers peeping just over the horizon, and, in the middle of it all, a knight on a rearing horse raising his sword high above his head, a dragon cringing at his feet.

Right now, Lucy rather knew how that dragon felt, cornered, frantic.

"Well?" said Matron, and Lucy fought the urge to tell her thank you very much, but this wasn't what she wanted at all, and flee down the back stairs, her smart heels click-clacking on the worn treads.

But this *was* what she wanted, she reminded herself, through a haze of heat and confusion. When she had heard that the old Pratt mansion had been turned into a women's boardinghouse, with rooms to let, it seemed nothing short of heaven-sent.

Even if the temperature in the room was more reminiscent of the other place.

That was, after all, where her German grandmother believed she was headed. *Lipstick, paugh!* Just one little slip . . . no corset . . . skirts up past the ankles . . . And that typing course—what did she need with more school? The bakery had been good enough for her father; it should have been good enough for Lucy, too. It was that mother of hers, putting ideas in her head, making her think she was more than she was.

Mother . . . Lucy felt an ache in her chest, beneath the place where her corset wasn't. They hadn't been particularly close, but her mother's death the previous summer had left her reeling, for more reasons than one.

Lucy gathered herself together, drawing herself up to her full height. "It's exactly what I wanted," she lied. "How much is it?"

"It's eight dollars a week," said Matron, and Lucy had to pinch herself to hide her surprise. Eight dollars for a cubby in an attic? She had known prices were higher in Manhattan than Brooklyn, but she'd had no idea how much. "Will that be acceptable, Miss . . ."

"Young," said Lucy briskly.

It was Jungmann, really, but a German name was hardly an asset, not now, with so many still mourning their dead. She wasn't lying; she was merely Anglicizing.

Lucy had left her German name behind in Brooklyn with her grandmother's disapproval, with sauerkraut and sausages and the squish of dough between her fingers. An entire life, gone with a twist of the tongue.

But what of it? If her grandmother was to be believed, she had no more right to Jungmann than to Young.

Lucy raised her head high. "It's Young. Lucy Young. And yes, it is acceptable."

"In that case, Miss Young"—Matron held out a hand—"welcome to Stornaway House."

"Stornaway House?" Lucy couldn't quite hide her quick look of surprise. "I thought this house belonged to the Pratt family."

She had done her research, thumbing through back issues of the *World*, the *Sun*, and the *Herald*, in which the Pratts were frequently featured, richly garbed, attending the opera, departing for Newport, returning from Newport, playing tennis, creating scandal. Even the house itself had been notorious, a nasty squabble between Mr. Pratt and his architect that dragged through the papers, and led, it seemed, to the suicide of the architect.

A house born in blood, one paper had dramatically termed the house on East Sixty-ninth Street, and so it would seem, given all that had happened after.

Lucy had snuck out from her work in the stenographic pool at Sterling Bates, squinting at old papers in the library, putting the pieces together.

All except the one piece she needed.

"It used to belong to the Pratts," said Matron placidly, closing and locking the door of the room behind her with one of the many keys she wore at her waist. She ushered Lucy to the back stair. "The house was bought by Mr. Stornaway five years ago, and dedicated for use as a home for respectable women."

Was it Lucy's imagination, or was there just a hint of emphasis on those last words?

Lucy held carefully to the banister as she picked her way down the steep, narrow stairs. Aside from the matter of her birth, she was as respectable as they came. She had no beaux; the boys back home found her too hoity-toity.

If by hoity-toity they meant that she wanted something other than to bear their children, to live from payday to payday, to pretend she didn't smell the beer on their breath or know what went on in the pool hall down the street, well, then, yes, she was hoity-toity. And she wasn't ashamed to admit it.

"Fortunately for me," she said. "When may I move in?"

"The room is available for immediate occupancy." Matron led Lucy out of the servants' stair on the fifth floor, to the grand circular stair that spiraled through the main floors.

Lucy could feel her lungs expanding here, in the quiet of marble and polish, with the sun casting multicolored flecks of light through the stained glass dome high above. Off the staircase hall, heavy oaken doors led to grand bedrooms, bedrooms with high ceilings and long, sashed windows, nothing like the little cubby upstairs for which she was to have the privilege of handing over more than half her weekly pay packet.

But it was done. She was in. Where she slept was immaterial. What mattered was that she was here.

A little voice in the back of her head whispered that this was folly, that there was nothing she could hope to learn here, but Lucy silenced it. She had come too far down this particular path to turn back now. Her belongings, such as they were, were contained in an ancient carpetbag and a cardboard box in her friend Sylvia's apartment. She had given up her job of four years at Sterling Bates and the prospect of advancement for a junior position at Cromwell, Polk and Moore.

Cromwell, Polk and Moore, among other, larger accounts, handled the affairs of the Pratt family.

They liked to keep the family in the family, did the Pratts. The junior partner in charge of the Pratt estate was the stepson of the notorious Prunella Pratt—the last remaining member of the once-thriving Pratt family.

The last remaining acknowledged member.

"My parlor is down that hall," said Matron, and Lucy nodded obediently, turning her head in the indicated direction.

And stopped.

There was a terra-cotta bas-relief set into the wall. Against a stylized background, a dragon cowered at the feet of a knight on a plunging charger.

Not just any knight. Her knight.

Her dragon.

"Excuse me," Lucy said, and had to clear her throat to get the words out. "But what is that on the wall?"

"Oh, that?" Matron looked at the mural incuriously, and Lucy wondered how she hadn't realized that the temperature in the hallway had dropped at least thirty degrees, the world frozen around them. "I believe it is Saint George. The Pratts appear to have been rather fond of him. He appears in various forms throughout the building."

Lucy made a noncommittal reply.

She remembered, very long ago, her father praising her mother's painting. Her father had always praised her mother, her elegance, her grace, her cleverness, perpetually in awe that she had chosen him, married him.

To say that her mother had tolerated his praise was too harsh, too unkind. It was more that she deflected it, gently and kindly.

It was the day her mother had finished the mural in Lucy's room. Lucy's father had been loud in his admiration, but Lucy's mother had only shaken her head, raising her hands as if to ward off further plaudits.

I am no artist, she had said ruefully. *I can only copy. Mine is a very secondhand sort of talent. Not like—*

She had stopped, abruptly, like a clock with a broken spring.

Lucy's father had swung Lucy up in his arms and swept her away to make bun men from bits of dough, and the conversation had been forgotten.

Until now.

"Miss Young?" Matron was regarding her with concern.

"I can bring my things tonight," Lucy said brusquely. "I get off work at five, although sometimes they need me later. Will that be acceptable?"

"Just let me get you your key," said Matron, and Lucy followed her down the winding marble stairs, past a long drawing room with an elaborate, gilded ceiling, and dark paneled walls that seemed cool even in the heat of the summer day.

In the middle of the day, all the tenants were at work. The stairwell was still and quiet; the woodwork smelled of beeswax and lemon oil. If Lucy closed her eyes, she could imagine that the house was as it had been twenty-eight years ago.

When her mother had been here.

"I will need a deposit," said Matron matter-of-factly, and Lucy dug quickly in her purse.

"How much?" she asked, hoping it wouldn't be more than she had.

"Two weeks' rent is standard," said Matron, and Lucy counted out the crumpled bills, grateful that she was frugal about lunches and dinners and streetcar rides.

The front hall, once so grand, was marred by the addition of hastily constructed cubbies on one side, each marked with the name of a resident. On the other was a curious sort of concierge booth.

Lifting the hinged counter, Matron ducked behind it. Unlocking a tin cash box, she put Lucy's hard-earned money inside.

"Room 603," said Matron, and made a note on a piece of paper. "Miss Lucy Young." Reaching beneath the desk, she drew out a key, frowning through her spectacles at the little tag attached to one end. "Your key, Miss Young."

They key was a modern thing, the metal shiny with newness.

"Thank you," said Lucy, and took it, feeling as though she had just crossed a mountain range and arrived on the other side, only to find that the campfire was dying low and there were wolves in wait just beyond the wagon train.

Wolves? Or dragons?

Deep in her heart, Lucy had half hoped she was wrong, that, once here, she would find that the house was just a house and nothing to do with her.

Had her mother danced in the great drawing room on the second floor? Had she dined in state beneath the dark beams in the formal dining room? Lucy didn't know. All she knew was that, somehow, her past lay in this house, with the mural of a knight on the wall.

With the man whose name her mother had uttered with her dying breath.

Harry.

Four

JUNE 1944

Kate

A golden thread of sunlight wound its way through the side of a blackout shade, cutting a line of light across the attic room and into my eyes. It must have been what had awakened me, or perhaps it was the knowledge that I wasn't alone.

I uncurled myself from the threadbare chaise longue and its faded chintz pattern. It had probably once been a very fine chair, much used and loved, but now it was worn past its usefulness. A spring had found its way through the bottom cushion, and one of the arms hung on by mere threads. I was careful not to put undue stress—or cause myself bodily injury—as I eased myself from where I'd spent most of the previous night.

Captain Ravenel had slept deeply, mostly due to the morphine I'd administered. The previous night I'd had to reopen his wound to clean it thoroughly, and thought the bliss of unconsciousness would be a relief to us both. The leg was badly damaged, the wound worse for having been sutured before all the bone and bullet fragments could be removed, the infection worse because of the delayed use of penicillin. I had doubts I could save the leg, but I kept them to myself. I continued to see his eyes as he'd begged me to save his leg, and I couldn't allow myself to think of failure.

I looked at my watch pinned to my blouse, realizing it was time for another dose of morphine. Nurse Hathaway, a girl just past twenty who was too young to have formed any traditional opinions about the way things *should* be and didn't seem to mind taking orders from a female doctor, had brought several syrettes of the pain medication the previous evening, sparing me yet another dash up and down the stairs.

When I stopped by the side of Captain Ravenel's bed and checked his chart, I realized that the nurse had been in while I'd been sleeping, had already administered the medication, and had placed a tray filled with a stack of gauze, cotton balls, and disinfectant on the bedside table. I grinned to myself, too thankful to try to figure out her motive.

The patient remained asleep as I slid down his bedclothes to expose his wounded leg so I could examine it, allowing a view of his body, barely covered by a hospital gown. I'd seen up close nearly naked young men thousands of times since I'd arrived at Stornaway Hospital, but this was the first time I'd felt a tinge of self-consciousness. He moaned something unintelligible and I paused, studying his features. He was almost too beautiful to be a man, but the broad shoulders and heavily muscled arms and torso assured me that he was definitely male.

My mind had always been focused on my goal of becoming a doctor, and I'd never allowed myself to be perceived as one of those silly girls swooning over a fine male form like my best friend Margie Beckwith had done since we were twelve and probably would continue to do until she finally found a husband. Her task had been made all the more difficult by war and the exodus of most of the eligible young men from the city, not to mention her job as a librarian at the New York Public

Library, which kept her surrounded by old records and other females in the same predicament.

I stared at his face, at the beautiful straight nose and olive skin, at his strong chin and dark brows, and wished he'd open his eyes so I could see them again. I quickly looked away, ashamed at how my purpose had been taken captive by the sight of an attractive male. My wavering brought back the unexpected memory of my mother and me standing wordlessly in front of this building, staring up at the windows of this very room.

I had spent a lifetime trying to understand my mother, to comprehend how she seemed to pine for something just out of her reach. I knew she'd loved my father and me, yet there had always been a barrier between us, a wall that sealed off half of her heart from us, as if she were holding it in reserve. I knew from an early age that I never wanted to be that way. And when I'd decided I wanted to be a doctor, I threw my entire heart into it. The difference between my mother and me, I'd decided, was that I didn't believe in half measures.

I studied again the beautiful man in front of me, reminding myself of all that I'd accomplished and sacrificed, and all that I could still do as a female doctor, and a familiar calm settled on me. I would do my job, and do it well, and work even harder not to derail my focus.

I took his vitals and, being satisfied with the results, I picked up his chart again from the table at the foot of his bed to make notations. Despite my frantic and constant reading of the chart during the night in an attempt to guide his treatment, I hadn't noticed his full name or where he was from. My eyes drifted to the top of the form where I'd read earlier that he was a captain and that his last name was Ravenel—a name that sounded oddly familiar. My gaze slid to the space on the form for a first name. Cooper. And he was from Charleston, South Carolina.

He hadn't said enough the previous night for me to determine whether he had a Southern accent, but in my newly awakened imagination, I thought that he would and that his dropped consonants and slurred vowels would sound wonderful emerging from those lips.

I clenched my eyes, reminding myself to remain focused, inordinately thankful that I was alone in the room with nobody to witness my foolishness.

"Victorine."

The word startled me, and I almost dropped the chart on the wounded leg. His eyes were open but still glazed from fever and morphine, and although I knew he was oblivious to his surroundings, the way he was looking at me made me feel again as if he *knew* me.

I placed the chart back on the table and moved closer to him. "Captain Ravenel? Can you hear me?"

"Victorine," he said again, his eyes focused on my face, the name filled with hope and wonder, making me want to answer *yes*. But for the first time in my life, I couldn't speak. None of my resources, or my authority as a medical doctor, gave me whatever it was I needed to answer the longing in the soldier's voice. It unnerved me, made me feel the loss of something I never knew existed.

He continued to look at me as I recovered my composure and slipped back into my Dr. Kate Schuyler persona. "Captain Ravenel, you're in a hospital in New York City. Your leg is badly hurt, but we are doing our best to save it."

As if he hadn't heard me, his hand gripped mine, and I knew I couldn't pull away even if I'd wanted to.

"It's you," he whispered, his eyes settling on my face.

A sensation like hot chocolate sliding down my throat cocooned me so that I was aware only of this man, and me, and the heat of our clasped hands. My logical mind tried to reason with me, to tell me that Cooper Ravenel was in a feverish delirium and had no idea who I was.

But there was something in his eyes that made me cling to the fallacy that there was something more.

"I'm here," I managed to say. "I'm here to take care of you."

"I know," he said through dry lips.

I knew there was a glass of water on his bedside table and that I should give him some to drink, yet I couldn't look away or drop his hand. Not yet.

His words rushed out, like they'd been held back for a long, long time, his sentences broken in the middle as he fought for the energy to speak them. "I've been . . . waiting a long time . . . to meet you." With great effort, he lifted his other arm and touched my hair. "Take it . . . down."

Since medical school, I'd worn my long hair twisted into a tight bun and held securely with a large comb at the back of my head. My hair was my only vanity, and I couldn't cut it even though I knew it would be so much easier than putting it up every morning. But it was long and dark like my mother's, which had framed her face with a pronounced widow's peak just like mine, and I remembered how as a little girl she'd allowed me to brush it before bedtime, giving it one hundred strokes, until it crackled. Nobody at the hospital had ever seen it down; to allow them to do so would have seemed like a nod to my femininity, an admission of weakness. I clung to that thought, the word *no* hanging on my lips as he reached for me.

"Take it . . . down," he said again. Before I could pull away he reached up with his free hand and dislodged the large comb.

I reached up with my hand to keep it in place, but I was too slow. It fell below my shoulders, almost to my waist, long enough for him to grab and pull a handful toward his face and breathe in deeply, keeping me pinned to his side.

"It's how . . . I always thought . . . it would be," he said, and I heard the soft cadences of his words, his accent touching briefly on each syllable, just as I'd imagined.

As if unaware that he was hurt, and lying in a hospital bed, he moved to sit up, grimacing as the pain coursed through him.

His words startled me, making me forget where I was. Who I was. "How do you know me?" I asked, transfixed by his eyes and his accent and the way he breathed in the scent of my hair.

His eyes drifted closed, and I wanted to protest, not ready to stop staring into them no matter how inappropriate it was.

His lips moved again. "I've always . . . known you," he said, his words slurring as he fell back to sleep, my hair sliding from his grasp.

I became aware of footsteps on the stairs leading up to my attic room, and for once I was grateful that the elevator didn't come this far. It was too quiet and I would have been aware of visitors only right before they entered.

As it was, I'd just finished twisting my hair in a knot and fastening it to the back of my head with the comb when the door was thrown open without a knock. I knew it was Dr. Greeley and didn't give him the satisfaction of turning around with surprise. Instead, I leaned forward toward the washbasin Nurse Hathaway had brought up the previous night, and dipped a cloth into the water before gently dabbing at Cooper's face. He was drenched in perspiration from the fever, and it was warm in the attic despite the electric fan I'd purchased at Hanson Drugstore and guarded greedily.

"How's the patient?" he asked, his tone carefully guarded. It wouldn't do for a doctor to want a patient to deteriorate. He picked up the chart and began to scan the latest notations.

"No change, which means he's not getting worse," I said optimistically.

Dr. Greeley grunted, then replaced the chart on the bedside table. He crossed his arms, lifting one hand to his chin. I was sure he thought it made him look scholarly, but I had the feeling that he did it to hide the slight paunch he'd begun to develop despite his relatively young age of thirty-one. "But he's not getting better, either."

I shook my head. "He's been here less than twenty-four hours. He's feverish, but I can tell he has a strong will. That will go far in his recovery."

He looked bored. "Medicine heals, not wishful thinking. Eventually his leg will have to come off. I'm keeping operating room one open just in case."

I focused on wiping Cooper's face, glad my hands were otherwise occupied so I wouldn't be tempted to throw something at the doctor.

In an attempt to change the conversation, I said, "He keeps saying the name 'Victorine.' It must be a Southern name because it's not one I've ever heard before. Do you know if his family in Charleston has been notified that he's here? Families are usually notified as soon as the ship docks, but his situation is different because he was sent here instead of on a train home. I'd hate to think of his family worried about him and not knowing why they haven't heard from him." I had been about to say that his Victorine must mean a great deal to him, which was why her name was always on his tongue, but I couldn't bring myself to say it. I didn't know this man at all, and there were no logical reasons why I'd be feeling a sense of jealousy toward a woman I would never meet.

"You could always write to them yourself. In your spare time, of course. I came up here to remind you that you're late for your rounds."

I dropped the cloth into the basin and stood quickly. "Of course. I lost track of time. I'll be right there."

"We'd be delighted for you to join us, of course. And if you need the captain's home address, I have his personnel file in my office. You can stop by after rounds."

I knew better than to ask him to bring it to me. The whole point of this exercise was to get me alone in his office again so he could try to pin me against his desk. This had happened twice before, and both times I'd been successful in outmaneuvering him and making it out of the office unscathed. The sheer fact that he was my superior was the only reason I hadn't used his gold letter opener for a greater purpose.

"I'll do that," I said, my mind already trying to figure out a way to obtain the folder without having to actually go into his office. My problem was solved when I passed Nurse Hathaway on the stairwell leading toward the mansion's ballroom on the second floor, which was now used as a patient ward. I disliked taking advantage of her willingness to help, but I knew I didn't have the energy needed to fend off the doctor's advances.

"Nurse Hathaway—may I ask a favor?"

"Yes, Doctor." She gave me a helpful smile, so different from what I'd grown used to from most of the staff at Stornaway.

"Captain Ravenel's personnel file is in Dr. Greeley's office. When you have a moment, would you be so kind as to get it for me? I have rounds now, and so does Dr. Greeley."

I added this last part so she'd know he'd also be out of his office and she would be safe entering. I wasn't under any illusion that his attentions were directed only toward me. "Captain Ravenel was admitted last night," I added. "So his file should be on top of Dr. Greeley's desk or on the filing cabinet."

"Yes, Doctor," she said again, her gaze telling me that she knew exactly what I was saying.

I managed to get through rounds without thinking about Cooper Ravenel. The patients were mostly young, many not much older than I was. Yet their faces had aged prematurely, a permanent reminder of what they'd seen and done. The wounds they'd sustained were bad enough to have them sent home—amputations, mostly, and burns—and several men had lost their eyesight in at least one eye. One man, a first lieutenant from Muncie, Indiana, was twenty-eight and now profoundly deaf from an exploding bomb. When I'd first started treating these patients, I'd expected to see them grateful to be home permanently, and I'd seen a few like that. But there were some eager to return to their comrades, disappointed not that they were missing a leg or an arm, but that they would never again be sent to the front.

When we were through, I managed to escape without Dr. Greeley noticing that I'd left the group, and headed toward the stairwell. As I'd expected, Captain Ravenel's file was waiting on the top step, and I picked it up before quietly entering the attic room.

I could tell that Nurse Hathaway had been in, had cleaned up the patient and tidied the bedside table. He slept in a sheen of perspiration, his condition apparently unchanged. I checked his chart and noticed the nurse had taken his vitals and all was stable. His temperature hadn't decreased, but neither had it risen. For now, all was good.

I remembered the look in his eyes as he'd called me Victorine and asked me to let down my hair. I had to remind myself that Victorine was another woman, a woman who was probably waiting to find out where her captain was, and that the sooner she came, the sooner I could regain my focus on what I wanted in life.

I moved the file to my makeshift desk and pulled out a piece of stationery and a pen. With a deep breath, and taking time with my unruly penmanship, I began to write, hoping my letter would reach Charleston as quickly as possible, while a small part of me wished that it would not.

Five

December 1892

Olive

The room at the top of the stairs.

Olive expected an attic of some sort, filled with furniture and objects that hadn't found a home in some other corner, or else boxes and crates that still awaited unpacking. She'd never seen the seventh-floor blueprints. Why bother? Architects saved their best work for the principal floors, the floors that counted. They didn't waste magic where no one would admire it.

So when she stepped through the doorway, she lost her breath.

"You don't mind, do you?" said Harry, brushing past her to busy himself at the other end of the room.

Olive turned in a circle, coated in moonlight from the long Palladian windows. The brick walls—they were like a secret garden. She gazed upward at a beautiful dome, a smaller version of the one at the top of the staircase, except this one was paned in clear glass, suspending her in the center of a velvet star-flecked Manhattan night. A beautiful and unexpected gift. *Thank you, Papa.* "Mind what?"

"If I sketch you."

Olive whirled around. "*Sketch* me?"

"Please?"

He stood near the wall, dangling a white rectangle from one hand and a short dark pencil from the other. His hair spilled onto his forehead, and his eyes were winsome. She took in his white shirt, which was unbuttoned to a point just below the hollow of his throat, and his loose pajama trousers, and she thought, *Good God, I shouldn't be here. This is quite wrong.*

She swallowed. "Of course not. This is quite wrong. I should return to bed immediately."

She began to turn away, and as quick as a June bug, Harry darted around her and stood akimbo before the door. "I said please."

"I don't know what sort of girl you think I am, Mr. Pratt . . ."

"The very best sort. I promise, I won't touch you. It's just your face. You look exactly like the woman I've been wanting to imagine, and I couldn't quite see you until now, and if I lose you at this moment, the moment of invention . . ."

His voice trailed away, and his expression was so contrite and beseeching, she wavered, just an inch or two, physically *wavered* there in the moonlight.

"Please," he said again, more softly.

"How long will it take? Mrs. Keane might come back upstairs to check on us."

"No, she won't. She never does. Trust me, I've spent enough nights up here, and in the attic I used in the old house." He held up the sketchbook. "I just need to make a study of you, and then I can paint you in from the sketch."

"Paint me in what?"

His eyebrows lifted, indicating the rest of the room, and Olive, who had been so transfixed by the architecture—the multitude of windows, the glass dome, the bricks, the beautiful tin ceiling—saw for the first time that the walls were stacked with canvases.

"Oh," she said, a little faintly, and she turned in another circle, aiming her gaze lower. She couldn't see the details, not in this pale wash of moonlight, but she saw the images: men on horseback, intricate landscapes, strange creatures. Behind her, Harry busied himself. She heard the crisp strike of a match, the sudden yellow glow of a lamp, and the color jumped away from the paintings, blues and reds and greens, like a handful of jewels. She gasped. "They're beautiful!"

"They're junk, mostly. Practice. I'm working on something, this idea of an idea, and I can't seem to get it right. I can't hold it in my head long enough. But I know it's there, waiting for me to find it. Like you."

"Like me?"

"Your face, I mean." He laughed. "I don't know *you*, of course. But your face is just how I imagined it, even if I couldn't quite see it until now. Does that make any sense?"

Of course she turned back to him then. He stood there holding the kerosene lamp, smiling from the corner of his mouth, almost apologetic, and the light turned his hair into gold. The smile smoothed slowly away. "My God," he whispered. "Please. Just thirty minutes, I swear it."

Olive touched her face, her ordinary face. Except that it wasn't ordinary anymore, was it? It was now, apparently, extraordinary. In the eyes of Harry Pratt.

"Very well," she said. "Where do you want me to sit?"

He moved so quickly, he was like a dervish. "Right here," he said, clearing away a pile of papers from a wooden chair. He set the lamp on a small table.

Olive sank into the chair and looked up at him.

"I'm sorry," he said. "Do you mind—I assure you I don't mean to be indelicate—but if you could perhaps loosen your dressing gown?"

Olive looked down at the thick and ungainly folds of her robe. "Certainly not."

"Miss Olive, I'm an artist. A professional. There's nothing improper, I assure you. All for the sake of art."

She squashed her lips together. "Is it necessary?"

"Not necessary, exactly. But the nightgown is closer to the effect I hope to achieve."

Olive considered the white flannel nightgown beneath the robe, a plain, high-necked affair, almost matronly. "I suppose it won't make any difference, since you have me in your clutches already."

"There's the spirit." He grinned and plopped himself in the opposite chair, a respectable five yards away, and crossed one leg high over the other. He leaned the sketchbook against his raised knee and poised his pencil, while Olive undid the belt of her dressing gown and let it slip a careful few inches below her flannel shoulders.

"Is that enough?"

"Perfect. Thank you." He touched his pencil to the paper and began to frown in concentration. "Loosen your hair a bit, could you?"

Olive frowned again and removed the narrow ribbon from the end of her braid.

"That's it," he said. "Undo the braid. And don't frown quite so hard. I'm not so awful as that, am I?"

"No. It's just that I really shouldn't be here."

"Yes, you should. You're doing nothing wrong."

"Mrs. Keane won't think so, if she finds out."

"Well, she won't." His voice was full of calm assurance.

"She'll dismiss me without reference."

"And I'll take the case straight to my father."

Olive thought that was a little strange. Wouldn't this be Mrs. Pratt's task, to sort out trouble in the domestic staff? But maybe things were different that way, among the upper classes. Olive came from a good family, a respectable professional family, well educated, well dressed—at least before Papa's disgrace, anyway—but they weren't anything like the Pratts. On the other hand, hadn't Mr. Pratt sorted out that little rumored difficulty with another housemaid? Which brother *was* that, anyway? Olive wondered, and she shifted her bottom uncomfortably against the chair, suddenly conscious of the thin barrier of flannel between her collarbone and the rapacious male gaze of Harry Pratt.

I shouldn't be here, she thought again.

Harry went on sketching, looking even more beautiful with his brow creased like that, his sleeves rolled up to expose a few inches of each forearm, his capable long legs crossed to support the sketchpad. *Scènes de la vie de bohème,* Olive thought, and she smiled.

"That's better," said Harry.

"What's better?"

"Your smile. It transforms you. I may have lost my breath a bit just now." That little curl was back at the corner of his own mouth, and combined with the studious crease in his brow, the disorder of his hair, it took a little of Olive's breath, too. She was still a bit stunned to find herself here at all, doing this, with a man she didn't know. It was daring and shocking, something the old Olive wouldn't have imagined, even as mischievous as she was. Alone in an attic with a beautiful young man at midnight? *In her dressing gown?* Unthinkable. But here she was.

"Still, I'm afraid it's not what quite I need at the moment," Harry said.

"What isn't?"

"Your smile."

Olive realized she was still smiling, that a silly wide grin hung from her mouth like a clown's mask. "I'm sorry," she said, stiffening her back.

"Don't be. How long have you been with us, Miss Olive?"

"Only a few weeks."

"Ah, that explains it. I would surely have noticed you if you were around this summer. Are you from New York, or elsewhere?"

"Elsewhere." Which was true, if you counted Miss Ellis's Academy.

"But you're not going to tell me where?"

She hesitated. "I went to school in Connecticut."

"But you haven't been in service long, have you?"

"What makes you say that?"

"The way you talk. The way you don't lower your eyes when you speak to me. A thousand things, really. Am I right?"

She started to rise from the chair. "I think that's enough for now."

"No, please." He started up, too. "No more questions, I promise. Please. Just a few more minutes."

Olive realized, in horror, that she was going to sit down again. That she couldn't say no to that charming voice, that humble *please*.

His voice dropped, shedding the charm, turning earnest. "Miss Olive, I assure you, I'm not like my brother. You have nothing to fear."

"Your brother?"

"I'm sure you've heard the rumors." He went on sketching, glancing at her and then at the paper before him, pencil stroking furiously. His mouth turned tense at the corners, his knuckles white around the edge of the sketchbook.

"You mean about the housemaid last year?" Olive asked daringly.

"That, among other things. I expect he'll drink himself to death by the time he's thirty. Poor devil." He glanced up from under his brow. "Stay away from him, do you hear me? If you have any trouble, come to me."

Olive huffed. "I've only just met you. How do I know *you're* not the one to stay away from?"

The pencil paused. Harry looked up at her and flashed that smile again, the old smile, lopsided and irresistible. "You don't, do you? You'll just have to take me on faith. Now. There we are. Would you like to see it?"

"You're done already?"

"I told you I'd be quick, so you can get back to the nunnery."

"The nunnery!" She laughed, because it was true. The little locked hallway of tiny bedrooms was exactly like a convent.

"Old Mrs. Keane learned her lesson last year." He lifted the sketch-book and turned it around. "Here you are, my lady."

Olive rose from the chair and stepped across the clean wooden boards. He held out the book to her, still smiling, and she took it from his hand and gasped.

"That's not me!"

"Yes, it is."

"But she's beautiful!"

"Olive, you *are* beautiful."

She looked up. "Not like *this*."

"What do you mean, like this?"

"She looks wild. She looks like . . . I don't know, someone medieval."

"Exactly. You have that quality, don't you know? Hasn't anyone told you? Your skin, the angle of your face. It's very noble, very clean. Otherworldly. What's the word? Pure."

Olive thrust the sketchbook into his chest, realizing as she did so how close he stood, only a foot away, and the smell of his soap filled her head. She watched his pulse move the golden skin at the hollow of his throat, just above the top of the sketchbook. Around them, the room was still and silvery, except for the pool of yellow lamplight in which they hovered. The stacked canvases against the wall, the warmth of the bricks, the worn old furniture, the intimate dimensions. It was like a separate flickering world from the house below, a small, enchanted square only the two of them could enter. Where Olive was a noble maiden, and Harry was a knight *parfait*.

Except it wasn't, was it? She was neither noble nor pure. She stood beneath this beautiful domed roof with a false name, under false pretenses, determined to ruin this charming young man's father. To ruin Harry Pratt's enchanted life.

"That's ridiculous," she said. "I'm going back to bed."

"Olive, wait." He took her elbow. "I'm sorry. I didn't mean to offend you. I spoke as an artist just now, nothing more. You just have a certain quality, that's all. It—It moves me." He said the last words so quietly, she had to strain to hear them.

Olive pulled her elbow away, and the motion caused her dressing gown to drop another few inches. She hoisted the sleeve back up over her shoulders and yanked the sash tight, and then she whipped the ends of her hair back into an obedient braid. "Well, you've captured it now, whatever it is. Am I free to go?"

Harry closed the sketchbook and said in the same soft, deep voice, "You were always free to go, Olive."

Six

◊

Lucy

"Where have you been?"

The senior partner's secretary pounced on Lucy as Lucy slipped through the door of the office. Miss Meechum's usually tidy hair had escaped in gray wisps from the knot at the back of her neck; her crisp collar was wilted. She looked, in fact, thoroughly frazzled.

"I'm very sorry, Miss Meechum." Lucy hastily set her bag on the floor by her chair, tugging at the fingers of her cotton gloves. She felt flushed and disheveled from the run from the El, made worse by the summer heat. But the room was hers. She had her entrée into the Pratt house. "If it's the memo for Mr. Cochran—"

Miss Meechum shook her head, her glasses slipping down to the tip of her nose. "Never mind about Mr. Cochran. It's Mr. Schuyler."

Electricity prickled down Lucy's spine. Or perhaps it was just the damp cotton of her blouse. "Mr. Schuyler?"

After three weeks at Cromwell, Polk and Moore, Lucy could still count her interactions with Mr. Schuyler on the fingers of one hand. He was out a great deal. Meeting with clients, Miss Meechum said piously, although Fran whispered, "Golf," between her fingers.

Once, he had breezed past Lucy into the office, handsome in evening wear, to pick up a box of chocolates and a black leather box that his secretary had purchased at his request, passing so close by Lucy's desk in the secretarial pool that she could smell the sandalwood of his cologne.

Another time, he had stood next to her at the elevator, pausing only to smile down at her and say, "You're the new girl, aren't you?" before tipping his hat to her and standing back for her to precede him, as though she had been a debutante rather than a secretary.

His eyes were a very deep blue in his tanned face.

Not, thought Lucy sternly, that she had any designs on Mr. Philip Schuyler's person. Everyone knew he was engaged to a Philadelphia debutante whose photos appeared regularly in the papers. Lucy had seen those pictures. Didi Shippen was always impeccably turned out, whether in tennis whites or an evening frock, her perfectly waved hair framing a face whose symmetry was spoiled only by a certain hint of a pout about the lips.

All the gossip columnists agreed: A Shippen was a fitting match for a Schuyler.

Not Lucy Young, who had grown up above a bakery in Brooklyn, who had spent her first few years fist deep in bread dough. She might as well sigh for the moon as for a Schuyler.

Besides, it wasn't Mr. Schuyler she was interested in; it was his files. Specifically, the files pertaining to the Pratt estate.

So far, however, there had been little opportunity. When Lucy had offered, casually, to bring Mr. Schuyler's coffee, she had been subjected to a freezing stare from his secretary, Meg, who had informed Lucy that she was *quite* capable, thank you very much, and hadn't Lucy any documents to type?

Meg, however, was nowhere in evidence. Her desk chair was empty, the cover over her typewriter.

Miss Meechum wrung her hands. "The worst *possible* timing—the Merola deal closes on Tuesday—they want several changes to the contract—"

"Meg is in the hospital!" chimed in Fran from the next desk.

"The hospital?" Lucy echoed, looking from one to the other.

"A taxi swerved and—smash!—there she was, just white as a sheet and all crumpled on the ground," jumped in Fran. "Right outside!"

Miss Meechum glared at Fran. "Frances is, unfortunately, correct."

"Oh, goodness," said Lucy helplessly. "I hope she's all right."

"If one can call a fractured leg and broken wrist all right," said Miss Meechum tartly. "I suppose it might have been worse, and, for that, one must be grateful, but—"

"They say she won't be back to work for *months*," contributed Fran. "And she might have a limp."

"The limp," said Miss Meechum, "is the least of our worries." She thrust an armload of files at Lucy. "Mr. Schuyler needed these fifteen minutes ago."

Lucy ignored the implied reproach. Breathlessly, she said, "But what about Mr. Cochran and Mr. Vaughn?"

"I've assigned Frances to Mr. Cochran and Eleanor to Mr. Vaughn," said Miss Meechum briskly. She gathered herself together, sounding a bit more like her old self. Looking over her spectacles warningly, she said, "This is a position of trust. Treat it accordingly."

Lucy clasped the files to her damp chest. "Yes, Miss Meechum."

Her heart was pounding beneath her blouse. The room at the Pratt house . . . and now Mr. Schuyler. As though it were meant.

"Sometime today, Lucy," warned Miss Meechum.

Lucy shook herself out of her reverie. "Yes, Miss Meechum. Of course, Miss Meechum. Right away, Miss Meechum."

From far away, she could hear Fran giggle. Lucy ignored it.

There was no such thing as fate. One made one's own luck. And she was going to make hers.

For now, that meant making sure Mr. Schuyler got the Merola contracts.

Lucy suppressed the wish that she had had time to go to the washroom, refresh her lipstick, brush her hair. That didn't matter. She wasn't here to vamp Mr. Schuyler. In fact, she was fairly sure that was part of the reason she had been chosen as Meg's replacement, even though Frannie and Eleanor were both more senior. But all of Eleanor's meager mental powers were devoted toward her own upcoming nuptials—everyone in the office had already heard of the great bridesmaid dress debacle—and as for Frannie . . . Well, Frannie was on the hunt for a husband.

Miss Meechum was very protective of her employers.

Tentatively, Lucy knocked on Mr. Schuyler's door. The brass plate read PHILIP C.J. SCHUYLER, ESQUIRE.

She wondered what the *C* and the *J* were for. Charles James? Cornelius Justinius?

There was no answer from within. Lucy heard the scrape of a chair being pushed back, then the sound of Mr. Schuyler's voice, distinctly irritated. "I already told you—not again." A pause. "Yes, I know. But it's not my decision."

"Sir?" Lucy poked her head around the door.

The wide mahogany desk in front of Philip Schuyler was littered with documents. Mr. Schuyler himself was kicked back in his chair, the telephone receiver in one hand, a grimace on his handsome face.

"Come in!" he said, and then, back into the phone, "*No*, Prunella."

Prunella? Lucy's ears pricked up. It wasn't precisely a common name. Prunella Pratt was the sole living scion of the once illustrious Pratt family—and Philip Schuyler's stepmother.

She had been a debutante in the 1890s, still living in the family home. If Lucy's mother had lived in that house, had stayed there, Prunella would know. And she might—Lucy clung to the frail hope— just might be the most likely person to know what had become of Harry Pratt.

Yes, and Lucy could just see herself taking the receiver from her startled employer and saying, *Pardon me, Mrs. Schuyler, you don't know me from Adam, but do you think I might be the illegitimate child of your brother? And, by the way, do you happen to know if your brother is still alive, and, if so, where he might be?*

That would certainly go over well. As in being handed a pink slip and booted out into the street well.

Holding up the files, Lucy mimed moving back toward the door. "I can come back," she mouthed.

Mr. Schuyler shook his head, gesturing her forward as he spoke into the phone. "Look, I'm sorry the people at Cartier's are giving you nasty looks, but there are three other trustees."

Mangled by the receiver, the sounds coming through sounded like the chickens Lucy's grandmother had once kept in a coop behind the bakery.

Philip Schuyler held the phone away from his ear, grimacing expressively at Lucy.

Lucy kept her face deliberately impassive, her spine very straight. Miss Meechum didn't approve of secretarial staff fraternizing with their employers.

As the squawking died down, Mr. Schuyler put the receiver back to his ear. "Look, we'll discuss this tomorrow, all right? I've a client waiting for me." He winked at Lucy. "Yes. Right now. A very important client. No. It can't wait. Yes, I know it's terrible to have to work for a living."

His smile invited Lucy to share the joke.

"Yes, yes, I'll see you at *Tosca*. No, darling, I won't forget. Ta-ta to you, too." Dropping the receiver into the cradle, Philip Schuyler let out an exaggerated breath. "Hello, hello. It's Linda, isn't it?"

"Lucy. Lucy Young." Lucy took a half step back. "If you're busy, I can come back . . ."

Philip Schuyler waved her forward. "No, no, come in. I needed an excuse." His teeth were very white and very even. Almost as white and as even as those of Didi Shippen, who smiled out from a silver frame on the corner of his desk. "Those have the unfortunate look of work about them."

Charm. That was the word for it. Philip Schuyler had an easy charm that was nearly impossible to resist.

But Lucy was very good at resisting.

Stepping briskly forward, she dealt out the files like a hand of cards, laying them out on the cluttered surface of his desk. "The Merola draft contract . . . Mr. Samson's letter of intent . . . and Mr. Cochran's memo."

Mr. Schuyler turned the files over in his hands. "Read it . . . read it . . . rubbish." Looking conspiratorially at Lucy, he said, "Cochran means well, but what he doesn't know about lease law would fill—well, something extremely large. Don't tell him I said that."

Lucy clasped her hands behind her back. "Of course not, sir. Is there anything else I can do for you?"

"Other than smother my stepmother?" Mr. Schuyler kicked back in his chair, looking Lucy up and down from her sensible pumps to the hair she had knotted up at the base of her neck. She was uncomfortably aware of the curls escaping in damp wisps from her usually neat coiffure. "So you're to be Meg's replacement, then."

The way his voice dropped made it sound strangely intimate.

"Yes, sir." Lucy kept her eyes focused on the studio portrait of Didi Shippen. "I am available to assist you in any way that Meg did."

Mr. Schuyler eyed her speculatively. "And some ways she didn't? Don't look so horrified! I didn't mean it like that. It's just . . ." He rested his elbows on the discarded files, looking up at her from under his blond lashes with boyish candor. "I'm in a bit of a bind. And you might be just the person to help me out."

"I can type a hundred words per minute, take shorthand dictation, and operate a telegraph machine." She knew she shouldn't, but she couldn't resist adding, "I don't smother."

Philip Schuyler rolled his shoulders. "This is a . . . different sort of favor." Another flash of those white, white teeth. "No smothering involved."

Lucy's heart sank a little. So he was going to be one of those? She'd dealt with them before, at Sterling Bates. Mr. Gregson, who seemed to think that the role of secretary was merely an audition for that of mistress—she'd soon seen him off, with high collars, a pair of false glasses, and an unflattering hairstyle—and Mr. Danzig, who pinched indiscriminately, and often inaccurately.

Didi Shippen's face smiled serenely from its silver frame.

"I am delighted to assist in any way that is appropriate to my position," said Lucy woodenly.

"Spoken like a true Portia." Mr. Schuyler's smile broadened into a grin. "It's nothing like *that*, Miss Young. Whatever you might be thinking."

Lucy could feel the color in her cheeks deepen. She wasn't accustomed to being teased. "I wasn't—"

"Oh, yes, you were. And I can't blame you. Lawyers can be old goats, can't they?"

"I wouldn't say—"

"No, of course you wouldn't." Fran had said Mr. Schuyler could charm the bees off the trees. At the time, Lucy had thought scornfully that it was more that anything in pants could charm the blouse off Fran. But she was beginning to understand just what the other woman meant. It was very hard to maintain the suitable air of professional detachment when Mr. Schuyler was looking at one with that mixture of boyish earnestness and mischief. "I wouldn't ask you to do anything I wouldn't myself. It's just a bit of . . . client development."

"Client development?" Lucy echoed.

"Yes." Mr. Schuyler steepled his fingers in front of him. "You know how busy we've all been with Merola—"

Not too busy to squire Prunella Pratt to *Tosca*, thought Lucy, but didn't say it.

"Well, there's this Mr. Ravenel, from Charleston. He has an art gallery down there, and he's thinking of expanding his operations to New York. Mr. Cromwell is particularly concerned that he should be extended every courtesy. Now"—Mr. Schuyler heaved a long-suffering sigh—"Ravenel just wired to let us know that he arrives in town on Friday."

Lucy tilted her head, indicating she was listening.

Mr. Schuyler fiddled with his silver pen. "Mr. Cromwell is taking him to lunch—but he's on his own for supper Friday night." Glancing up, he said, "I'll be honest with you. I was meant to take him out. But my stepmother's making a nuisance of herself. And when she makes a nuisance of herself . . . Well, are you sure you don't want to reconsider your professional stance on smothering?"

Lucy wasn't quite sure she liked where this was going. Quickly, she said, "Perhaps Mr. Ravenel might enjoy the opera?"

Mr. Schuyler pulled a comical face. "From what I've heard of the man . . . I doubt it. I've spoken to him on the phone. He sounds a bit like Huck Finn. Mark Twain," he added.

"I've read it." She didn't want to get off on the wrong foot with Mr. Schuyler on the first day, but . . . "I seem to remember something about whitewashing fences."

"You've found me out." Mr. Schuyler cast her a look of mock repentance. "What do you say, Miss Young? Are you willing to cancel your plans on Friday night?"

Her plans for Friday night included such fascinating activities as washing her stockings and mending her second-best blouse, where a seam had split beneath the arm.

Mr. Schuyler's gold cuff links glittered in the light of the window. They were very new, with his monogram engraved with suitable flourishes and curlicues. "It shouldn't be too onerous," he said encouragingly. "Just a few cocktails . . . dinner . . . Keep him happy."

Lucy could hear her grandmother's voice. *No better than she should be . . . going out to work like a man.*

She'd had employers like that before. But she hadn't expected it of Philip Schuyler.

"Would you have asked the same of Meg?"

"Meg," said Mr. Schuyler firmly, "is a great girl, but she has an accent that could curdle cream. And that unfortunate fringe. We're trying to entertain Ravenel, not torture him—even if he is being a damned nuisance."

Just what kind of entertainment did he have in mind?

Taking her silence for assent, Mr. Schuyler leaned back in his chair. "It's only for Friday night. We just need someone to hold his hand, make sure he has a good time."

Lucy fought a wave of disappointment. She'd so wanted to make a good impression. But not at the expense of her self-respect.

"I'm sorry, Mr. Schuyler," she said, and there was a hint of steel in her voice. "But I'm afraid you'll have to find someone else. I'm not a good-time girl. And I don't hold hands."

"Not even for the greater good of Cromwell, Polk and Moore?" The charm was turned on full bore.

Politely but firmly, Lucy said, "I am happy to be of service to the firm—during business hours."

She felt sick to her stomach—she couldn't lose this job, not now—but made herself meet his eyes, coolly, levelly.

"Well, then." Sitting back in his chair, Mr. Schuyler regarded her with speculation, and just a hint of admiration. In a very different voice, he said, "Miss Young, I'm not asking you to do anything I wouldn't myself. I'd trade with you, if I could. What would you rather? Steak at Delmonico's or opera with my stepmother?"

Daringly, Lucy said, "I've never seen *Tosca*."

"Don't tempt me." More seriously, he said, "Are you sure you won't reconsider? I give you my word that if Ravenel doesn't behave like a gentleman, I will personally see that he never does business with this firm again."

Something about the way he said it made Lucy think of the knight her mother had painted for her, the knight in the mural in the Pratt house, raising his sword against all comers.

"Well . . ."

Mr. Schuyler saw his advantage. "If you do this," he said fervently, "I will owe you the biggest martini Manhattan has to offer."

Lucy looked at him from under her lashes. "Martinis are illegal."

"Not if you know the right people." Bees from the trees, Lucy thought dizzily. This was the world her mother had known, a world where people knew people and the ordinary rules didn't apply, a world away from the mundanities of making sure the rolls were shaped and bread was baked. "What do you say, Miss Young? A dinner in exchange for a drink?"

It was about winning his confidence, Lucy reminded herself. About winning his confidence and winning her way into those files.

"All right," she said slowly, and saw the expression of triumph on Philip Schuyler's well-bred face. "But only this once."

What was one dinner, after all?

Seven

Kate

I felt a meager ray of sun on my face but kept my eyes shut just one more moment; one more moment to extend my dream where I was lying in my comfortable bed in my comfortable house with my mother and father in the room next to mine, my dog, Sassy, sleeping at my feet. There was no war, and no shell-shocked soldiers with missing limbs stumbling through the city, no blackout windows shutting out the light. It was a memory of when I was a girl, a memory of *before*, and my exhaustion of the last week was making me far too susceptible to having hopeless dreams.

A scratching sound made its way through my dream state, and briefly I thought it was Sassy's nails on the wood floor of my old bedroom, trying to dig her way to China. It was a habit Sassy had had since she'd been a puppy, and one my mother would scold her for, usually followed by a threat that she would put Sassy out on the street. But we both knew that Sassy was beloved by both of us, and spoiled rotten to boot, and the worst that would happen would be Sassy getting another soup bone to gnaw on in the kitchen.

But Sassy was long gone, a victim of a mule pulling a milk wagon that had been spooked by the honking of a car horn. I opened my eyes, staring at the faded chintz of the chaise longue that had been my bed for the last four nights, sure now that the scratching wasn't in my head but most likely in the walls. *Rats!*

I catapulted out of the chaise, catching the hem of my lab coat on the unruly spring, and miraculously landed on the floor with both feet. With one giant leap, I reached behind my desk for the cast-iron skillet that I'd found in the corner of the attic room. Because of its heft and telltale dings on the back of it, I assumed it had probably been used as an effective weapon against all intruders, not just the furry four-legged variety.

I paused, listening for the scratching again, trying to find which wall it was coming from and hoping the rat wasn't *too* big. Not that I was afraid of something like a rat, just that the large ones made such a mess and took time to clean up.

Slowly, I turned toward the sound and found Captain Ravenel in bed sitting up against plumped pillows, an empty breakfast tray on the table next to him. He was holding his chart, the attached pen poised above it.

"I hope you have more modern medicine than that to knock me out with," he said with a soft drawl.

"I heard scratching . . ." I stopped, suddenly realizing that he wasn't delirious with fever, and was sitting up in bed and speaking. "How . . . ?"

"Nurse Hathaway came in about an hour ago, and pronounced my fever broken. I was also starving so she brought me breakfast. No grits, but I managed to eat it all anyway. I'm weak as a foal and I'm pretty sure I couldn't shoot straight to save my life, but I'm feeling much better."

I took a step toward him, too shocked to speak. The night before he'd been clammy with sweat and I'd begun to finally admit to myself that Dr. Greeley might have been right all along.

"But . . . ," I finally managed to say.

He looked at the skillet. "You can put that away. I promise you that I'm stronger, but most definitely not strong enough to ravish you. Just strong enough to doodle a little bit with pen and paper while you slept. Nurse Hathaway and I both agreed that we should let you sleep. She said you've been taking care of me without a proper rest." He tilted his head. "Although I must say that your rumpled appearance and sleepy eyes are very alluring. I'm almost tempted to start all over."

"Oh," I said, the skillet sliding to the floor with a thud as my hands reached for my hair. My comb had been dislodged while I'd slept and I was almost grateful for the lack of a mirror in my attic room.

My gaze moved to his chart and the pen in his hand and I suddenly remembered who I was and who he was. Trying to muster as much authority as I could with my hair half-hanging down my back and my eyes still puffy with sleep, I approached the bed. "Excuse me, Captain. But what are you doing? No one is supposed to mark on your chart except for medical personnel . . ."

I stopped as I reached his side, realizing the source of the scratching noise. The page had been flipped over to the blank side, but instead of an empty sheet of paper, elegant strokes of a pen like the gossamer threads of a web now filled the middle of it. Leaning closer, I recognized a remarkable likeness of my own face.

"You're very good," I said, my admiration superseding my need to reassert myself as a medical professional.

His hand began to tremble, the exertion of sitting up and sketching too much for his weakened body. I took the chart from him and settled him back against his pillow, already knowing that I would meticulously copy everything onto a clean chart so I could keep the sketch. I told myself it was so Dr. Greeley wouldn't see it and make conjectures where none should be, but there was something intimate and familiar about the way Captain Ravenel had drawn my face, something *raw*. And I remembered again the first time he'd looked at me, and how it seemed as if he knew me.

"You saved my leg," he said quietly, moving his foot under the sheet.

I moved aside the sheet to examine the wound that I had cleaned and rebandaged the night before. The adhesive was loose, telling me that Nurse Hathaway had also already examined the wound, but I needed to see for myself. Pushing aside the bandage, I was amazed by what I saw. Instead of the red inflamed skin around the sutures that I'd grown used to seeing, it was merely pink now, a thin scab already beginning to form. If I'd believed in miracles, I would have said that I had just witnessed one. Or maybe this soldier's strength of will was more powerful than any medicine.

I replaced the bandage and the sheet. "I wish I could take credit, but I can't. It was a group effort by all the nurses and doctors at Stornaway—"

"It was you," he said, gently cutting me off.

I started to protest, but he said, "When I was first brought here, I remember you. It was raining . . ." He closed his eyes and I waited as I remembered, too.

"You were soaking wet," he said slowly, his eyes still closed. "And it made your clothing transparent."

I sucked in my breath, disturbed and titillated all at the same time. He spoke to me as if we were old acquaintances, as if familiarity was taken for granted. As if a mention of my transparent dress could be said with the same tone of voice as he might use to tell me that I had a crumb on my chin.

He opened his eyes and I saw there were brown flecks in the marsh green depths, as if even his eye color couldn't be simple and straightforward. "There was a man, too. A disagreeable man if I'm remembering correctly. You were defying him and saying you would take over my care."

I straightened my back, determined to be seen as not a woman, but a professional. "I'm a doctor, and I thought your leg could be saved. And besides, you asked me to."

His lopsided smile would have appeared boyish on another face, but there was nothing boyish about Captain Cooper Ravenel. "Do you always do what you're asked?"

"Hardly." I moved back from the bed, determined to put space between us. "I've written to your family in Charleston to let them know of your injury and where you are. I wasn't sure if the Army had notified them, or if your family expected you in South Carolina by now. You weren't supposed to come here. It was a bit of an emergency and I'm afraid the paperwork might not have been a priority." I put the chart down on the chaise longue and began reparations to my hair before anybody else saw me. "We haven't heard anything back yet, but it's been less than a week. I would expect a telegram any day now, or they're already on their way to see you."

A shadow flickered behind his eyes, and I wondered if he was thinking of his Victorine and wondering why she hadn't written back, or if she was on the first train to New York. I hoped she was. The sooner she got here, the sooner I could refocus my efforts on being the best doctor I could be without the frivolous thoughts and feelings this particular patient seemed to evoke.

There was a small knock on the door before it was pushed open by Nurse Hathaway carrying a tray of syringes and small paper cups of water. "Good morning, Doctor," she said cheerily as she made her way to the captain's bed. "I hope you don't mind that I let you sleep. I took Captain Ravenel's vitals and his fever was completely gone. And he was complaining of being hungry and he managed to talk me into bringing him breakfast. I brought it from the doctors' dining room since the food there is typically more appetizing. Dr. Greeley wasn't there yet, so it's probably his. I saved yours in the kitchen so nobody would eat it. I hope that's all right."

She winked at me, and as much as I wanted to, I didn't wink back. "Thank you, Nurse. If he throws it all up because his stomach isn't ready for solid foods yet, I'll know who to get to come clean it up."

"Yes, Doctor." She busied herself with the patient, taking his temperature again and giving him water to drink. "I also thought you should know that Dr. Greeley is on the warpath this morning. Apparently a file was taken from his office and he wants to know by whom. But I think he'll discover that he simply misplaced it, and if he searches for it again he'll find it where he thought he left it."

She picked up the breakfast tray and placed it outside the room before picking up the medicine tray again and heading toward the door. "I'll be back later to sponge bathe the patient. Unless you'd prefer to do it again?"

Heat flooded my cheeks as I remembered the frequent cold baths I'd given Captain Ravenel to bring down his fever. I hadn't even paid attention to his muscled torso or long, lean legs. At least, not in a non-medical way.

"That will be all, Nurse Hathaway. Thank you. For everything."

I moved to the windows to push aside the blackout curtain, hoping my complexion would return to normal by the time I was done. The city sprang to life beneath the window seven stories above the street. Since nearly the beginning of the war, New York at night became a tomb of dark-clad people moving silently throughout the dimly lit city, headlights of cars half-covered with black paint. But in the daylight people became like hibernating animals after a long winter, emerging from their caves into the sunshine. I wondered how much longer the war could last. With news of German defeats and the success of the Allied invasion of France, I felt sure it would be over soon. But we'd all been saying that for more than a year.

When I turned around again, my gaze fell on the sketch. I picked it up, unable to resist, and studied it as my mother had once taught me to study artwork. *The skill of the artist can be determined from the lightness of his paint strokes and the delicate lines of his sketch work.* "Are you a professional artist, Captain Ravenel? You really are very good."

He shook his head, his face marred with something I could only think of as regret. "No. I just dabble in pen-and-ink sketches. Before Uncle Sam asked me to visit Europe and shoot Germans, I was an art dealer with a gallery in Charleston. My grandfather, however, was a well-known painter. You may have even heard of him. Augustus Ravenel."

I stared at him for a long moment, wondering if I'd heard correctly. I remembered how his last name had seemed familiar to me, and now I knew why. "Augustus Ravenel was your grandfather?" I sat down in the chaise, mindful of the errant spring. "My mother loved his work. Whenever one of his paintings appeared in a gallery here in New York, she would take me so I could study it. I always wondered why we didn't own any of his work. My father was a lawyer, and I know we could have afforded a small painting at least. But my mother wouldn't even consider it. I daresay it would be an odd coincidence if I owned a piece of your grandfather's artwork now, and here you are, my patient."

He smiled, his odd eyes watching me closely. "You said your mother would take you to galleries so you could study the artwork. Are you an artist, too, Doctor?"

"Sadly, no, despite my mother's deepest wishes. She had a love for art although no talent for it. She hoped that I might, so I spent years taking art lessons, but I was a severe disappointment. And then my father died of lung cancer when he was only fifty, and that sealed my fate. I decided then that I was going to become a doctor."

"That couldn't have been easy, going against your mother's wishes. And to pursue a career not many women aspire to. You must be a very strong woman."

When Dr. Greeley said the same thing, it wasn't meant as a compliment. But coming from Captain Ravenel's mouth, it sounded as if he were calling me Cleopatra, the Queen of Sheba, and Mata Hari all at once. I felt my cheeks coloring again, and looked down at the sketch to hide my face. "The likeness is remarkable. If I hadn't known for sure that you've been unconscious for most of the time you've been here, I'd accuse you of spending a lot of time studying me."

He was silent for a long moment, and I glanced up, thinking he must have gone back to sleep. Instead, his eyes were focused on me with an intensity I was unfamiliar with but from which I couldn't look away. Quietly, he said, "That's because I've been drawing your likeness since I was old enough to pick up a pen."

Afraid he might still be suffering from delirium, I opened my mouth to ask him to explain, but froze as I stared at the wall behind his bed.

I could debride an infected wound, amputate a limb, and wipe up bloody vomit without batting an eye. I could even flatten a rodent with an iron skillet and not blink. But the one thing I could not abide was a cockroach, most likely stemming from a childhood incident involving one of the six-legged bugs that had fallen into my bathtub while I was in it. And at the moment one of the mahogany-colored insects was currently crawling up the wall behind the captain, its long antennas casting grotesque shadows onto the white wall.

Before I could think, I screamed.

Captain Ravenel sat up suddenly, his face paling from the sudden movement of his still-injured leg, then looked at the wall behind him. He snagged a square of gauze from his bedside table, then reached out his hand and cupped it over the cockroach, effectively imprisoning him within his long-fingered fist.

Utterly humiliated, I wanted to whip out my diploma and tell him that I'd graduated from medical school with honors, that I had replaced my own shoulder in its socket without passing out, and that I thought that people who fainted at the sight of blood shouldn't be allowed to have children.

His voice belied the smile behind his words. "Don't worry, Doctor. The only reason why I didn't scream is because I'm used to them in Charleston. Except there they're so big you could saddle them. And they fly."

Completely annoyed now with him and myself, I yanked up the wastebasket and brought it to him, hoping the bug was at least dead before he discarded it. He kept his hand by his side so that I had to lean over to give him a better aim.

"Closer," he said, his voice weak.

I turned my head to see him better. "Are you all right?" I asked with concern. Our noses were almost touching.

"I am now," he said, lifting his head slightly, then touched his lips to mine.

I told myself later that it was the surprise of it, the shock of his lips against mine that created a warm light exploding behind my eyes. Or more likely it was from the anger I remembered to feel a split second afterward when I realized what was happening.

The door flew open and Dr. Greeley stood in the threshold, his balding forehead glistening with sweat, his cold eyes quickly assessing the scenario in front of him.

"Dr. Schuyler," he said, his voice full of pompous righteousness. "I'll see you in my office."

Waves of anger and humiliation wafted through me, most of it directed at myself. All of those years of focus and determination possibly erased in one moment of stupid recklessness. I didn't try to defend myself or explain anything, knowing it wouldn't make any difference.

"Dr. Schuyler is entirely innocent, I assure you," Captain Ravenel said, his soft consonants deceptively sweet. "I'm afraid in my delirium I've mistaken her for someone else."

Without saying anything or looking at either one of them, I carefully put down the chart on the bedside table, hoping Nurse Hathaway would take the sketch before anybody else could see it, then replaced the wastebasket before leaving the room. Slowly, I walked down the steps, ignoring the elevator so I could delay the inevitable as long as I could. My shoes tapped quietly on the marble circular staircase as I slowly descended to the fifth floor, pausing briefly to view the bas-relief of Saint George slaying the dragon.

I stared at the frozen pair, wishing for the first time since my father died that I had a knight who would slay my dragons for me. But I'd given up those childish fantasies the day we buried him, along with hair bows and pinafores. I turned on my heel and headed toward Dr. Greeley's office, Captain Ravenel's words still echoing in my head. *I've been drawing your likeness since I was old enough to pick up a pen.*

I paused outside the office door, then took a deep breath before going inside, wondering if my mother had been right and that I should have become an artist after all.

Eight

Olive

The greengrocer's name was Mr. Jungmann, and his face always brightened when Olive walked into his shop on Lexington Avenue and Sixty-fourth Street to place the order for the next day's vegetables. She liked that. How nice it was, to escape from the House of Disapproval—frowning housekeepers, frowning cooks, frowning Prunella and her frowning mother—and have someone's face actually *brighten* when you entered a room.

Ironic, wasn't it? All of New York society longed to be invited inside the Pratt mansion, and Olive wanted only to escape from it. And her own father had built the place! Didn't it belong to her just a little bit, not in a material way but in the way a house always belonged to all those who had lived and loved and suffered in it? As if it had kept behind a small part of your soul.

"Miss Jones! I was beginning to lose the hope of you."

Olive realized she had already entered the shop and was staring at a pyramid of apples. She looked up and tried to return Mr. Jungmann's wide smile, but failed by at least half an inch. "Good morning, Mr. Jungmann. I had a late start today, I'm afraid. I have Cook's list right here." She pulled the paper from her coat pocket and held it out in her mittened hand.

"Ah, there we are." He was so hearty and jovial, such a nice big bear of a man, loyal to the consonants of his homeland: each *w* rendered lovingly as a *v*, each *j* softened into a *y*. (*Yovial,* she thought.) She always imagined him with a wife and ten red-cheeked children who crawled all over him when he returned home at night (did he live above the shop, or somewhere else?) and checked his pockets for sweets, though of course she never asked him such familiar questions.

"Cook also wanted to know if you have any peaches. Something's gone wrong with the trees in the hothouse in Newport, and we haven't gotten a crate from them in weeks."

He studied the list, which seemed much smaller in his enormous paw than it had inside her mitten. "Peaches? Why you want peaches in December?"

Olive shrugged. "Peaches Melba, I think. It's all the rage these days. They're having a dinner party."

Mr. Jungmann looked over the top of the list with his bright blue eyes. "When you need these peaches?"

"Saturday?"

He folded the paper and tucked it into his breast pocket. "For you, Miss Jones, I will find these peaches. Not for that terrible Valkyrie, Mrs. Jackins!" He shook his finger at the cook, though she was several blocks away. "But for you, Miss Jones, I find peaches in December. I deliver them Saturday morning."

"I hope that's not inconvenient. I'm sure you'd rather spend the time with your family."

He spread his hands before her. "What family, Miss Jones? I am a poor bachelor. Is no trouble."

Something about the way he said the word *bachelor* made the blood prickle into her cheeks. "Well, thank you. Mrs. Jackins will appreciate it, I'm sure."

"I already tell you. The peaches, they are not for the happiness of Mrs. Jackins."

From another man, this might have sounded like an invitation of some kind: an invitation of the improper kind, or at least of the indelicate kind. But Mr. Jungmann had already turned away and was sorting through the potatoes, plucking out the choicest ones and placing them in the slatted wooden box that would be brought in a wagon later that afternoon to the modest delivery entrance at the extreme left-hand corner of the Pratt façade. He didn't expect any kind of return for his trouble. He was simply providing her with peaches to make her happy.

"Do you know what you are, Mr. Jungmann?" she said. "You're a gentleman."

"Bah. Away with you, Miss Jones. You have some chores to do, I think?"

"Yes. But I do need to bring back a few things for the soup. Do you mind?" She held out her basket.

"What do you need?"

He filled the basket and gave her a beautiful rosy-cheeked apple to eat on the way home, and when he handed it to her he peered into her eyes. "Everything is good, Miss Jones? You need something?"

"No, no. I mean yes. Everything is excellent."

"You need to make smile more. That is how to be happy. You smile, you are happy."

"I thought it was the other way around."

He shook his head. "No, no. Smile first, that is how."

"I'll try to remember that, thank you."

Outside, however, it was too cold to smile. Olive's face froze at once in the chill wind blowing down Lexington Avenue from the north. She turned up Sixty-fourth Street, seeking relief, and as she walked along the quiet sidewalk, basket bumping rhythmically against her leg, she considered what Mr. Jungmann had said, and whether you could force happiness on yourself, simply by arranging your mouth in a happy expression.

And yet, she didn't feel unhappy, did she? You couldn't feel unhappy, exactly, when you were as physically busy as Olive was, up and down stairs, making beds and tables and fires, forever cleaning, cleaning, cleaning. You might be frustrated and bothered and exhausted, but that was a different world entirely from the black hole in which she'd existed since she found her father's body slumped over his desk in the cold January dawn last winter. She had begun climbing out of that hole from the moment she arrived on the service steps of the Pratt mansion—oh, that feeling of resolve, when she had let the knocker fall!—and she hadn't slipped since.

So what had Mr. Jungmann seen in her face that had caused him such concern?

The air was crisp and cold, smelling of smoke. Manhattan always smelled of smoke, even up here, away from the offices and factories, and especially near Fourth Avenue, where the railway cut through, chugging toward New Haven and Boston and points north, filling the air with dirty steam. In the country, the air would smell like snow, white and sharp.

She crossed Fourth Avenue—no trains passing, thank goodness—and continued up the street. The houses began to enlarge as she left the noisome tracks behind; trees began to sprout up from the neat new pavement. At Madison Avenue, she should have turned right, but instead she continued toward Fifth Avenue and the bare vegetation of Central Park.

Harry.

The name slipped free from deep in her mind, where she tried to keep it locked. It was the trees, wasn't it? The beckoning fingers of the park, where you might almost forget you were a New York housemaid who had no business receiving notes under her door from a scion of one of the city's most prominent families. Still less keeping the latest note, which had appeared just that morning, tucked in the pocket of her skirt so it could brush unseen against her leg—the opposite leg from the vegetable basket, one leg naughty and the other leg dutiful—as she went about the business of her day.

> *You seem to think I am some kind of satyr. I assure you I am not. I have no designs on you, only an admiration that borders on veneration. Can you please have a little pity for me? At least return my glance when we pass in the hallway, so I know I still exist for you. A smile, I suppose, is too much to ask for, though I admit I harbor a secret hope that you are only saving one for Christmas. Listen to me. I am an idiot. I have never written notes like this before, and I'm afraid I don't know how it's done. I have been working on my sketch of you, but I can't seem to get the way of your eyes anymore. You are slipping away, and I don't know what to do. Except hope.*

Not that she had memorized it, or any of the others. Not that she could picture his quick handwriting, or hear the sound of Harry Pratt's voice as he ate with the family in the massive paneled dining room a few yards away from her, a world away from her.

Not that she remembered each time they had passed in the hallway: the flash of the electric light on his wheat-colored hair, the brightening of his face—like Mr. Jungmann, only lit by a thousand more watts—and the glimpse of his smile before she looked down at the rug and hurried on, and on, and on, usually forgetting where she was going.

Hoping he would touch her arm and stop her.

Praying to God that he would not.

He never did, and sometimes she wondered if she had imagined the whole thing: the quiet star-filled night in the room at the top of the stairs, the pencil that moved in eager little jerks, the expression on Harry's face, the things he had said. The way he had looked at her, as if she were a goddess instead of a housemaid. An angel, instead of a bitter young woman contemplating a sordid revenge on the family under whose roof she lived.

But it was better this way, wasn't it? Better that she pretended it hadn't happened. Better that the door to the room upstairs remained shut, because what beckoned beyond it—she had a vague impression of colors and vibrancy and imagination and laughter, something extraordinary and never ending—was nothing more than a fairy tale. Medieval allegory, that was what Harry called it, but what was medieval allegory except a fairy tale?

The kind of fairy tale her father used to read to her at night, before he died.

Olive crossed Fifth Avenue, dodging a pair of clattering half-empty omnibuses, and turned to walk northward with the park at her side. The basket was heavy now, but she didn't care. She gazed over the wall and across the brown thicket of winter trees, the distant towers of Belvedere Castle. Above them, the sky was gray, contemplating snow. For a moment, she imagined walking through that empty demi-wilderness next to Harry, not saying anything, simply existing in a tender equilibrium in which there were no such things as housemaids and mansions and—

"Olive."

A figure rose from the bench ahead, and Olive had just enough time to gasp before Harry Pratt appeared before her under a peaked wool cap, smiling and woeful at once, his jaw square against the folds of his India cashmere scarf, looking so much like he had in her imagination that she hovered, for an instant, in a kind of delicious netherworld of hope. A medieval allegory.

"Mr. Pratt! What are you doing here?"

"Waiting for you. Freezing to death."

"But that's ridiculous."

"Yes, it is, isn't it? You haven't left me any choice, however." He slapped his gloved hands together. "Haven't you read my notes?"

"I don't know what you're talking about, and I'm going to be late."

He laid his hand on her elbow. "Please, Olive. Only a moment. We'll go into the park, if you like."

She glanced at the world to her left, and back at Harry's pleading face.

"Say yes," he whispered, lifting the basket from the crook of her elbow.

She heard herself break in two. "Just for a minute."

What a smile he gave her, what a reward for giving in. He held her basket with one hand and took her arm with the other, and they slipped through the gap in the wall and into the artificial urban forest, all by themselves, and Olive thought, *This is so foolish. What am I doing?*

Harry said, "You're going to model for me again."

"What?"

"You must. I can't sleep. I've never had so many ideas, never been so ready to work. Do you know what that's like? As if my fingers and my brain are going to burst. Every time I see you, it all spreads in front of me with so much clarity, this perfect vision of what I have to paint. What I was *meant* to paint, what I was put on this earth to create. And then you disappear, and it's gone. No, worse. It's there, like a dream when you've just woken up, and you can't quite touch it."

He stopped to catch his breath, as if he'd been keeping the words at bay for too long, and they had come out of him too quickly. His arm was snug around her elbow. He smelled a little bit like the house itself, of wood and smoke but also soap, that same intimate scent that had drawn her in a week ago. She turned her face away, but it was too late. Her ribs hurt. Of all the stupid things, to be in love with the smell of soap.

"This is the most ridiculous thing I've ever heard."

"Go ahead and pretend you don't feel it."

"I don't feel anything at all, except a big heap of admiration for your technique. Tell me, how many housemaids have you lured in this way?"

He stopped in the path and set down the basket and turned toward her. His white breath curled around hers, and his cheekbones were stained the most edible shade of apple pink. "None."

"Well, you sound like an expert."

Harry was frowning down at her, in such a way that even the most cynical and sensible girl in the world would want to smooth away the furrow in his brow, to push back the lock of hair on his forehead and tuck it under his cap. To let him do whatever he wanted to her.

Until the next girl turned up.

"All right," he said. "Fair enough. I know I sound like an idiot. I'll take you back to the house, and we can pretend we've never met before. If that's what makes you feel better, Olive. If that's what will make you happy. I guess, if we do, I'm only back where I was a week ago, all restless and frustrated, wanting to just get drunk and forget about everything. Thinking there was no point in anything, that I was all by myself in the middle of a wilderness. But just tell me one thing, Olive. Give me one little word."

"What word is that?"

"Just that you felt it, too, even if it was only an instant. Tell me I wasn't alone up there, Olive. God knows I'm sick to death of being alone in a crowded room."

She picked up her basket and turned away, back up the path toward the gap in the wall on Fifth Avenue. "I can't."

"Why not?"

She started walking. "Because you won't leave it at that, will you? You'll want me to come up and pose for you again, and you won't stop until I do, and it will ruin me."

He tried to take the basket back, but she wouldn't let him, and they walked in silence out of the park and up Fifth Avenue. When they reached Sixty-ninth Street, she said, "You'll have to go on without me. We can't be seen together."

"But you'll come upstairs tonight. You must."

She didn't reply.

"I won't touch you, I swear. I won't say a single word until you see the finished painting, and you can see for yourself what I mean. You'll see that you can believe in me."

She turned and stood on the corner, waiting for a delivery wagon to pass by. The horse's hooves thudded in the road; the wheels creaked. A gust of wind caught the edge of her hat, swirling with the first snowflakes of winter, and as she grabbed the crown with her hand and started across Fifth Avenue, she heard Harry's voice floating behind her.

"Excellent! I'll see you tonight!"

Nine

Lucy

"Shouldn't you be putting on your glad rags?"

"My—?" Lucy was elbows deep in a pile of documents, looking for the latest rider to the Merola contract.

"Your sparkling raiment." Philip Schuyler rested a hand against the edge of the desk, his gold signet ring tapping against the dark wood. "Or, at the very least, your dinner dress."

Lucy looked at him blankly. "I don't have a dinner dress."

That wasn't a problem for Philip Schuyler. Her employer was elegant in evening dress, his white tie impeccably tied, discreet mother-of-pearl and ebony studs marching the way up his lean chest. The stark black and white set off his light tan, his blond good looks.

"Then you'd best find one, hadn't you?" he said, and, for a mad moment, Lucy's mouth went dry and the color rushed to her cheeks as bedtime upon bedtime of fairy tales came flooding back to her.

But it was only in fairy tales that Cinderella was invited to the ball.

Mr. Schuyler said jovially, "Have you forgotten? You're wining and dining that art dealer fellow, Ravenel—or dining, at least." He pulled a long face. "I regret to report that Delmonico's sold off their wine cellar last year thanks to those Philistines in Congress."

Delmonico's. Ravenel. Lucy drew in a deep breath, thankful for the pile of documents that ostensibly demanded her attention, thankful for the heat of the day that explained away the flush in her cheeks.

Thank goodness Mr. Schuyler had no inkling of what she had been thinking! What a fool she would look, daydreaming of being plucked from her papers by the prince, like Cinderella from the ashes.

Lucy concentrated on shuffling the documents on the desk into a neat pile. "But, surely, with everything that needs to be done—"

"Merola can wait a day." Mr. Schuyler plucked the pile out of her hands and held the papers just out of her reach. "You did forget, didn't you? Don't try to lie to me. Your cheeks tell all."

"I—" Lucy made a grab for the papers, but he dropped them onto the blotter with a decisive thunk. "We've had so much to do."

And it was true. They'd both been working every hour God gave them, at the office before Miss Meechum, there long after the janitor made the rounds of the hall, his mop bumping gently against the woodwork. Mr. Schuyler might play at being a dilettante, but when the situation demanded—and it had demanded—he had buckled down with the sort of fierce concentration that Lucy had once imagined that he would accord only a tennis match or an act at the opera.

And it was the opera tonight, wasn't it? In the scrum of work, of papers to be typed and retyped, every clause a crisis, every comma crucial, Lucy had forgotten about Mr. Schuyler's engagement to see *Tosca* with his stepmother.

And her own with Mr. John Ravenel, the art dealer from South Carolina.

Or was it North Carolina? Lucy couldn't remember. She'd never been as far south as Jersey.

Mr. Schuyler grinned at her. With mock seriousness, he said, "Don't deny me my moment of triumph." His eyes meeting hers, he added softly, "It's a relief to know that you aren't entirely perfect."

"Far from it," said Lucy repressively, putting the lid on the treacherous flutters his words made her feel. Mr. Schuyler flirted as easily as he breathed. It was a habit with him. And she'd be a fool to assume otherwise. "I'm just as fallible as anyone else."

A secretary didn't fall for her employer. Her engaged employer, Lucy reminded herself.

Mr. Schuyler didn't seem to notice anything out of the ordinary. "The reservation is for eight, which means you have plenty of time to don your gay apparel." Reaching into one of the desk drawers, he dropped a pile of bills on the desk. "That should cover your cab fare."

Bad enough that she was going out to dinner, alone, with a strange man. But the pile of bills on the table . . . They made her feel cheap.

Lucy's shoulders stiffened beneath the boxy fabric of her suit. "I couldn't possibly—"

Mr. Schuyler chucked her under the chin. "You're doing this for the firm, remember? It's a business expense. A legitimate business expense," he added, his lips quirking.

Despite herself, Lucy couldn't quite help smiling back. She'd had some queries about his expense reports when they'd started working together last week. "You mean like your greens fees?"

"Just like my greens fees," said Mr. Schuyler solemnly. He pushed the bills toward Lucy. "Don't make me slip it into your purse."

This money, Lucy was quite sure, wasn't coming out of the firm coffers. This was direct from Mr. Schuyler. She knew what her grandmother would say about that. But . . .

"All right," said Lucy, and, belatedly, "Thank you."

Averting her eyes, she scooped up the pile of singles. During the day, working together, Mr. Schuyler's tie askew, his hair rumpled, a mess of papers between them, it was easy to forget the difference in their stations.

But not now, with the detritus of his largesse on the desk between them.

"Righto, then. I'm off." He whistled an unfamiliar tune as he rooted through his pockets.

"Here." Lucy scooped up his opera glasses from the desk and handed them to him.

"You're a treasure, Miss Young." Mr. Schuyler swirled a white silk scarf around his neck. "What would I do without you?"

"Squint," Lucy said succinctly.

Mr. Schuyler chuckled. "Touché, my dear. Touché." He paused with a hand on the doorjamb, the late-afternoon sunlight slanting through the window turning his hair to gold. "By the by, will you do me a small favor? Our little substitution—I haven't mentioned it to Ravenel. Or Mr. Cromwell. If either of them asks, you will tell them that something madly important came up at the last minute, won't you?"

Lucy felt the bottom fall out of her stomach. "But I thought— You said you'd arranged—"

Her employer deliberately misunderstood her. "You're all set at Delmonico's. You'll find the reservation in my name. Just tell them to put it on my account." He grinned. "Or, better yet, on Mr. Cromwell's. Have a steak for me!"

And before Lucy could protest, he was gone, sauntering down the hallway, his hands in his pockets, a whistle on his lips—and every head in the stenographic pool turning to watch him go.

There were times when Lucy dearly wished that she were the cursing kind. Since she wasn't, she contented herself with stomping back into Mr. Schuyler's office and closing the door with a muted but decided click.

Wonderful. Not only was she having dinner with a strange man; she was having dinner with a strange man who was expecting her employer.

On the plus side, thought Lucy, staring tight-lipped at the impeccable countenance of Miss Didi Shippen, it might be a very short dinner.

And she had the office to herself.

The week had been such a blur of work that she hadn't even had time to think of her own private quest, much less pursue it. Mr. Schuyler might have grumbled, but he had been there, right along with her, from dawn to dusk. He'd even taken his lunch at his desk—sandwiches and coffee from the deli down the block. Lucy had made sure that the man at the deli remembered to leave off the mustard and put two sugars and cream in the coffee, and she'd always brought a piece of something sweet as well, coffee cake or cookies that were hard and flavorless compared to the ones her grandmother made, but which Mr. Schuyler received with exaggerated exclamations of gratitude.

Just as he would for Meg, Lucy reminded herself. He was charming, and he wasn't quite the dilettante he appeared, but that didn't change the fact that he was a means to an end, and there wasn't the least reason she should feel guilty about using him to get to the Pratt files. Not that she did feel guilty.

Or maybe just a little. She could feel those dollar bills burning a hole in her purse. It felt wrong taking money from him.

She knew what her grandmother would say.

Like mother, like daughter.

Enough. Lucy walked briskly to the file cabinet. To anyone watching, there was nothing amiss, nothing at all. Just a secretary working late.

For all her other shortcomings, Meg did keep the files in order, everything sternly alphabetized, not a letter out of place. *N . . . O . . . P* was all the way down on the bottom of the third rank of cabinets. Lucy had to kneel down on the worn carpet to scrabble through the files. She could feel the wool of the carpet prickling through her stockings, leaving marks on her knees. But there it was, just where it was meant to be. Pratt.

The file was a substantial one. The papers didn't spill over—Meg had been too well organized for that—but they strained against the cardboard confines.

Lucy resisted the urge to sit back on her haunches and scour through it then and there. That would look odd if Miss Meechum or one of the junior associates were to pop their heads around the door. Instead, she carried it over to the desk, turning it carefully so that the label faced away from the door. One folder looked just like another.

Oh, just the correspondence relating to the Merola contract, she imagined herself saying. *Mr. Schuyler wanted me to find the draft language for the third rider.*

But the door remained chastely closed.

Quickly, quickly. Hands shaking, Lucy drew the papers out of their cardboard casing. Invoices and accountings, that was what most of it seemed to be, and none of it older than—she flipped hastily through the pile—1912. The Pratt trust paid out monies quarterly to Prunella Schuyler, nee Pratt. The correspondence consisted largely of bills from tradesmen, demanding payment from the Pratt trust, and formal letters from Mrs. Schuyler, demanding advances on next quarter's payment. Mrs. Schuyler, it seemed, lived considerably outside her income.

It was an income that would have kept Lucy in stockings and carfare for a very long time, but, judging from the documentation, Mrs. Schuyler hadn't the least problem blazing through an entire quarter's allowance in one visit to Cartier.

Fascinating, in its way, but none of her affair. Tearing herself away from descriptions of diamond clips and sapphire and emerald brooches, Lucy set the pile relating to the Pratt trust aside. Which didn't leave terribly much. There were papers concerning the sale of the house, all of the proceeds from which had gone into the Pratt trust.

Well, what had she expected? Henry August Pratt's personal diary? Letters to his lawyer? *Dear Mr. Cromwell: My wastrel son has impregnated a guest in our home . . .*

Had her mother been a guest? She must have been. She knew the house too well, had described it too fully, to have been a mere visitor.

But who was she? Strange to be asking that about one's own mother. Lucy knew her mother as a brush of serge, as her small hands clutched her mother's skirt; she knew her as the scent of lavender; as a low, sweet voice singing lullabies, and later, much later, as a quiet, withdrawn presence, the sound of pages in a book being turned, a darkened room, a cough that wouldn't go away.

Sometimes, Lucy wondered if the mother she had known was only a shadow, if the real woman had been left somewhere, across the bridge in Manhattan. There had been a hint of something vital about her, but only a hint, like the impression of a flower in an old book, long after the actual petals had faded and crumbled away.

Her mother loved her; she had said so, time and again. But Lucy had never been able to shake the feeling that there was someone her mother loved more, someone who had taken the best of her, leaving only a husk for Lucy and her father.

Lucy's knuckles were white against the dark wood of the desk. She forced herself to relax her hands, finger by finger.

The file, Lucy reminded herself. She still had a dinner dress to acquire, a client to charm. She drew in a deep, shuddering breath, scrunching the old hurts down, as far as they would go.

There wasn't much left in the file. Miscellaneous financial documents—apparently, Mr. Pratt's investments hadn't fared that well in the nineties—and, at the very bottom, a copy of Henry August Pratt's will.

It was surprisingly short. There were no charitable bequests, no recognition of old servants. In fact, the only legatee—the sole legatee—was Pratt's daughter, Prunella.

Had she missed a page? Lucy leafed back through the closely typed pages. No. It was all in order. *To my daughter, Prunella* . . . and then a complicated spate of legalese, which, when translated to English, seemed to be the provision of a trust that kept her from touching any of the principal. There were four trustees, of whom one was Philip Schuyler.

There were no bequests to his wife or to his other children. It was as if they had never been.

One son had died, hadn't he? Lucy struggled to remember. A bar fight on the Lower East Side? The papers had only hinted, but it had been something vaguely sordid. An angry husband?

But there had been two sons, twins. What had the other twin done to be excluded from his father's will?

The date on the will was 1893, the year Lucy had been born.

There was a sharp rapping on the door. "Yoo-hoo? Anyone in there?"

Lucy jammed the file into the drawer and kicked the cabinet closed with her foot. "Yes?"

Fran poked her head around the door. She already had her hat on and was drawing on her gloves. "We're going for chop suey. Want to come?"

Lucy pressed her eyes shut. Only Fran. Fran wouldn't know a file if it bit her. "I would, but . . . I have a dinner engagement."

Fran's eyebrows went up. "A dinner engagement? You've been holding out on us. You never said you had a fellow. Hey, El! Miss Dark Horse has a dinner engagement!"

Lucy cut around Fran, yanking the door of Mr. Schuyler's office firmly shut behind her. She walked purposefully toward her desk. "No, no. It's not like that. It's just . . ."

"Just . . .'?" Fran trailed after Lucy, scenting fresh gossip.

Blast Philip Schuyler and his schemes. Philip Schuyler, sitting seraphically in a box at *Tosca*, his stepmother in silk and diamonds beside him.

Lucy improvised. "It's just . . . a friend of the family. He's visiting from out of town."

Fran pursed her lips significantly. "An out-of-town friend."

Lovely. It would be all over the steno pool by Monday.

There was no strategy like distraction. On an impulse, Lucy said, "Fran, do you know where I can get a cheap dinner dress in the next"— Lucy glanced at the clock above Miss Meechum's desk—"hour and a half?"

"What sort of dinner dress are we talking about?"

"A respectable one. Something I can wear to Delmonico's."

"Delmonico's! I wish my family had friends like that." Fran craned her neck to call back over her shoulder, "Hey, El, did you know we had a Rockefeller in the office?"

"We do?" Eleanor appeared behind Fran, searching in her purse. "Have you seen my gloves?"

Fran rolled her eyes. "Never mind your gloves. Miss Butter Won't Melt here has a date at Delmonico's!"

She oughtn't to have said anything. Briskly, Lucy jammed her hat on her head, securing it with a long pin. "Never mind. I can just wear my suit. It's no one I need to impress, after all."

"Oh, no, you don't." Fran linked an arm through hers. "Delmonico's! I'll send you off right. I know this little woman on Delancey who can make you look like your dress came straight from gay Paree."

Given that Fran had been no closer to Paris than the Bronx, Lucy took that with a grain of salt, but she let herself be towed off to the elevator, Eleanor trotting along behind.

※

Fran's dressmaker might not be Parisian, but she was reasonably cheap. Passing up the gaudier options, Lucy settled on a dress of sapphire blue, with long chiffon panels over a silk slip.

It was only an imitation, she knew, but looking at herself in the long mirror, she could imagine herself at the opera with Philip Schuyler.

She couldn't do anything about her sensible shoes or her battered leather bag, so different from the wisps of beads and silk the other ladies were carrying. But at least her dress looked right. As long as one didn't look too closely.

Delmonico's was housed in an imposing building on Forty-fourth and Fifth. The maître d' took in Lucy's old hat and cheap gloves at a glance.

"Yes?" he said.

Behind the maître d', Lucy could see the dining room, the walls hung with pale yellow silk—*Ach*, she could hear her grandmother say in her head, *such waste!*—the windows shaded with cream lace. An onyx fireplace dominated one side of the room. Large palms provided an illusion of privacy for the well-dressed diners, who spoke in muted tones by the light of yellow-shaded lamps.

Lucy tried to look as though she dined out every day. "Do you have a reservation for Schuyler?"

The name appeared to have a magic effect. The twin furrows disappeared from between the man's brows.

"Schuyler . . . ," said the maître d', checking his book. "Ah, yes! Mr. Schuyler reserved a table in the Palm Trellis. If you would come this way?"

The Palm Trellis, it appeared, was on the roof. The maître d' handed Lucy over to a uniformed elevator operator, who whisked her upstairs to a vast room where white fans turned lazily overhead, dispelling the July heat. Window boxes spilled over with hydrangeas, and sweet-scented wisteria twined around white-painted trellises.

Back at Stornaway House, her attic room would be hot and close. The shared kitchen would be even hotter, with the depressing smell of day-old boiled cabbage that seemed to have sunk into the very walls.

On an impulse, Lucy tugged her mother's ruby pendant from its hiding place. It was heavy and old-fashioned, but the ruby was real. It made her feel, a little bit, as though she belonged here.

Through the long windows, the sky was shading gently toward dusk.

The breeze from the fan ruffled the long chiffon panels of Lucy's dress as she followed yet another attendant through the long room, to a choice table at the back, framed in an arch of wisteria, shaded by two tall palms.

As they approached, a man unfolded himself from his seat at the table. The light was against her; Lucy could make out only a dark suit, dark hair, a broad set of shoulders.

What would Didi Shippen do?

Pinning on a stiff social smile—and trying not to trip on the hem of her gown—Lucy held out a hand. "Mr. Ravenel?"

Mr. Ravenel made no move to take her hand. He stood frozen, an expression of surprise amounting to shock on his face.

In a voice so low that Lucy could hardly hear it, he said, "Your eyes are blue."

Ten

June 1944

Kate

"Well, he *is* a doctor."

I stood in the middle of the tiny single room of a three-floor walkup in a dubious East Side neighborhood south of Park and stared into the pretty freckled face of my best friend, Margie Beckwith, her eyes wide with possibilities.

"So am I," I reminded her. "But I'd rather kiss a cockroach."

She shuddered with an empathy that only sisters or best friends who'd known each other since they were in diapers could have. Our mothers had met on a bench in Central Park when we were babies, our prams parked next to each other by happenstance, and then by design as the women discovered they had much in common. Or, more specifically, that they both had the same delusions of grandeur.

Whereas my father had been a lawyer with a respectable pedigree, most of our family money had been lost in the crash of '29, and while we weren't penniless, we had most definitely become middle class. It had always been apparent to me that while both of my parents had minded our social demotion, my mother had been much less forgiving of our circumstances. She'd been a loving wife and mother, but I'd never been able to completely shake the feeling that she always believed that there had been another life, a bigger, brighter life, waiting for her somewhere around the corner.

Mr. Beckwith sold men's suits at Bergdorf's, while Mrs. Beckwith taught piano to the privileged—and mostly tone-deaf according to her—children of those who'd managed to hold on to their money, or the newly rich. The latter she considered beneath her and were tolerated only because they paid well. Although neither the Schuylers nor the Beckwiths lived anywhere near Fifth Avenue and Sixty-ninth Street, their bench in the park was somehow fitting.

Margie turned toward her closet. "I don't know why you're asking to borrow clothes from me—we're nowhere near the same size. And I certainly don't have anything appropriate for dinner at 21."

"Exactly," I said, eyeing her curvy figure, which had gone out of style during the Victorian age. "I'm not trying to look attractive."

She pulled out a dark gray skirt and examined it before putting it back with a dismissive shake of her head. "That's not something you say to a friend from whom you're borrowing clothes, you know."

"I'm sorry, Margie. I didn't mean it that way. It's just that Dr. Greeley makes me so angry. He's practically blackmailing me to go out with him. Otherwise, he's going to do his best to ruin my career."

"Well, maybe you shouldn't be kissing patients." She sounded a bit peeved as she roughly slid hangers over the rod in her closet.

I blushed at the memory of Captain Ravenel's lips on mine. Despite my best efforts to forget it, I could still taste him every time I closed my eyes. Which is probably why I hadn't had much sleep in the past week. A week where I'd happily delegated his care to Nurse Hathaway and the other staff doctors, ignoring his requests to see me.

"It wasn't like that. He . . . surprised me. And then excused the whole thing to Dr. Greeley by saying he confused me with someone else."

Margie looked over her shoulder at me. "I wish some good-looking man would surprise me with a kiss. That sort of thing doesn't happen in the archives at the New York Public Library, unfortunately. And if it did, it would probably be from some old man wearing tweed with suede elbow patches and smelling of mothballs." She screwed up her face, her good humor returned. "Of course, I'd probably still be grateful. It's been a good deal too long since I was last kissed. This war is taking far too long."

"Send a Western Union to Hitler, why don't you? He probably hasn't realized."

"I just might," she said, turning around and holding up something brown, wool, and indescribable. The only way I could tell it was some sort of garment was because it was on a hanger.

"Whatever it is," I said, "it's perfect."

"It's a dress that was my mother's, and not only is it blatantly out of style, but it's also hideous. And it's about two sizes too big for you."

I was already unbuttoning my blouse. "Then let me borrow a belt, too."

"I'm still not sure why you agreed to go out with this guy, Kate. Just tell him no and let him say what he wants. You're a brilliant woman—one of very few, I'd bet, who've graduated from college in less than four years. And you're a good doctor, too. Surely your work will speak for itself."

I slid the rough material over my head, grimacing in the mirror as it settled on my shoulders. "In a perfect world, maybe. But I'm a woman, and a young woman at that. People will believe what they want to believe. They're already prejudiced against me because I'm only twenty-three and already a doctor. They think I haven't paid my dues because I graduated from medical school in two years—along with just about every other MD candidate since the war started—which they conveniently don't remember. Like it's my fault there's a shortage of doctors. I'm constantly made to feel as if I need to wear my Vassar diploma around my neck as well as my MD to prove myself."

I turned to the side and back, making sure the heavy material hid all of my curves. "So, no, my work doesn't count, only the word of my male colleagues." I leaned forward and plucked Margie's cigarette from the ashtray and took a long drag before regarding myself in the mirror again as I blew smoke at my reflection. "Which is why I'm being forced into this charade tonight. I just need to make sure that Dr. Greeley is left with no illusions. I plan to talk about my thimble collection and my crooked toes all night."

Margie took the cigarette and took a drag before placing it back in the ashtray, studying me with a tilted head and narrowed eyes. "I hate to tell you this, Kate, but even in that awful dress you still look beautiful." She took a folded handkerchief from the top drawer of her dresser. "Maybe if you wipe off your lipstick."

I did as she instructed and faced her again. "How's this?"

She shook her head. "It's no use. Maybe you should show him your toes just in case." Margie stuck her head back into the closet and when she turned around she was smiling triumphantly.

"Here are a pair of my librarian shoes—only seen on elderly women over eighty and younger women who are on their feet all day and work in libraries—and which will look perfect with those old stockings with the ladders running up and down your legs."

I smiled, knowing the thick, clunky heels and manlike uppers would be perfect with the dress. "I hope they don't turn me away. The 21 Club is pretty ritzy." I'd wanted to go to my mother's favorite restaurant—one she'd told me about again and again when I was a child yet where to my knowledge she had not been since I was born—but I'd sadly discovered that Delmonico's had closed in 1923.

Margie took another drag from her cigarette, then blew the smoke up to the ceiling. "Why's he taking you there? It's not like he couldn't take you to some dive—you had to say yes anyway."

"His cousin's the bartender, so he can get us a table. Dr. Greeley is trying to show me how important and well connected he is, I suppose, even though we'll probably be put in some corner by the kitchen." I slid on the shoes and sighed. "I can't believe I went to med school for this."

"Sure. You could be living the glamorous life of a librarian like me instead. What I wouldn't give," she added under her breath.

As I folded up my skirt and blouse to tuck into my pocketbook, she said, "Maybe I should stop by the hospital and meet your Captain Ravenel. Since you're not interested."

"He's taken," I said, a little too quickly. We hadn't heard back from any member of his family, or any Victorine. I'd decided that if something hadn't arrived by today, I would send another letter to let them know that he was on the road to a full recovery and that arrangements could be made to bring him home by the end of the month if his recuperation continued on the same path.

According to Nurse Hathaway, he'd not requested a pen and paper to write a letter himself, and I tried not to read anything into it. I had no interest in the captain except as his doctor. *I've been drawing your likeness since I was old enough to pick up a pen.* I gritted my teeth, wishing I could stop hearing his words. But they haunted me, a ghost that accompanied me during my rounds and at night in my dreams when I was finally able to fall asleep.

Margie stood back from me, eyeing me critically as I pinned my hat to my hair and pulled on a pair of kid gloves that had once belonged to my mother. They had once been expensive, purchased years ago by my father and given as a Christmas gift. They were worn now in the fingertips, and I'd resewn the seams along each finger several times, but I couldn't bear to part with them. There was precious little of my mother's I still had. And when I wore the gloves it was like having her hand in mine, guiding me like she had when I was a child.

Margie shook her head. "You look positively awful, but still better than most women. Are you sure you don't want to spend the night here? You know I'm always up for a midnight gab session."

I leaned forward and hugged her. "I know, and I appreciate it. But I have early rounds in the morning so it's better that I sleep at the hospital. We'll have lunch next week and I'll let you know all about it—down to the last gory detail."

"All right. But if you change your mind, just ring the bell. I'm a light sleeper."

We said our good-byes and I hurried down the three flights of stairs and out into the humid night and began walking toward the nearest subway. I'd refused to leave the hospital with Dr. Greeley, knowing it would only fuel the gossip mill, and I was already prepared for the argument we'd have about him not bringing me back to the hospital. Not that he would necessarily offer, of course. He made a big deal out of me being a "new" woman, an educated doctor of independent means. I suppose he thought those were insults, too.

I walked in the early-evening drizzle, futilely trying to avoid the drips from shop awnings as I passed beneath them, then quickly ducked into the station. I bought chewing gum from the vending machine on the subway platform so I'd stop gritting my teeth, hoping Dr. Greeley wouldn't think I'd freshened my breath for him. After a short wait, I boarded my train and sat down. *I've been drawing your likeness since I was old enough to pick up a pen.*

What had he meant? I shook my head to mentally erase the words and attempted to focus on the evening ahead, where I would at least be getting a free meal. Instead, all I could see were eyes the color of winter grass, and hear words spoken with a soft Southern drawl.

<hr />

I struggled through the heavy wood doors of Stornaway Hospital, feeling—and probably closely resembling—a rat drowned in an overflowing gutter. I was soaking from the rain, and bone weary from trying to stay mentally sharp during the interminable dinner where I had fielded off innuendoes, hands on my thighs, and blatant attempts to kiss me—only one that I'd allowed to be successful. I had to give him *something* to chew on, to make him think there was hope. Otherwise, I had no doubt I'd be asked to pack my bags and find another hospital where fraternizing with the patients wasn't frowned upon. Most likely on the corner of Never and Ever.

I wondered how long I could take a steaming hot shower for without using up all the hot water in the building. Probably not long enough to scrub every inch of my skin the number of times required to erase Howard Greeley's clammy touch and rubbery lips.

The night nurse at the reception desk gave me a disapproving glare as I walked past her, too tired to attempt a smile or share any pleasantries. It didn't matter. News of my appearance so late in the evening would be spread among the nurses and staff by morning rounds. Hitler had nothing on the nurses at Stornaway—perhaps he should consider using them for his propaganda machine.

In my exhaustion-induced delirium, the thought made me giggle, and I was awarded with an outright scowl and then a loud *shhhhh*, complete with a fat index finger pressed to the nurse's lips. Ignoring her, I used the central marble steps to climb to the nurses' quarters on the sixth floor. The small space was filled with six metal beds, three of them occupied, including the one I'd been using and under whose pillow I had just that morning tucked my pajamas. The bucket I used for my toiletries was nowhere to be found.

I peeled off my gloves and stuck them into my pockets, then slid out of my dripping dress and slip, letting them fall to the ground because there was nowhere to hang them. I was still wet, and I smelled like a damp sheep. My gaze fell upon a bathrobe at the foot of what had been my bed. Without remorse, I grabbed it and wrapped it around my body, feeling mildly mollified.

I thought longingly of my peaceful attic room filled with light and the lost treasures of the people who'd once lived in the building. But it certainly wouldn't do if I spent the night up there now, not since Captain Ravenel had awakened and begun his long road to recovery.

With a heavy sigh, I crawled under the covers of one of the unoccupied beds and closed my eyes. I should have been able to fall asleep immediately. The week had been long, my workload heavy. And tonight's battles simply exhausting. But my thoughts kept drifting up toward the attic and to the solitary figure in the metal-framed bed. I kept picturing him as I'd last seen him, propped against the pillows, his face very close to mine. I remembered the sketch he'd drawn of me, and I wondered what had become of it. I was fairly sure it hadn't fallen into Dr. Greeley's hands or I would have certainly heard about it by now. I needed to remember to ask Nurse Hathaway if she had it. I wanted to keep the sketch. Not as a memento, I told myself, but as a reminder of something I might want to remember later in life. A reminder of the time a kiss had made light and color explode inside of me, a brief second when I'd questioned my chosen path in life.

I threw back the covers, knowing sleep would continue to evade me the longer I sought it. So as not to wake my sleeping companions, I stepped out into the deserted hallway and stood, listening to the nighttime pulse of the building, the soft hum like the memory of voices trapped inside its old walls. I crept out toward the elegant marble stairway, looking upward toward the glass skylight, and imagined I could hear the sounds of one of the grand parties that must have once been held in the mansion. I closed my eyes—just for a moment—and imagined I could see the handsome men in their tuxes and the beautiful women in their elegant clothes and jewels, smiling and dancing.

I opened my eyes, feeling dizzy. My imagination had seemed too real, as if I'd been remembering an event from my own past. I itched for a cigarette, to give my hands something to do more than from any real craving. But the night nurse would serve my head on a platter if I were discovered. I had almost decided to call Margie when I remembered the promise I'd made to myself earlier, about how I'd write to his family again if I hadn't heard back by today.

I'd already begun stealthily walking down the stairs, listening for the night staff, and was almost at Dr. Greeley's office door before I realized what I was doing. All correspondence was usually placed on his desk until he found the time to open it at his convenience. I happened to know that he was most likely already asleep in his bachelor's apartment, and that he also routinely didn't lock his office door—not because he was forgetful, but because he assumed his exalted position meant nobody would dare enter his office without his permission.

I turned the doorknob and opened the door. After making sure nobody was watching, I flipped on the light and locked the door behind me. I quickly went through the stack of mail on his desk, but there wasn't anything from South Carolina—Charleston or elsewhere. I was about to admit defeat and try getting to sleep again when my gaze fell on an Army duffel bag shoved under a table heaped with books and papers.

All of the officers in the hospital had their duffel bags on the floor at the foot of their beds. All except for one. I bent down and read the name stamped in bold black letters on the side: CPTN CJ RAVENEL.

I sat back on my haunches, trying to justify what I was about to do. Maybe I didn't have the correct address and my letter had not reached his family, and there might be something inside with another address. With the same bullheadedness that had made me apply to medical school despite what everybody else said, I unzipped the bag, making myself believe that if I didn't do this, then Captain Ravenel's family would be worried sick, possibly believing the worst.

I didn't even pause before peering inside. It was mostly clothing—not recently cleaned judging from the odor that drifted out of the opening. I wasn't sure what I was looking for, but I was fairly certain that it would be relatively easy to find in a bag full of soft clothing. I stuck my hand into the bag and began shifting everything like a spoon stirring a soup pot. I lifted out a canteen, a book—Mark Twain's *Huckleberry Finn*—a hardened package of Wrigley's chewing gum, and a Dopp kit.

I was about to give up when my fingers brushed against something hard. I knew it was a picture frame before I held it up to the light and saw the tinted photograph of a woman who looked a lot like Carole Lombard.

She was beautiful, with icy blond hair and clear gray eyes, but whereas one could picture Carole Lombard laughing in one of her screwball comedies, the woman in the photo didn't appear to be one who smiled easily. Her hair was dressed for evening, her head poised looking over her shoulder, her left hand lifted. And on her third finger sat a giant round diamond she seemed to be holding up like a trophy.

Victorine, I thought, even as my fingers quickly undid the clasps at the back of the frame. I slid the photograph out from behind the glass and turned it over, my breath held as I looked for the name I was sure had been written on the back, most likely in an elegant script and as unlike my own pigeon scrawl as possible.

But it was blank. I flipped it around to the front, thinking maybe I'd missed a signature or endearment, but all that was there was the name of Estes Photography Studio embossed in the bottom-right corner.

Feeling oddly despondent, I reached my hand inside the bag one last time, digging in the corners just in case I had missed something. My fingernail clipped something solid and light, something that had been carefully wrapped in an article of clothing, then tucked in place rather than being haphazardly thrown.

Carefully, I pinched the object between my thumb and forefinger and brought it out of the bag before placing it faceup in the palm of my hand. A fine linen handkerchief—the monogram CJR hand-embroidered in a corner—was wrapped around the object. I studied the handkerchief for a moment, briefly wondering if Victorine had lovingly stitched his initials, then pulled it away from the small square object so I could see it.

It was a miniature oil painting, set in a gilded frame, of a woman with dark hair and green eyes who stared up at me. Her expression eluded me, the emotion displayed there unknown to me. If I'd been a poet, I would have called it passion, or perhaps lust. Or maybe even love.

I remembered all the journeys to art galleries and museums my mother had taken me to, the lectures and art lessons, and for the first time in a very long while I wished that I had paid more attention. There was something eerily familiar about the paint strokes, about the way the colors blended together when one stared closely, the features of the face discernible only when held at arm's length.

The woman appeared to be nude, her long dark hair tumbling around her shoulders, her only accessory a filigree gold necklace about her slender, pale neck, a perfect large ruby dangling from the center.

I stared at the miniature for a long time, the air thinning around me. It wasn't the woman's expression, or the necklace, or even the fact that this had been found with Cooper's possessions. What stole the breath from my lungs was the simple fact that the woman in the portrait looked exactly like me.

Eleven

DECEMBER 1892

Olive

An enormous gilt-framed mirror hung above the mantel of the Pratt dining room, expertly scattering the light from the brilliant electric chandelier, and Olive kept catching her reflection as she hurried past with the serving dishes. She couldn't seem to recognize herself. Who was that ruddy-cheeked young woman with the lacy white cap and the dark hair and the frown occupying the space between those harried green eyes? No one she knew.

She bent next to the thick black shoulder of August Pratt—the younger, not the older—and presented to him the bowl of creamed peas. He was deep into a loud and good-natured argument with his father, brandishing his wineglass to illustrate a point, and didn't notice her. "Sir," she said. "Mr. Pratt. Would you care for the creamed peas?"

She didn't know how to serve, really. She'd been pressed into duty today because Hannah, the more senior housemaid, whose job it was to attend the family in the dining room (along with beetle-browed Eunice, who bore a plate of sliced goose at the other side of the table) had taken sick after lunch and was now confined to her room upstairs. At home, even before Olive's father died, meals had been a much more casual affair, served all at once instead of fashionably à la russe, in separate courses, as the Pratts insisted on dining even when en famille. Mrs. Keane had given her a two-minute course of instruction. Serve on the left, pick up on the right (well, she knew *that* much already; she wasn't a barbarian), and never, ever disturb the family while they're eating. Or talking. Or listening to someone else talk. How Olive was supposed to serve and clear up six different courses (soup, fish, meat, game, roast, salad, dessert) without once intruding herself on the family's notice, Mrs. Keane never quite made clear.

The peas were heavy, swimming in a thick cream broth. August went on talking and gesticulating (something about railroads, or banks, or perhaps both) and paying her not the slightest notice. The fire sizzled and popped a few yards away, and Olive felt the first trickle of perspiration begin its slow, inevitable journey down her temple. In another moment, it would either roll underneath her jaw or drop from the edge of her chin. Possibly into the peas themselves.

"Gus, you big lummox, the peas are to your left," said Harry Pratt.

Harry.

She had done her best to ignore the third man at the table, radiant and laconic in sleek black dinner dress, though his burnished hair kept catching the electric light, as if (so it seemed to Olive, anyway) to signal her, or else to taunt her. Every time she leaned next to his shoulder, offering him the newest dish to arrive steaming in the dumbwaiter, she felt the warmth of his neck on her arm, and smelled the curious mixture of pomade and shaving soap that characterized his evenings; every time she passed around the other side of the table, his face would half turn toward her, catching her gaze in an amused way that communicated the length and breadth of their secret in a single instant. (She snapped her eyes away at once, of course, but never soon enough.)

Harry.

"What's that?" said August, wineglass raised.

Harry nodded at Olive. "The *peas*, idiot."

August jerked to the left, knocking his elbow into the dish. Olive staggered and caught herself, while the creamy pea ocean sloshed dangerously to the edge of its Meissen shore.

"Clumsy girl," said Mrs. Pratt.

"She wasn't clumsy," said Harry. "Gus was the clumsy ox who knocked into her. Are you all right, Olive?"

"Yes, sir."

"How on earth do you keep all their names straight?" said Mrs. Pratt. "Especially the new ones."

"Not difficult at all when they're as pretty as this one," said Mr. Pratt. "Eh, Olive?"

Olive's cheeks burned. She righted herself, steadied the sloshing of the bowl, and then hesitated at August's unpredictable elbow, not certain whether he had actually rejected the peas or forgotten she was there.

Mrs. Pratt said icily, "Well, as far as I'm concerned, I can't tell them apart. I suppose it's different for you gentlemen." There was a slight ironic weight on the word *gentlemen*.

"For God's sake, Gus, spoon yourself some peas and let poor Olive continue on her way," said Harry.

"*Poor* Olive, is it? Friend of yours?" demanded Gus, in his voice that sounded like cigar smoke passed over gravel. He shared Harry's golden good looks, but already his excessive habits were beginning to grind down and tarnish the gifts nature had bestowed on him. He ate too much and drank too much and—judging from that voice—smoked too much. In another hour, he would be off in a cab, visiting a series of establishments and acquaintances that knew him all too well, each one lower and rougher than the last. In another year, his last football season a distant memory, he would start churning all that robust muscle into fat.

Meanwhile, August, ignorant of either the corpulent future that awaited him or of Olive's nearby disapproval, plunged the silver serving spoon deep into the creamed peas, carried them perilously to his plate, and went back for another spoonful.

"It's not so different, is it?" Mr. Pratt was saying to his wife. "A gentleman notices a pretty woman, and I understand it's much the same for the ladies. Noticing a pretty fellow. Don't you think, Mrs. Pratt?"

Mrs. Pratt pressed her lips together and stared at her plate.

Mr. Pratt smiled and turned to his daughter. "Isn't that so, Prunella? Your fiancé is handsome enough, for all he's twice as old as you are."

"Yes, Papa," said Miss Pratt. That was all Olive had ever heard her say: *Yes, Papa* and *Yes, Mama*, and sometimes the opposite, when the occasion called for respectful negation. If Prunella Pratt had formed any chance opinions of her own in her eighteen years on this earth, she kept them to herself. The other housemaids liked to moan about her— *she'll catch you out; she likes to stir up trouble*—but housemaids were always moaning about something, weren't they?

"You see, my dear?" Mr. Pratt directed his jowly, bland face back to his wife. "It seems a woman's head can be turned by a handsome face after all. Who'd have thought it?"

"Speaking of Prunella's unfortunate victim," Harry said, a little quickly, "does he have any idea what's waiting for him at this engagement ball you're planning? I happened to meet him yesterday over at Perry Belmont's place, and he seems to be under the impression that it's just a small family New Year's Eve kind of thing. Bottle of champagne and canapés and everybody kisses at midnight. Won't he be surprised by those swans? Ha-ha. Why, thank you, Olive. I believe I *would* enjoy a dollop of those delightful peas you're offering."

❉

"You should be careful how you speak to me," Olive said, closing the door behind her.

Across the room, Harry was busying himself with his chair and easel and a set of charcoals. He was either nonchalant about her arrival—and she almost hadn't done it, almost hadn't come at all—or trying exceptionally hard to seem as if he were. "Careful? How?"

Olive leaned back against the door and took in the scene before her, not wanting to miss a single detail in her haste, in her anticipation, which choked up her throat and made her fingertips tingle. "Your family will think there's something between us."

Harry straightened and turned toward her, wearing that broad and radiant smile that made her heart freeze in her chest. He had changed into a simple white shirt and brown trousers, terribly bohemian. His sleeves were rolled halfway up his forearms, and his teeth were as white as his shirt. "There *is* something between us."

"Don't be a fool. You know what I mean. I'll be dismissed on the spot." She could hardly get the words out, he was so beautiful.

Harry put his hands on his hips and tilted his head. His smile dimmed, almost mortal. "Olive," he said slowly, "do you think for a single moment that I would let them hurt you in any way?"

And that was it. For the past several days, and especially the past few hours, Olive had argued with herself endlessly about Harry Pratt. Whether she was simply blinded by his pretty face and his pretty manners and his flattery and his social position, or whether this attraction she felt for him was genuine. Whether she should visit him again in his studio, or ignore him and continue on her mission to rescue her father's memory and reputation. Whether she was right to be in this room at all, whether she was being weak or brave, whether Harry was a good man or simply a good seducer, whether Harry meant her salvation or her downfall.

And now, as he stood there before her in his billowing white shirt, glowing gold from the lamplight, surrounded by canvas and paint and brick walls and old furniture, in that beautiful and intimate room her father had designed at the top of the Pratt mansion, she realized that not only did she no longer care about the answers; she couldn't even remember the questions.

She belonged here. That was all.

"I don't know," she said. "I don't know much about you at all."

"Well, you're going to. You're going to know everything about me, and I hope you'll tell me everything about you. Not that I need to know it. I already know who you are."

"What?"

"I mean the essence of you. Come here. I've set up a little background for you, a little more comfortable than last week. And I built the fire up, so you won't be cold."

Olive wanted to ask why she would be cold, since she was wearing her thick flannel nightgown topped by an even thicker dressing gown, but perhaps she didn't want to know the answer to that, either. She walked obediently in the direction of Harry's gesturing hand, where a pile of cushions lay on the floor, flanked by a pair of potted palms. "Of course they won't be palms in the actual painting," Harry said. "It's just for perspective."

"Of course." Olive lowered herself carefully onto the cushions, which were upholstered in silk and threadbare velvet and released a comfortable scent of dusty lavender as she sank among them.

"They're from my aunt's old house in Washington Square, I think. I salvaged them myself when Uncle Peter died and she moved uptown. There was something old and decadent about them; I couldn't resist."

"I thought everything about this house was decadent already."

"Not in the same way. It's all gilding and no gold. That's it. You can recline a little. On your elbow, yes, like that. Look as if you're settling down to daydream. Beautiful." He circled around behind her and put his hands to her head, unpicking her braid. "Do you mind removing that dressing gown?"

"Yes, I do!"

Harry stepped around the cushions and bent on his knee in front of her, bracing his elbow against his thigh, almost as if he were playing football. "Olive, will you do me a very great favor? Stop thinking about the stupid people downstairs, all the stupid people in the world outside this door. They don't exist. There's only one opinion that matters anymore, and that's yours. Your opinion, Olive. That's all I care about, and that's all you should care about. What do *you* think will happen if you take off this robe?"

"I don't know."

"Do you think I'll turn into a slavering beast and ravish you on the spot?"

She laughed. He was smiling and genial and serious all at once, and the lamplight hit his head like a halo. "No."

"So you trust me?"

She studied him a little longer, and he didn't waver. How could he be a danger to her, when his blue eyes reflected hers so steadily?

She reached for the belt of her dressing gown. "Yes."

Harry said nothing as she slipped the thick brocade over her shoulders and freed it from around her legs. He took the robe from her hands and folded it carefully, leaving it atop the fraying rush seat of the chair in the corner.

"Now come here," he said, holding out his hand.

She put her fingers in his palm, and he drew her upward. Her cheeks were warm, but she held otherwise steady, though her limbs felt naked under the white flannel of her nightgown. *Because they* are *naked, you fool*, she reminded herself, but not even that thought disturbed her tranquility. The flutter in her belly was only a benign and eager anticipation. She had made her decision, hadn't she? She had crossed the Rubicon. Now she had only to see what lay on the other side.

Harry led her to the wall next to the small fireplace, where a pile of angry coals hissed heat into the room, and pointed to the three square tiles above the mantel. Olive hadn't noticed them before, and now she wondered why: They were beautiful, full of color, depicting intricate heraldic shields on either side and a central figure of Saint George bearing his crimson white-crossed flag.

Harry's hand moved downward. "See this section of brick here? It's loose."

He released her hand and worked the bricks free from the mortar in a single irregular shingle, revealing the cavity within. "You see? There's a hollow here, as if the builder forgot to put in a few bricks. Well, he didn't forget. I got to know the architect a little bit, when they were building this place, and he showed me. I guess he liked to do that when he designed houses, to put in some little secret. So, if you need anything, if you want to leave me a message of any kind, just put it in here. I'll find it, I promise."

Olive stared at the hole, unable to speak. Unable, almost, to breathe. *I got to know the architect a little bit.* Oh, Papa. Papa, my God. Papa knew Harry. Papa made a little secret and shared it with Harry. Shared it— maybe—with *her*, with Olive, from wherever his soul now existed? To tell her—what? To perhaps say: *Harry is a fine man, a man who can keep a secret, a man you can trust, Olive.*

A sign. *This is the way, Olive.*

If she looked hard enough inside this small cavity in a brick wall, would she see her father inside?

At last, a whisper: "Yes."

"And I'll do the same. I'm sure you can find an excuse to sneak up here during the day, can't you? Just check behind the bricks, and I'll be there."

"Right under Saint George," said Olive. The fire warmed the flannel of her dress, or maybe it was Harry, robust and full of life, inches away.

Harry replaced the bricks. "Three up, five over. Now let's get to work, shall we? I don't want to keep you up too late. I know you start work early around here."

They returned to the cushions. Olive lay on her back, still stunned, leaning slightly to one side. Harry drew one arm above her head and arranged her hair around her shoulders. His hand touched the drawstring of her nightgown. "May I?" he asked solemnly, and she thought about the cavity among the bricks, and she nodded.

He untied the ribbon, and the nightgown loosened about her chest. Without touching her skin, Harry slid the gown over her shoulder, so that it pooled loosely around her breasts. Olive stared upward at the tin ceiling, the neat repeating pattern of squares, stamped with scallops and intricate trailing vines, and tried not to think about how she must look. Like a wanton, like one of those bad women you read about in novels and magazines, a cautionary tale. Was this how August's housemaid had fallen? One little step at a time, until she lay half-naked and helpless on a cushion at midnight. Stupid Olive. Thrilled and daring Olive. Who knew she had even existed until now?

A pair of large hands touched her cheeks, dry and warm and inexpressibly gentle.

"Olive, look at me."

She turned her eyes.

"Do you know what captivates me? This. You, like this. I don't know what to call it. Your artlessness, your decency, it's everything I've been dreaming of, the exact opposite of that world downstairs, the world I've been living in all my life. Every night this week I have lain in my bed, thinking about you. How I want to paint you, to capture—no, that's not the right word. To express this essence, this wonderful nobility here"—he drew his thumb along her cheek and jaw—"and here." He touched her collarbone.

"I'm not noble," she whispered.

"That's what's so innocent about you. You don't realize. You don't know what you *are*; you don't realize everything you could be. You think you're one thing, but my God, you're another. I want to show you what I see." He picked up her hand and kissed her fingertips. "I want to thank you for showing yourself to me."

Olive wanted to say that she wasn't showing herself to him, not at all. That this nobility he saw was just an illusion, a hallucination of his own making, because Olive happened to look like a girl he saw in his dreams.

But she couldn't say the words. His eyes reflected her image, white and clean against the blue irises, and maybe it was just possible, while she was here with him, in this room where nobody knew her, that she could be that girl. The snowy white girl reflected in Harry Pratt's eyes.

The girl, perhaps, her father wanted her to be.

"You see?" Harry said.

He rose to his feet, picked up his charcoal, and began to sketch.

Twelve

⸎

Lucy

"Your eyes are blue," John Ravenel said.

At first Lucy thought she must have misheard him. Not *Hello, how are you*. Not *How do you do*, but *Your eyes are blue*. It sounded almost like an accusation.

What color were her eyes meant to be? Of course they were blue. They'd always been blue. And why were they talking about eyes anyway?

"Mr. Ravenel?" Lucy withdrew her hand, assuming her most forbidding expression. "It *is* Mr. Ravenel, isn't it?"

He had to be drunk. There was no other explanation. Drunk or mad. The man in front of Lucy wore a conventional suit, but there was something about him that made her think of bandits and brigands, highwaymen and pirates. It might have been his hair, black and soft, not parted and slicked down as fashion commanded. Or it might have been his skin, browned by the sun to the color of well-crisped toast. His eyes—since they appeared to be commenting upon eyes—were a deep, velvety brown.

Right now, they were staring at her as though she were a ghost instead of a woman in a cheap dinner dress, disheveled from her sprint across town.

Mr. Ravenel blinked, and said, unevenly, "Yes, ma'am. Forgive me—I wasn't expecting—"

His voice was different from the voices she was accustomed to, deep and slow. He took his time with his words, letting them spin out like syrup from a jug.

"Lucy Young," said Lucy briskly. "From Cromwell, Polk and Moore. Mr. Schuyler was unavoidably detained. He sent me in his place."

"From Cromwell, Polk and Moore," Mr. Ravenel echoed, as if the words didn't quite make sense. Mr. Ravenel's eyes dropped to the pendant at her neck. A strange expression crossed his face. Calculating. Wary. "Mr. Schuyler sent you?"

"He sends his apologies," Lucy lied.

And wasn't that just like Philip Schuyler, to wiggle out of the disagreeable tasks and foist them onto someone else. He might have warned her that Mr. Ravenel was what her mother would have charitably termed "simple." Her grandmother used rather less charitable terms, in her native German.

No wonder Mr. Ravenel needed to be entertained on his visit to New York. Mr. Cromwell was probably afraid he would wander off if left unattended, Lucy thought tartly.

The waiter was holding her chair for her, waiting for her to sit.

Have a steak, Philip Schuyler had said. Lucy decided she deserved one, right on Philip Schuyler's tab. No, not a steak. Lobster. And champagne and all the most expensive things on the menu.

"Thank you," Lucy said to the silent waiter, and sat, fixing Mr. Ravenel with her most forbidding stare. "Good evening, Mr. Ravenel."

"Shall we start again?" Instead of sitting, he took her hand with a courtly gesture that was more an homage than a shake. "I am honored to make your acquaintance, Miss Young."

There were callouses on his thumbs. Lucy wondered how it was that an art dealer came to have such muscular arms. Hauling canvases? Art dealer, it seemed, might be a very broad term.

What had Mr. Schuyler said about him? Something about his father being a famous artist. Lucy had seen it often enough at home, sons who weren't the sharpest knives in the drawer being taken into the family business.

"Thank you, Mr. Ravenel." Lucy crossed her legs at the ankle, sitting primly on the edge of her chair. "I understand that you were expecting Mr. Schuyler."

Mr. Ravenel seated himself on the other side of the table, moving with the easy grace of a sportsman. "And instead I see a vision in blue."

Or just a vision. He had looked like a skeptic who had seen a statue of a saint weeping, a rationalist who saw a blurry face in a window of a deserted house, a man confronted with an impossibility that had become possible.

"I trust you had a comfortable trip?" said Lucy, determined to make polite conversation if it killed her. Open a gallery in New York? The man would be lucky if he could cross the street by himself.

"Not so very bad," allowed Mr. Ravenel, drawling out the words so that the sound was as thick as the scent of wisteria from the flowers twining around the trellis on the walls.

Lucy reached for her napkin. The waiter whisked it away, shaking it out over her lap, leaving Lucy grasping at air.

Amusement glinted in Mr. Ravenel's brown eyes.

Perhaps he wasn't so simple, after all.

Lucy seized on her water glass to hide her confusion, taking a prim sip. "Is this your first time in New York, Mr. Ravenel?"

"I passed through in 'seventeen, on my way to France."

Mr. Ravenel said it so casually, but there was no mistaking his meaning. Lucy remembered those days, the troops in their khaki, shipped through New York from Minnesota, Missouri, Maine. Men who had never left their hometowns, desperate to sample the pleasures of the big city before facing death in the trenches.

"I'm finding it a great deal more pleasant this time around," said Mr. Ravenel, and Lucy couldn't quite tell if he was making fun.

"Yes, well, I imagine one would, not having to worry about being shot at and all," said Lucy and winced at how callous she sounded.

She was saved by the waiter, who appeared unobtrusively at the side of the table. "If madam and sir are ready . . ."

Defiantly, Lucy ordered lobster Newburgh. If Philip Schuyler wanted a steak, he could have one himself.

John Ravenel ordered in French. Not the rough sort of French picked up by a soldier trying to finagle a loaf of bread out of the locals, but impeccable, perfectly accented French. The sort of French Lucy's mother had spoken.

"Your French is very good," said Lucy. Hers wasn't nearly as good, but at least she spoke enough not to disgrace herself among the Philip Schuylers of the world. Her mother's lessons had been erratic, but they had stuck.

"Does that surprise you?"

"I—" It did, actually. It was Philip Schuyler, she realized, calling Mr. Ravenel "Huck Finn." It had set an image in her mind, one their first meeting had done nothing to counteract.

But Huck Finn, she ought to have remembered, was cannier than he had appeared. And she might not know much about anything outside the five boroughs of New York, but she knew enough to be aware that Charleston was hardly a backwater. Mr. Ravenel was the son of a famous artist, owner of a gallery.

And she was just a secretary.

"I suppose it shouldn't be surprising." Lucy scrambled to regain her footing. "Given that you were, er, over there."

"My father insisted we learn the language."

"We?" She'd lost control of the conversation somehow.

"My sister Anna and my brother Oliver." Mr. Ravenel was watching her with a calculating expression, quickly replaced by a self-deprecating smile. A Huck Finn smile, all *Aw, shucks* and *Don't mind me.* "We started off on the wrong foot, didn't we? When I saw you . . . you have the look of someone . . . someone I used to know. It startled me. That's all."

Reluctantly, Lucy asked, "Were her eyes blue?"

John Ravenel smiled at her. "Green," he said.

Mr. Ravenel couldn't know that Lucy had always secretly wished for green eyes, like her mother's, instead of a pedestrian pale blue. Growing up in an area populated by immigrants from Northern Europe, blue eyes were about as unusual as having two feet.

Lucy hadn't wanted to be like everyone else. She had wanted to be exceptional. Different.

Mr. Ravenel raised his glass to his lips. "When I saw you walking toward me, I thought I must be dreaming."

Lucy wondered who the mystery woman was. A fiancée who had died while he was away at war? Someone lost at sea? Whoever she was, she must have been very dear.

"She sounds very glamorous."

"Well, yes," said Mr. Ravenel, and this time, Lucy didn't miss the amusement in his expression. "She looks very like you."

All too late, Lucy saw the trap she had walked into. "I didn't mean like that," she said quickly. "I would hardly—"

Mr. Ravenel looked at her quizzically. "Are all New Yorkers as leery of compliments as you?"

"Are all Southerners as free with them as you?" Lucy countered.

"Only when they're deserved." John Ravenel's voice was an intimate drawl. Above, the fans swirled lazily, sending a pleasant draft of cool air down the back of Lucy's neck. The air was sweet with wisteria and hydrangeas, the light low and soothing.

"It's not polite to tease," said Lucy sternly. "I thought Southern gentlemen were supposed to be the soul of chivalry."

"Ah, but you're a Yankee." John Ravenel grinned, a pirate's grin, all white teeth. His smile faded as he looked at her. He was studying her as though she were a painting he couldn't quite place, a work of art without a signature. But all he said was, "That's a fine necklace you're wearing. Might I ask where you acquired it?"

Lucy's fingers closed protectively over the pendant. "It was my mother's."

For you . . . Her mother's voice had been so weak Lucy could hardly hear her. She had reached beneath the pillow, fumbling at the sheet, falling back as a fit of coughing bent her double, red blood on white linen. Red blood and the glint of gold. *For you* . . .

Lucy had never seen the pendant before, never known her mother had it. It wasn't the sort of thing worn by a baker's wife in Brooklyn.

Father . . . Her mother had managed to gasp out. With the last of her feeble strength she pushed the pendant toward Lucy. *Legacy.*

And then Lucy had run for a glass of water, the pendant hastily thrust inside her skirt pocket, as though water might have any effect against those horrible hacking coughs, wrenching up her mother's blood and guts, coughing, coughing, coughing. She'd had the pitcher in her hand, the glass in the other, when it happened, a gush of blood, a rattle of breath.

Harry . . .

And then nothing. Nothing but a pendant in her pocket and a name she didn't know.

Mr. Ravenel nodded at the necklace. "A family heirloom?"

"Yes, something like that." It was just polite chitchat, but Lucy found that she didn't want to talk about her mother or her necklace. It was too close, too raw. "I understand that you wanted to speak to Mr. Schuyler about opening a gallery?"

For a moment, it looked as though Mr. Ravenel would pursue the topic of the necklace. But he relaxed back in his chair, saying, "I've been considering opening a branch of my gallery in New York, yes. But I may have misled Mr. Cromwell just a bit. My reasons for being in New York . . . They're a bit more complicated than that."

"Complexity is our specialty," said Lucy brightly. "I'm sure, whatever it is, that Mr. Cromwell and Mr. Schuyler will do their utmost."

Mr. Ravenel turned the glass around in his hand, candlelight sparkling off crystal. "It's not necessarily a legal problem."

The waiter appeared with a small procession of underlings, and for a moment, they were silent, as porcelain plates were whisked into place and water glasses refilled. The pale damask tablecloth was nearly invisible beneath bowls of green vegetables swimming in butter, golden-brown slabs of potatoes Anna, and large crimson lobster shells, brimming with a mysterious concoction of creamy lobster meat.

Mr. Ravenel waited until Lucy reached for her fork before lifting his own. "I suppose you could say this visit is something of a pilgrimage."

"Artistic or otherwise?"

"Both, you could say." Mr. Ravenel's lips twisted in a reluctant smile. "I don't mean to make a mystery of it. It's just difficult to find a way to explain. Do you know of my father?"

"Only by reputation," Lucy hedged. She hadn't heard of him at all until a week ago. Her mother's artistic interests had skipped a generation; she was her father's daughter, efficient and practical.

At least, she had thought she was.

Mr. Ravenel's calloused fingers traced the delicate stem of his water glass. "My father made his reputation painting in Cuba in the nineties. Pictures of village life, local festivities. When war broke out, he painted what he saw. Those same villages burnt-out, scarred, destroyed. There are some who credit his paintings with bringing the U.S. into the war with Spain."

"That is . . . impressive."

"I wouldn't know. I was only just born at the time, and I was too concerned with making sure I had a regular milk supply. At least, as my mother tells it." He glanced up, a hint of a smile on his face. "She had a time of it, getting us out. She dragged my father and his easel with one hand, and hauled me with the other, clear up to the Texas border."

"She sounds like a formidable woman."

"She is." The fondness in his voice was unmistakable. "She's currently the terror of several ladies' auxiliary committees and a constant thorn in the side of my sister."

"You're lucky," Lucy said. "To have a sister."

She used to imagine brothers and sisters for herself, a whole household full of companions. But no matter how hard she wished or imagined, it was always just her. There had been a miscarriage—twins, Lucy knew, from what she had overheard from behind the door, clinging to her doll—and then nothing. Her parents had shared a room, but not, apparently, anything more.

Mr. Ravenel was watching her with a little too much interest. Hastily, Lucy said, "But what does this have to do with your visit to New York?"

Mr. Ravenel regarded the baroque curlicues on the handle of his fork. "As I said, it's hard to explain. Cuba made my father's career—but it was more than that. He never spoke of his life before Cuba. It was as if he sprang full blown as a grown man, with an easel on his back and a paintbrush in his hand." He shook his head. "Most artists have early works. Old sketches, experiments that failed. My father—we have only one painting that predates Cuba. And I only found that one by accident. He was," he said, as if by way of apology, "a very private man."

Lucy's mother had been like that, too. Lucy had always had the sense of her mother as a traveler at a wayside inn, hugging her past to herself like a precious bundle she was afraid to lose.

"Do you think your father has something to hide?" Lucy asked practically. "Was he wanted by the law?"

Mr. Ravenel lifted both hands. "If I knew that . . . All I do know is that he was originally from this part of the world. He never said it in so many words, but . . . there were details he let slip. Mentions of Central Park, of the smell of the tanneries on the East River. Little things." Parallel lines appeared between his brows. "And my mother said she once saw him writing a letter addressed to someone in New York."

"About his paintings, perhaps?"

A shadow crossed John Ravenel's face. "He hid it when he saw her coming. There was something—or someone—in his life in New York that he didn't want her to know. I've wondered sometimes if Ravenel is even our name." He gave a little shrug. "It's the name on my birth certificate, so I suppose I'm as entitled to it as any other. But . . . it would be nice to know for certain."

There was a lump in Lucy's throat that had nothing to do with lobster. *I understand*, she wanted to say. But she couldn't. Not to a stranger.

Instead, she said, with false brightness, "Why don't you ask him?"

His eyes met Lucy's. "My father passed. While I was away in France."

"My mother died last year." The words came out of nowhere, from deep in Lucy's chest. She set her fork down on the side of her plate. "Consumption. She had been sick for some time. I—I wish I had known her better."

She felt instantly mortified. Mr. Ravenel didn't want to know her history. But he answered easily enough, "You never really think of them as people, do you? It's hard to imagine your parents being—well, anything but your parents."

He seemed to require a response, so Lucy nodded, even though she wasn't sure she entirely agreed. Her mother had always had that air of mystery about her, of not quite belonging where she was. Maybe it was because her grandmother had been so very forceful, had made it so clear that the bakery was her province, had inserted herself so strongly into Lucy's upbringing.

Her mother had fought a little less every year, had drifted back and back and back until it was as though she wasn't there at all.

Mr. Ravenel was caught in his own memories. "By the time I was old enough to remember, we were already in Charleston, Anna and Oliver were squalling in the nursery, and my father was a household name." His expression turned thoughtful. "Sometimes, it seems like my father just leapt into being in Cuba in 'ninety-three, as if there was nothing before then. But there must have been." He sat up a little straighter, his expression determined. "One thing I know about painters, Miss Young. Painters paint. They'll scribble on the walls if there's no canvas for them to paint on. I've never met an artist who hasn't had a portfolio of youthful embarrassments tucked away somewhere."

"If they're so embarrassing, might he not have done away with them?" Lucy toyed with the contents of her lobster shell. She ought to have been feasting on the succulent lobster, but her appetite had fled. "Filed them in the fire, so to speak?"

I'm no artist, her mother had said.

"No, I don't believe so." Mr. Ravenel seemed very sure. But, then, it was his father. Perhaps Mr. Ravenel senior had been the sort who couldn't be brought to throw away a scrap of brown paper or a frayed roll of twine. He leaned forward, one elbow wrinkling the creamy tablecloth. "If I tell you something . . . can you keep it to yourself?"

"I keep everything to myself, Mr. Ravenel." Her entire life was a lie. Remembering that she was there in her professional capacity, Lucy added virtuously, "As long as it doesn't compromise the firm in any way."

"Not the firm." Mr. Ravenel turned his fork over and over in his hand, the heavy silver catching the light. "Recently, a series of paintings appeared on the market. They were unsigned—but they were unmistakably my father's work."

He was watching her closely, looking for a reaction. Lucy frowned at him. "How could you tell? If they were unsigned?"

"I know my father's work the way you know your own handwriting. And it wasn't just me. A colleague brought the first of them to my attention. The technique is unmistakably my father's. But the subject matter is . . . different."

"How different?" Something in the way he said it made Lucy wonder just what these secret paintings might be. Nude ladies? Scurrilous sketches?

"In Cuba," said Mr. Ravenel, "my father became known for his realism, for painting what he saw as he saw it. These are . . . I guess you could call them allegorical. Fairy-tale scenes. Knights and ladies and Arthurian legendry."

A knight raised his sword in the mural on Lucy's wall. Brave Saint George, perpetually poised to rescue the maiden, eternally chained to the rock.

Lucy felt a sudden surge of frustration with it, with all of it. Why didn't the maiden just break her chains and save herself? Why hadn't her mother said anything, done anything?

"Miss Young?" Mr. Ravenel was regarding her with a little too much interest.

Flushing, Lucy recalled herself to the present. "That was a popular subject," she said quickly. "But if these are so different from your father's other works, can you be sure . . . ?"

"Yes," said Mr. Ravenel. "Do you remember that I mentioned that I had one of my father's early works? It's a miniature. A portrait miniature. One of these new paintings—the lady in the painting is the same as the lady in that miniature. I would know her anywhere. In fact . . . Well, let's just say it's a distinctive face."

Lucy looked keenly at Mr. Ravenel, intrigued despite herself. "That's why you're here, isn't it? Those paintings."

The waiter slipped silently between them, taking their empty plates away, but Lucy didn't need Mr. Ravenel's nod of corroboration to know she was right.

The waiter brought them coffee in delicate china cups. Lucy toyed with the handle. "Are there details in the paintings, physical objects, that might give you a clue as to where your father came from?"

"I'm hoping I can do better than that. I'm hoping that if I can trace the paintings themselves, find out where they came from, I might be able to learn something about my father's secret life." His lips twisted wryly. "You must think it sounds absurd, a grown man chasing after a ghost. I've been told as much before."

He didn't specify by whom.

"No," said Lucy. "No. It's not absurd at all. Sometimes . . . sometimes knowing matters. Knowing where you came from." *Father . . . Legacy.* Taking a quick sip of coffee, Lucy said, "Shouldn't it be simple enough, though? All you have to do is find the seller and find out where he acquired the paintings."

Mr. Ravenel's lips set in a grim line. "You would think. But these paintings weren't sold through conventional channels. There are men in the art world who deal with . . . well, they call them works of dubious provenance."

"What do you call them?"

"Stolen," said Mr. Ravenel bluntly. "It doesn't look like the seller knew what they were—they weren't marketed as Ravenels—but there's something about the business that smells wrong. You don't go under the table unless you have something to hide."

Lucy hated to say it, but . . . "It sounds to me that what you need is a private investigator, not a lawyer. I am sure that Mr. Schuyler could provide a referral for you."

For a moment, she saw the shrewd businessman behind Mr. Ravenel's easy façade. "I have one of those. He's located the seller."

"And you need Mr. Schuyler to put the fear of the law into him?"

"Something like that," said Mr. Ravenel. He drained his coffee. "I'd meant to discuss it with him tonight, over dinner . . ."

"But you got me instead." Lucy felt wretched, thinking of Mr. Ravenel expecting Mr. Schuyler, hoping for answers, and seeing her walk out of that elevator instead. Given how disappointed he must be, he'd been more than decent about it. "I'm sorry."

"I'm not." The waiter came with the bill. Before Lucy could tell him to put it on Mr. Schuyler's account, Mr. Ravenel dropped what seemed an alarming number of bills on the table.

"You mustn't. Mr. Schuyler—"

"Isn't here," said Mr. Ravenel firmly, and came around the table to pull out her chair for her before the waiter could reach it. "And it's my pleasure."

"He really was unavoidably detained. I'm sure if he'd known, he wouldn't . . ." Lucy floundered, torn between loyalty to her employer and guilt. "I can clear a space on his calendar for you on Wednesday. If that wouldn't be too long?"

"That wouldn't be too long at all." When Mr. Ravenel offered Lucy his arm, it would have seemed churlish not to take it. "It may take some time to arrange a meeting with the seller of those paintings. And . . . I'm rather taken with the idea of spending a little time here in New York."

Lucy glanced up at him. "Getting to know your father's city?"

"Something like that." They paused before the cage of the elevator, beneath the great gilded wheel that slowly revolved as the elevator clanked and groaned its way from one floor to the next. Mr. Ravenel studied Lucy's face as though it were one of his father's paintings, until Lucy was sure he could read all of her guilty secrets beneath the brush-strokes, that he knew that Mr. Schuyler was currently training his opera glasses on the second act of *Tosca*, and all of that rubbish about an emergency was just that, rubbish. "Miss Young, I know this is presumptuous of me. I don't want to impose—"

"Don't be silly," Lucy broke in brusquely. "I'm happy to do anything I can to help."

Mr. Ravenel cocked a brow. "Anything?"

Lucy shrugged. "Anything other than getting you an appointment on Monday. I don't think even Saint Peter could manage that."

Mr. Schuyler had a standing game of golf on Monday, followed by a trip down to Philadelphia to squire his fiancée to some dinner or other, a dinner that would undoubtedly be chronicled in loving detail in the society pages by Wednesday.

"Well . . ." Mr. Ravenel drew the word out, several syllables long. "I wasn't thinking so much of Monday as tomorrow. There's a whole long day ahead of me—and I've already been to the Metropolitan Museum more than once. Is there any chance I might persuade you to sacrifice some of your time to the entertainment of a lonely traveler?"

Thirteen

July 1944

Kate

"Dr. Schuyler? Dr. Schuyler?"

Two gentle shoves on my shoulder brought me awake, although it took a long moment for me to recognize where I was—inside the nurses' sleeping quarters at Stornaway Hospital. But just a few minutes before I'd been standing on the sidewalk below, holding hands with my mother and looking up at the tall, Gilded Age mansion, while my mother told me to pay attention. She was telling me the old story about the mural of Saint George in her childhood bedroom, and that it was important that I understood.

I had been about to ask her what she'd meant when the shoves on my shoulder had begun.

"Dr. Schuyler?"

"I'm awake," I said in a matching loud whisper, blinking several times to clear the sleep from my eyes, and recognized Nurse Hathaway. "What is it?"

"It's Captain Ravenel, Doctor. He's having one of his nightmares and Nurse Houlihan and I can't calm him down. I could give him a sedative, but you told me not to—that I should come to you first."

I was already standing and sliding my arms through my bathrobe's sleeves. "Is he feverish?" I asked, furtively searching with one foot for my slippers, then finally giving up and dropping to my knees. I retrieved both from the farthest reaches under my bed and put them on.

"No," she said.

"Good. Wait for me outside. I'll be right with you."

She gave me a brief nod, then waited outside the door while I carefully slid my hand into my pillowcase and pulled out the linen-wrapped miniature portrait I'd taken from Captain Ravenel's duffel. I had no intention of keeping it, but I couldn't leave it in Dr. Greeley's office. I couldn't imagine his blunt fingers pawing around the captain's possessions and discovering it. And seeing the resemblance to me. At least that's what I told myself.

Pushing back my inner voice, which kept reminding me about curiosity and the cat, I slid the miniature into the pocket of my robe, then quietly exited the sleeping quarters. I began to walk as quickly as I could in slippers toward the staircase, Nurse Hathaway keeping pace beside me.

"It's the old nightmare. The one where he thinks he's landing on the beach again." She paused as our feet clattered up the stone steps. "And he's calling that woman's name again."

I stopped for a moment to look back at her. "Victorine?"

"Yes. That one. That's how I knew to come get you. He always seems to think it's you and calms down once you speak to him."

I gave her a brief nod. "Thank you. You did the right thing."

We reached the top of the stairs, then moved quickly toward the smaller staircase that led to the attic of the old mansion.

A bare bulb burned in the hallway to light our way. With all of the windows painted black or covered with dark shades, the bulb burned night and day, so it was nearly impossible to determine the time of day. I had no way of knowing how long I'd been asleep, or how close to dawn it was.

I heard him even before we reached the door, shouting out men's names as if he were still commanding his soldiers on a beach somewhere in France. I entered the room and saw in the dim light of the bedside lamp the other nurse on duty, a fresh Irish immigrant whose name was Mary or Margaret Houlihan. It's not that I didn't bother to learn the nurses' names, but with the rapid turnover it was impossible to keep them straight.

Her accent thickened vowels and tripped on consonants, but I was familiar enough with an Irish lilt from living in New York City my entire life that I could still understand. She pressed a compress against the captain's forehead, the water dripping down his temples. I quickly approached the bed. "I thought there wasn't any fever," I said.

The Irish nurse shook her head. "No, Doctor. But I thought he'd find a cool compress a wee bit soothing."

I snatched it from her. "He nearly drowned at Normandy. I don't think splashing cool water on his face is going to help him."

His troubled face moved from side to side on his pillow, seemingly searching for a way out from a hell nobody could see but him. He clutched at his sheets, his knuckles white. He lay still for a moment, his eyes moving rapidly beneath the lids. "Victorine," he said softly.

Gently, I pried his hand from where it gripped the edge of the sheet and wrapped it in mine. He was a large man, but his hands were long and elegant. Artist's hands. "I'm here," I said softly. "It's Victorine."

His body relaxed, his face softening. "I knew you'd come." His words slurred as he seemed to drift back to sleep, still holding my hand as a drowning man would grasp a rope.

I turned to the nurses. "You may go see to the other patients. I'll stay with him for a while to make sure the nightmare doesn't return."

Nurse Mary Houlihan—or was it Margaret?—looked scandalized, but Nurse Hathaway pulled on her arm. "It's all right, Bridget. Dr. Schuyler knows what she's doing."

I wasn't all that sure I agreed as far as Captain Ravenel was concerned, but I nodded my thanks and watched as they left the room.

I sat on the side of the bed and continued to hold his hand while he slept. I told myself that it was because he was gripping it so tightly that I would have awoken him if I'd pulled away. But I knew there was something else, something in the way he looked at me. Something about the way he recognized something in me. His face relaxed in sleep, making him no less handsome but more boyish, less troubled. More intriguing. But it seemed that it was more than the war that had added the lines to his face and the shadows in his eyes. There was perhaps something before that, perhaps even in his boyhood, that made him look out at the world, searching for the familiar.

And there was the miniature, of course. The painting of the woman that was as familiar to me as my own face. *I should go*, I told myself. I even tried to extricate my fingers from his, but he held firm. I resigned myself to a night spent staring at the blacked-out window, waiting for dawn to emerge around the edges. I'd awaken him then, after I was assured he'd had a restful sleep and before anybody realized I was in there, dressed in only a bathrobe. I sat back against the headboard, trying to find a comfortable position, and began to count the scrolls on the tin tiles of the ceiling.

For an indeterminate amount of time, I rotated between counting scrolls and tiles, allowing my gaze to drift downward to the captain's face, and then forcing my eyes upward again to begin counting over. Every once in a while I tried to pull my hand free, vigilantly aware that the light outside had shifted and that I'd have to awaken him soon. I'd just started with another round of counting tiles when I was interrupted by a decidedly masculine voice.

"Dr. Schuyler?"

My time spent with mostly men in medical school and then soldiers for the last few years had taught me several expletives of which my mother certainly wouldn't have approved. But I used several of them then as I jerked my body off the bed, managing to slide onto the floor, taking most of the bedding with me.

"Didn't mean to startle you, Doctor. I was just going to say that if you want your bed back, I'll be happy to move over."

"I thought you were sleeping," I said through gritted teeth as I hastily rearranged the bedclothes, doing my best not to notice the unclothed captain or his long, muscular legs. I gave up trying to tuck everything in with jittery fingers and just focused on covering up anything I shouldn't be noticing.

"I was, but when I awakened I didn't want to interrupt your counting."

I glared at him. "I'm sorry, Captain. I shouldn't be here—not dressed like this at any rate. You were having a nightmare again that the nurses weren't able to pull you out of, so they came and got me."

"No apology needed, Doctor," he said, his morning stubble doing nothing to detract from a grin that Margie would describe as wicked. "There are worse things than waking up in bed with a beautiful woman."

"I wasn't sleeping," I said in my defense, and realizing my error too late. I closed my eyes for a moment, trying to block out his grin, then jerked them open again as I raced to the window and pulled away the side of one of the blackout shades. I hoped it was light enough outside already or that the civil defense warden didn't happen to be looking up at the moment to see a contraband sliver of light, but I needed to know how much time I had to race back downstairs to change my clothes before anybody saw me.

The sky was still dark, with tiny pinpricks of stars shooting a feeble light down upon the sleeping city. The moon was a slender fingernail nudging its way across the horizon, with no sign of a rising sun to ruin its fun. I let the shade fall back, then pressed the heel of my hand against my chest to slow my hammering heart.

"It's three twenty," he said with a slow drawl. "You could have just asked."

I looked back and saw the captain holding up his GI-issued Bulova wristwatch.

Despite my best intentions, I barked out a laugh. "Captain Ravenel, you are incorrigible."

"Thank you," he said with a quick bow of his head, as if I'd just given him the most sincere compliment. His smile softened. "I've missed you. You seem to have deserted me, leaving me at the mercy of the much less attractive Dr. Greeley. I hope there wasn't any misunderstanding."

Had he forgotten? "You kissed me."

"Not properly, but I enjoyed it. And if you keep avoiding me, there won't be a chance for another."

"I could have been fired, you know."

"I know. That's why I made sure Dr. Greeley knows that you were an unwilling participant and that no disciplinary action is needed. You just need to be more careful next time, Doctor. There's something about you that I find so . . . captivating."

I stepped toward the bed to let him know in no uncertain terms that there wouldn't be another kiss, but stopped as I felt the weight of the miniature in my pocket. Having prepared no statement to explain why I had possession of it, I simply pulled it out and handed it to him.

I watched his beautiful fingers slowly unwrap the linen handkerchief and take out the small portrait. "Where did you find this?" he asked, shadows moving behind his eyes.

"In your duffel bag. I was searching through it looking for more contact information for relatives in Charleston and I came across it." I put my hands behind my back like a little girl about to be scolded. "I thought you might want to have it with you."

He held it toward the light and I bent my head toward it to get a closer look.

"It's uncanny, isn't it?" he asked.

I pulled back, wondering if he saw what I saw. "What is?"

"How much you look like her."

Our eyes met, and in the dim light his seemed more gold than green, like a chameleon. "Who is she?"

He studied the portrait again, tilting it in the light. "I'm not sure. It belonged to my grandfather, the great artist, and then to my father. And now it's mine. All I know is what my father told me—that the woman was my grandfather's great and true love. You can tell by the way he painted her, that there was true passion between the artist and his subject."

"Your grandmother, then?"

His lips quirked upward. "Perhaps. Perhaps not. It was given to my father by an old friend of my grandfather's after my grandfather's death. The friend had been a fellow artist living in Cuba before the Spanish-American War, and he had possession of this portrait and my grandfather's journal." His eyes brightened. "The journal contains quite a few salacious details regarding my grandfather's amorous activities while in Cuba—mostly revolving around a beautiful Cuban girl, Maria, who eventually became my grandmother. I never met her, but I'd like to believe she's the woman in the portrait. Except . . ."

"Except?" I asked, leaning closer.

"Except that in my grandfather's journal he mentions Maria's beautiful brown eyes."

I took a step back, having the sensation of a cold breath on my neck. "You said you've been drawing me since you first picked up a pencil. Is this who you meant?"

He was silent for a moment. "Yes. I found her intriguing, mesmerizing. Mysterious. I felt compelled to draw her. And when I first saw you . . ."

"You thought you'd found her," I finished. I licked my dry lips, wondering if I should tell him more. Wondering how I could not. "There's something else . . . ," I started to say.

I was interrupted by a brief knock and then Nurse Hathaway stuck her head around the door. "Dr. Schuyler? The first-shift nurses will be up soon. I thought you might want to be downstairs before they awaken."

I looked at her with sincere gratitude. "Thank you. You have no idea . . ."

"I think I do," she said with a sparkle in her eyes. "You go on downstairs and try to get some sleep."

I turned back to the bed. "Good night, Captain."

"Good night, Doctor," he said with a secret smile.

I headed toward the stairs, chill bumps erupting on my skin, as I felt again the unmistakable sensation of a cold breath of air running down my spine.

❊

I scooped up my stack of change from the nickel thrower in the glass booth at Horn & Hardart Automat, her rubber-tipped fingers impatiently tapping the counter as she stared past me without any expression whatsoever. Hurrying over to the long wall of square glass compartments, I quickly selected my coffee, macaroni and cheese, cucumber salad, and tapioca pudding, sliding in my nickels and turning the chrome-plated knobs with porcelain centers. I waited briefly before each glass door opened and I pulled out my food.

After scanning the crowded room, I found Margie already seated at one of the highly lacquered tables, her feet and pocketbook on the only available chair. As I approached she slid her feet to the ground and removed her purse.

"Sorry," she said. "It was the only way I could keep it from being taken." She scowled up at a matronly woman who approached the chair with an expectant look. The woman stepped back in alarm, then continued her hunt for a chair.

"I'm sorry I'm late," I said. "Dr. Greeley doesn't want to let me out of his sight. I had to sneak away just to telephone you to set this up. And he wants me back in thirty minutes."

She watched as I settled myself in the chair, dropping my pocket-book on the floor beside me. "Well, that's an idea."

"What's that?" I asked, arranging my dishes and placing a napkin on my lap.

"The telephone. Why don't you just call Captain Ravenel's family?"

I quickly stuck a forkful of macaroni and cheese into my mouth so I'd have time to think. "I don't believe that information was on any of his paperwork."

"But you're not sure."

I met my best friend's gaze. "I don't think I looked."

Margie sawed into her Salisbury steak, then dipped it into mashed potatoes. "Because for some reason you're not too eager to get them here, despite your protests to the contrary." She smiled. "Even though it gave you a good excuse to snoop through his duffel."

"I wasn't snooping. I had a legitimate reason. The man nearly died and yet there's been no contact from his family whatsoever."

"But he hasn't suggested calling them, either."

I paused. "No."

Margie smiled as she chewed, her expression like the clever cat who'd figured out where the mouse lived. She picked up her pocketbook and opened it, then took out a small, rectangular, robin's-egg-blue-colored box. It was worn and frayed along the edges, but I knew the inside was lined with white silk and bore the name of Tiffany & Co. jewelers. She slid it across the table to me.

"I'm just dying to know why you need this now. Your date with the doctor was last night."

I quickly began shoving the cucumber salad into my mouth, desperate to eat every morsel of my lunch since I wasn't sure when I'd be eating dinner. I took a quick sip of tepid coffee, then slid the box into my own pocketbook. "In the miniature portrait, the woman is wearing a ruby necklace. One that looks remarkably like this one."

Margie sat up straighter. "No fooling. Where'd it come from?"

"It's the only thing of real value—besides the mink coat—that I inherited from my mother. She never wore it—which is why I'm pretty sure my father hadn't given it to her. But sometimes I'd catch her trying it on and looking at herself in the mirror. I always assumed it came from her mother, but my grandmother was a baker's wife. I can't see how he could have ever afforded a piece of jewelry from Tiffany's."

Margie leaned toward me, her eyes wide. "Maybe it was stolen. And maybe you're about to open a can of worms that you can't shove back once they're out."

"Or chances are it's just a similar necklace and means nothing. I just want to show him. He's not sure who the woman in the portrait is, but maybe he knows something about the necklace."

"Or maybe you're just looking for an excuse to talk to him." Her wide eyes gleamed.

"The woman looks *just like me*—complete with dark hair, green eyes, and a pronounced widow's peak. I can't simply ignore it." I took one bite of my tapioca, then slid it across to Margie. "I've got to run—it's yours if you want it."

But Margie wasn't looking at the pudding. "Be careful," she said.

I paused. "Of what?"

"I'm not sure." A deep vee formed between her brows. "It's just that this is all so . . . strange."

I stood and pushed my chair under the table, my hand barely leaving the top of it before the chair was taken by a tall man in a dark suit and hoisted over his head. "Don't worry. I can take care of myself."

We said our good-byes and I left, but it was her frown I was still seeing when I returned to the hospital only one minute past the time I was supposed to have returned. I looked around, waiting for Dr. Greeley or the reception nurse to scold me, but was surprised to find the foyer completely empty.

I dropped off my things in the nurses' quarters, then slid the jewelry box out from my pocketbook and carefully clasped the necklace around my neck. I'd never worn it, always feeling as if it belonged to my mother and not me, that I was somehow just its caretaker. But the gold filigree and the bright red stone felt heavy and cool against my bare skin, falling neatly below my collarbone, as if it had been made for me. As if it had always belonged there.

I buttoned up the collar of my dress, not wanting anyone to see it, then ran all the way up to the attic floor, unable to hold in my anticipation. I paused for a moment outside the door, trying to catch my breath, and was surprised to hear a low murmur of conversation on the other side.

I knocked briefly, then stepped inside, immediately wishing that I hadn't. Dr. Greeley stood at the foot of the bed, expounding on his extraordinary efforts to save Captain Ravenel, while Nurse Hathaway stood back at a distance, as if unsure whether she should correct the doctor.

But my attention was focused on the woman sitting in my chair, which had been pulled up to the side of the bed, her graceful red-tipped fingers gripping Captain Ravenel's hand as if it belonged to her. Her almost white-blond hair was worn in a gentle flip, the curve of it around her face exactly like Carole Lombard's. Even before she turned to look at me with ice blue eyes, I knew it was the woman in the photograph.

"I'm sorry. I didn't mean to interrupt," I said as I hastily attempted to retreat from the room.

"Oh, no. Do come in, Nurse. I believe Captain Ravenel needs some water."

The woman's voice was slow and rich like honey, but I also imagined it was full of bees waiting to sting. I paused with my hand on the doorknob. "Actually, I'm Dr. Schuyler. But I see all is taken care of here . . ."

"Dr. Schuyler, please. Come in." Cooper's voice held an unfamiliar note to it, something that sounded a little bit like panic. "I'd like you to meet Caroline Middleton. My fiancée."

The news that somebody had come for him should have made me happy enough to kick up my heels and brush my hands together. But instead, my feet felt leaden, taking all of my effort to cross the room to greet this woman. The whole time the ruby seemed to burn my skin where it lay under my dress.

She placed cool fingers in my hand, not bothering to stand as she greeted me. "The pleasure is all mine, I'm sure. Dr. Greeley here was mentioning how you helped a little with my fiancée's recovery."

I looked at Dr. Greeley and could see Nurse Hathaway behind his shoulders, rolling her eyes. "Yes," I said. "I helped." The necklace quivered against my skin as I turned to Cooper and then back to the ice queen in confusion. "Your name isn't Victorine?"

She threw back her head and laughed, the sound low and throaty. "Oh, no, my dear. Victorine is the name of the artist Manet's muse, a woman he dearly loved." She turned her attention back to Cooper. "Just like yours is Caroline, isn't it, darling?"

I grabbed the empty water pitcher by the side of the bed, said a hasty good-bye while avoiding Cooper's gaze, then left the room. I was halfway down the steps before I thought to wonder why the woman he called out for in his dreams wasn't Caroline.

Fourteen

Olive

When Olive first set foot in the kitchen of the Pratt mansion, her jaw had fallen straight to the floor.

Of course, she'd already seen the plan in her father's architectural drawings, so she shouldn't have been shocked at all. Her fingers had once slid lovingly along the generous dimensions, lingering on the cupboards and counters, the massive oven—or rather ovens, for there were two of them—the larder, the silver closet, the wine cellar. Wondering what it might be like, to command a kitchen like that, so modern and large and efficient, lit and ventilated by special windows and shafts, so that you hardly noticed you were in the basement of a New York City town house at all.

But it was one thing to sigh over a set of two-dimensional drawings, and quite another to don apron and cap and walk through the doorway into the enormous and bustling three-dimensional room, presided over by a cook who might have sent Genghis Khan to the devil.

In a household that revolved around the precise and formal succession of splendid meals, the kitchen was the pulsing center, the steam engine driving the propeller that was Pratt family life. (Or was Pratt family life the steamship itself, and the food the propeller?) Regardless, just presenting herself in the doorway each morning, apron crisp and cap pinned in place, was enough to make Olive's heart fail at the magnitude of the work looming before her, the same damned Sisyphean boulder she would have to push up the hill yet again, just as she had the day before, and the one before that, unto (so it seemed, anyway, at five o'clock in the bleak winter morning) eternity.

The task seemed especially impossible this morning, which happened to be both Christmas Eve (more work!) and the day after last night: a night that had concluded only three hours ago, as Olive tiptoed down the back staircase to the nunnery, slipped her Bible from the doorjamb, and crept into her cold bed. Except she hadn't noticed it was cold, had she, because she was aglow, aglow, dizzy with the promising adoration in Harry's eyes, the warmth of his smile, the understanding that filled the attic room in the sizzle of the coal fire. The smell of oil paint and human skin. The scratch of pencil, the rumble of laughter that moved her heart against her ribs. As she laid her head on her early-morning pillow, she had never felt warmer. She had never felt more alive.

It was only upon waking, a few scant hours later, that Olive found the cold.

"Having trouble sleeping, are you?" snapped the cook.

"I beg your pardon?"

"You've got circles under your eyes the size of quarters." The cook's face was red and suspicious, and her thin black hair was already wisping away from the side of her cap. Christmas was her Armageddon, the annual life-and-death climax of her struggle against the towering demands of an Important Family during the festive season.

Olive wanted to say that she had already laid the fires and scrubbed the floors and polished the silver for Christmas Eve dinner, and all before nine o'clock in the morning. She had served breakfast to Mr. and Mrs. Pratt and Miss Prunella Pratt at nine thirty (really, how many cups of coffee could a man drink?) and cleaned up the table afterward. She had done all this on exactly two hours and forty-eight minutes of sleep, and if she had circles under her eyes, she had damned well earned them.

On the other hand, if anyone in the Pratt mansion was working harder than Olive just now, it was Mrs. Jackins.

"I couldn't sleep," she said instead. "It's so exciting, my first Christmas here."

"It's a load of bother, is what it is," the cook said, conciliatory. She tucked the loose hair back under her cap and glanced up at the clock. "And them boys not even awake yet. Up to no good last night, I don't doubt. Boys that age is never up to any good."

Was it Olive's imagination, or did the cook put a bit of emphasis on those words?

She shrugged. "It must be nice, being rich."

"Well, and so it *is* nice, but it's not for the likes of us working folk. Do you hear me, Olive? Now—"

But the sharp ring of a bell interrupted her words, and she glanced up at the row of them on the wall.

"Master Harry," she said, sighing. "He'll be wanting his coffee."

"I'll get it," Olive said quickly.

"Oh, and you will, will you?"

"It's my job, isn't it?"

Mrs. Jackins put her hands on her spacious hips. "You and the half dozen other housemaids who might take Master Harry his morning coffee."

Olive took a tray from the cupboard and began to collect the coffee service. "Well, I'm here, aren't I? I might as well."

"Now, Olive," said the cook. "You stop banging that china around for a moment and listen to me. *Olive!*"

Olive sighed and set down the sugar bowl.

Mrs. Jackins's right index finger appeared out of nowhere, scolding the warm kitchen air. "I've been in service near all me life, and I've never seen it turn out well."

"Seen *what* turn out well?"

"You know what I mean."

Olive marched to the nearest stovetop, where the enamel coffeepot sat on a round back burner, keeping hot. "I don't have the faintest idea."

"You and Master Harry. I've seen the way the two of you look at each other. Like I said, I've been in service me whole life, and I knows a look when I sees it." Under moments of emotion, Mrs. Jackins's original accent slipped out, a relic of her upbringing an ocean away. She had moved to America when she was eight or nine, she'd once told Olive over tea one evening, and had started as a scullery maid in a house off Washington Square, moving both upward and uptown as she grew apace with Manhattan itself. While Olive couldn't guess how old the woman was—her hair was still dark, but her face was red and wrinkled—she could well imagine that no aspect of downstairs life hid for long from Mrs. Jackins's experienced eye.

Still, Olive had no choice but to brazen it out. She poured hot coffee into the elegant porcelain pot, replaced the lid, and set it carefully on the tray, without so much as glancing in Mrs. Jackins's direction. "You're imagining things. I wouldn't dream of looking at Master Harry, and as for *him*, why—"

A hand closed gently around her arm. "Now, Olive. You just listen to me one minute. One single minute; that's all. I'm not casting no stones. I'm not after tattling on you to herself. But I seen all this before, masters and servants, and trust me, my dear, no good can come of it. No good, do you hear me?"

"It's not like that," Olive whispered.

Mrs. Jackins removed her hand and sighed. "And there it is. All you girls think it's different for you, that you're the special one. It'll all work out for you, won't it? But listen to me, dearie. Listen good." She leaned toward Olive's ear. "It never does. You ain't special. The world don't work that way. Masters and servants, mixing together. Never did, never will. Take my advice, Olive dearie. If you want to be happy, set those sights of yours a wee bit lower. A fine man like Master Harry might fancy a pretty housemaid like you, but curse me if he ever marries her. Why, we had a housemaid just last summer, didn't we, who set her cap for Master August and wound up in a right fix—"

Olive pulled away and picked up the tray. Her face was hot and tight. "Thanks very much for your advice, Mrs. Jackins. I'll just run this coffee upstairs, now, won't I?"

Mrs. Jackins rolled her eyes upward and turned away. "Have it your way, dearie. But Master Harry leaves for college in less than a fortnight, and where will you be? Right here on Sixty-ninth Street, ironing them tablecloths, hoping you ain't in a fix of your own."

❖

The tray was heavy, but Olive was strong. She bore Harry's coffee up the five long flights of stairs until she arrived at his door, which was closed. Propping the tray against one arm, she knocked with the other. "Coffee, sir!" she said, into the paneled wood.

"Come in!" called Harry's familiar voice.

She turned the knob awkwardly and backed her way in.

She had entered Harry's room before, of course. Many times, in fact, since he had returned home from college. Dusting and polishing the family's rooms was part of the ordinary course of her duties, and while one of the more senior housemaids usually attended the boys' rooms—or so they were called, anyway, though both Harry and August had long lost any resemblance to their innocent younger selves—she often filled in. She knew the details intimately. There was Harry's bed, still unmade, probably still warm, hung in green damask and plump with white pillows. There was his desk, covered with sketches and half-finished letters. His wardrobe stood open, in need of a thorough thinning out, or perhaps the services of a professional valet. The bookshelves at one end were crammed full in a comfortable, messy-scholar way that Olive found endearing. She set down the tray and turned to the chair, where she expected to find Harry himself, dressed and smiling, but it was empty.

"Oh, it's you."

Olive spun around and gasped, filling her eyes with the sight of Harry's bare chest, which gleamed a beautiful pale gold between the open edges of the dressing gown that hung from his shoulders. His face was half-spread with shaving soap, and the wicked edge of a razor hovered above the other side, ready to strike. He grinned and turned back to the mirror above the sink, framed by the open doorway of his private bathroom. (Her father's own design, naturally.) "I was hoping they'd send you up. I don't suppose you have a moment or two before you have to go back?"

Olive was too astonished to speak. Harry stroked the blade in confident lines across the foam that adorned his cheek, while the soap-fragrant steam from his recent bath billowed around him. He looked radiant and well rested, lean and marvelously built: each contour immaculate, like an Italian marble touched by God's finger and brought to life. Her eyes dragged helplessly along the width of his shoulders, the lines of his waist, the curves of his calves beneath the edge of the robe, and she felt as if someone had doused her in kerosene and set her quietly alight. Her mouth watered and her insides melted. He was too much.

He was too exalted, too magnificent. He was unreal, a different species altogether.

Mrs. Jackins's voice echoed in her head: *Masters and servants. Masters and servants, mixing together. A right fix.*

Harry set down his razor, patted his cheeks with a towel, and turned toward her. "Why, what's the matter?" he said, stepping forward.

Olive stumbled back. "I should leave."

"No, you shouldn't." Harry grinned his most charmingly piratical grin and strode toward her, robe swinging dangerously. He lifted his arms and spread his palms as if to grasp her by the cheeks, to pin her to his lips like a butterfly in a collection, and Olive turned and flew out the door, out of Harry's comfortable room, out of sight of that bed that had only just been vacated, that bookshelf full of volumes a mere housemaid would never, ever have time to read.

❄

By the time the multitude of Pratt clocks struck a united eleven o'clock, the glorious Christmas Eve dinner had been served and cleared, the coffee had been drunk, and the family had gathered together in the drawing room, trimming the tree under the imperious direction of Mrs. Pratt. (Christmas trees, apparently, must be trimmed *just so* for the proper effect, which, according to Mrs. Pratt's taste, might best be described as baroque.)

Not that Olive cared. She was worn to pieces. She had just brought down the last tray of coffee cups and saucers and been dismissed by Mrs. Jackins, who thought she looked a little peaked. Peaked! She could hardly stand, and her mood was not improved by a glimpse of the Pratt family as she dragged herself past the open double doors of the magnificent second-floor drawing room (*ballroom* might be a better word, and indeed Miss Prunella's engagement party was due to take place there next week), richly dressed, laughing and making merry. Well, Harry was laughing, anyway, balancing on a stepladder to light a few more candles on that twenty-foot tree brought down from the Adirondacks on a special railroad car. The tip nearly brushed the ceiling plasterwork. A nearby phonograph played a tinny Christmas carol, and the air swelled with the scent of pine and cigar smoke and prosperity.

As Olive paused, heart bursting, Harry glanced inevitably toward the doorway from his perch, and his eyes met hers. His smile widened, and he winked—yes, actually *winked!*—as if it were all a great joke, and Olive had also been celebrating her Christmas Eve amid ten-course meals and the loving rituals of her gathered family, instead of dragging her weary body about a mansion that was not hers, seeing to the comfort of people she did not especially like.

She turned and hurried down the landing and up the stairs, away from the ring of tipsy Pratt laughter and tinny Pratt phonographs, and as she arrived at the third-floor landing she came face-to-face with the closed door of Mr. Pratt's study.

Closed, but not locked.

She rested her hand on the newel post and stared at the door, and for an instant she almost thought she saw her father's face, gazing at her in reproach. A line of Shakespeare drifted through her head—*Oh, Shakespeare!* she thought with a pang—like a passing ghost: *Do not forget. This visitation / Is but to whet thy almost blunted purpose.*

Thy almost blunted purpose.

She had always scorned Hamlet, just a little. Five acts of vacillation, scene after scene of contemplation instead of action, putting on silly plays instead of simply confronting the usurper that was Claudius: man-to-man, face-to-face. But she was worse, wasn't she? One smile from Harry Pratt, and she had forgotten almost entirely what she was here to do. She was willing to labor all day, to iron Pratt linens and scrub Pratt boot prints from the floor, and for what? For the chance to meet Harry in the hidden room at the top of the house? To bare herself before him, to serve Harry's needs the way her father had served those of Mr. Pratt?

Because she hadn't taken a single step toward justice, had she? Not since she had sunk herself a week ago into the lavender-scented cushions in the attic room and taken off her dressing gown for Harry Pratt.

Harry and his wink.

Master Harry leaves for college in less than a fortnight, and where will you be?

She was weak, wasn't she? A weak, deluded little fool: extracting Harry's tender little notes from the hole in the brick wall as if they were jewels, leaving one or two in return. Stealing upstairs when she should be sleeping, dreaming about Harry when she should be planning his family's just deserts.

Atop the newel post, her hand curled into a fist. She stepped forward with determination and opened the study door.

She was not entirely unprepared for this moment. Around her neck, on a simple silver chain, hung the key that fit the lock on Mr. Pratt's desk: a key obtained at great effort, from a wax imprint of the original during one of Mrs. Keane's rare inattentive moments. Every morning she had looped it over her head; every day it had dangled on her chest, beneath her neat starched uniform, waiting for the opportunity to strike. That opportunity hadn't arrived, of course. She was always too busy, or the family too close by, or her body too enervated. Or an appointment upstairs with Harry too imminent.

But now. Now the family was busy trimming the Christmas tree in the drawing room, while the phonograph drowned out any untoward noises with its hollow rendition of "The Bottom of the Punchbowl." Harry was trapped on a stepladder, doing his mother's bidding. There was no question of anyone wandering into Mr. Pratt's study, tonight of all nights.

She was familiar with the room now and needed no light to find her way to the massive desk. Her hands shook. She was doing this, actually doing this. She drew the key out from beneath her collar, and the metal warmed her skin. Where was the drawer? There it was, the lock solid beneath her fingertips. She guided the key inside, holding one hand with the other to keep it steady, moving quickly so she wouldn't have time to think about it, wouldn't have time to lose her nerve.

The lock turned; the drawer slid obediently open. Now she needed a light. She straightened and found the lamp on the desk and switched it on, hoping the thin bar of light beneath the door would go unnoticed, should someone—a maid, the housekeeper—pass by the landing.

The drawer was full of leather portfolios, each one labeled at the top by a small rectangle of cardboard set in a thin metal frame. She flipped through them all—BAKER, HANSBOROUGH CO., KEYSTONE STEEL, NEW YORK CENTRAL—and closed the drawer again.

The next drawer yielded nothing, nor did the next. Her pulse knocked furiously in her neck. The reek of leather was beginning to make her feel ill. She stuck the key into the lock of the final drawer and yanked it open.

AMES, HARDING CO., NORTHERN PACIFIC. Another railroad; railroads were all the rage on Wall Street, weren't they? PHILADELPHIA & READING, STRATHCOTE & HARPER.

And then: VAN ALAN.

Olive fell back on her heels. She hadn't really expected to find it; she had even, in her heart, perhaps been hoping she wouldn't. Finding something meant . . . well, *finding* something. Discovering the true story, forcing herself to act. She had spent the past year in righteous fury, trembling with the need to destroy the man who had destroyed her father and her family. And now the whole affair lay before her in a plain leather portfolio, the documented scale of Mr. Pratt's perfidy, and all of a sudden she didn't want to know. Didn't want to bring the poisoned chalice to her lips.

Didn't want this at all.

But you have to, she told herself, staring at the leather, the black block letters spelling out her own name, her own lost family. She could still hear the phonograph, straining through the floor below. Somebody broke out in hearty male laughter.

Thy almost blunted purpose.

She reached into the drawer and set her hands on either side of the portfolio.

The doorknob rattled.

In a flash, she slammed the drawer shut and turned the lock. From above the desk came the faint creak of hinges, a wedge of light from the hallway beyond. Olive swallowed back her heart and pressed her fingers into the floor, to keep her body from shaking.

"Olive? Is that you?"

Harry.

She let out a long column of air, the full contents of her lungs.

"Olive, darling. It's just me." The click of the door closing again. "I'm sorry it took me so long to get away. I had to make up an excuse about too much eggnog. I'm not sure if anyone believed me." A chuckle. "You're not hiding, are you?"

There was no point in pretending, was there? Olive rose slowly from behind the desk. Harry stood just outside the circle of light from the desk lamp, tall and reassuring in his black-and-white dinner dress, hair glinting gold.

"I didn't want anyone to catch me," she said shakily.

"Well, you chose the right spot. I never would have guessed if I didn't see the light beneath the door." He held out his hand. "Come along. I've got a special Christmas surprise for you upstairs."

"A surprise?"

He came around the corner of the desk and took her hand. "Why, you're shaking like a leaf. Poor Olive." He kissed her hand. "You must be exhausted, and I'm keeping you up like a scoundrel. But don't worry. That will all be over soon."

"Over?"

Harry turned off the lamp, leaned down, and kissed the tip of her nose. "Just come with me, will you? I promise it will be worth your while."

She had no choice but to follow him as he led her by the hand toward the door. He opened it, peeked out, told her the coast was clear, and drew her out before him into the empty glamour of the third-floor landing.

As he shut the door behind them, Harry gave a little shudder. "I never did like that room very much," he whispered in her ear.

Fifteen

❧

Lucy

"Miss Young? Will you escort Mr. Ravenel to the elevator?"

"Yes, of course." Lucy hastily pushed back her chair as the door to Mr. Schuyler's office opened and her employer motioned to Mr. Ravenel to precede him.

The two were a study in contrasts, Mr. Schuyler fairer, thinner, taller; Mr. Ravenel with his velvety eyes and his rugby player's muscles. He wore a suit in a lightweight fabric; the pale color brought out the sun on his skin, making Mr. Schuyler seem pale and office bound in comparison.

"Thank you for your assistance in this matter, sir," said Mr. Ravenel, holding out his hand to Mr. Schuyler.

"Not at all, not at all." Mr. Schuyler was smiling—smiling with his teeth, but not his eyes. "I'll be in touch as soon as I have some answers to your questions. Miss Young?"

"Yes, sir." With brisk efficiency, Lucy handed Mr. Ravenel his hat. "If you would be so good as to follow me?"

"With pleasure, Miss Young," said Mr. Ravenel, and tipped his hat courteously to Mr. Schuyler. All very proper, all very correct. As the office door closed, he said in a lower voice, a voice for Lucy's ears only, "I enjoyed our outing on Saturday."

Lucy cast a quick, nervous look over her shoulder. Silly of her. It wasn't as though there had been anything illicit about the outing. Not even her grandmother could find anything compromising about a walk in the park in broad daylight.

They had stopped at a street cart for ice-cream sandwiches, Mr. Ravenel teasing Lucy for the dainty way she licked the ice cream from the sides first, so the melting treat wouldn't drip on her gloves. He had taken great bites of his sandwich, the way it was meant to be eaten, he said provocatively, driving Lucy to a demonstration of her own highly superior technique. Mr. Ravenel nobly refrained from gloating when the ice cream dripped on her all the same.

With sticky fingers, they had taken to the carousel, queuing behind girls in hats with long ribbons and boys in knickerbockers for their chance at two of the brightly painted horses. Rosinante, Mr. Ravenel had called his, with a grin that told Lucy that there was a joke she was meant to understand. They had raced their steeds all around the circle as the calliope played and small children squealed with excitement around them.

Somewhere between the ice-cream sandwich and the carousel, Lucy had forgotten that Mr. Ravenel was a client, forgotten that she was meant to be entertaining him for Mr. Schuyler, and just tipped her head back to the bright summer sky and enjoyed the day as she hadn't enjoyed anything since her father had died last fall, and, with him, the last sense of belonging she had.

But now, back in the office, Lucy felt as though a shadow had been cast over their bright outing, as though there were something clandestine about it.

Taking a deep breath, Lucy said primly, "All of us at the firm want to make sure that you enjoy your stay in New York."

Mr. Ravenel paused with her before the elevator, his dark eyes meeting hers with quiet amusement. "Is that so? How very public spirited."

Lucy could feel the color rising in her cheeks. The way she had laughed and shouted on the horse—it hadn't been public spirited at all. Or terribly ladylike.

But Mr. Ravenel hadn't seemed to mind.

"Would you," said Mr. Ravenel solemnly, leaning one palm against the wall, "consider being an angel of mercy, and, out of the goodness of your heart, devoting another day to entertaining a stranded traveler?"

Lucy tried to squelch the flare of pleasure his question evoked. "Aren't you going back to Charleston?"

"Not quite yet," said Mr. Ravenel, and while his face didn't change, she saw his eyes flick briefly back to the hallway that led back to Mr. Schuyler's office. "There are matters still to be resolved."

"Well, in that case . . . If it's for the good of the firm . . ."

"I'll meet you on Saturday at noon. By the carousel." His gaze dipped to the prim collar of her blouse. "You're not wearing your necklace."

She was, actually, beneath her shirt, as she had since her mother had given it to her. It made her feel closer to her mother, as though carrying around this key might somehow unlock her past.

Lucy ducked her head. "It's not the sort of thing one wears to work."

Mr. Ravenel grinned at her. "Ah, yes. Work." There was a ping as the elevator arrived. The elevator man cranked open the grill. In formal tones, Mr. Ravenel said, "Thank you very much for your assistance, Miss Young. You are a credit to Cromwell, Polk and Moore."

Lucy tipped her head. "Mr. Ravenel."

And he was gone. But only until Saturday.

Noon. At the carousel. Lucy suppressed a silly smile. Had there ever been so innocent an assignation?

Not that it was an assignation, she reminded herself hastily, and picked up her pace as she walked briskly back to her desk. She had a forty-three-page contract to type, in triplicate, before she could call it a night.

And Mr. Ravenel was a client, just a client.

Lucy took the cover back off her typewriting machine, but before she could spool a piece of paper into the machine, Philip Schuyler poked his head out of his office, his usually genial face grim. "Where did you take him? Timbuktu?"

It was so unlike his usual manner—even on their longest evenings, Mr. Schuyler was nothing but polite—that Lucy couldn't think what to say.

"I—," she began. "The elevator—"

"Never mind." Philip Schuyler gave his head an irritable shake. "Get Mrs. Schuyler on the line."

Usually, he requested. This was a command. Lucy stood a little straighter. "Yes, Mr. Schuyler. Right away, Mr. Schuyler."

Philip Schuyler pressed his fingers to his temples. "I didn't mean to snap at you." He gave a forced laugh. "Any more of this, and you'll be begging Miss Meechum to reassign you."

Lucy felt something tight in her chest unclench. "I've worked for the others. I wouldn't trade."

Philip Schuyler gave a crooked smile. "I suppose that's something, isn't it? Just put the call through, will you, Lucy?"

It was back to work, then. "Right away, Mr. Schuyler. Would you like some coffee with that?"

"No," said Philip Schuyler grimly. "Gin. And make it a double."

The door of the office clicked sharply shut behind him.

Lucy was fairly sure he was joking about the gin. At least, she hoped he was. She decided, in lieu of strong spirits, to make him that cup of coffee. And it had nothing to do with the fact that she couldn't hear his conversation through the thick oak of his office door. A good secretary anticipated her employer's needs, and if that need involved walking quietly into his office while he was in the middle of a phone call . . . well, that was just the sort of thing good secretaries did.

She could hear his voice through the door, not the words themselves, but the rhythm of it, a crisp staccato entirely unlike his usual bantering tones.

Coffee cup balanced in one hand, Lucy gently turned the knob with the other, just as Mr. Schuyler said, "What the devil were you thinking?"

Mercifully, the words were directed to his stepmother and not to Lucy. Lucy didn't think she wanted to be on the receiving end of that tone. He sounded like a man at the end of his rope, a good-natured man pushed to cracking.

Seeing Lucy with the coffee, he gave her a curt nod and gestured to her to set it down on the desk, mouthing, *Thank you*, before saying sharply, "Not this time, Prunella."

Lucy wondered what Mrs. Schuyler had landed on her stepson's lap this time. Another Cartier bill past due? A demand that he squire her to a charity ball? Over the past few weeks, Lucy had seen Mr. Schuyler deal with both of those scenarios and more, fielding his stepmother's demands with patience and humor—if, occasionally, with a roll of the eyes.

But not this time. Whatever it was, Prunella Pratt Schuyler appeared to have gotten on her stepson's last nerve.

Mr. Schuyler's other telephone buzzed. Lucy picked it up. "Mr. Schuyler's office."

"Miss Young?" It was the breathy girl in the telephone exchange. Lucy didn't know them by sight, but she knew them by voice. This voice sounded like a cross between a pinup and a consumptive. "I have Miss Shippen for Mr. Schuyler."

She said *Miss Shippen* the way one might say *Mary Pickford*, with that same tone of breathy reverence. Or maybe it was just that she made everything sound breathy.

Didi Shippen's beautiful face smirked at Lucy from the silver frame on Mr. Schuyler's desk.

"Just a moment," said Lucy. "Miss Shippen for you."

Philip Schuyler broke into whatever his stepmother was saying with a terse, "I have to go." To Lucy, he said, "Have them put her through."

Lucy could hear Prunella Schuyler's voice down the line, squawking in well-bred indignation.

"Here," she said, and held out the earpiece to him. Usually, Philip Schuyler took the base of the phone in his hand, turning away slightly in his chair, his voice dropping indulgently as he said, "Hello, sweetheart."

This time, he picked up the receiver with a terse, "Yes, Didi?"

He sounded less than thrilled. Or maybe that was just the aftermath of his conversation with his stepmother.

Without bothering to put a hand over the mouthpiece, he said, "Miss Young, do you have the Kiplinger contract?"

Lucy took the hint. "Right away, sir."

Loudly, Philip Schuyler said, "They want it tomorrow morning, remember."

"Tomorrow morning—but I thought—"

"Yes, I'll be right with you, Miss Young." Philip Schuyler held a finger to his lips. Ostensibly to Lucy, he said, "I know you need those documents initialed. Sorry, Didi; we're very busy here just now."

Quietly, Lucy moved toward the office door, ignoring Philip Schuyler's flapping hand. She didn't like the idea of helping Mr. Schuyler lie to his fiancée. Bad enough that she had lied to Mr. Ravenel for him.

Not that they were big lies, either of them. They were just little lies, lies of convenience. But maybe that was what made her so squirmy, knowing that a little lie could grow and grow until everything became a lie.

She was living proof of that.

Philip Schuyler was arguing with his fiancée, in a voice from which the smooth patina was beginning to rub off. "Tomorrow? But I— Yes, I know you told Mrs. Reinhardt, but . . . I can't just— Bother it, Didi, they call it work for a reason. That's what I do here; I work."

An ominous pause. "I'm sorry, honey, I didn't mean to imply— Of course you come first, but . . . I can't just drop everything."

Lucy slipped out the door and back to her desk. Through the open doorway, she could hear Philip Schuyler desperately trying to get a word in, reduced to disjointed monosyllables. "But—I— Really, Didi! You can't— Right. Fine."

Down went the receiver, hard enough to send a jolt straight through to the girls at the switchboard.

Lucy rapidly began typing, as loud and as fast as she could.

The door of the office crashed open. "I can't take another minute in this damn—this blasted office."

"Sir?" Lucy said, looking up from her typewriter, the efficient secretary ready to leap into action.

Philip Schuyler gestured imperiously at her. "Come on. Get your hat. We're going out."

"But . . . sir." Lucy's typing faded from a rapid staccato to a muted peck. "I thought you wanted the Kiplinger contract."

"It will wait until tomorrow."

Lucy raised her brows. "I thought you said they wanted it tomorrow."

"They want it next Thursday." Philip Schuyler grabbed the typewriter cover and dropped it over the machine, half-written page and all, as Lucy made a noise of protest. "I lied. Come on. I promised you the biggest martini in Manhattan, didn't I?"

"I'm not sure if it was a promise or a threat," said Lucy with some asperity. She was going to have to type that page all over now; the heavy cover had crumpled it beyond repair.

"Is that your hat? Get your gloves on and we'll go." With some of his old charm, Mr. Schuyler held out a hand to her. "Didn't Miss Meechum tell you that it's your obligation to keep your employer happy?"

"She didn't advise the application of gin," said Lucy tartly, but she put on her hat and gloves all the same, glad that she had worn her new hat, a straw hat, trimmed with green ribbons the color of her mother's eyes.

"Gin, coffee, it's all the same." Philip Schuyler was walking so quickly that Lucy could scarcely keep up, hurrying behind him to the elevator. "Lord, what a day. It's enough to drive a man to the bottle. Let's get you that martini, shall we?"

"Don't you mean let's get you that martini?" Lucy protested breathlessly.

Mr. Schuyler flashed her his most winning smile. "I don't like to drink alone."

Before Lucy could argue, he bustled her into the dark depths of a taxicab, giving the driver an address in the West Fifties, an area Lucy knew not at all. As the crow flew, it might not be that far from her lodgings on East Sixty-ninth, but Manhattan was fiercely territorial. East was east and west was west and never the twain would meet.

Mr. Ravenel had teased her about that, about her ignorance of the city she called home. He had taken her down paths in the park she hadn't known existed, pointed out buildings she had never noticed before.

Lucy hadn't wanted the afternoon to end. She could have roamed the paths of the park forever with Mr. Ravenel for an escort and a melting ice cream for sustenance, forever in the sunshine, forever summer.

Except that summer ended, sunshine gave way to rain, and Mr. Ravenel would, eventually, go back to his home in Charleston, his visit to New York nothing but a pleasant memory.

Perhaps, Lucy told herself, perhaps that was why she had enjoyed herself so much, not because of anything inherent in Mr. Ravenel, but because he was only passing through, because she didn't have to worry with him.

That was all. That had to be all.

As if he had read her thoughts, Philip Schuyler asked, abruptly, "What did you think of that Ravenel fellow?"

"Mr. Ravenel?" Lucy played for time, thankful for the murky interior, the sunlight barely filtering through the soot-grimed windows. "He seems nice enough."

Nice. Such an incredibly inadequate word. He was an intriguing mix of old-fashioned courtliness and schoolboy mischief. He gave the impression of openness, but Lucy suspected that it was as much of an act as his Huck Finn impression that night at Delmonico's. There were depths there, and secrets, and the more she saw of him, the more she wanted to unravel them.

Which was silly, given that he was just a chance acquaintance.

Mr. Schuyler didn't seem to notice her abstraction. "Nice." He turned the word around on his tongue. "You might just be right about that. Let's hope you're right about that."

The cab screeched to a halt outside a nondescript redbrick building with a faded awning. There was a storefront advertising sewing machines for sale. It was closed, the door locked and the store dark.

"If you want me to sew on your buttons," said Lucy, turning to Mr. Schuyler, "there are easier ways to ask."

"Watch and learn, Miss Young; watch and learn." The jauntiness was back in his step as her employer went to a small door on the side, a service door, and knocked three times, one slow, two fast.

The door opened, but only by inches, revealing a man who could have doubled as the troll in one of her father's stories, thick of neck and arm. Instead of holding a large club, though, he held a notebook.

"Yeah?" he said, looking forbiddingly at them.

Behind him, a steep flight of stairs rose into darkness. The hall was dingy, with a smell to it that Lucy didn't like. "Mr. Schuyler, are you sure—"

"Philip," he said. "It's Philip." To the man at the door, he said, "The cat's pajamas are the bee's knees."

The magic phrase had been spoken. The troll stepped back, letting them through. The door clanged shut behind them, although not before Lucy saw Philip press a folded bill into his hand.

Behind them, Lucy heard the ominous sound of locks turning. *Bad things happen to fast girls,* Lucy's grandmother liked to say. Despite her attempt to maintain a veneer of sophistication, Lucy felt a little trickle of unease.

Stop it, she told herself. The idea of Philip Schuyler—Philip Schuyler!—selling girls into white slavery was so ludicrous that it almost made her smile.

Almost.

"We're in," said Philip Schuyler, with satisfaction.

"Lovely," said Lucy weakly, and her employer laughed.

"It's better upstairs, you'll see. This is just for atmosphere. Well, and to keep the cops away."

"Cops?" Lucy looked at him with alarm. She'd seen the stories in the news, clubs raided by police, men and women gasping their last breath after drinking tainted gin.

Mr. Schuyler squeezed her arm. "Don't worry. No one is going to bother a couple of virtuous citizens." When Lucy didn't look reassured, he said cheerfully, "They wouldn't come on a Wednesday. They only raid when it's worth their while."

Lucy looked at him sideways. "You seem to know a lot about it."

Mr. Schuyler shrugged modestly. "I get around."

He pushed open a door at the top of the stairs, and Lucy found herself in an entirely different world. A long bar ran down one side of the room, the wood gleaming in the muted light. The walls were wood paneled, with the subdued opulence of a gentleman's club. It was relatively empty at six o'clock on a Wednesday. Two businessmen had their heads together at one of the round tables, and a bored-looking society girl powdered her nose at another, while the man with her sipped morosely at his drink.

A small stage in the corner was unoccupied, a music stand devoid of music.

"It doesn't really get going until later," said Mr. Schuyler. He led her to a small table in the corner, standing courteously as she settled herself on the black leather banquette. "Well, Miss Young? How does it feel to enter a den of iniquity?"

"My grandmother would never approve," said Lucy, looking at the man and woman together, her dress dipping in a daring vee in the back.

"Mine would," said Philip Schuyler. "She was a ripping old soul. And she did like her drink. What's your poison?"

"Er—a gin fizz." Lucy wasn't quite sure what it was, but she'd heard the name somewhere.

"That's my girl," said Mr. Schuyler approvingly.

No, Didi Shippen was his girl. Lucy wondered if he would take Didi to someplace like this, up a secret stair, whispering together in the shadows, or if Didi was for sunlight and tennis courts and brightly lit ballrooms.

Lucy glanced covertly around as Mr. Schuyler ordered their drinks, both nervous and exhilarated. There was a curious unreality about it all, about the dark, tobacco-scented room, the low lights, the small table, Mr. Schuyler so close to her she could feel his knee—unintentionally, of course—brushing hers.

Not Mr. Schuyler, Philip, Lucy reminded herself, and forced herself to relax her hands. She looked, she knew, like a nervous spinster paying a call on a crotchety maiden aunt, not a woman of the world about to have a clandestine drink with a handsome man.

Deliberately, she set her bag on the table and drew the pins from her hat. Little enough in the way of debauchery, but at least it made her feel less like an Irish schoolteacher.

A waiter set their drinks in front of them, the contents icy cold, the glasses already sweating gently in the warm room.

"Bottoms up," said Mr. Schuyler—Philip—and drained half his glass in one swig. He set it down with a satisfied sigh. "That's better."

Lucy sniffed cautiously at her own drink before taking a very small sip. "I don't want to pry . . . but is something wrong?"

"You're the least prying person I know," said Philip, and Lucy felt a small flush of shame.

If he knew why she had taken the job . . . If he knew that she had gone through his files when he wasn't there . . .

He raised his glass in a salute. "What's wrong is that my father married the Hag from Hell. And then the old so-and-so had the nerve to die and bequeath her to me. Cheers."

"The Hag from Hell?" Lucy took another small sip from her drink.

"Demanding Witch will also do." Philip Schuyler drained the last of his martini. "God, I needed that."

It was the perfect opening Lucy needed to ask about the Pratts. "Is she really that bad?"

Mr. Schuyler waved for the waiter. "It depends on how you define *bad*. She never locked me in the attic or sent me to my room without my supper. Of course, she would have had to be aware that I was having supper to send me to my room without it."

Tentatively, Lucy asked, "How old were you when your father married her?"

The waiter set another martini down in front of Mr. Schuyler, the astringent smell of undiluted spirits strong enough to strip the varnish from the table.

"Eight. I was eight when my father married her." Philip wrapped his hands around the stem of the martini glass, his shoulders hunching forward, and, for a moment, Lucy saw not the confident man she saw in the office every day, but a lonely little boy. "I remember him telling me that he'd found a new mother for me. Mother. Ha. She's about as maternal as a mongoose."

If Philip had been eight when his father had married Prunella Pratt, that meant he was old enough to remember the family; old enough, perhaps, to have noticed Lucy's mother. Prunella Pratt had announced her engagement to Harrison Schuyler in the winter of 1892. Lucy's mother had married her father in early 1893.

Did you ever meet a woman there? Lucy wanted to ask. *A woman who looked like me?*

If her mother was a houseguest, she would have been included in family events. But Philip Schuyler, eight years old and confined to the nursery, wasn't likely to remember.

Philip was still musing over his martini. "She had me fooled for a bit. You wouldn't think of it to look at me now, but I was a very pretty child." There was a mocking note. "Blond ringlets and all. Prunella liked to dress me up in a little velvet suit and take me to tea with her friends, so they could all exclaim over how maternal she was, how sweet. Then she'd send me back to the nursery as soon as we got home. I used to wonder what I was doing wrong. I'd try to find ways to get her attention, to make her love me. Stupid."

"It's not stupid," said Lucy softly. "I—"

She bit her lip on what she had been planning to say. The drawings she had made, trotting to her mother with them like a dog with bones. She'd known her mother loved art, and she'd thought, maybe, if she could create it, then her mother would pay attention to her, would look at her as though she really saw her.

"It's not stupid," she repeated.

Philip shook his head. "Wasted effort. She'd make up to you when she wanted something and then forget you a moment later. It took me years to realize it."

"What about your father?" She was wandering away from the Pratts, but she was curious. This was a side to Philip Schuyler she'd never imagined. He'd always seemed so untouchable to her, a man in control of himself and his destiny.

Yes, she could hear the strain in his voice sometimes when Prunella would call for the second or third time that day, but he had always covered it with a smile.

But not now.

Philip gave a short laugh. "My father was besotted with her. Thought she was the embodiment of all womanly virtue. He couldn't believe his luck when she passed up all the others and chose him instead. He didn't know that her father was about to go broke."

Lucy's head went up. "I thought Mr. Pratt was one of the wealthiest men in New York."

"New money," said Philip dismissively. "Easy come, easy go. They put on a good show . . . but by the time my father married Prunella, it all came out. There was nothing left but the house."

Lucy remembered that file in the cabinet, the Pratt trust, funded by the sale of the house on East Sixty-ninth Street. It had never occurred to her to wonder why there was nothing else.

So much for any hopes of being a long-lost heiress, she thought wryly.

"What happened?"

"Railroads," said Philip Schuyler succinctly. "One minute they were up and the next they were down. August Pratt went down with them." With a stiff wrist, Philip knocked back his second martini. "My father wasn't the love of Prunella's life. He was her lifeboat."

He looked so miserable that Lucy cast around for something that might comfort him. "That doesn't mean she didn't love him."

"Prunella loves Prunella." He considered for a moment. "Also diamonds."

Lucy saw her chance. Artfully, she said, "There were brothers, weren't there? Surely she must have loved them."

Mr. Schuyler—Philip—let out a very ungentlemanly snort. "There was no love lost there. Prunella used to snoop around, look for things she could use against them." He leaned forward confidingly. "When you're eight, no one pays any attention. You fit in cracks and corners. I heard all sorts of things I wasn't supposed to hear." He nodded emphatically. "All sorts."

Lucy's heart was in her throat. "What sorts of things?"

Philip leaned back against the banquette, squinting at the smoke-wreathed ceiling. "I 'member—I remember—Prunella threatening her brother that she was going to tell his father about some of his less lady-like lady friends."

Lucy tried to ask casually, tried not to show how much it mattered. "Which brother?"

"Gus. August. He reeled in drunk that night, smelling like a brothel. I was sitting on the stairs, playing with my top—they didn't want me in the drawing room." A shade of childhood hurt passed across Philip's face. He shrugged. "So I saw them. Prunella told Gus she'd make it all right if he got her a ruby brooch she wanted. Or maybe it was a necklace? Doesn't matter. Prunella smashed a glass when Gus laughed at her."

"They don't sound like very nice people." Somehow, Lucy had always assumed that life must have been better in the Pratt household, that wealth brought with it gentility, in the muted clank of silver against porcelain, in the soft swish of the servants opening the drapes. Rudeness, lewdness, those belonged to squalor and noise, not to a place where the very sound of footsteps was swallowed up by the vastness of soaring marble ceilings.

Apparently, she had been wrong.

"Do you know the worst of it?" Philip leaned his elbows on the table, so close that Lucy could smell the gin sharp on his breath.

"There's more?" Lucy braced herself for some new revelation.

Philip's face was bleak. "Didi is just like her. I didn't realize it before—I don't think I wanted to realize it—but when I heard her on the phone today . . . *Christ.* They might have been twins." He looked up, fiercely. "Do you know what Didi wanted?"

Lucy mutely shook her head.

"She wanted me to drop everything tomorrow and go down to Philadelphia to take her to buy a hat."

"A hat?" Lucy nodded her thanks as the waiter set a fresh round of drinks in front of them. She had barely touched her first, but Philip seized on his third martini gratefully.

"A hat," he repeated grimly. "She saw one that was just too darling and wanted me to cancel my meetings to come to the milliner with her. In Philadelphia."

"Perhaps she was joking?" suggested Lucy, with more optimism than hope.

"Ha," said Philip. "It's a test, you know. Show of devotion. She liked to do that sort of thing to her beaux—wait till they were in the middle of a conversation, then send one to get her a drink, another to find her gloves. . . . She liked to keep 'em hopping. But I'd thought, well, it was just a game. I thought, she's young, she'll grow out of it. But she won't, will she?" He looked owlishly at Lucy over the rim of his martini glass.

Lucy wished she could tell him otherwise, could give him some comfort. But basic honesty prevented her. "No," she said. "I think people are who they are. It's a mistake to marry someone and believe you can change them."

Her father—the man she had believed to be her father—had tried, so very hard, to win her mother's love, to make her smile.

She missed her father. She missed her father so. He might not have been a Pratt, he might not have lived in a grand house or worn a starched cravat and a diamond stickpin, but he had been warm and loving and as reliable as a fresh loaf of bread.

"You're right. People don't change, do they?" Philip sank back against the banquette, his long legs brushing Lucy's under the table. "'S no use. 'S no use pretending that anyone thinks I'm a real lawyer."

"What on earth do you mean?" Lucy discreetly moved Philip's glass out of reach. She didn't think she had it in her to carry him downstairs. "You went to Harvard Law. Surely that makes you a real lawyer."

He had the diploma on the wall to prove it, magna cum laude and all.

"Thass jus' a degree." Philip shoved himself back up to a sitting position, squinting for his martini. "Prunella's right—'s not like I do real work. Old Cromwell just gave me the job as a favor to m'father. Needed someone to handle the Pratt estate."

"But you do so much more than handle the Pratt estate!" Wasn't the last month proof of that? They'd spent long hours in the office, longer than anyone else. Mr. Schuyler—Philip—might pretend to be a dilettante, but he'd been working like a dog. With a smile and a starched collar, yes, but still working, and working hard. Lucy wished that

Prunella Pratt were in range to hear a piece of her mind. "Mr. Cromwell always speaks highly of you. I've heard him."

"He was friends with my father." Philip gestured for another martini. "They don't take me seriously, any of them."

Lucy absently took a sip of Philip's old martini. The gin made her cough. "That's nonsense," she said crisply. At least, she tried to say it crisply. If it came out just a bit slurred, Philip was in no state to notice. "You're a wonderful lawyer."

"Oh, I know," said Philip moodily. "No one deals with the clients like I do. By which they mean that I can keep the drinks coming, tell jokes in four languages, and play a good game of tennis."

"No." The gin was remarkably freeing. Without conscious volition, Lucy's hand was on Mr. Schuyler's arm, her fingers making creases in his perfectly pressed jacket. "That's not it at all. You're not just a good host; you're a good lawyer. You know what Mr. Cochran's drafts look like."

"Well . . . Cochran," said Philip with a shrug.

"I won't have you selling yourself short. You're good at it. And I know you care, even if you pretend you don't."

Philip's eyes focused on her face. There was a curious, wistful expression on his face. "I do, do I?"

"Yes."

"You're a good woman, Lucy Young." Philip toasted her with his new martini, baptizing the table with gin. "Where were you when I was proposing to Didi?"

Commuting from Brooklyn.

"On my yacht in the South of France," Lucy quipped. She hadn't minded telling John Ravenel that she'd grown up above a bakery, but she still, even with her tongue loosened by gin, found that she didn't want Philip Schuyler to know. She liked when he spoke to her like this, like an equal, with that admiring light in his eyes, a light that would go away if he knew the truth about her.

New money, Philip had said dismissively.

She wasn't money at all, new or old, just a working girl with sensible shoes and an attic room that cost too much of her weekly salary.

As for being a Pratt . . . Maybe she had thought, once, that that would provide some social cachet, but she was reluctant to blurt that out, not just because she didn't want Philip to know she'd been using him, but also because they sounded like horrible people. She didn't want him to look at her and see Prunella Pratt. She didn't want him to talk about her the way he did Didi.

Philip Schuyler reached across the table, took her hand, and, before Lucy realized what he was doing, raised her knuckles to his lips. "I don't know when I've ever been so grateful to anyone for breaking her leg. Here's to Meg and her multiple fracture!"

"You can't mean that," protested Lucy, flattered and appalled—but she left her hand in his.

"Oh, I'm sorry about her leg—don't get me wrong—but I can't be sorry about you." Philip's hand tightened on hers, his thumb moving in an intimate caress against her wrist. "There you were, in the secretarial pool, all that time, and I never saw you."

"You said hello to me once," said Lucy, and then wished she hadn't. It made her sound like a besotted teenager.

"Did I? If I'd known better, I wouldn't have just said hello. I would have asked you for a drink."

There was something mesmeric about the way he was looking at her, his face so close to her, his hand on hers, the culmination of a thousand guilty daydreams. This wasn't happening, not really. Philip Schuyler flirted, yes, all the time, but this was more than flirting, this was . . .

Not right.

Reluctantly, Lucy drew her hand away. "And I would have said no."

"Don't say no, Lucy." Philip touched a finger to her lower lip, and Lucy felt the tingle of it, stronger than the gin, so exciting and so wrong all at the same time. "These lips weren't made for saying no."

And before Lucy could say no, before Lucy could say anything at all, Philip Schuyler leaned in and kissed her.

Sixteen

JULY 1944

Kate

The whine of sirens pierced the still night, jerking my eyes open. I was on call and still wore my clothes, making it easier to exit the sleeping quarters with only a quick hand-swipe of my eyes and a brief toe-search for my shoes before sliding them on. The air-raid drills were a weekly occurrence, and I moved through the mansion still half-asleep, my motions automatic. I no longer had to look at the drill instructions taped on most doors inside the hospital at the instruction of Mayor La Guardia; the familiar words and graphics of various siren sounds seemed to be imprinted on the inside of my eyelids.

I joined an orderly and a nurse as we each picked up a flashlight from the bucket on the landing, and I began systematically turning off all lights I passed as the steady scream of the siren continued outside. I peered through one of the drawn shades in a blackened room and spotted an air-raid patrol car racing down the street, pausing so its air-raid warden could jump out and douse a phantom fire.

One of the men from the ballroom turned hospital dormitory

screamed from a nightmare, an unholy side effect of the drills. So many of the patients returned to their recent battles when they closed their eyes, the innocuous sounds of sirens more menacing to them, transforming into the sounds of falling bombs and spiraling planes.

I was headed in his direction when I spotted Nurse Hathaway and an orderly in the doorway. "We've got this," she said.

I nodded, listening to the sound of scrambling feet throughout the hospital. I looked up the stairs, knowing I should make sure that Captain Ravenel was prepared to move if the siren sound began to waver, signaling us that it was no longer just a drill. Still, I paused. Since meeting his fiancée, I'd done everything in my power to avoid the attic room except to retrieve personal items when I knew he was sleeping and his fiancée wasn't there. But nobody was running up to the attic. The captain hadn't been coherent during the last drill and I pictured him up in the attic room, in the dark and alone, wondering what all the commotion was about. I had my foot on the first step when I heard my name.

"Dr. Schuyler?"

I groaned inwardly as I turned. "Yes, Dr. Greeley?"

"Where are you going?" he asked, although it was clear he knew exactly where I'd been heading.

"To see to Captain Ravenel. The attic room wasn't included in the original drill plans because it wasn't a . . ."

Dr. Greeley took my elbow. "The patient is fine. I saw to him myself. It looks like all that's still needed is for you and me to find a safe place."

"I'm quite . . ."

Before I could finish my sentence, he'd opened a door—to what had once been a cloak closet outside the ballroom but had been converted to store medical supplies—and pushed me inside, making me drop my flashlight in the process. He closed the door behind us and I had two sudden thoughts: He'd had onions for dinner, and the space was too small for him to do much of anything.

I tried to turn to the side but managed only to elbow him slightly in his soft abdomen. "I'm sorry," I said. "But this is quite unnecessary . . ."

"You've been avoiding me, Kate." I'd always liked the sound of my name. Until now.

"I haven't been avoiding you. I've just been incredibly busy, as you are aware."

"You haven't accepted my invitations to dinner." He sounded genuinely hurt. As if he really believed that the two of us had a future together.

"We are overloaded with patients right now, and I need my sleep so I can be the best doctor they need me to be. I really don't have time for leisurely dinners, as lovely as they sound."

He was my height, so that when he smiled his sparse mustache tickled my ear. I found myself almost hoping that a bomb would actually fall nearby just so I'd have a reason to get out of this closet.

I felt his fingers playing with my hair. "I hope you understand that it's in your best interests to make me happy. I don't think dinner with me would be so hard for you to manage."

Damn. It wasn't fair. Nothing about being a woman was fair, especially not a woman whose only dream was to be a good doctor. But none of that would matter if I didn't give Dr. Greeley what he wanted. "I'll check my schedule. I'm sure I can find an hour."

"Or two," he said.

I kept my head turned to the side so when he tried to kiss me, he got only my cheek.

Reaching behind him, I grabbed the doorknob and twisted it, but his hand on mine stopped me. "Before you go, I just wanted to let you know that I've received word that we are scheduled to be getting more patients. You're going to have to make room for two more beds up in the attic. No more private quarters for Captain Ravenel, and you'll have to make other permanent arrangements for yourself."

The siren stopped, lending an uneasy stillness to the air. I turned the knob hard and pushed the doctor, making him stumble backward. I grabbed hold of his upper arms to make it look like it had been an accident. "Sorry, Doctor. I'll get started on that first thing in the morning." I picked up my flashlight and began jogging up the flight of circular stairs, not really sure where I was going, just that I needed to get *away.*

He recovered quickly and called me back again. I paused, looking past the banister at him, and hoped he knew I could see his bald spot from my elevated position on the stairwell. "We're short staffed tonight. Another nurse has defected to the WAVES. I'm afraid I'm going to need you to empty all the bedpans in the main ward."

I knew that to argue, to remind him that I was a medical doctor, same as he was, would do no good and would only set me up for even more "selective" duties. I took a slow step down.

"And when Caroline Middleton arrives in the morning, I want you to make yourself available to her. She has all sorts of questions about New York—where to shop and where to eat; women things—and I told her you'd be happy to answer any of her questions."

I smiled, even though I had the flashing visual of him tumbling over the banister. "Yes, Doctor." I flipped on lights as I made my way to the main ward. Nurse Hathaway was still there, holding the hand of a patient and humming softly. I nodded in her direction, then began checking bedpans.

"We already took care of it, Dr. Schuyler." The orderly I'd seen with Nurse Hathaway was at the far wall turning on the overhead lights. As if noticing them for the first time, I saw how ugly the fixtures were, how out of place against the rich wood paneling and elaborately molded ceilings. They were an abomination, I thought, glad the architect of this masterpiece wasn't around to see the desecration.

"Thank you," I said, nodding to him and then the nurse. I looked down at my watch, pinned to the front of my lab coat, and realized that it was almost six o'clock. Since I was due for rounds at seven, it made no sense to toss and turn for such a short time before reporting back to work. At least I had time to wash and change clothes.

After hesitating only a moment, I ran up the servants' stairs to the top floor, pausing only briefly to make sure there was no sound or movement before entering the attic room. It was pitch-black inside, with only the slow, steady sound of Captain Ravenel's breathing to let me know I was in the right place. I aimed my flashlight at the floor and quietly crept to the corner of the room. I'd found an old, empty trunk and was using it as a place to store my clothes as well as a dressing table. I'd managed to find a cracked gilt-framed mirror and hung it on the wall behind the trunk, which made me feel a lot more elegant than circumstances allowed. It must have once hung in the main house, and whenever I peered at my reflection, I couldn't stop myself from wondering who else had sought to see themselves reflected in the old glass.

I fiddled one-handed with the trunk's latches and popped them open, then shone the flashlight inside to pull out clean clothing. I had just grabbed my last clean slip when I heard the switch of a lamp and found myself and the room clearly illuminated in pale yellow light.

"Glad to see you're not a German." Captain Ravenel was sitting up in bed, grinning as if he were privy to a very funny joke.

"Sorry. It's only me. And that was just an air-raid drill. I hope you didn't really think the Germans were coming."

"Would you protect me from the Germans if they came?"

"Yes," I said without thinking. "I mean, it's my job. To protect my patients."

As if it were even possible, his grin widened. "I'm flattered, I'm sure."

I rolled my slip inside the dress I'd pulled from the trunk, then placed the bundle on top of a tall casement clock with no face before approaching the bed. "How are you feeling this morning?"

"Now that you're here, like I could run a mile. If you'd smile at me, then I could probably run three."

"Captain, please. You shouldn't say things like that."

His grin faded, and I found myself missing it, found myself wishing I'd said nothing so that I could continue my fantasy. That was impossible, of course. His fiancée had come to him. Had come to take him home.

"No," he said. "I shouldn't." His eyes searched mine, as if he'd heard my thoughts.

Since I was already there, I decided to help out Nurse Hathaway and take the patient's vitals. I avoided looking at him but felt his eyes on me like I imagined a flower felt the sun. "I'll need to examine your wound. I know you must be eager to return home, but I'm afraid I can't discharge you until there is no sign of infection." I raised my eyes to meet his, to let him know how serious I was. "If we do not kill all of the bacteria, the infection will return. And there will be nothing left to do except amputate."

"Yes, Doctor," he said slowly, and there was no sign of sarcasm.

I pulled back the covers just enough so I could examine the leg, then carefully removed the bandages, doing my best to concentrate on the wound and not the beautifully muscled leg. Focusing on my work, I cleaned the wound as I examined it, pleased with his progress.

As I washed my hands in the bedside basin, I said, "It's looking very good. I'm thinking you should be able to leave in about a week—two weeks, tops." I smiled, wondering why the good news didn't make me feel as happy as it should. Turning away from him, I wrote my short report on his chart, my handwriting shakier than usual. *Lack of sleep.*

I replaced the chart on the bedside table, feeling the weight of the ruby necklace under my dress, the stone burning my skin. Until I could return it to Margie, I wore it to keep it safe, having convinced myself that I didn't need to show it to Cooper. *It's just a necklace. There must be dozens, hundreds, just like it. Stop thinking of reasons to tie him to you.*

With the pretend smile I normally reserved for seriously ill patients, I said, "You'll have company soon. We're getting more patients, and the only room for two new beds will be up here. I've been instructed to clear out some of this mess."

He raised a dark eyebrow. "I thought you were a doctor. Surely clearing out an attic shouldn't be part of your responsibilities."

"It probably shouldn't." I bit my lip, the words I wanted to call Dr. Greeley ready to pour out of my mouth. "We're horribly short staffed, so everyone must do his—or her—part."

"Including Dr. Greeley, I'm sure. He doesn't seem the type of man who thinks of women with the same credentials as equals."

"No. He's not," I said bluntly, still too angry to sugarcoat the truth.

"I find a woman with brains enormously attractive and not threatening in the least. A pretty face is nice, too, but having somebody to converse with and share thoughts for thirty or forty years is very appealing to me." His voice sounded wistful, as if he were still searching for that woman.

"Your fiancée is a lucky woman, Captain, to have found a man with such progressive thinking."

He was silent for a moment, studying me. Quickly changing the conversation, he said, "I'll help." He sat up and placed his feet on the floor.

"Absolutely not. You're a patient here, not an orderly. I promise to be as unobtrusive as possible . . ."

As if I hadn't spoken, he stood, wearing only his hospital gown, and I turned my back to him. "Captain Ravenel, please . . ."

"It's Cooper. And if you will give me just a moment, I'll put on my shirt and pants—I do believe they will fit over my bandages—and then you won't have to act like you've never seen a naked man before."

"Captain . . ."

"Cooper. You said yourself that my leg is mending. And if you don't let me get out of that bed and do something useful, I'm afraid that I can't be responsible for my actions."

I slowly let the breath out of my nose, tired of dealing with too many obstinate men in one morning. "Fine. But you are not moving heavy furniture or anything that might impede the healing of your leg." I headed to the corner of the room, where many of the mansion's remnants had been piled. "I'll get an orderly to clear out most of the larger items that I can't move myself, but first I wanted to go through the trunks and armoires and pull any clothing out. I'm sure it's all mostly moth-eaten, but I know the ragman will welcome any donations. It's amazing what they're collecting these days for the war effort—even gum wrappers and silk stockings. I'm sure if I donated my mother's old fur, they'd be able to turn it into a parachute or bomb or something useful." He'd moved to stand near me, making me babble like a young girl on her first date.

"All very much appreciated, I assure you."

"I really don't think you should be standing . . ."

"Are you going to let me finish?"

The words were spoken very close to my ear, and when I turned I found those fascinating eyes watching me closely. "Finish what?" I asked, forcing myself to remain upright instead of leaning toward him.

"Your sketch. It's not quite done. I've been working on it from memory, but I really need you to sit for me so I can finish. There's something about your eyes . . ."

I reached past him and yanked open the door of a towering armoire, its mahogany finish cloudy with dust, glad for the coughs the movement generated. Anything was better than continuing this conversation. He'd already sketched me while I slept. *While I slept.* The only thing more intimate would be for me to be aware of him as he sketched me, to allow our eyes to meet for long periods.

I coughed again, then jerked open the second door. "I've been dying to see what was in here. When I first moved up to the attic, I was going to use it to store my clothes, but it was so jam-packed that I realized it would take too much time." Blindly, I reached inside, grabbed an armful of material, and lifted the garments from the hanging rack.

"These aren't heavy," I said behind a pile of crinolines and lace. "If you could just place them on the floor by the door, I'll bring them downstairs and have the nurses sort through everything to see if there's anything salvageable, and the rest goes to the ragman."

He lifted the load from my arms while I turned back for another handful until the armoire was empty. "Thanks for your help," I said, swiping my hands together. I closed one door and, while reaching for the other, looked at the floor of the piece of furniture, where a crumpled pile of yellowed satin lay in a heap. "Hang on. We have one more."

I lifted the errant garment in my hand, the smell of dust and age wafting past me, and heard myself sigh. It was a ball gown of the softest cream-colored satin, with tiny handcrafted rosettes along the neckline, the skirt gathered in waves of satin into a small train at the rear, where tiny buttons lined up the back from the top to the bottom of the bodice. The waist was tiny, possibly made tinier by the strategic use of a corset, with a delicate embroidery of roses in the palest pink, almost too faint to see, splashed all over the gown.

"What have we here?" Cooper asked, taking the gown from me and holding it up so I could get a better look at it.

"I would say a wedding gown, except I don't think it was ever a true white. Maybe a gown for a very special occasion." I leaned forward, examining a dark stain of brownish red on the front bodice. It was a garish blemish on the pale satin, like a scar. "Possibly worn only once because of a wine spill. What a shame."

"Should I put this in a pile for you?"

I actually thought about it for a moment before shaking my head. "No. I have no use for it, and certainly no place to put it. But it is lovely, isn't it?"

He'd taken two steps toward the pile before he stopped. "There's an embroidered label inside." He fumbled for a moment with the collar, bringing it closer to his face. "It says, 'Made Expressly for Prunella J. Pratt.'"

"Prunella?" I said, the name jarring.

"Not the most attractive of names; that's for sure. It's a good thing she was wealthy. I've found that people will overlook a lot if one has money."

I barely heard him, my brain too busy racing. "That's odd," I said. "It *is* an unusual name, yet when I was growing up I remember having an Aunt Prunella. I don't know what her exact relationship was—she could have been a great-aunt or something—but I called her Aunt Prunella. I don't recall if her last name was Pratt—it wasn't something I ever thought to ask. She seemed ancient even back then to my four-year-old self and smelled like mothballs. My parents would take me for an obligatory Sunday afternoon visit and I'd have to kiss her cheek and then sit still for a whole hour gnawing on stale cookies and listening to her talk about how wonderful her life had once been, and how many times she appeared in the society pages labeled as a 'great beauty.' She had a scrapbook she'd always bring out just to prove to us that she was telling the truth. And my parents usually brought her a check. She must have always been asking for money, because I remember that part very clearly."

I paused, the memory not wholly unwelcome. My father and mother had both been alive then, and if the weather was nice, on the way home we'd walk through the park and my father would buy me an ice-cream cone. And when I was very small, he'd lift me up on his shoulders for the last block, pretending to stagger under my weight.

I slammed the armoire door shut. "We stopped visiting her when my father died—I always got the sense that we did so only out of my father's sense of duty, and my mother saw no sense in extending the misery after his death. I have no idea if Aunt Prunella is even still alive."

"She sounds delightful," he said, the laughter in his eyes again.

I looked down at my watch. "I really need to get started on rounds . . ."

"What's this?" he asked as he pushed aside a hanging rack of more garments, these draped with an old sheet. But the object he'd focused his attention on was hiding behind it—a short and squat Chinese chest with two drawers, its ornate mother-of-pearl design nearly obliterated by what appeared to be splattered paint. Each drawer had a lock, but no key.

"I really should go downstairs now," I said, my voice sounding half-hearted even to me.

"Or I could open this top drawer," Cooper said as he tugged on the ornate drawer pull and it slid open as far as it would go.

"It's sketches," I said with surprise. Of anything I anticipated being inside the drawers, that wouldn't have been it.

Cooper reached in and took out a small pile of various-sized papers, then began slowly flipping through them, showing them to me before moving on to the next.

"They're sketches of this room," I said. "Before it became a store-room."

Cooper pointed at one of the far wall where the tall blacked-out windows with fanlights sat recessed within the brick walls and under elaborate gilded keystones. "And before there were dimouts in the city."

Each sketch was a detailed analysis of various parts of the room—

the brick fireplace with the painted medallions over the mantel, the delicate scrolls of the ornate ceiling, the domed skylight that magnified the sun, shooting prisms of light throughout the room. I stared at the last one for a long moment while I searched for my voice. "It's exactly what I thought it would look like. Before they painted it black."

He was quiet for a moment. "They look . . . familiar somehow. Like I've seen them before, or at least the artist's work. Look," he said, tapping the bottom right corner of the top sketch. "They're all signed."

The signature was tiny, making me squint as I tried to read it. "I think it says Harry Pratt," I said, handing it back to Cooper.

"Harry Pratt," he said slowly. "I'm pretty sure I don't know his work. Most likely some relation to Prunella Pratt, who owned the dress. He's quite good, whoever he is. Or was." His glance fell to the second drawer. "Would you like to do the honors?"

With my rounds having been completely forgotten, I knelt in front of the chest and pulled, but nothing happened.

"Is it locked?" Cooper asked.

I shook my head. "No. It looks like something's stuck. It might be a sketch, and I'm afraid that if I pull on it, it might get damaged."

I stood back and allowed Cooper to take a look. "I think you're right." He began tipping the chest forward to study its back, and then tilted it on its side to look beneath it. "If you can get me some kind of chisel, a hammer and a screwdriver, I should probably be able to take it apart without damaging anything inside."

I was about to remind him that he was a patient when we both heard the unmistakable clicking of high-heeled shoes in the corridor outside. Cooper limped back to his bed as quickly as possible, and I followed him, not really sure why I felt like we'd been caught doing something wrong.

He slid beneath the sheets and as I leaned forward to tuck the blankets beneath the mattress, I felt the ruby slowly slide from its hiding place. I stood quickly, hoping to tuck it back inside my dress before he noticed. His hand grabbed my wrist, his eyes meeting mine.

The door flew open. "Well, isn't this cozy?" Caroline Middleton stood near the pile of discarded clothes, the light from the hallway behind her outlining her form like a halo.

Cooper dropped his hand as I straightened, tucking the necklace back into my dress. "Good morning, Miss Middleton. I'm happy to report that Captain Ravenel is making wonderful progress. I expect that we will be able to release him in no more than two weeks."

I stepped away from the bed, feeling his eyes on me but knowing that looking back would mean acknowledging that he'd seen the ruby. That there was a connection between us, a connection I couldn't begin to understand.

I busily tidied the bedside table as I prepared to leave. "It's a little early for visiting hours. Perhaps you'd like to come back later?"

Caroline's lips curved upward. "Dr. Greeley told me that I could come at any time. And because those awful sirens woke me up at such an ungodly hour, I thought I'd just come straight here to see Cooper."

I used my foot to slide the pile of clothes out of the way and against the wall, then stepped past her. "Well, then, I see Captain Ravenel's in good hands, so I'll leave you. If you'd like coffee, there's usually a fresh pot at the nurses' station on the first floor. And it's the real thing, too. New York City managed to get an exemption on a few rationed items, thanks to the Society of Restaurateurs. Being that we're a military and war production area, and all. But it's still in limited supply, so go easy on it."

Caroline sat down in the chair by the bed and slowly slid off her gloves. "Oh, just one cup should do me. I like mine black with two sugars."

I paused in the threshold just for a moment, then turned back to her with a wide smile. "So do I," I said, before quickly heading down the corridor toward the stairs, listening to Cooper's laughter echoing off the plaster walls.

Seventeen

꧁꧂

Olive

The fire in the grate was already lit, and the room radiated a homely warmth. Harry released her hand—they had raced up the stairs together like guilty lovers, Harry's fingers wound so tightly around hers that she could hardly breathe—and closed the door behind them.

"This had better be quick," Olive said. "I've got to be in bed by eleven for Mrs. Keane's inspection. And if she catches me stealing down the stairs . . ." She let her words trail away, because she couldn't quite say what the consequence of this malfeasance might be (too horrible to contemplate—immediate dismissal without reference, possibly a public flogging) and because Harry was hurrying across the room to the squat old Chinese cabinet by the wall, and why on earth would he be doing that?

A surprise, he'd said. Well, she couldn't help but flutter a bit, could she? She was human.

"Don't worry about Mrs. Keane," Harry was saying, as he took a key from his pocket and unlocked the bottom drawer of the cabinet.

"I've already set her up with a bottle of Christmas brandy and an entire mince pie all to herself. With my grateful thanks for a year of service, of course."

Olive tried to imagine Mrs. Keane drinking a glass of brandy. "And she accepted it?"

"She's always had a soft spot for me. God knows why." Harry rose from the cabinet and turned, smiling his brilliant smile.

"You know very well why."

"Well, I shared the first glass with her, just to get her started, and I can promise you she won't be in any condition to make an inspection this evening." He saluted. "You are hereby dismissed from your duties, Miss Olive, and have only yourself to please."

"Until five o'clock tomorrow morning."

For a moment, he was silent, and a little of the smile faded from his mouth. He still stood before the cabinet, holding something in both hands behind his back. "Are you really up so *very* early?" he said at last.

"Didn't you know?"

"I didn't think five o'clock. And I've made you stay up so late."

"It was worth it."

"Was it?"

She dropped her gaze to the worn Oriental rug. "You know it was."

The floorboards creaked as he stepped toward her. She counted each one, because they belonged to Harry, because the floorboards were so lucky to bear the touch of Harry's feet. Her hands twisted together atop the wilting white face of her pinafore apron. When he stopped before her, she admired the curve of his shoes.

"I have something for you. But you're going to have to look up first."

Olive looked up slowly, but only as far as his hands, which now held a small framed miniature portrait.

"I painted it from the sketches. It's the best one yet. I think I'm finally getting it right. Getting *you* right, I mean. The lines of your face and figure, the pose, the way your nightgown drapes against your skin, although of course it's not a nightgown here, it's more like a—a medieval garment that— Anyway, do you like it?"

Her gaze darted upward to Harry's face, because he was *nervous*; he was actually babbling like a schoolboy. His brows slanted upward, anxious for her approval.

She looked back down at the miniature and took it from his fingers. "It's wonderful. It's like magic. It's not even me."

"It's yours."

"I can't take this. You need it for your painting."

"I'll make another. I want you to keep this. I want you to keep this in your trunk in your awful grubby room in the nunnery, and to take it out every night when I'm gone and look at it and say, *Harry loves me, Harry's coming back in June to take me away to Europe, Harry's going to make up for all this work and misery and make me as happy as a man ever made a woman.*"

Olive stepped back. *"What?"*

He caught her hand. "Listen to me, Olive. I'll be twenty-two in April, and I'm coming into a little money then, a tidy little nest egg my grandmother left me. It's not a fortune, but it's a start. Right after graduation, I'm taking you away from here—"

"But you can't!"

"Yes, I can." He kissed her hand and went down on his knees, pulling her to the floor with him. "I can't stand watching you in your uniform, working the way you do, serving us like this. We should be serving you. The way Prunella sneers at you—"

"She *sneers* at me?"

"When you're not looking. That's just the way she is. She's jealous of anyone who's prettier than she is, and she's seen me looking at you—"

"Oh, no!" Olive put her face in her hands, but Harry pulled the fingers gently away and tilted up her chin.

"Because she knows you're her superior, Olive. She knows I love you." He placed his palms on her cheeks. "I love you, Olive. What do you think of that? I'm taking you away with me. It's going to be the biggest scandal. We're going to live in Europe together, and we'll be the happiest two people on the face of the earth, the king and queen of happiness."

"I can't," she whispered. "Don't be silly. I'm just a—just a house-maid. You're Harry Pratt—you have your future before you—"

He was shaking his head. "No, I'm not Harry Pratt. Not *that* Harry Pratt, the fellow who swans about Manhattan, pretending to be what people expect of him. The college boy, the ladies' man, ready to follow his father onto Wall Street and marry some heiress and own a big fat mansion uptown filled with ten kids and a safe-deposit box filled with railway shares. Old drawings packed away in a crate somewhere. That's not me. I want to *paint*, Olive. I want to paint for a living; I want to paint for life. I want to live with you in an attic in Florence and paint all night until I make something real, something almost perfect, and then tramp through the hills with you and lie naked in the vineyards. I want to see your face every morning and draw your face every day. I want to see the sunshine on your skin. Now, that's what I call a grand future."

"You don't know what you're saying."

"Oh, I know what I'm saying, all right. I've been thinking about it every second. I can't imagine living without you. I want to know every inch of you and give you every inch of me, if you'll have it. The real me, the Harry that's hidden beneath all the shirtfronts and the dinner jackets." He leaned forward, and his lips touched the tip of her nose. "You're about the only one who's ever met him, I think."

"I'm just a passing fancy. You'll go back to Harvard and forget me by February."

"You know that's not true. It would be like forgetting my own arm."

He kissed her nose again, a little longer, a little more tenderly. "Forgetting my own heart."

"Stop." His breath was sweet on her face, brandy and mincemeat and adoration. "You promised not to—not to—" *Not to touch me. Not to kiss me.* Not to do *this*, the one thing she couldn't afford. The final line she couldn't possibly cross.

Unless she did.

He pulled away a few inches, and his smile and his blue eyes came into shining focus. He pointed to the tin ceiling above them.

"It's Christmas, Olive. Look up."

She looked up and up, into the skylight that showed the black Christmas night and the tiny bright stars, and the little sprig of green that hung with painstaking care in the exact center, several feet above.

"You're a devious man, Harry Pratt."

"When I have to be."

He brushed his thumbs against her cheekbones. "I've been plotting all day. The mistletoe. The miniature. The darned brandy and mince pie—and she takes a lot of buttering up, that Mrs. Keane, you know, and for a moment there I thought she'd never give in—and then tracking you down before it was too late."

"Just for a kiss?"

"Just one little kiss, Olive. A tiny Christmas miracle. What do you say?"

Olive had never kissed anyone on the lips. Her heart was striking her ribs, maybe twice every second, panicked and thrilled. Her fingers were cold. She thought, *If he tastes like he smells, it can't be so bad.* Brandy and mincemeat and adoration.

"Well, Olive? Kiss me?"

She placed one brave hand against his shirtfront.

"I guess you've earned it," she whispered, and his lips sank against hers, so much softer than she had imagined.

❖

Olive wasn't an only child, but her two brothers and a sister had all died before her. The usual scourges of childhood, and a little bad luck besides. Arabella, her sister, had had a weak heart, and it gave out during a scarlet fever epidemic when Olive was three. Olive had woken up one morning and found herself alone, and ever since—because she had been almost too small to remember Arabella at all, really, except as a kind of shadow, smelling of sugar cookies—ever since, she had always wondered what it would be like to have siblings. To have someone to share your troubles, to have someone who knew you intimately. You would quarrel and make up, and you would lie side by side on the attic floor on rainy days, sharing your dreams, sharing the silent space between them. And the missing piece of your heart—Olive had imagined it so many times—would simply fall into place, making you whole.

Well, maybe she'd had it all wrong about siblings, but lying on the cushions with Harry seemed a lot like she used to imagine, except more: more pulse, more life, more fullness in your chest until you almost couldn't breathe, this beautiful warm *burstiness* that crowded everything else out. Her lips still tingled from his kisses, and her right hand was tucked in his left. His jacket had been tossed on the floor somewhere, and his waistcoat lay open, and it was all so natural and perfect, so exactly as they were meant to be.

Except they were not. Except there was that portfolio downstairs, marked VAN ALAN.

But she pushed the portfolio away, because it was Christmas, and because she could still taste Harry's kisses and smell Harry's breath, and the warmth of Harry's shoulder merged into hers.

"We'll be like two new people," he was saying. "The real Harry and the real Olive. I can just see us, waking up in the sunshine. Not having to pretend anymore, not having to be nice to people you despise. There's this fellow I know there, an old professor who moved to Fiesole last year. He'll help us get started, I'm sure."

"It sounds wonderful," said Olive, wondering what Fiesole was.

Harry turned his head. "Does it, Olive? Do you really want it? Not just because I do, I mean, but because you want it for yourself."

"I do. I do want it." It was the truth. She thought about lying next to Harry's warm body in a sunlit Italian attic, and her whole chest ached, her limbs pulled with longing. And then her practical mind whispered: *What about marriage? What about children?* He hadn't mentioned those. But children would surely follow, wouldn't they, and how would Harry feel about a squalling baby interrupting his artistic paradise? Would he still admire his darling nymph when her belly was swollen with child?

But that was why she loved him, wasn't it? His dreams, his beautiful ideals, soaring so far away from what was real and possible. If she tried, she could hold him carefully moored to earth, just close enough that he didn't fly away entirely. She squeezed his hand and said again: "I do want it. I want it so much, Harry."

He lifted himself up on his elbow and grinned down at her. "Take off your clothes."

"*What?*" (For the second time that evening.)

"I'm going to draw you, right now."

"In the—in the—" She couldn't say *nude*.

"Yes, all bare and true. With a sheet draped over you, of course." Harry sprang to his feet. "Go on. I'll avert my eyes, I promise. For now, anyway."

She couldn't be certain, but she thought he leered. She sat up and looked down at her black dress, her white pinafore apron, the ruffles now crushed and guilty. *But it's Christmas,* she thought recklessly. *It's Christmas, and in two weeks, I'll never have the chance again.*

She rose and went behind the screen to take off her pinafore and her dress, her corset and petticoat and stockings. "Everything?" she called, over the screen.

"Everything."

"You won't look?"

"Of course I'll *look*, Olive. That can't be avoided, even if I wanted to." (She imagined he was grinning.) "But I'll drape you with a sheet, and I promise to be a gentleman."

She pulled her chemise over her head, and her skin crawled and tingled against the air, as if she could distinguish the delicate rub of each molecule. "Oh, the same way you were a gentleman just now?"

"Trust me, those were the most gentlemanly kisses a fellow ever bestowed on the girl he adores. Come along, now."

Olive looked down at her belly and limbs, shockingly bare. The tips of her breasts had crinkled into tiny nubs, the way they did when she climbed into the bath. What would Harry think? He had probably sketched dozens of naked women already. That was part of his training, wasn't it? To transform the female form into art. Olive had never imagined her body as a thing of art, as a collection of curves and lines designed to entrance the viewer, to express some sort of human or feminine ideal. What if she wasn't ideal enough? What if her bones and flesh were all wrong? What if the fraud in her soul had somehow warped her exterior, in a way that would be instantly recognizable to Harry's true blue eyes?

She crossed her arms over her chest.

"Would it help if I removed my own clothes?" called out Harry in a stage whisper.

"No!"

"An article or two. Only fair." His waistcoat winged into view, skidding across the floor, followed by his necktie.

"Harry, no!"

A shoe tumbled past. The other shoe.

"I'm going to keep going, Olive. Do you want me to keep going?"

"No!"

"Then come out of there. I'm picking out the studs of my shirt right now." A few pings sounded, as of metal hitting the floor.

"Harry!"

"Do you think I'm bluffing?" A flash of white flew past, landing on top of the waistcoat.

She thought, *My God, he's serious.*

And then, in horror: *Trousers next.*

She snatched up her pinafore, clutched it to her breasts, and stepped from the screen.

"That's better," Harry said warmly, but she couldn't look up, she wouldn't look up. She made for the cushions on the floor and sank down, trying to arrange her pinafore for the maximum possible effect, and not succeeding particularly well. A flush began to spread over her skin.

"Here, let me." Harry's hands appeared, pulling away the pinafore gently, like a doctor examining a wound. An instant later, a sheet of fine white muslin replaced the pinafore, and Harry's long fingers arranged it over her shoulder, down along her breasts, under her opposite arm. Olive couldn't breathe. Harry's bare chest balanced before her, a very pale gold, flat with elegant muscle, exactly as beautiful as it had looked that morning, only far less frightening. His bent knees, covered with sleek black wool, appeared enormous. "Now lie down on your side," he whispered, and she did, and he adjusted the sheet again, and this time she was quite sure that her right breast was now open to the air, but she didn't look down, and she didn't protest, because she could tell by the expression on Harry's face that he thought she was perfect.

The broad hands moved lower, draping the sheet over her hip, and then he moved back and surveyed her.

"Am I up to your standards?" she said.

"Yes." He reached for the pins in her hair and slid them free, one by one, until the curls tumbled over her shoulders and down her back, and he rose to his feet. "One more thing."

She watched him pad across the room to the Chinese cabinet and admired the flex of muscle in his back, the little secrets of him she hadn't even suspected. When he returned, she was watching his bare feet: not because she was shy, but because they fascinated her.

"Hold up your hair," he said, and Olive's eyes flew to his face, and then to his hands.

A delicate gold filigree chain hung from his fingers, weighed down by a prodigious crimson stone.

"Tell me that's just a garnet," Olive whispered.

Harry smiled and reached around her neck with both hands. "But that would be a lie, Olive dear. And I can't tell you a lie. Anyway, it's yours." He settled back on his heels and touched her cheek. *"For her price is far above rubies."*

The stone settled into the hollow of Olive's throat, like an enormous drop of blood, cool and heavy. She touched it with one finger, not daring to look. A coal popped in the fire behind her. Harry lifted a curl of hair from her shoulder, pressed it to his lips, and picked up his sketchbook.

❖

The air was warm, and Harry worked in a state of silent concentration, until Olive, exhausted and relaxed on the old velvet cushions, drifted to sleep, started, and drifted back.

"That's all right," said Harry. "Sleep if you like."

So she allowed her heavy lids to close, terribly grateful, to the sound of the sizzling fire and the scratch of Harry's charcoal pencil, and the utter peace of the sanctuary around them.

❖

When she awoke, the world was black, and a woolen blanket was tucked around her, so snugly that she thought for a moment she was safe in her bed in the nunnery.

But the bed was far too comfortable, and then there was no accounting for the weight that lay like a bar across her stomach, and the warmth at her back and shoulders. The stir of breath at the nape of her neck.

Her eyes flew open. Her limbs went stiff.

"Harry!" she whispered.

But there came only a faint snore in response, a reflexive twitching of fingers at her waist. The arm, she perceived, rested over the blanket, and Harry's body did not quite touch her back. A few respectful inches lay between them. The velvet cushion was soft under her cheek.

What time was it? There was no telling. It might be midnight or half past four; she might have hours left or none. How daring and delicious, to lie here quietly with Harry, while the rest of the house slept, while the rest of the world had to endure some ordinary bedfellow.

Well, so would Olive, in two more weeks. In two more weeks, there would be no more Harry, and she would return to the leather portfolio marked VAN ALAN. She promised herself that. She made a bargain with God, or Saint Nicholas, or the baby Jesus, or whoever was keeping vigil with her, in the warm, black, brandy-scented Christmas night. A fortnight of Harry, just Harry and nothing else, no guilt or regrets, no anxiety about tomorrow. And when the carriage had left for that stinking great terminus on Forty-second Street, for the waiting train to carry him to Boston, why, that very morning she would steal into August Pratt's study and take those Van Alan papers. This time, for good.

But until then. Harry.

Her stiff limbs had gone limp and soft, absorbing him. She should have been ashamed, but she wasn't: all those nights of posing, all that intimacy. They were in their room, their own sanctuary at the top of the stairs, where Olive could shed her old skin and be someone she'd never known before, someone she never imagined she was.

"Olive."

She should have been startled, but she wasn't.

"You're awake?"

"Not really."

She smiled. She was filled with heat and certainty, and a flutter deep in her belly that she could not name but supposed was anticipation.

She turned beneath his arm, until they were facing each other, and the scent of Harry's skin blended with the scent of hers, warm and salty and sleepy. The ruby slipped along her collarbone. With one hand, she lifted the blanket and enclosed him; with the other, she touched his cheek. She couldn't really see his face, but she heard the damp sound of his lips, parting in surprise.

"Merry Christmas," she whispered.

Eighteen

꧁꧂

Lucy

Lucy tasted gin.

Tingling on her tongue. On Philip Schuyler's lips as he kissed her, his hand cupping her cheek, his other arm snaking around her waist, pulling her close despite the interfering curve of the table. The black leather of the banquette encased them, shielding them from the rest of the room.

Those were Philip Schuyler's fingers on her cheek, the gold of his Yale class ring cool against her skin; it was Philip Schuyler's lips against hers, murmuring her name as he kissed her, the culmination of a thousand guilty daydreams, daydreams in which he took her hands in his and declared that he'd been a fool, a terrible fool, that she was the girl for him and he didn't care who knew it, like something out of the serial stories in the papers, where the shopgirl always won the love of the heir to the fortune.

But this wasn't a daydream.

This wasn't a ball; she wasn't wearing a silver-spangled gown and diamond clips in her hair. She was in her work suit, crammed into a corner of a dark speakeasy where the floor smelled of spilled spirits. She wasn't floating; there weren't violins. There was no rapture, just the side of the table biting into her rib cage and a nagging sense of the wrongness of it all, the wrongness of kissing a man who was engaged to someone else.

Three tables away, the bored socialite laughed, a high-pitched whinnying laugh. Lucy gave Philip Schuyler a push, hard enough to make the table rock, gin sloshing over the sides.

"Philip—Mr. Schuyler—don't."

"Lucy . . ." The banquette creaked and groaned as he lurched after her, falling against the spot where she had been.

He was drunk. She'd never seen him drunk before, never imagined he could be drunk. Drunkenness was for the louts who used to swill beer from the barrel behind the bakery, singing rude songs straight from the beer garden. Drunkenness was for red-nosed old men and high school dropouts, not for Philip Schuyler, the epitome of all that was elegant and refined.

"Lucy . . . Sweetheart . . ." He reached for her, his smile a parody of that easy charm she knew so well.

Miss Young, if you wouldn't mind . . .

Miss Young, be a sweetheart and . . .

And she had. She'd brought his coffee; she'd taken his meetings; she'd even gone to dinner with John Ravenel.

The thought of John Ravenel—smiling down at her in the sunshine of the park—made her push with renewed energy at the hands clasping her waist.

"I'm not your sweetheart." Lucy's voice rose as she struggled to free herself. "Mr. Schuyler—*stop.*"

The waiters stopped in their tasks and the bored socialite threw a glance over her shoulder and then said something in a low tone to her companion that made him throw back his head and laugh.

Lucy could feel shame, hideous shame, rising red in her cheeks. *Your mother's daughter*, her grandmother said.

"You called me Philip before," said Mr. Schuyler, looking like a disappointed little boy.

"Before, you hadn't tried to kiss me." Lucy reached below the table, rooting for her bag. It had fallen in the scuffle, somewhere under the table.

"Lucy . . . Lucy, wait." Philip Schuyler grabbed her hand, pulling her up to face him. He twined his fingers clumsily through hers. "I thought you liked me."

He was looking up at her with such big eyes, all vulnerability. A little boy, rejected by his stepmother. Indignation warred with pity, and, worst of all, flattery. "I did like you. I do like you. It's just—I can't—"

Philip's hand tightened on hers. "Sit down." He gave a little tug. "Have another drink."

Lucy stared down at him, fighting a crushing sense of disappointment. "And what? Be your little bit on the side? Kiss you in the dark and then take your calls from your fiancée? No, thank you, Mr. Schuyler."

Philip Schuyler stared at her in genuine consternation. Or perhaps that was just the gin, slowing his wits, wrinkling his forehead. "I never thought— You're a girl in a million, Lucy. Has anyone ever told you that? You're the bee's knees. The cat's meow." Grandly, he declared, "You're the best secretary I've ever had."

And whatever last illusions Lucy had cherished shriveled and died.

What had she thought, really? That Philip Schuyler was going to sweep her into his arms and declare he loved her, only her? She'd seen the pictures of him with Didi Shippen.

It wasn't that Didi was beautiful. In themselves, Didi's features were pleasant but pedestrian. It was what she had made of them. It was the arrangement of her hair, the set of her mouth, the pearls in her ears, all of which proclaimed her status as loudly as any number of entries in the social register.

Didi was the sort of woman a man like Philip married. Maybe, in the end, he wouldn't like her all that much. Maybe, after a few years, he'd take to kissing his secretaries at speakeasies.

But Lucy wouldn't be that secretary.

"What? Lucy? What did I say?"

Lucy's head was beginning to ache. The smell of gin and Turkish cigarettes was strong in the air, clinging to her hair and clothes. "Nothing," she said. "Nothing but the truth. I'm your secretary. You are my employer. Which is why I shouldn't be here right now."

"No reason not to be." Philip Schuyler was still clinging to her hand. He tapped a finger against his nose. "After business hours. No one's going to know about it."

Lucy yanked her hand away. "No one is going to know because this never happened." She wanted to cry with shame, to drum her fists against the scarred wooden tabletop, but she kept her back straight and her voice level. "Meg comes back in another month. Until then—I'm your secretary. And this never happened."

"Can you really say that?"

A crazy laugh bubbled up in Lucy's throat. "I have to say that! Don't you think I wish it were otherwise? Don't you know that it's going to make me crazy, every day, seeing you, and having to pretend this never happened? But I can't afford to do otherwise. If I ask to be reassigned, Miss Meechum will know something happened! And who do you think she'll blame? Not the junior partner. She'll blame me. And I'll be out on the pavement, looking for another job and wondering how I will pull together the money to pay my rent!"

Philip Schuyler stared at her, frozen in tableau against the banquet.

Once started, the words kept bubbling out. Lucy couldn't stop them. "I need this job. I'm not one of your debutantes. I don't work on a whim. I work because it's how I keep myself alive. Do you think I enjoy typing and filing? Do you think anybody enjoys typing and filing?"

"I didn't—" Philip Schuyler shook his head as though he were trying to clear it. "Lucy—"

"Don't you mean Miss Young?" Lucy's tone was as acid as the bootlegged gin. "I thought you were different. Everyone knows that Mr. Cochran pinches and Mr. Gregson isn't to be trusted after a few drinks. But I thought you—I thought you were something special." More fool she. "I thought you were a gentleman."

She had the satisfaction of seeing Philip Schuyler flinch. She had done that at least. She had torn a strip off his smooth façade. But it was a Pyrrhic victory. She would have done anything never to have come here, never to see what he could be, never to have known what he thought she could be. She had liked it before, when he was her preux chevalier, Saint George on the wall, unreachable and untarnished.

"Lucy." The gold light winked off Philip Schuyler's class ring as he reached out a hand to her. "I never . . ."

Lucy slapped his hand away. "No, you never. And I never." Reaching into her purse, she flung a dollar on the table. "For my drink."

It was an absurd amount of money, money she couldn't afford to spend, but it was the only way she could think to salvage her pride, to claim some control over the situation.

She grabbed up her hat, her bag. "Have a martini on me," she said over her shoulder, and made for the stairs before Philip could extricate himself from the banquette, his long legs tangling against the legs of the table.

The waiters had seen worse scenes; they looked the other way as she ran from the room, down the malodorous stairs, past the gatekeeper in his loud checked suit.

The air on the street was little better than it had been inside, stinking in the July heat, thick with the scent of yesterday's garbage. It had grown dark when she was inside, the creeping dusk of the city summer. It wrapped around her like damp flannel. The dark brought no relief from the summer heat; it only pressed it in more closely around her.

Lucy clutched her bag in both hands and started walking, as quickly as she could. But not fast enough.

Philip Schuyler came trotting along behind her, face flushed, tie askew. "Let me put you in a taxi, at least."

"Like you do all your girls?"

"You're not just any girl." He darted around, in front of her, forcing her to a halt before the shuttered front of a greengrocer's establishment. "There haven't been other—I mean, there were, before Didi, but since then—there hasn't been anyone. Not like that—"

He was floundering; polished, glib Mr. Schuyler, who could talk the most contumacious client into good humor. He didn't look smooth and polished now. The veneer was off, his face raw and confused. He looked, Lucy realized, lost. As lost as she felt.

"You've had a spat with your fiancée," she said, as matter-of-factly as she could. "And I happened to be there. That's all."

He shook his head, adamantly, the blond locks disarranged. In the light of the streetlamp, Lucy saw gray, gray she had never noticed before, beginning to thread its way into the blond.

"It's not like that. Didi's not—you're not—"

Pity took the place of her anger, pity and an incredible sense of weariness. "Go home. Take a glass of soda water and an aspirin," she advised. "You'll feel better in the morning."

This time, when she started walking, he didn't follow. He stood beneath the streetlight and watched her go, his face a mask of confusion.

❧

When Lucy arrived at the office the next morning, there was a message with Miss Meechum. Mr. Schuyler had been called away to Philadelphia for an urgent meeting with a client.

Lucy had a shrewd idea of just who that client might be.

It was right, wasn't it? she told herself, slamming the typewriter shuttle from one side to the other so hard that it nearly jammed. It made sense for Mr. Schuyler to go to Philadelphia to make his peace with his fiancée. She'd all but told him to. In fact, she had told him to, hadn't she?

Either way, he'd done the right thing. He'd done the gentlemanly thing, removing himself from the office for a few days.

Why did it make her more angry, then?

When Lucy went into Mr. Schuyler's office—always Mr. Schuyler now, never Philip—to leave him a stack of neatly typed copies of the Kiplinger contract, she found a folded piece of paper in the middle of the desk, with *Miss Young* written, in Mr. Schuyler's elegant hand, across the outside.

Inside lay the same worn, crumpled dollar she had tossed on the table the night before.

No note. Just that dollar.

The phone on Mr. Schuyler's desk rang. Didn't that idiot at the switchboard know better than to put calls through when he was out of the office?

Lucy snatched up the phone. "Mr. Schuyler's office," she snapped.

"Miss Young?" The voice had a warm Carolina drawl. "You sounded so fearsome I hardly knew you."

She hardly knew herself these days. Lucy glanced quickly over her shoulder. "I shouldn't be talking with you at work."

"I am a client, aren't I?" said Mr. Ravenel mildly. Then, "Bad day?"

"Bad week." Bad month. Bad year.

Nothing had been right since her father had died. His absence was a hollow in her heart. No matter how she had fought with her grandmother, no matter how she had yearned to move to the city, to try a new life, her father had been home for her.

She had lost him twice. Once when he died, and again that afternoon after his funeral when her grandmother had unleashed her terrible secret.

A cuckoo in the nest, her grandmother had called her. *Your mother— no better than she should be.*

And Lucy had remembered the pendant so hastily shoved in her pocket only a few months before, and her mother's dying words. A legacy from her father, yes, but not the father she had believed to be hers.

"Let's make it a good weekend, at least." Ravenel's rolling Southern accent felt like a balm after Philip Schuyler's clipped, boarding school cadence. It conjured up memories of the weekend before, of sunshine and ice cream and innocent pleasures. "I have a surprise for you on Saturday."

"I don't know . . ." Lucy ran her finger along the blunt edge of the embossed blotter. She'd thought those drinks with Philip Schuyler were innocent, until they weren't. "I shouldn't."

She could hear the amusement in his voice, all the way through the wires. "Be surprised?"

"See you." She was amazed by the effort it cost her. "It isn't really appropriate."

"Isn't there an old adage about horses and barn doors?" When Lucy didn't say anything, John Ravenel added, "I promise, there's nothing that your mother wouldn't approve of."

That was what she was afraid of. "I don't . . ."

"One forty-seven West Fourth Street. Meet me there at noon. I promise you"—John Ravenel's voice was warm and persuasive—"you won't regret it."

Nineteen

July 1944

Kate

Margie wiped her mouth with a napkin before folding it neatly and tucking it into her lunch pail. We sat on the same Central Park bench where our mothers had met all those years ago, a habit we'd fallen into after I'd begun working at Stornaway Hospital. It was a nod to a past we both remembered fondly while dealing with a present that seemed uncertain at best.

The day was saved from the murderously hot summer heat by a layer of thin, wispy clouds, as if even the sun agreed that the world below in all its turmoil didn't deserve all of its light. The city was merely a shadow of its former glory, with even Lady Liberty and Times Square darkened at night. On my walk to the park I was assaulted with advertisements to buy war bonds on the sides of trolleys and buildings. Metal signage and ornamentation had been vanishing from the city since the first call for scrap metal, and I'd begun to wonder if New York would ever be the same again.

Margie shook out her cigarette case and took one, then offered it to me. I hesitated for a moment and then shook my head. "No, thank you. If I have one, I'll only want another."

"What?" she asked over the sound of a crowded bus jerking its way down Fifth Avenue.

"Never mind," I said, latching my pail.

"So," Margie said, blowing out a puff of smoke. "How's your captain?"

"He's not *my* captain. His fiancée is here. From Charleston. I doubt I'll be seeing much of him until he leaves." *Are you going to let me finish?* I kept hearing his words, asking me to let him finish his sketch of me. And each time I heard them I had to remind myself to say no.

"Um-hmm," she said, a knowing smile tilting her lips.

I looked at her cigarette and she handed it to me. I took a long, calming drag, then handed it back to her. "He has a *fiancée*. Why would you think I'm interested in him?"

She looked at me fully. "Because when you talk about him there's something about your eyes."

There's something about your eyes. I startled. "He said the same thing. When he told me he wanted to finish the sketch of me."

She raised a plucked eyebrow as she took another drag from her cigarette and didn't say anything. She didn't need to.

Eager to change the conversation, I checked my watch. "I need to get going. But first I need to ask a favor."

She leaned back, narrowing her eyes. "This won't involve me going on a blind date in your place, will it? The last time that happened I got stranded on Coney Island with a short, bald man who only spoke Russian and called me Martzie."

"I know. And I still owe you. This favor doesn't involve blind dates or Russians—promise. I need you to look up a name for me in the newspaper archives. Harry Pratt. He might be an artist. I found a few of his sketches in the attic, and I believe his family might have once owned the hospital building. He might be related to Prunella J. Pratt—I found a ball gown in an armoire with her name embroidered on the inside."

"Prunella?"

"I know. It's not the sort of name that rolls easily off the tongue, is it? I had an aunt named Prunella. Must have been popular way back when."

Margie took one last puff of her cigarette, then crushed it under the toe of her shoe. "Thank goodness its popularity had waned by the time we came along." She gave an exaggerated shudder. "Why are you so interested in the Pratts?"

"I'm not really sure. Curiosity, maybe. The sketches are so good that I'm wondering if he might have become a renowned artist."

"And?" she prompted. Margie was the one person in the world who knew me enough to know when I was holding something back.

"And I think I've heard the name Pratt before. I didn't think so at first, but then I had a memory of my mother and me standing in front of the building when I was small. I think she called it the Pratt mansion."

"Interesting," she said, raising both eyebrows. "I rather like searching through the archives. If I turn up something interesting, I might even forgive you for the Russian."

"You're a peach. I owe you dinner."

"I'll put it on your tab."

We hugged good-bye and went our separate ways—she back to the library while I headed to the hospital, trying to lose myself in the sounds of the city instead of hearing Cooper's voice echoing in my head. *There's something about your eyes.*

I was reaching for the outer door of the hospital when I heard my name called.

"Dr. Schuyler?"

I recognized the soft Southern voice before I turned around, and prepared myself. "Good afternoon, Miss Middleton. What can I do for you?" She wore an elegant light blue suit that matched the color of her eyes, the tightly fitted bodice hugging her tiny waist. A stylish hat with netting sat perched at an angle on top of her neat chignon, and impeccable white gloves and silk stockings completed the look. I tried not to think about my own bare legs and hands, or straggly hair that stuck to my forehead after my walk from the park. Sighing inwardly, I remembered Dr. Greeley saying that he wanted me to make myself available to Miss Middleton, to answer any of her questions about where to eat. And shop. Like I would know. I doubted we ate or shopped at the same kinds of establishments.

Her blue eyes remained icy despite her smile. "I was hoping we might have a chance to chat—woman to woman."

"Of course," I said, trying to remember the names of all the shops Margie was always telling me were the places she'd go once she married her rich husband. "Let's go inside and out of the sun . . ."

"No. I'd rather not. I'd prefer privacy. Why don't we walk down the block together?"

I looked at my watch, not bothering to hide my impatience. Some of us weren't women of leisure who didn't march to the hour hands of a clock all day. "All right. But I'm afraid I can't be long. I'm due back in five minutes."

Her smile widened. "Not to worry. What I have to say won't take long."

Attempting to hide my reluctance, I walked toward her, her arm claiming mine as soon as I was close enough. We began to walk in the same direction I'd just come from, our sides pressed against each other as if she were afraid I might try to escape.

"It's a lovely day, isn't it?" she asked as we strolled leisurely down the sidewalk.

"It's a bit warm," I said, wondering why she was wasting my time talking about the weather.

"Not if you're from Charleston. The heat and humidity in the summer are like a wet blanket that's been resting on coals. It takes some getting used to if you're not a native like Cooper and me. We were born and raised in Charleston. As a matter of fact, my family has been in Charleston for over two hundred years—isn't that something? We've had a cotton plantation on the Waccamaw River in Georgetown County since the Revolution, which means we have a lot of family connections. Important connections that can make or break an art gallery or even an artist."

She paused a moment to smooth the loose hair under her hat. "Has Cooper told you that we've known each other since we were in diapers? We have so much in common. Our families are even next-door neighbors at our summer retreats on Edisto."

We continued to walk, but I was becoming less and less aware of my surroundings as she spoke, understanding seeping through me like water through sand.

"Cooper and I are two of a kind, Kate. May I call you Kate?"

I nodded numbly.

"You see, Kate, the best marriages are those that are made between two people from the same world. They understand the same things." She turned her face toward me and her eyes seemed bleached by the sun. "That's how I know that Cooper and I are meant for each other." She placed a slender gloved hand over her heart. "Of course, it helps that he's mad about me and I'm mad about him."

I stopped suddenly, causing an old man in a worn brown suit that smelled of pipe smoke to stumble into me. He said something under his breath as he walked past, but I was too focused on Caroline's perfect face to care. "Then why didn't you come? The moment you knew Cooper was here, you could have come. But you waited."

Her face seemed carved from marble, her skin bloodless. I knew her answer before she spoke, by the way she hesitated and didn't meet my eyes. "Because your letter said that . . ." She stopped. "Because there was a chance he might lose his leg, and I didn't think I could stand to see him that way. See him as . . . less than a man."

I stared at her dumbly, unable to think of a single word to respond.

She tugged on my arm and we continued our walk back the way we'd come. "His mother doesn't travel, but she asked me to come. I had already packed my bags and was preparing for the journey when your second letter arrived, letting us know that his leg had been saved. So, you see, I was prepared to come regardless."

Because his mother asked you to. It was pointless to argue the obvious, so I kept my mouth shut. None of this was any of my business. Captain Ravenel was a patient of mine. A patient whose leg had been saved and who would be out of my life forever in a few short weeks.

We'd reached the front of the hospital again and stopped. I quickly slipped my arm from hers. "Why are you telling me all this?"

She smiled like a patient mother with a wayward child. "Because I don't want you to be hurt. I see the way you look at Cooper and I just want to make sure you understand that you're not his kind. He's grateful to you for helping to save his leg, and might even think he's a little in love with you because of it, but that won't last. As soon as he is back in Charleston, everything will return to normal and he'll forget all about you. I just wanted you to know that."

I felt the blood rush to my face. "I think you've misunderstood, Miss Middleton."

"Have I?" She smiled brightly, and I noticed that she had a small chip in her front teeth. I was relieved, somehow, as if this slight imperfection were like a chink in her armor. As if any of this really mattered at all.

"I'm late," I said, moving past her.

She caught my sleeve. "We're getting married on November tenth, and I'll be wearing his mother's wedding veil. The engraved invitations have already been ordered."

I pulled my arm away and hurriedly jerked the door open. I'd wanted to turn around and ask her why she hadn't said that she loved him and that he loved her, but I hadn't. I hadn't because I was afraid that the emotion coursing through me wasn't disbelief, but hope.

※

I sat at Dr. Greeley's desk with bleary eyes, my cravings for a cigarette reaching mythic proportions. My father had been a heavy smoker, and although nobody had ever said it was linked to his death from lung cancer, I wasn't completely convinced it hadn't been. But that didn't mean that I didn't crave them.

Dr. Greeley was, presumably, at home in his comfortable bed, finally giving me an entire evening where I didn't have to creep around corners or tiptoe down hallways. He'd left a stack of charts and reports for me, enough to ensure that I wouldn't get any sleep. I rubbed my face, eyeing the full ashtray on the corner of the desk, then picked it up and dumped it into the trashcan.

My head had been throbbing ever since my confrontation with Caroline Middleton. It had taken nearly an hour before my shock and embarrassment had turned into righteous anger. How dare she? How *presumptuous* of her. I was a *doctor*. It was expected that a certain level of intimacy would form between a doctor and a patient. It was unavoidable. But I was always a professional first. A healer. Not a woman so desperate for a husband that I would steal another woman's fiancé. I certainly hadn't gone to medical school to find a husband. I ground the heels of my hands into my throbbing temples, wishing I'd thought to grab a couple of aspirin before holing myself up in the airless office.

I stacked another folder on the edge of the desk and had just decided to take a break and find aspirin when Nurse Hathaway knocked on the door. "I'm sorry to disturb you, Doctor, but Captain Ravenel is having another one of his nightmares."

"Yes, of course," I said, smoothing my skirt as I stood. After that horrible conversation with Caroline Middleton, I'd sworn to myself that I wouldn't see Captain Ravenel again, to prove to her that I could stay away. And, if I were to be honest, to prove to myself that I could. But I was the doctor on duty, and he was a patient. I couldn't very well say no.

"I won't be too long," I said, walking past her. "If anybody needs me and it's not an emergency, tell them I'll be back shortly."

I could hear Cooper's shouts as I reached the top landing and hurried toward his room. The sickly scent of fear assailed my nostrils as soon as I entered, emanating from the thrashing form on the bed. The bedside light was on, its bulb flickering like a movie projector. Most of the bedclothes had slid to the floor, revealing a bare-chested captain clad only in what appeared to be light blue pajama bottoms. A gift from his fiancée, no doubt.

He was glowing with sweat, his head moving back and forth on the pillow, his arms lashing out at an unseen enemy. "Get down, goddammit, get down!" His voice was raw, as if he'd been in the thick of battle for hours.

I sat down on the edge of the bed. "Captain Ravenel?"

He continued to thrash, making me stand again to avoid his flailing limbs. "No, no, no, no." His voice weakened as his shoulders hunched forward, and for a moment I was with him on the beachhead, half-immersed in salt-flavored water, the waves tinted red with the blood of my fellow soldiers.

"Cooper?" I said softly, desperate to bring him back from the dark places his nightmares brought him.

"Victorine?"

I took one of his hands in mine. "Yes. It's me. Victorine. You're safe now. You can stop fighting."

His eyes were open, but I knew he wasn't seeing me as he lifted his other hand and brushed my face with the tips of his fingers, as gentle as a butterfly. "Victorine," he said, his hand falling and capturing my free hand, his voice lighter.

"Yes. Go to sleep now. Nobody is going to hurt you."

"Stay," he whispered, his eyes closing.

The words fell from my lips before I could recall them. "I'll stay. For as long as you need me, I'll stay."

His breath slowed to an easy rhythm, his hands tightly clasping mine. *Just a few minutes.* I'd wait for just for a little bit, until he was in a deep sleep, and then I'd leave. With my hands still held tightly to his, I found a comfortable spot on the headboard to lean against and lifted my legs on the bed. I left the light on and began counting ceiling tiles again, trying to ignore the heaviness of my eyelids. *Just for a minute,* I told myself as I finally allowed them to close.

When I opened them again, the room seemed dipped in black ink. A warm body pressed against my back, a heavy arm pinning me to the bed. Disoriented, I rolled to my back as the body behind me shifted. I blinked, waiting for my eyes to grow accustomed to the dark. Looming over me, I saw the outline of Cooper's head.

I was about to close my eyes and go back to sleep when the realization of where I was and with whom struck me. I tried to rise but found myself restrained by a firm hand on my shoulder.

"Don't worry. You haven't been asleep very long." I heard the smile in his voice.

I tried again to rise, but he continued to hold me down. "It's not yet dawn. You don't have to go."

"Of course I do. I shouldn't be here."

"This is your room. I feel guilty for kicking you out."

"That's not what I meant and you know it. I shouldn't be here. With you. And you don't have a shirt on."

"You noticed?"

I could feel the warmth of his skin, his chest close enough that if I leaned forward just slightly I could press my lips against the soft skin under his neck. *No.* I jerked back, his hand holding me tightly.

"I just wanted to thank you. I know tonight isn't the only time you've come to me during one of my nightmares. Nurse Hathaway told me that you're the only one who can calm me down."

I relaxed into the pillow, the Southern slurring of consonants somehow reassuring in the blackened room. "I didn't think you knew it was me. You always call for Victorine."

"My muse," he said.

"You mean Manet's muse."

His face hovered over mine. "No, mine. Ever since I saw that miniature, she became my muse. I named her Victorine. The dark-haired beauty with green eyes." Gentle fingers brushed my throat, lifting the heavy ruby stone. "Where did you get this, Kate?"

I should go. But there was something otherworldly about this room in the summer night, my bones suddenly limp in the languid heat. His voice soothed me like a hypnotist's, and I found myself suspended in the darkness, where morning and war and fiancées didn't exist. Where my career aspirations seemed very far away. I placed my fingers over his and it was as if he knew my touch, and I knew his.

No! The word was so loud in my head that I imagined I'd shouted the word. I struggled to rise but he held me back. "Don't go. Please. I know you've felt it, this connection between us. I can't explain it. You look just like the woman in the miniature, the woman I've always called my Victorine. And you wear her ruby necklace."

"It might not be the same . . ."

"Kate. Don't. You and I both know it is. Please stay. Just a little longer. And tell me how you came to own this necklace."

I lay back down, unable to walk away from him no matter how much I knew I should. He lay down, too, our faces only inches apart. I took a deep breath, smelling the laundry detergent clinging to the pillowcase and the alluring smell of man and sweat and *him*. "It belonged to my grandmother, and then to my mother. It passed to me when my mother died. She never wore it, although several times when I was a little girl, I'd see her take it out of her jewelry box and put it on for a little while. But she never wore it outside the house."

His fingers lifted the stone from my throat, feeling its heft, turning it around in his hand, the brush of his skin against mine like tiny flaming matches. "It's a large stone, probably worth a great deal."

"I never really thought about it until I showed it to my friend Margie—she keeps it in her apartment for me. She said the same thing and she and I agreed that it didn't make any sense. You see, my grandmother was a baker's wife. I never could figure out how a baker's wife would come by such a beautiful and expensive piece of jewelry."

He gently rested the stone against my neck, then placed his arm around my waist as if it belonged there. He was silent for a long time, and I wondered if he'd gone back to sleep. "What are we going to do, Kate?"

For a moment I imagined the ruby crushing my chest, squeezing the air from my lungs, feeling for the second time since I'd met Captain Cooper Ravenel suddenly bereft.

I swallowed. "You'll continue to heal and then you will leave and go back to your home in Charleston where you will marry Miss Middleton in November and forget all about me. And I will continue to nurse the wounded officers that the war will spit out until there are no more bodies to throw into the war machine. I hope to become the best doctor that I can be and continue to practice medicine until I'm too old to see straight."

I'd tried to make my tone light and flippant, but my voice had caught on the last word, as if I imagined Cooper seeing the bleak world I'd painted for both of us.

"Then let me finish your sketch, so I won't forget you. But I want you to wear the necklace. Would you do that for me? As a parting gift."

I pulled away and sat on the edge of the bed, my back to him. I should say no. I should stand up and walk out of the room without saying anything. But the ruby lay heavy around my neck, as if all the unanswered questions lay trapped inside of it. He would be leaving in two weeks and I'd never see him again. It was a small thing, really. To allow him to sketch me wearing my grandmother's necklace. It would be a fitting way to say good-bye.

"Yes," I said without turning around. "I'll let you finish the sketch, and I'll wear the necklace." I'd made it to the door before he spoke.

"Kate?"

I turned the door handle.

"You feel it, too, don't you? This thing between us. This connection."

I closed my eyes, seeing my face in the miniature, remembering how I'd felt the first time I'd seen him being pulled from the ambulance in the pouring rain. But he was promised to another, and my life's path was never meant to intersect with his.

"Good night, Cooper."

I closed the door behind me with a soft snap before I felt compelled to answer.

Twenty

CHRISTMAS DAY 1892

Olive

The tracks of the New York Central Railroad lay like an open scar all up the length of Fourth Avenue, and to cross over this dirty gulf by one of the steel bridges was to cross into another world.

Well, maybe the transition wasn't quite so dramatic as that. Nobody wanted to live next to the stink and steam of the railway line, after all, so the houses began shrinking once you walked across Madison Avenue. But the inhabitants of the western side of the tracks still had some aspirations to grandeur. They lived within gazing distance of the mansions around Fifth Avenue. They passed these limestone palaces on their way to a morning stroll in Central Park and rubbed shoulders with their well-heeled neighbors at every opportunity.

Like an old English ha-ha separating one pasture from another, however, the Fourth Avenue railway viaduct neatly separated the upper classes from the middle ones. On the eastern side lived the respectable professionals, the artisans and shopkeepers seeking a little more fresh air than could be found farther south, and here, in a narrow and neatly kept house on Seventy-eighth Street, between Lexington and Third Avenues, lived Olive's mother and the three boarders in the upstairs bedrooms, one of which had once belonged to Olive herself, in the long-ago days of her girlhood.

When Olive trudged up the steps to the front door on her afternoons off, she always remembered how her father had scorned this house, which the Van Alans had bought in the early days, when he was only an ambitious junior draftsman at McKim, Mead & White. He hadn't liked its narrow proportions, or its cheap construction, or the muddy brown stone of its façade. When the Pratt mansion was finished, he told Olive, he would buy them a beautiful wide house on the other side of Fourth, the *right* side of Fourth, made of noble white limestone with a proper garden in back. The commissions would come pouring in, once the Pratts' wealthy friends saw the beauty of the Pratts' new home, and they would have an upstairs and a downstairs maid, a trained cook and housekeeper, and even their own carriage. The Van Alans would take their place—this was her father's dream—among the very society that employed him.

A dream, of course, that would never be realized, and to Olive, returning week after week from the glory of the Pratt mansion, the color of the brown stones had become the exact shade of disappointment. The very sight of them, as she turned the corner, would turn her legs into lead. One by one, she would trudge up the steps, as she might drag her way into prison.

But today, Christmas Day, Olive didn't trudge up the front steps. She bounded. Her heart swooped along for the ride. She was too sore and exhausted and exhilarated to notice the ugly brown color of the wall before her. As she dropped the knocker against the door, and as the noise beat against her ears, she thought for the first time that perhaps her father's dream had always been impossible. That you couldn't really enter the hallowed halls just because you had designed them. And even if you could, you might perhaps find that this entrée wasn't going to make you happy after all. That it wasn't the beauty of the house itself, but the beauty of what lay inside.

The beauty of *who* lay inside.

A year after Mr. Van Alan's death, there was no downstairs maid to open the door on Christmas Day: only Olive's mother, groomed to her painstaking best in what had once been a fashionable gown of burgundy velvet.

"Merry Christmas!" Olive said, leaning forward to press a cheerful kiss on her mother's cheek. She did this mostly to disguise the flush that overcame her own skin at the sight of that familiar maternal face; her mother had always seen right through Olive's angelic expression to guess at the transgressions that lay beneath.

Transgressions that now seemed absurdly trivial, compared to what Olive had done last night.

"Why, Merry Christmas, darling," Mrs. Van Alan said, a little surprised. "Come into the parlor. It's so awfully cold outside. I've built up the fire, nice and hot."

If *this* was nice and hot, Olive thought, then what had the fire been like before Mrs. Van Alan built it up? She unwound her muffler and shrugged out of her wool coat and decided that it must be her imagination, how the ruby underneath her plain gray dress seemed to glow against her chest. Before her mother took the coat away, Olive reached into the pocket. "Here. They gave us each a little Christmas present."

Mrs. Van Alan looked down at the money in Olive's palm. "Ten dollars?" she breathed.

"Take it. I don't have anything to spend it on, anyway."

Her mother looked at her in wonder, hesitating, and then went to the small walnut desk in the corner, which was populated by Mrs. Van Alan's beloved china shepherdesses in various pastoral attitudes, along with a few pensive sheep, contemplating a woolly escape (or so Olive had always imagined). She unlocked one of the drawers and tucked the ten-dollar bill inside a leather purse, all without a single word. Just a kind of heartbroken gratitude in her posture, the declining angle of her neck, as if she were too embarrassed to express her thanks.

Olive stared at that vulnerable white nape, bent in humiliation, and a little of the euphoria ebbed away.

Mrs. Van Alan turned from the desk and straightened her woolen shawl around her shoulders. "Did you have a nice Christmas Eve?" she asked, with false brightness.

"Christmas Eve? Oh, yes. Thank you."

"They didn't make you work too late, I hope?"

"Work? No."

"Because you don't quite look yourself." Mrs. Van Alan stepped forward—it was not a large parlor—and took Olive's hand between hers. "You're not sick, are you? They're not cruel to you?"

"No, no." Olive looked away, to the collection of framed photographs on the mantel. Her father's was the largest, right in the center, looking impossibly youthful and handsome in his pressed black suit and neat beard. He had always seemed young for his age, had always bristled with energy and enthusiasm. You could detect his charisma even in the sepia dimensions of the photograph. A bit like Harry that way, wasn't he? Even the memory of him could draw Olive's adoration from between her ribs.

Mrs. Van Alan put her hand to Olive's forehead. "You're flushed. You don't have a fever, do you?"

"Of course not!" Olive stepped away. "I was just walking briskly, that's all. I didn't want to waste a moment."

Her mother didn't reply, and Olive had the queer sensation that

that quiet brown gaze was settling on her skin, sinking beneath her surface, rooting out the truth that lay inside.

That Olive was in love.

That Olive—shameless, glorious Olive—had lain with her love in the early hours of Christmas morning.

That she felt him still upon the hollows of her body, upon every patch of skin, in every nodule. As if she now carried him inside her.

The old story, a maid and her master. But it hadn't been like that, had it? No, it was Olive who had kissed Harry first, Olive who had placed Harry's hand on her warm breast. She was not an ignoramus. She had once had all her father's books at her command, even the ones not intended for young ladies; she knew what was about to happen. She had known it would hurt—and it had—but she had also known that there would be pleasure: that she could give Harry pleasure and he could give it to her in return, and that she might never have this chance again. She might live a hundred years and never again connect with a human being in this perfectly primitive way, this way she could connect with Harry. As if they understood each other better without the interference of language.

So she had gathered up all her bravery and placed Harry's hands on her skin, and when he had asked her if she was absolutely certain, she whispered back that she absolutely was. She had braced herself for the brutal moment, but he hadn't been brutal at all, only tender and grateful and enamored, and he had held her so close afterward, she thought that their veins were clicking in the exact same rhythm, that they had actually achieved the kind of union that would make them immortal.

Then she didn't think anything at all, until Harry kissed her awake just before dawn and helped her wash and dress. His chest was still bare, and she had put her hands on him in amazement. He had laughed softly and smoothed her hair and told her not to be shy, that she could touch him all she liked. He belonged to her now, like Adam belonged to Eve.

Then she had stolen back down to her cold bed in the nunnery, trying to encompass this thought. Trying to comprehend what she had just done. This trespass she had just committed, this sin that felt like the opposite of sin.

"He would be so dismayed to see you now," said Mrs. Van Alan.

Olive snapped her gaze back to her mother. "Dismayed?"

Mrs. Van Alan was looking at the photograph. "Yes. To see you as a servant to that family, at their beck and call. Serving their needs."

Was it Olive's imagination, or was there a certain inflection in the words *Serving their needs?*

"Only to find justice for Papa," Olive said.

"He would want that least of all." Mrs. Van Alan shook her head, making her earbobs jingle against the dark waves of her hair, which were gathered into the same gentle knot Olive had known all her life. "He would want you to find a better life. A husband and a family of your own."

"And if that's not what I want?" Olive said defiantly, conscious all at once of her undergarments, which seemed to chafe on the sensitive skin between her legs in an entirely new way this morning.

"Olive! Don't say things like that. You don't mean them."

"But I do mean them. I want to be free. I want to be independent and able to choose whom to love—"

"Olive!"

Her name bounced around the room, rattling the china, making the rows of sheep and shepherdesses shiver in shock. Olive planted her feet in the middle of the worn rug and returned her mother's horrified gaze with too much sternness. But she didn't feel stern. She felt as she had last night: as if she were finally telling the truth. Throwing off shackles. Contemplating the impossible.

What if she *did* follow Harry to Europe? What if they did live in Florence together, laughing at convention, repeating that strange and wonderful act as often as they liked, while the Italian sunshine poured down upon them like a benediction?

Italy. Where no one knew who she was. Where Harry might never find out how she came to live on Sixty-ninth Street.

"A parcel arrived for you yesterday," said Mrs. Van Alan.

"A parcel!" Olive's heart leapt.

Her mother turned back to the desk, and for the first time Olive noticed a small package resting among the china shepherdesses, wrapped in brown paper. "It's from Mr. Jungmann."

"Mr. Jungmann," Olive repeated. Her heart settled right back into its ordinary place. "The grocer, you mean?"

"Such a nice man. Do you remember how you introduced us after church, last month? He's been so kind. He calls on me every week, to see if there's anything he can do for me. He fixed that stopped drain in the kitchen a few days ago. There's something to be said for a fellow who's good with his hands, don't you think?" She handed the package to Olive. "I think he's rather handsome."

Olive stared dumbly at the brown box in her hands and tried to remember seeing Mr. Jungmann at church. Well, it was possible, wasn't it? She and her mother always met for the nine o'clock service at the Church of the Resurrection, right after the Pratts had bundled off for fashionable St. James' on Madison Avenue. "I—I suppose so."

"Well, open it."

Now she remembered. She had been a little surprised to see Mr. Jungmann there, because she hadn't noticed him among the congregation before. He had been friendly and red-faced and had greeted her mother with the reverence of an acolyte before the Virgin Mary. He had said many complimentary things about Olive and parted from them with a quaint and formal little bow. And then Olive had returned to her duties at the Pratt mansion and forgotten all about it.

But Mr. Jungmann, apparently, had not.

Olive slid the string free and loosened the paper, which had been folded in crisp brown angles around an oblong box.

"Ooh, look at that," said Mrs. Van Alan.

"It's a box, Mother."

"Dearest, the *best* things come in boxes. Go on, go on."

Olive opened the box and unfolded the tissue to reveal an ornate silver hairbrush, beautifully made, its bristles so white they disappeared against the wrapping. "I can't accept this!" she gasped.

"*Gracious*, Olive." Her mother's voice was slow with awe. "How beautiful!"

"It's too much! It's—it's far too intimate." She set down the box as if it were scalding her. "Far too expensive. It's improper."

Mrs. Van Alan snatched the box right back up and plucked the hairbrush from its nest of tissue. She laid it lovingly on her palm, turning it over, tracing the scrollwork with an admiring finger. "Don't be a fool, Olive. He's in love with you."

"But I don't want him to be in love with me! I certainly never encouraged him. And I can't possibly return his affection."

Mrs. Van Alan turned sharply. "And why not? Too good for him, are you?"

"It's not that—"

"You do realize we are *destitute*, Olive? Destitute. Your father's debts . . ." She pressed her lips together and shook her head. "The money from the boarders hardly covers the housekeeping. Every month I scrape and mend and make do. I've run out of credit at the butcher. I've had to sell off all my good clothes, all the silver, all the jewelry except my earbobs. The last thing I own from your father." Her eyes glimmered. "I shall have to sell the house next, and live in some dirty tenement—"

But Olive had stopped listening, because she had just taken notice of those earbobs in her mother's ears, hanging from the tiny lobes as they always did on special occasions, at holidays and at church. They were made of rubies, a small round one at the top and a larger, teardrop-shaped stone dangling below, in a delicate and distinctive gold filigree setting.

A stone exactly the same shape, inside exactly the same setting, as the ruby that now dangled between Olive's breasts.

❄

Mrs. Van Alan produced tea and brandy cake, which Olive chewed dutifully in a mouth that seemed to have lost all sensation. She replied like an automaton to her mother's questions, though she couldn't remember, later, a single word they had exchanged. At half past three she glanced at the clock and said she had better be going. She needed to return to Sixty-ninth Street by four in order to start preparing the house for Christmas dinner.

"Can't you wait a few more minutes?" said Mrs. Van Alan. "Mr. Jungmann promised to stop by this afternoon."

"Then I should leave immediately."

Her mother's soft and longing face turned hard. "Don't be stupid, Olive. Just listen to you! You're running off to serve Christmas dinner to the people who murdered your father, when—"

"They did *not* murder Papa!" Olive shot back, and then, shocked by her own words: "Not all of them, anyway."

"Oh." Mrs. Van Alan fingered the edge of her plate—the second-best china, because the first had been sold off last spring. "Oh, I see. I see it now. You're being drawn in, aren't you? Seduced by their riches and glamour, just like your father was. So they can swallow you inside and digest you and spit you out again—"

Olive rose from the table. "That's not true!"

"We have nothing, Olive. We *are* nothing, thanks to those—those *evil* people. You have this chance, this one chance, a kind and respectable man with a nice prosperous business—"

"Where did you get those earbobs, Mother?"

Mrs. Van Alan blinked and touched a finger to her right ear. "These? From your father, of course."

"I know, but when? When did you get them?"

"Last Christmas." The tears began to glisten again at the inner corners of her dark eyes. "He used the first installment from the Pratts to pay for them. Nothing left over for housekeeping, of course, oh, no. Your father never thought about the price of coal. Why buy coal when you could buy a beautiful—a thing of beauty—" Her voice faltered. She laid her hands in her lap and stared at the small and sizzling fire in the grate, a pitifully tiny pile of cheap bituminous lumps.

"Then why didn't you get rid of them?" Olive said cruelly.

"Because they reminded me of him. They were your father exactly. Dreaming of great things." She paused, folding her napkin over and over against the worn burgundy velvet of her skirt. When she spoke again, her voice had turned soft. "I loved him so. And it seems to me, when I'm wearing these . . ."

"Yes?"

Mrs. Van Alan whispered, "He's still here. A little piece of his spirit, anyway, right next to my head, speaking in my ear. A little piece of his beautiful soul."

Olive sank back into her seat and bowed her head over her halffinished tea. The smell drifted upward, the particular spice of her mother's favorite Ceylon blend. The tea probably cost more than the coal, but Mrs. Van Alan couldn't seem to give that up, either. Tea and rubies.

It was the bitterest thing, wasn't it, to come down in the world. To watch your extravagant dreams disintegrate into the rug of your cold and narrow parlor. Your favorite things disappear, one by one, until there was nothing left of you.

What would Olive's mother do, if Olive ran off to the sunshine with her lover?

A heavy knock sounded from the hallway, and it seemed to Olive like the final scene of a Mozart opera, when Death pounded like a bass drum upon Giovanni's sinful door.

Mrs. Van Alan placed her napkin next to her plate and rose from her chair.

"That will be Mr. Jungmann," she said.

Twenty-one

JULY 1920

Lucy

"Miss Young?"

John Ravenel was waiting for her by the El, standing on the top of the steps, his hat in one hand, unconcerned amid the dust and the grime, the stream of people leaving the train. They eddied around him as he stepped easily forward, taking Lucy's arm and tucking it comfortably beneath his own.

Lucy pulled away a little. "How—how did you know I would take this train?"

"It's the nearest to the studio." John Ravenel smiled down at her as if he hadn't a care in the world, and, despite herself, Lucy felt her spirits rising in response, all her carefully cutting arguments as to why she shouldn't be here dissolving.

"The studio?"

"Shoot. I've gone and given it away." John Ravenel's teeth flashed in a grin. "Never mind. Pretend to be surprised when I open the door, won't you?"

"I won't need to pretend." Lucy held on to her hat as she hurried to keep up with him. "I haven't the faintest notion of what you're talking about!"

Apologetically, John Ravenel slowed his steps. "My favorite place in New York. It's—well, you could call it my refuge. I never showed it to— Let's just say that I've never showed it to anyone before."

"My." Lucy couldn't think what else to say. The block they were traversing, still at a brisk clip, was lined with old brownstones, houses that might have been workers' homes once. It was a part of the city she knew not at all. "You said studio . . . Do you paint? I can't quite imagine you in a floppy hat and a great bow of a necktie!"

John Ravenel laughed, a great rumble of a laugh, and the sunshine seemed to brighten on the stoops and windows. "It's not an official uniform, you know, any more than spectacles are for professors. But, no, I don't paint." As they reached number 147, he paused, looking down at Lucy. "But that doesn't mean I don't appreciate beauty when I see it."

Lucy could feel the blood rise in her cheeks. From the heat of the day, of course. And the exertion of the walk. Mr. Ravenel was an art dealer. Finding beauty was his business.

Beauty with a price tag.

"Is it hard," she asked, as Mr. Ravenel set his hand to the knocker, "finding beauty, only to have to give it away again?"

"I don't give it away; I sell it, hopefully for a profit." He leaned against the doorframe. "You learn a certain detachment after a while. And there's the excitement of knowing that there's always another and another and another. Ah, Luisa! I didn't know you were in residence."

A woman had opened the door. At least, Lucy inferred from the curves of chest and hip that she was a woman. Her hair was shingled and she wore trousers. Smoke rose from the cigarette that she held in one hand.

"The work," she said, gesticulating with a trail of ash, "it struggles to be born."

"And Mrs. Whitney provides a good free meal," said Mr. Ravenel, sotto voce. In his normal voice, he said, "Show it to me when you're done. I might be able to find a home for it." To Lucy, he added, "Luisa is a sculptor."

"Does she own this house?" Their hostess, if such she was, was already trailing away, through a door into a room dotted with easels.

Mr. Ravenel laughed. "Lord, no. Welcome to Mrs. Whitney's studio. She provides the space for deserving artists—and if anyone has the eye, she does. There's a reference library and a sketching studio, even a billiards table."

"A billiards table?" Lucy knew she was staring shamelessly, but she couldn't help it. She'd never seen anything like this house before. It must have been a town house once—or two town houses—but walls had been knocked through and ceilings lifted, walls painted white and skylights put in.

"Apparently, the muse likes pool," said Mr. Ravenel. "Ours not to reason why. Ours just to admire."

Another and another and another, he had said. Always the next painting, the next beautiful thing. But never to keep. It made Lucy feel deeply uneasy. "To admire and then to sell?"

"And sell." He nodded to two bearded men, deep in argument, before looking back to Lucy. "You sound as though you disapprove."

"I just—" It was hard to encapsulate what bothered her about it. "Maybe it's because we had so little. I was raised to hold on to things."

Stability. That was what had been pounded into Lucy throughout her youth. To her grandmother, that meant the reliability of having a shop, a trade, a family, church on Sunday, and gugelhupf at Christmas.

But it wasn't just her grandmother. Lucy remembered, in one of those rare moments of communion, her mother telling her, soberly, "You don't know what it's like to see your world disappear, piece by piece, item by item. Watching it all go, bit by bit. It's terrifying, like clinging to the wreck of a ship." Her hand had gone to the high collar of her dress, as though touching a necklace that wasn't there. "In the end, you seek what port you can."

She had always impressed upon Lucy how lucky she was, how lucky to have a home, a father, food on the table. But her words had always been at odds with the longing in her eyes. There was something, something else, to which her mother wished she had held.

Some grander past, Lucy had always thought. A house like the Pratt house. Jewelry. Gowns.

But maybe it had been something else, something more. Someone more.

"But these paintings aren't mine," said Mr. Ravenel, and Lucy recalled herself, with difficulty, to the present. "Art doesn't belong to anyone in particular. It's a gift to the world."

Fine words, but Lucy wasn't ready to let him off that easily. She raised her brows at him. "A gift with a price tag?"

"Artists have to live—and there's only one Mrs. Whitney." With a hand at the small of her back, Mr. Ravenel escorted her through a room crowded with plaster models, into another, dominated by the aforementioned billiards table. "Selling their paintings is how artists survive to paint once more." He spoke simply, but there was no mistaking the genuine emotion in his voice. "And the world gets something wonderful."

Lucy didn't entirely see the wonder in some of the pictures in front of her, but the wonder on John Ravenel's face was real enough.

"I don't have the talent myself, but I have talent enough to recognize it. Getting to see this," he said, gesturing around the room, the partially dried canvases on their easels, the paintings on the walls, "humbles me. The idea that I might do something, anything, to promote this kind of talent . . . It's like getting to shake Michelangelo's hand."

Lucy cocked her head. "I thought your gallery sold your father's pictures."

"My father's pictures started the business, but this"—John Ravenel waved a hand at the paintings on the walls—"this is the future. If I held on to my father's paintings, I'd be running a museum, not a gallery. There's a place for that—but it's not my place. It's not what I want to do. It's not what I want my legacy to be."

"Then—" Lucy rested a hand on the green baize of the billiards table. The felt was springy beneath her fingers, virtually unworn. "I'd thought you were here to search for your father's past."

John Ravenel lifted a billiard ball, turned it between his fingers. Light winked off the surface. "Do I want to know where I came from? Yes. But that doesn't impact who I want to be. My past—that's the work of other people. What I do—that's up to me." Setting the ball down, he looked sheepishly at Lucy. "My apologies, Miss Young. I promised you art and instead I go baring my soul."

"No," said Lucy slowly. "No, you've given me just what I needed."

She had thought of the future once. When she'd fought her grandmother and taken that secretarial course. When she'd won the job at Sterling Bates and forged her way into Manhattan, feeling like a pioneer, like an explorer, every morning as she rode the train in from Brooklyn, swaying from the overhead strap, evading the pinches of men who thought that working girls were fair game. It had been exhilarating, exciting. And her father—her father had been so proud when she had graduated from high school.

And then her father had died.

She hadn't realized how much his quiet presence had bolstered her, how much just knowing he was there had mattered to her, until he was gone. After the funeral, the barber had brought back his shaving mug, caked with the remnants of the soap that smelled like her father's chin, his name in gold on white porcelain.

Lucy, who had remained straight-backed through the funeral, found herself brought low by the smell of that soap. She had managed to murmur the right words to the barber, her fingers clutched tight around the mug, the paint with her father's name already chipping and flaking, faded in parts. She had clung to that mug like a child with a doll, smelling that smell, wanting her father badly, so very badly. She could close her eyes, and smell the soap, and imagine him there, her quiet, loving father, the blond hair grizzled with gray, the blue eyes a little dimmer since her mother's death, but still, always, her father, her port in a storm.

And that was when her grandmother had uttered those hateful words. *Did you think he was really your father?*

She had spoken in German, as she always did at home, partly, Lucy always suspected, as a means of excluding Lucy's mother.

Did you think he was really your father?

And with that one spiteful phrase, her world had collapsed in on itself. She had lost her father. She had lost herself.

"I—" Lucy spoke hesitantly. "I've been chasing the past. When my father died"—she licked her dry lips—"well, he might not have been my father. I've been trying to find out what I can about the man who might have been my father."

It sounded so garbled put like that, so silly. She couldn't believe she was blurting it out to a virtual stranger, the fact of her illegitimacy, her confusion.

But John Ravenel didn't recoil or look at her with disgust. Instead, he took her gloved hand in his and gave it a squeeze. "You poor kid," he said softly.

Lucy managed a crooked smile. "I'm twenty-six. I'll be twenty-seven in November."

"Even so. When it comes to our parents we're all still children, aren't we?" His voice was so warm, so understanding, his hand on hers so comforting. Lucy let herself lean into him, into the support he offered. His hand tightened on hers. "It knocked me sideways when I found out that my father had a life before Cuba. I'd always heard the stories about Cuba and I'd never thought to ask about what came before. Then he died, and a friend of his gave me—"

Lucy tilted her head up at him. "Gave you what?"

"A picture of a woman. Not my mother. It was just a miniature, but the fact that he'd kept it secret—well, that said something."

"My mother was in love with someone before my father." The words came out before Lucy thought about them. She felt the color rising in her cheeks and gave an uncomfortable laugh. "Obviously. I'm here, aren't I?"

"Whoever he was"—John Ravenel squeezed both her hands in his—"he was a very lucky man to have you as a daughter."

"If I can ever find him." Harry Pratt had disappeared off the map so many years ago. Dead? Missing. "And if I do find him . . . what if he doesn't want me?"

John Ravenel didn't make light of her fears. "People make new lives for themselves. Look at my father, with a new name. If he doesn't want a daughter appearing out of nowhere—then it's to do with him, not you. Never you."

Lucy looked up at him through a haze of tears that made the lights in the chandelier jump and dance. "Would you claim me?"

"If you were mine, I would never have let you go."

His hands were on her shoulders now, her head tilted toward his. Dimly, Lucy realized that they weren't talking about fathers and daughters anymore. And that they were smack in the middle of the billiards room of the Whitney Studio.

With a jerky movement, she stepped away, lifting her gloved hands to her damp cheeks. "If you succeed in finding your father's people," she said in a muffled voice, "what will you do?"

"I—" John Ravenel shook his head, as if to clear it. "I don't know. I thought once that I wanted to wave my father's achievements in their face, show them what they'd lost. Now? I'm not sure I even need to see them. I just want to know who they are, who my father was. Just to know."

It sounded so wise, but there was something about it that rang false to Lucy. "You can tell yourself that, but it's never just knowing, is it? Everything you know changes you. And you can't go back."

His face clouded. "No, you can't. I'd thought, after the war—but when I came back . . ." With an attempt at levity, he said, "Who made you so wise, Miss Young?"

"The school of hard knocks." The moment of intimacy was over. Lucy rubbed her gloved knuckles beneath her eyes, striving to match his tone. "You must think I'm very silly. Talk about baring your soul!"

"No," said Mr. Ravenel lightly, stepping back, away from her. "I think you argue like an attorney. There's no judge in the world could stand up against you."

He had begun moving, strolling toward the door, as though they were two sightseers at a museum. Lucy fell into step beside him, groping after her lost poise. "I'd like to see that," she said. "A woman attorney."

"Why not? I met a woman doctor when I was serving overseas." Mr. Ravenel glanced down at her. "She was doing twice the work of the men and just as well."

Lucy had never hankered after bloodstained bandages or bottles of pills, but the idea of being the one sitting behind the desk, dictating memos, making the decisions, had a powerful appeal.

Regretfully, Lucy banished the image. "Maybe my daughter will be the attorney. Or the doctor."

"Not you?"

She might as well have sighed for the moon as for a college education. That was for other women. Women whose fathers had money to burn. "I had to fight to finish at the high school. My grandmother didn't believe in education for women. She thought it would give me the wrong sort of ideas."

A woman didn't need education, her grandmother had said. She would only marry anyway. It was a waste of time when she might be helping at the bakery.

A good gugelhupf. Now, there was a way to a man's heart.

John Ravenel looked at her thoughtfully. "But here you are, a model of the new woman."

The new woman. Scarlet women, according to her grandmother. Lucy squirmed at the memory of the scent of gin, Philip Schuyler's lips on hers, the high-pitched laugh of the woman in the backless dress.

"Not entirely. I like being useful. I like working. But I'm *not* fast," she said fiercely. "I'm not."

John Ravenel looked at her, puzzled. "I never thought you were." His lips lifted in a half smile. "You can tell just from looking at you that you're a lady."

"Even now that you—know my background?"

"What your parents did isn't who you are." They were back in the front hall. Lucy could hear the sound of a gramophone from somewhere up the stairs, and a spirited argument coming from the room with the sculpture. "Aren't I proof of that?"

Lucy looked at John Ravenel, wanting to say yes, wanting to agree with him, but she couldn't help thinking, traitorously, that he was what his parents did. "Would you have found art if your father hadn't been a painter?"

"I don't know. But I do know that I love art for its own sake, not my father's. He gave me my start, but—" John Ravenel shook his head. "I guess we can't get away from them entirely, but we can pick and choose what we want our legacies to be. What do you want your legacy to be, Miss Young?"

The words came out in a rush, out of nowhere. "If I have children, I want them to feel like they belong to something." She had never felt as though she belonged. Not in Brooklyn. Not in Manhattan. Not with the Jungmanns. Not with the Pratts. She was betwixt and between and adrift. She took a deep breath. "I want them to know where they come from. No mysteries, no secrets. I want something solid, stable. It sounds pretty petty, doesn't it? Here you are, planning to change the world one painting at a time—and all I want is a safe home."

John Ravenel didn't mock her. "My mother was an artist's model." A rueful smile creased his lips. "Well, my father's model. She made pictures that made history. And, in the end, she claims her greatest success was making a home for us. She made order out of chaos. She kept us all safe and fed. She kept my father—and me—alive. She's the strongest woman I know. She wouldn't find your ambition petty at all. She would admire you for it." His eyes met hers. "I admire you for it."

It was like staring at the sun. Lucy looked away, down at her shoes. Such sensible, workaday shoes. "You're a kind man, Mr. Ravenel."

His brown eyes crinkled at the corners. "My mama tried to raise me right. Whether she succeeded . . . not everyone would agree." There was something grim about the way he said it. But before Lucy could inquire further, he said, "Shall we see if we can find something to eat? All this soul baring is making me hungry."

Astonishingly, so was she. They said confession was good for the soul, but she'd never realized it also stimulated the stomach. "I wouldn't mind an ice-cream sandwich," Lucy admitted, adding shyly, "Thank you for taking me here. I never knew this was here."

John Ravenel stepped out into the sunshine, holding the door open for her. "It hasn't been here long. Mrs. Whitney only opened the studio club two years ago." Letting the door swing shut, he offered Lucy his arm. "One of these days, I'd love to do something similar in Charleston."

Charleston. The name hit Lucy like a slap. It felt like Mr. Ravenel had always been here, would always be here.

Trying to sound casual, she said, "Are you going back to Charleston soon?"

There was a pause before he answered. "I've booked my berth on the train for Tuesday."

"Tuesday!" Lucy tripped over a bit of loose paving. "That soon?"

Mr. Ravenel steadied her effortlessly, his hand on her elbow. "I've been here longer than I intended. There are . . . responsibilities at home that I've left too long." He snaked a sideways glance at her. "What do you say, Miss Young? Do you fancy a trip to Charleston?"

"Oh, certainly," mocked Lucy, even as her heart screamed with loss. Which was mad, wasn't it? She hardly knew him. "Are you looking for a secretary? A manager for your gallery perhaps? I might be needing a new job."

And that, she realized grimly, was nothing more than the truth. The bright day seemed to darken; the sunlight was hard and flat, the heat itchy and oppressive. Her job, the job for which she had schemed— she couldn't face the thought of facing her employer.

She had no home in New York, only an overpriced attic room in a building that meant nothing to her. Her mother's voice didn't whisper from the walls. Her lost father wasn't leaping out of the woodwork to enfold her in his arms and sweep her into society with a capital *S*.

And John Ravenel was leaving New York.

There would be no more walks in Central Park, no rides on the carousel. He would go to Charleston, and she . . . she would look for another job, another room. And on and on and on.

They had wandered their way to Washington Square. Lucy could see courting couples, arm in arm, taking advantage of the nice day.

John Ravenel came to an abrupt stop just inside the entrance to the park, swinging her around to face him.

"Lucy—" It was the first time he'd called her by her name. "I know it's mad, but—what if you did come to Charleston?"

Lucy stared at him. The sun was behind him, casting his face into shadow, dazzling her eyes. "I—I've never been south of Brooklyn."

"We're not so savage, really. There's indoor plumbing and all." Together, they moved aside to let others pass. "I never meant to be in New York for more than a week. And then I saw you and— It's a damnable complication. It's not anything I intended. But it's there. Isn't it?"

He didn't have to explain what it was. It was there between them, that invisible bond, that strange sense of ease, as though she had known him always. As if her life would be immeasurably the worse for not having him in it.

"Oh, yes," whispered Lucy. "Yes."

It was inexplicable, and illogical, but it was there.

His hands grasped hers, pressing tightly through her gloves, holding on to her like a lifeline. "It takes a nerve, I know, to ask you to leave everything you know. But I can't face the thought of never seeing you again."

It was the sun in her eyes, the sun dazzling her, making her lightheaded. Only it wasn't. It was Mr. Ravenel, his nearness, these mad, wonderful words. "Mr. Ravenel—"

"John."

"John." Such a prosaic name, but it sounded like music on her lips. They had only just met. She scarcely knew him. But that wasn't true, was it? She did know him, somehow, deep down in her bones. "John, I—"

"Wait." His hands were on her shoulders, holding her and holding her away all at the same time. "Before you say anything, there are two things you should know, two things I have to tell you."

"Do you have eight wives in the attic like Bluebeard?" Lucy couldn't imagine anything that would blunt the incredible pull she felt toward him.

Was this what the novelists wrote about? This crazy euphoria? Was this what made kings abandon their thrones and tycoons throw everything away for a chorus girl?

Lucy wanted to take her hat and fling it into the summer breeze, to lift her skirt and twirl in circles, to fling her arms around John Ravenel's neck and kiss him, kiss him right there in the sunlight, in the middle of Washington Square.

John touched a finger to her lips, his touch feather soft. "I haven't been entirely honest with you." He took a step back, the brim of his hat casting his face into the shade. "This business about my father's paintings—it's all true. But I didn't tell you the whole of it. The person who's been selling those paintings—it's Mr. Schuyler's stepmother."

Whatever Lucy had been expecting, it wasn't that. It took her a moment to make sense out of his words. "Prunella Pratt had your father's paintings?"

John was watching her, watching her closely. "That's why I needed to speak to Mr. Schuyler. Not for his legal expertise. And that's why—" He broke off, taking a deep breath. With difficulty, he said, "That miniature I told you about, it's of a woman wearing a ruby necklace. The same necklace you were wearing that night at Delmonico's. When I saw it on you—well, it seemed that you must be involved in it somehow. And I had to find out—"

"Involved?" whispered Lucy.

John Ravenel had the grace to look abashed. "I'd thought Schuyler might have given it to you—that they'd found the necklace when they found the paintings."

"You mean that you thought I—that you thought he—" She could feel the sweat prickling beneath her arms, spots dancing in front of her eyes. She forced herself to say the words. "You thought I was his mistress."

Their Saturday. Their beautiful Saturday in the sunshine. The carousel. The ice cream. All of those questions about her work, her life. She'd thought it was because he was genuinely interested.

"Well, no," John said, and Lucy could tell that he was lying. "Not his mistress, not exactly. But as his secretary . . ."

A sick feeling threatened to overwhelm her. Lucy felt as she had as a child when she'd broken into the bakery at night and gorged on the candied cherries. She'd had the same feeling then, the wild energy, followed by that horrible plunge into sickness. Except then it had been a sickness of the stomach, not the soul.

This was worse. Infinitely worse.

"That's why." Lucy stared up at John Ravenel, feeling as though she'd never seen him before. "That's why you were wasting your time with me. You wanted to see what I knew. You were using me."

Twenty-two

Kate

I ducked into the elevator just as Dr. Greeley's office door opened. We'd had another disastrous dinner date the previous evening where he'd spent much of the time talking about what a great catch he was while I'd been busy pushing his hand off my knee and keeping my face out of reach of his roving kisses. He'd totally missed my point, as he'd conceded that he respected me for my reticence. Apparently, he believed this was caused by a good upbringing instead of any repulsion or complete disinterest on my part.

The elevator chugged its laborious way down to the first floor, opening just in time for me to see Captain Ravenel and his fiancée walk in from the street. I hadn't seen him alone since the night a week ago when I'd promised that I'd allow him to finish his sketch of me. It wasn't that I was planning on reneging on my promise; it was just that every time I thought about him going back to Charleston my lungs seemed to collapse and I found myself gasping for air. I knew that was the reason I couldn't sign his release papers, knowing there was unfinished business between us.

But if I saw him while other people were in the room, I could almost pretend that he was just another patient, just another soldier wounded in the war whom I had helped piece back together. Almost.

Happily, the new patients hadn't yet materialized so I hadn't had any reason to go up to the attic room. I'd prescribed exercise for Captain Ravenel to restore his strength, and Nurse Hathaway brought his chart to me so I could follow his progress. Except for a daily visit with the other doctors on our morning rounds, I hadn't seen or spoken to him. But that didn't mean I didn't miss him like the winter earth missed the sun.

"Captain Ravenel. Miss Middleton," I said formally, as if we were only passing acquaintances. I tried not to notice how handsome he looked in his olive drab Army dress uniform, his silver captain's bars on his shoulders, his dark brown hair nearly hidden by his cap. Ribbons decorated the left breast of his jacket; a Bronze Star, a Silver Star, a European Theater ribbon. Caroline looked like an unnecessary and utterly frivolous decoration in a pale pink suit and matching hat. He gripped a cane in his right hand.

After tucking his cane under his arm, Cooper took off his hat. "Dr. Schuyler." His eyes probed mine in open question and I looked away.

"We made it all the way to the park and back," Caroline said, unable to hide the triumph in her voice. "He still needs the cane but Dr. Greeley said that's normal and that in a couple of months with regular exercise, he won't need it at all." She squeezed Cooper's arm, her face like a child's on Christmas morning. "I think he's ready to go home now."

My chest hurt, the way it did whenever I felt like crying. I took a deep breath. "That's very good news. I'll consult with Dr. Greeley and determine how much longer. It will be soon, I'm sure, and his physical strength is a good sign. But the wound has to have healed completely."

Caroline's lips compressed, but I imagined I saw relief flit across Cooper's face. She was about to say something when the front door flew open and Margie barged into the foyer, her face red and glowing with perspiration as if she'd run all the way from the library.

"Margie? What are you doing here? I thought we were meeting tomorrow for lunch."

She put her hand over her heart, trying to catch her breath, and I noticed she carried a leather-bound journal.

"Come on, Cooper. Let's take the stairs. It will be good for you." Caroline began leading him toward the circular steps. I wanted to go after him, to tell him to be careful, to take the elevator once they reached the next floor so he wouldn't tire out. But I didn't. Caroline was there to take care of him, to see that he didn't overexert himself. He was hers, after all.

Margie's eyes widened as she looked at Cooper, immediately registering who he was. I shot her a warning look to be quiet. She continued to pant, so I started to lead her over to the foyer bench that served as a waiting area but stopped when I met the disapproving glance of the nurse on desk duty.

"Come with me," I said, leading her into the elevator.

We exited on the second floor, where two orderlies were arguing with one of the doctors about the heavy bookcase against the wall that made it difficult to move stretchers past it. I'd asked Dr. Greeley about having it moved several times, but it was an old antique and he was afraid it might get damaged if it were moved. I assumed his real reason for saying no was because I'd been the one to bring it up instead of him.

I led Margie to a deserted office with beautiful stained glass doors. Hopefully if Dr. Greeley saw me, he'd think I was having a discussion with the next of kin of a patient.

"So that's your captain." She smacked her lips together as if she'd just eaten something delicious.

"He's not mine. And that was his fiancée."

Margie snorted. "That ice queen?" Smiling smugly, she said, "In the few short minutes I saw them, I could tell that he looks at you a whole lot differently than he looks at her."

Ignoring her, I said, "Why are you here—is something wrong? Is it your mother?"

She shook her head and slapped the journal onto my lap. "I just couldn't wait to show you this. I've been working on it since I saw you, but this morning I found something that will blow the dots off your dominoes."

I started to open the journal, but she slapped her hand down on top of it. "Not so fast. These are my notes that I jotted down while doing my research, and you can take it with you to read later. But I just couldn't *wait* and had to tell you it all myself."

We both looked up as two nurses scurried by outside the door.

"Well?" I said, not having seen Margie this excited since she'd found a pair of shoes on sale at Bergdorf's that she could actually afford.

"I found your Harry Pratt in the library's archives," she blurted out. "Let's just say that one last name was like poking a hole in a dam."

"What do you mean?" Little tingles of anticipation marched up my spine, yet I wasn't sure why. Maybe because this was a little mystery that Cooper and I had discovered, something that only he and I shared.

"Well, it wasn't because he was a renowned artist, if that's what you're wondering. Or if he was, I can't find anything connecting his name with the art world. His family was exceedingly wealthy—well, at least for a time—so it was most likely just a hobby for him."

"Oh," I said, leaning back in my chair, feeling oddly deflated. Harry had been so talented that I found it sad that he'd never realized his potential.

She patted my hand. "Don't worry—it gets better." She looked up at the ceiling above us. "This hospital used to be called the Pratt mansion, built in 1891 and home to Mr. and Mrs. Henry August Pratt and their three children—Harry, Gus, and . . ." She held her breath, her cheeks puffed out with air.

"And?" I prompted.

"Prunella." She wagged her eyebrows. "She was in all of the society pages during her debutante year. Quite the beauty of her day, although I'm sure her fortune would have been enough to attract potential swains."

"The owner of the dress," I said.

She nodded. "We'll get to her and the house in a minute—but first there's poor Harry. He apparently fell off the face of the earth in 1893. His father hired the Pinkerton Detective Agency to find him, but no trace of him was ever found, living or dead. It was quite the tragedy. It was right after his brother, Gus, was killed in some kind of brawl—it was definitely whitewashed in the newspapers, no doubt due to his family's prominence, but I could read between the lines enough to figure out it was something wonderfully unsavory."

"That's so sad," I said, preparing to stand so I could get back to work. It was all interesting, but somehow removed from what I'd thought it would be. Poor Harry. I couldn't help but wonder what had happened to him, and if he ever thought about the room at the top of the stairs of the Pratt mansion where he'd once created such beauty with only charcoal and paper.

Margie yanked my arm and pulled me back down in my chair. "Not yet, Kate. I haven't even scratched the surface. I'll be quick—but you need to be sitting down."

My right leg began bobbing up and down as it did when I was impatient, and I pressed my hand on my knee to get it to stop. "All right. Shoot."

She took a deep breath. "As I said, when I looked up the last name Pratt there were tons of articles about the family. But there was one subject that dominated most of the articles, and that was the mansion itself—this hospital that we're sitting in now. About its architect." She stared at me as if she were waiting for me to finish her thoughts.

I shook my head. "And . . . ?"

Margie looked vaguely disappointed. "He apparently felt cheated by Mr. Pratt and was never paid for his services. The details in the paper are murky, but the scandal resulted in the architect's suicide."

"That's awful," I said, "but . . ."

She cut me off. "The architect was Peter Van Alan." Her eyes widened as if to emphasize her point.

"Peter Van Alan? That's my great-grandfather's name." Our eyes met in mutual understanding. We both knew the name only from my mother's repetition of it in her quest to make sure that I comprehended the importance and pride of family lineage despite a lack of money or assets. I'd always thought that it was her way of letting me know that I came from something grander than an immigrant German baker and a grandmother who'd reminded me as a child of brightly colored wallpaper faded by the sun. I remembered standing on Sixty-ninth Street with my mother and staring up at the mansion, and suddenly it all began to make sense.

An icy breath trickled down my spine, making me shiver. "She never told me about how her grandfather died, or that he'd designed this building. Maybe she was ashamed about his suicide and wanted to spare me."

Margie leaned closer, her eyes so wide I could see the whites around her irises. "That's not all."

She reached over and opened the journal, flipped through several pages before replacing it on my lap. "I copied this one verbatim from the society pages of the *New York Times* from their January third, 1893, edition."

I peered down at Margie's neatly formed Catholic school penmanship and began to read.

Mr. and Mrs. Henry August Pratt of New York City announce the engagement of their daughter, Prunella Jane, to Mr. Harrison Charles Schuyler, widower of the late Cassandra Willoughby Schuyler and father of Philip C. J. Schuyler. An elegant engagement ball was held at the Pratt residence on Sixty-ninth Street on New Year's Eve. The date for the nuptials has been set for October 10th at Saint James's Church.

I looked up, meeting her eyes. "But Philip Schuyler . . ."

"Is your father," Margie completed for me. "Which makes Prunella Pratt your father's stepmother, which I suppose means that Harry Pratt was your stepgrandfather? Or something like that."

"Actually, that would make him my stepgranduncle." I shook my head. "Why didn't my mother ever tell me any of this?"

Margie shrugged. "Well, there's the architect's suicide, and then Harry Pratt's disappearance and his brother's tragic death—it's all rather sad if you think about it. Maybe she was trying to protect you."

"Maybe," I said. But I knew that wasn't it. The ruby necklace alone told me that my mother had kept secrets from me. Her reasons were now silenced by the grave but whispered in my memories of a mother who'd always seemed to be waiting for something; something *more*. I pressed my fingers against the ruby beneath the collar of my dress as if it held all the answers. But it lay heavy and still against my throat, a mute talisman of my mother's past.

Margie reached over again and flipped a page in the journal. "Prunella Pratt Schuyler was listed in the last census in 1940, widowed and living alone. I couldn't find a death certificate so I'm assuming that means she's still alive. Here's her address."

I stared down at the page, the words barely registering. I met Margie's eyes. "You're amazing, you know. I don't know how to thank you."

She brushed her hand through the air as if to erase the words. "It was fun. And you can take me to dinner. Or find out if your captain has a brother and introduce me."

I hugged her. "You're better than a sister—have I ever told you that?"

She shoved me away but her face had pinkened. "Yeah, yeah. Just don't forget that introduction to the captain's brother."

"You got it," I said, pulling her to her feet and escorting her out of the hospital. I needed to return to work, but first I had to write a note requesting a visit with Mrs. Prunella Pratt Schuyler. I wasn't sure if she'd remember who I was, or even want to see me, but I would try. She was quite possibly the only remaining person in the world who could shed light on the mother I thought I'd known, and into the dark corners of our past.

❖

I waited until I was certain the nurses in the cots around me were sound asleep. I wasn't on call and had allowed myself the luxury of sleeping in a proper nightgown. Not that I'd done much sleeping since lying down— but I'd have plenty of time for that as soon as I finished my errand.

I slipped on my wrapper and slippers, then carefully slid the hammer and screwdriver from under my pillow before stealing from the room. I'd taken the tools from the maintenance closet earlier that day, hoping they wouldn't be missed until I could return them the following day.

After pausing to listen for voices or approaching footsteps, I dashed out into the corridor, almost colliding with the corner of the large antique bookcase that I'd seen the orderlies and doctors discussing earlier. It looked as if they'd managed to pull out a corner of the large piece of furniture before simply giving up, leaving an even bigger impediment in the hallway.

I ducked into the servants' stairwell and ran quickly up to the attic floor. I'd seen Caroline leave after dinner, so I knew Cooper was alone. Two empty cots had been set up in the attic but had yet to be filled by incoming patients.

The door was slightly ajar and I pushed it open. There were no lights on in the room, but a pale, milky light settled on the room like a gentle benediction. The bed was empty, yet I knew Cooper was there, could feel him watching me, could feel his pull like the tides under the moon. I turned my head and saw him outlined against the window, where he'd pushed aside the blackout shades.

I stayed where I was, afraid to approach. Afraid to get pulled into the riptide that seemed to surround him. I cleared my throat. "I brought the tools to open the top drawer of the cabinet." I considered for a moment placing them on a trunk and leaving, but knew that I could not.

"I was hoping you'd come," he said softly. "I've been waiting to finish sketching you. You promised."

I swallowed, hoping he couldn't hear it. "I've been busy." I cleared my throat. "I found out that I'm related by marriage to Prunella Pratt. She was my father's stepmother."

"And Harry?"

"Her brother. He disappeared in 1893. And it looks like his artistic abilities disappeared with him."

"Interesting," he said, walking toward me. "What a strange coincidence. That you're related to the family who once lived here." He stopped in front of me, near enough that I could feel his heat. He was bare chested again, wearing only his pajama bottoms. The gift from his fiancée.

The reminder made me step back. Holding out the tools to him, I said, "Here. Let me know if you get that cabinet drawer open." He hesitated a moment, then took them. I turned to leave, but strong fingers captured my arm.

"Please. Not yet. Let me finish your sketch. It's a full moon and I'd like to capture you in the moonlight." I heard the tools clattering against the top of a trunk and then felt both of his hands on my shoulders, turning me around. "Please," he said again, and I was lost on that single syllable.

"Do you still have it?" I asked, hoping for a delay, or postponement, or any reason at all not to spend more time alone with him.

He grinned, apparently reading my mind. "Nurse Hathaway copied all of my medical information on the other side onto another page and gave the sketch to me. She's a very astute woman."

Cooper left me where I stood and walked over to a trunk that had been moved between the two new hospital beds to be used as a shared nightstand. He opened it and pulled out what looked like a sheepskin blanket and a single candle in a brass holder. "I found these in here and figured they must have been used by Harry for his sketch subjects."

"You have to close the blackout shades if you're going to light the candle." I was trying to be practical, to remind myself that I was a professional woman, that I was doing this only as a favor to a patient.

His teeth glowed white as he smiled at me, as if he knew what I was thinking. "The civil defense patrolman went by about ten minutes ago. We have about two hours before he returns."

"Oh," I said, watching him place the blanket in the puddle of moonlight by the window, then set up the candle on a small table he'd dragged to the middle of the room. The strike of a match was followed by the sharp scent of sulfur as he lit the candle. He grabbed a pillow from the bed and propped it against the wall beneath the window. "Come recline here. I want to make sure I see your eyes."

I began walking toward the window.

"Take off your slippers, too, if you don't mind. It ruins the effect."

I heard the smile in his voice, and it relaxed me, made me believe that he was simply an artist and I his subject. I reclined on the blanket, propping my head on my hand as I leaned against the pillow. It wasn't uncomfortable, although I wasn't sure how long I could stay in that position.

"Do you have a brother, by any chance?" I asked, remembering my promise to Margie.

His eyes widened with surprise. "No, I don't. Why do you ask?"

I shrugged, feeling silly. "Just wondering."

He nodded, his gaze brushing over me. "Your wrapper. It needs to go, too."

Looking down, I saw how matronly it looked. "Oh. Of course." I sat up and slowly untied my wrapper before taking it off and tossing it away from the blanket.

I heard him rummaging through a drawer—presumably for the unfinished sketch and the pen from his clipboard—so he wasn't looking at me when he issued his next directive. "And unbutton your nightgown."

I sat up quickly, clutching the neckline against my throat. "Excuse me?"

"I need to see the ruby necklace if I'm going to sketch it. I assume that's the lump I'm seeing at your neck."

I relaxed somewhat and unbuttoned the five small buttons that ran from the top of the neck to my breastbone, spreading the material so the ruby could be clearly seen.

"Perfect," he said, looking at me, his voice strained. He pulled over the bedside chair next to the candle and sat, then began to sketch.

The only sound was that of the mice in the walls and the scratch of pen on paper, and I found it soothing. Soothing enough that I felt my head grow heavy.

"Not yet," Cooper said. "Let me finish with your face and then you can sleep." He looked over the clipboard at me. "Perhaps if I talk, it will keep you awake."

"Perhaps," I said, giving him a groggy smile, watching how the candlelight softened his face, illuminated the boy beneath the soldier.

"So tell me about yourself. Tell me why you wanted to become a doctor."

It took me a while to answer, as I realized nobody had ever asked me that question before. "Because I hated feeling so helpless watching my father struggle with lung cancer." I thought for a moment. "And because my mother encouraged me."

"How did she do that?" he asked, his eyes focused on the paper in front of him.

"She told me . . ." I stopped, sensing how odd it would sound telling this to someone who hadn't known my mother and father; hadn't known that there was always enough love, but how there always seemed to have not been enough for my mother. My father had adored her, and she had loved him, but not in the same way. To me she'd been like a child who'd lost her favorite doll and been left to make do with her second best.

"She told you what?" Cooper prompted.

"She told me to do something with my life that could never be taken from me. To devote myself to something that involved every part of me, including my heart, so that I would never lose it. When I told her that I wanted to go to medical school, she almost seemed . . . relieved."

The scratching noise had stopped, and I looked up to find him watching me intently. "So you've never wanted to fall in love? To have a husband and a home? Children?"

"It's not that I never wanted any of that. It's just that I've always wanted to be a doctor more. When so many people along the way told me that I couldn't because I was a woman, it made me want to be not just a doctor, but the *best* doctor."

"And you never met a man who made you rethink your choices?"

Not until you. I bit the words back. I wanted him. Yes, I'd finally admitted it to myself. But did I want him enough to give up everything

I'd worked so hard for? Not that it mattered. He was promised to another, and my wanting of him was as impotent as a single raindrop in the desert.

I closed my eyes without answering him. "I'm so tired. Are you almost done?"

I listened as the clipboard was placed on the wood floor with a snap, then Cooper's bare feet as he padded toward me. "Can you move your nightgown off your shoulders? I need to see the ruby against your bare skin."

"Like in the miniature," I said, my tongue sticking to the roof of my mouth.

"Yes."

I sat up and pulled one side of my nightgown off my shoulder, knowing if I pulled the other one down, I'd lose the nightgown completely. Our eyes met, our thoughts in tandem.

Very quietly, he asked again, "Have you ever met a man who made you rethink your choices?"

We stared at each other for a long moment, listening to the sound of the candlewick flickering in melted wax and a lone car passing by on the street below.

"Just once," I whispered, my eyes not leaving his. I reached up to the fabric on my shoulder, but his hand against mine stopped me.

His face was that of a man in pain. "Don't," he said, his voice rough. "I can't . . ." He shook his head. "We shouldn't . . ."

I lifted his hand with my free one and brought the palm to my lips. Since my decision to become a doctor, I'd never been so sure of anything in my life. "My mother once told me that a lifetime of good enough was a fair price to pay for a single moment of pure happiness. This is my moment. Don't take that from me."

With deliberate slowness, I reached up and slid the nightgown from my shoulder, feeling the soft cotton puddle at my waist.

"Kate," he said, the word filled with wonder, and promise, and the single moments that were meant to last a lifetime.

He cupped my face in his hands and kissed me softly as I pulled him down with me onto the sheepskin blanket, cocooned in the light of the moon where wars and tomorrows didn't exist, and where one moment could be made to last until the fragile light of dawn.

Twenty-three

New Year's Eve 1892

Olive

This time, they hadn't even made it as far as the attic. The shame of it.

Sorry, Harry gasped into her ear, but she hardly heard him over the noise of her own blood, the thump of her own heart. *Sorry*: How could he be sorry? Olive wasn't. She wasn't sorry for anything, not the hardness of the wall against her back, not the dampness of Harry's forehead against her cheek, not the stairwell railing that pressed into her hip. Not for Harry's hands, which held her in place like a double-headed anchor, so that she didn't float right off into kingdom come.

Not for all the times they had come together this week, just like this, furtive and beautiful and primeval, like a pair of lovers resurrected from legend. Like Tristan and Isolde, like Lancelot and Guinevere: the kind of tale with which Olive, as a budding young lady, had always become impatient. Why would any sane woman give up everything for an object so chimerical as passion? But now she knew. She would give up anything for this. It frightened her, what risks she would take, what price she would pay, what conventions she would ignore, for this instant of joy in Harry's arms.

An instant of true happiness, before she returned to reality.

She tightened her fingers around his hair and whispered, "I have to go back. Someone's going to come looking for me."

"But not here. No one ever comes here, except us." His thumbs moved against her bottom. "One more minute."

"Why? You've had what you wanted."

"Not yet." He kissed her neck. "*This* is what I really wanted, Olive. This is what I can't get enough of."

"Harry—"

"Just be still, won't you? Don't spoil it. Trust me, for once."

Olive relaxed against the wall, against Harry's sturdy hands, and closed her eyes. Just for a minute. Because he was right, wasn't he? Harry was always right. This *was* the best part. This was what she couldn't get enough of, not if she lived forever: Harry on her skin, Harry's grateful kisses on her neck, Harry and Olive, teeming and sated, brimming over with each other, as if this house and this world had been built by God's hands for their love alone.

❀

But they weren't, not really. The world was more practical than that. Two minutes later she was hurrying back down the staircase, legs atremble, smoothing her rumpled skirt, to burst onto the fifth-floor landing and the maelstrom of preparation for the evening's festivities.

If anything, she thought, the house and the world had been built for Prunella Pratt's engagement ball.

A curl brushed against her cheek. Olive put her hands to the sides of her head and realized that her hair was damp and loose, that the pins had been dragged from the knot at the base of her neck: a natural consequence of repeated ecstatic abrasion against a plaster wall. She turned in horror to the gilded mirror that hung at the end of the landing, right where the winding staircase reached the floor, and began jabbing the pins in place.

"Olive! What's the matter? You're blushed to the gills!"

Olive spun around. It was Bitsy, one of the parlormaids, a quiet girl with a lilting Irish accent.

"Nothing! I was just fetching something, and the stairs . . ." She shrugged helplessly.

Bitsy rolled her eyes. "Well, you'd best clean yourself up right quick. Ellen's burned her hand on the curling tongs, the old galoot, and there's no one else to help Miss Prunella dress."

"But I'm not a lady's maid!"

"Seems you are now. I'd hop to it, if I was you."

Bitsy turned and hurried back down the stairs, without another glance, until she rounded the curve and disappeared. But her voice floated up in her absence: "Mind you straighten your cap, now, Olive!"

Olive turned back in horror to her reflection. Bitsy was right: She was flushed, and her cap sagged shamefully to the left. Upstairs, Harry had ducked into the studio to reconstruct himself back on orderly lines, but Olive had no such luxury, did she? She forced her fingers to stop their shaking and put each pin back in place. She drew in a long and steadying breath and straightened her white cap. There was nothing she could do about the blush. She had earned it, fair and square.

Miss Prunella's room lay only a single floor down from the nunnery but it occupied a different universe: high of ceiling, deep and intricate of molding, lavish of decoration. Olive knocked on the door and pretended not to notice that the entrance to Harry's room beckoned only a few feet away. He had left his door carelessly ajar. If she craned her neck, she could peek through the few inches of space and spy his bookshelf, the corner of his bed.

But the summons from Miss Prunella came at once, sharp and annoyed, and Olive had no time to waste on sightseeing. She put her hand on the knob and pushed open the heavy wooden door.

Olive had never entered Miss Prunella's room while its owner lounged inside, and she was surprised by the way the Pratt presence transformed the space: from tranquil sanctuary, upholstered in pleasing shades of green and yellow, to a bristling silk-strewn hive, dominated by an enormous cheval mirror and the tiny young woman who stood before it, dressed in her underclothes.

"There you are!" Miss Prunella spun around, hands on hips, in a white vortex of lace and satin. "Where have you been?"

Engaged in passion with your brother, in the attic stairwell.

"My duties," Olive mumbled.

"Well, help Mona here with my dress. She's so simple, she can't tell one end from another." Prunella spun back to the more agreeable contemplation of herself in the mirror, and for the first time Olive noticed Mona cowering in the corner, huge-eyed, next to a chaise longue that bore the holy of all holies: Prunella's engagement gown.

"It's that heavy," she whispered to Olive, lifting one scrap of a sleeve, and Olive sighed and slid her arms under the voluminous skirt. The gown was of cream-colored satin, embroidered with tiny pale-pink flowers, and trimmed at the neck and sleeves with satin rosettes that must have cost the Pratts' dressmaker weeks to create. All for a single night, for the care and feeding of Prunella Pratt's vanity.

With Mona's help, Olive bore the dress toward the mirror. "Don't let it touch the floor!" snapped Prunella, and Olive whispered to Mona to bring over the stool. She climbed atop and settled the satin folds carefully over Miss Prunella's elegant little head, fitting each delicate sleeve over an uplifted ivory arm, while Mona guided the delivery down below. Miss Prunella's corset had already been squeezed into an impossible circumference. Olive found the buttonhook amid the jumble of ribbons and jewelry on the bureau and fastened each satin-covered button, until the dress lay snug against Miss Prunella's artfully manu-factured figure.

She climbed down from the stool and stepped back. "There we are."

"Now the shoes."

Olive followed Miss Prunella's pointing finger and discovered a pair of miniature slippers, lying on the rug near the hissing fireplace. The satin was warm, whether by design or accident, and Olive carried them over to the young lady's waiting feet.

As she knelt and lifted the hem of the dress, she felt Miss Prunella's eyes upon the top of her head, the white cap that had come loose as she and Harry had tangled greedily on the stairs, trying to reach the attic door and not succeeding. Succumbing where they stood, because it had been hours, *hours* since breakfast, when they had come together last in their nest in the studio (Olive was supposed to be hanging garlands from the railing in the stairway), and hours then since the night before.

(Oh, the night before!)

"Mona," said Miss Prunella, "you may leave."

Olive looked up into a pair of blazing blue eyes, which were fixed on the space between her throat and her collarbone.

"Yes, Miss Prunella," gasped Mona, and an instant later the door clicked shut.

Olive started to rise.

"Where did you get that?" said Miss Prunella.

Olive's hand went to the gold filigree chain at her neck. "Get what?"

"You know what I mean. That necklace."

"I—I don't—"

"Oh, yes, you do. I know that necklace. There's a ruby pendant on it, isn't there? That was *my* necklace."

"*Your* necklace?" Olive stepped back.

"I recognize the chain. My mother gave it to me to wear on New

Year's Eve last year, for my debut, and the next morning it was gone from my dressing table."

"I don't know anything about that. This is my necklace."

"Let me see it."

"I— No." Olive straightened and allowed both hands to fall to her sides. "I won't. The necklace belongs to me. It was given to me a week ago."

"How dare you! Show me that necklace."

"With all possible respect, Miss Prunella, you have no right. The necklace belongs to me."

"No right? No *right?*" Prunella stamped her foot. She was shorter than Olive by several inches, and yet somehow, for an instant, she seemed to stand taller. No sign now of the dutiful daughter, the quiet and obedient flower of the house. What had Harry said? *She's seen me looking at you.* The ruby burned against Olive's skin.

"I am entitled, I believe, to a certain degree of privacy, even if I am a mere household employee."

The field of scintillating fury began to dissolve from around Miss Prunella's small body, replaced by something colder and far more dangerous. Olive took another step backward, unable to help herself.

"Ah, yes," Prunella said, far too softly. "The maid who speaks like a lady. Do you think I don't know who you are?"

Olive stared in horror at those chilly blue eyes, the exact same shade as Harry's, except that on Prunella they reminded her of little chips of arctic ice. And her voice, frostbitten, hanging in the air. *I know who you are.*

"I don't know what you mean. I'm Olive Jones, the housemaid."

Miss Prunella leaned forward. "Jones, indeed. You're the architect's daughter, aren't you? I recognize you, even if the others don't. I used to watch him while he was at work. My goodness, he was handsome. You have that same peak in your hair, in the middle of your forehead, and your eyes are exactly alike."

"That's ridiculous."

"I knew something was wrong about you, right from the beginning. The way you looked at us. And I turned it over and over in my head until I realized, watching you, that night at dinner, when my brother was so *obviously* in love with you . . ."

"That's—that's—"

"And your name. I remembered he had a daughter named Olive. He used to speak of you."

Olive's mouth opened without speech.

"Oh, I've kept it to myself, of course. Never fear. I've been waiting to see what you mean to do. And I suppose this is it, isn't it? Seducing my brother, as if *that* would ruin us." She laughed, a bitter sound. "As if disgraced housemaids aren't already a regular occurrence around here."

"That's not true."

Prunella didn't reply, except with her eyes, which narrowed in frosty contemplation. She looked so unnervingly perfect, so incongruously innocent with her round face ending in a pointed chin, with her silky curls clustered girlishly around that alabaster forehead and those dainty spiraling ears. Her lips formed a sweet pink pout. Only her eyes were hard, calculating the sums that lay on the other side of Olive's hot face, inside the nooks of her soul.

Until she laughed and turned away. "Fetch my gloves, Olive, and be quick. My father is waiting downstairs to lead me into the ball, *my* ball, where I will dance and laugh while you serve drinks to my guests and mop up the mess when they spill, because that's what servants do. Isn't it, Olive?"

"I—I—" Olive swallowed back the response that rose to her lips. What would Prunella do if she were crossed? Tell Harry? Of course she would. She would tell Harry, and Harry would know. He would look at her with bewildered eyes, a confusion that would turn to betrayal and then to hatred. "Yes, of course," she whispered, and her hands turned into fists at her sides.

Prunella laughed again. "You'll do whatever I say, won't you? You haven't any choice, because I know your secret."

Olive felt sick. She stumbled to the dressing table and searched for the gloves, while Prunella went on behind her, in a voice high with triumph. "I am going to be married, don't you know, into one of the oldest and best families in New York, right about the time you find yourself alone and abandoned, living in some miserable tenement downtown. Perhaps you'll read about me in the papers sometime, Olive. The wedding's in October. I'm sure the photographs will be everywhere."

Olive stalked back toward Prunella and thrust the gloves toward her beautiful cream-satin chest, then walked without pause straight on to the door, eyes blurring, while Prunella's vertiginous laugh rippled the air behind her.

❈

The grand second-floor drawing room had been transformed into a ballroom, filled with all the glittering jewels of New York society, but Olive—balancing a dozen glasses of champagne on a single silver tray—saw only one man: Harry Pratt, who was dancing with the most beautiful girl in the world.

Well, maybe the lady in question wasn't *quite* that beautiful, not on objective study. But she *seemed* so, swirling about the room in the shelter of Harry's arms, beaming and blushing at something he was saying to her, as if the glow of Harry's attention contained magical properties that altered its object into something better and more perfect than it was before.

Like Olive herself.

Olive looked away, because the sight was too much to bear. The girl had light brown hair set with brilliants, and her dress was made of a filmy pink stuff, so pale it was almost white. Not the sort of girl who would allow Harry Pratt to have his way with her on an attic staircase: oh, no. That was Olive's weakness, Olive's shame, though it hadn't felt like shame until this instant, when Harry danced with another girl. The sort of girl he was supposed to marry.

Harry had spoken often of Italy over the past week, and the eternal summer that awaited them there. But he hadn't mentioned marriage. Of course he hadn't. She had pretended not to notice the omission; she had perhaps convinced herself that the promise of marriage was implied in his offer.

But maybe it wasn't. Probably it wasn't. You ran off with housemaids, but there was no need to *marry* them, was there? No need to make it all legal and proper and binding. In case you changed your mind. In case you met another girl, a suitable girl.

Olive made her way along the edge of the crowd, bearing her champagne. A few hands reached out to pluck the glasses from her tray, without thanks, without recognition, without a single exchange of glances. And maybe this unexpected wound was the one that hurt the most: her invisibility. Once you donned a servant's uniform, you became invisible, not even quite human. This was necessary, of course, for the entire system of human servility to operate without friction, but still it rankled. She wanted to scream, *I'm just as good as you are! I speak French and I dance, I play the piano beautifully and recite poetry from memory and enunciate every consonant without flaw. A year ago, I was almost one of you!*

But that didn't matter, did it? If you fell, you fell.

On the other side of the room, along the windows, the crowd was thinning. Olive, stepping carefully so the bubbling glasses wouldn't tilt onto the polished parquet floor, approached a pair of men, identical in portly middle-aged formal dress. They stood next to one of the grand

French windows, heads bent together, smoking forbidden cigars, which they tipped out the open bottom sash in furtive gestures.

". . . magnificent, to be sure, but it will all go to the receivers quick enough if even one of his damned railroads fails . . ."

Olive slowed her steps.

". . . which ones . . . invest . . . ?"

The other man was speaking, the nearest one, who faced away from Olive's line of approach. She couldn't make out the words very well, but the lift in his voice suggested a question.

She was at his elbow now. She held out the tray, and both men, without a glance, without missing a single beat of their conversation, reached out in unison to swipe away two sizzling glasses of champagne.

". . . but the chiefest part is held in the damned P and R. He's up to his silly neck in it."

The other man laughed. "Fool."

"And so I told him, but he's got all this confounded faith in McLeod, thinks the expansion will pay off before they run out of money—"

"And the patience of creditors—"

"Well, that too, of course—"

Olive was forced to step away now, because even invisible serving maids might attract attention if they lingered too long. But she moved slowly, as if taking extreme care for the safety of the crystal, as a good servant should.

"Well, between you and me, I don't think the P and R lasts more than a week after Cleveland takes office."

". . . repeal . . . silver act . . ."

"Don't matter. Stretched too far, and I hear Morgan's about to pull the plug—"

The voice became muffled as the owner turned toward the window to knock away a length of ash from his guilty cigar. Olive's heart thumped into her ribs, making her dizzy. There was a little draft from under the sash, and it fluttered coldly against her long black skirt.

The P&R. That was the Philadelphia and Reading Railroad; even Olive knew that. Everybody knew the P&R; it was one of the largest companies in the world, transporting infinite tons of rich Pennsylvania anthracite coal from the rural mines to the mid-Atlantic ports, and now it wanted to extend its tentacles into New England. Its *expensive* tentacles, of course. You didn't build out a hundred miles of track without mountains of money. Railroads ate capital like Gus Pratt ate his breakfast bacon, and they were always one ill wind away from collapsing under the weight of their own debts.

Yes, even Olive knew that.

And she also remembered the fat file in Mr. Pratt's fat study, labeled PHILADELPHIA & READING.

The dancers blurred past, colorful and frenetic, whirling from prosperous and plentiful 1892 into the dazzling unknown riches of 1893. A handsome face winged before her and disappeared, and it was an instant or two before Olive realized that it was Harry. Harry, cradling his right arm around yet another beautiful girl, clasping her elegant gloved fingers with his left hand. He hadn't noticed Olive at all.

❖

Not until half past eleven o'clock did Olive find her opportunity to steal into the study upstairs. She had emptied another tray of champagne and made for the stairs to the kitchen, but instead of descending into the basement she had left the tray on the Chippendale lowboy and slipped upward and out of sight.

This time, no hesitation stayed her hands. She knew exactly what she was doing, exactly what she was looking for. The leather portfolios flipped beneath her experienced fingers, until the familiar words appeared once more in the minute glow of the candle: VAN ALAN.

Familiar, and yet foreign. The name hardly seemed to belong to her at all anymore; she felt as if she were no more than a disembodied Olive, belonging to no one and to no particular name. She had spent the last week in a kind of fairyland, knowing that it was a fairyland and entering into it anyway, and now that she was emerging back into the real and practical world, she found she didn't have a place there, either. That she would never be the same Olive Van Alan as before. That she might never again know who Olive was, or should be.

She opened the portfolio, and the tactile sensation of the leather and the papers within brought her back to the task at hand. The truth: the only thing left to her.

There were perhaps thirty papers in all, arranged immaculately by date. Olive sifted through the early correspondence, detailing the Pratts' specifications and her father's tactful responses, referring to blueprints and drawings that must have been stored elsewhere. Then the requests for payment, each one neatly marked PAID in the sleek brown-black strokes of a confident fountain pen. The sums were not large, which didn't surprise Olive. According to Mrs. Van Alan, the bulk of her father's fee had been due upon completion and inspection of the mansion, and the sum was large enough that he had agreed to this particular arrangement with a gentleman's handshake.

Until she came to the last two pages. There was a letter from her father, dated the twentieth of December 1891, noting the successful inspection of the house on the first of December and requesting payment of the balance of his fee for architectural services: nine thousand dollars.

But scribbled at the bottom of this particular letter was not the customary word PAID, which appeared on all the other invoices, followed by a date. Instead, the word—black, in thick, angry block letters—was REFUSED. Dated the second of January 1892.

Her father had shot himself the next day.

"Well, well."

Lost in contemplation of that single word, REFUSED, Olive had almost forgotten where she was. She started upward, knocking over the candle, righting it again. Hot wax spilled over her fingers.

"Oh, I beg your pardon," came the voice of Miss Prunella Pratt, followed by the young lady's white figure, emerging from the shadowed doorway. "Am I disturbing you?"

Olive drew her spine straight, her shoulders back. "No," she said.

Prunella stalked across the rug. She was holding a glass of wine in her hand, half-finished, and the reckless quality of her gait suggested it wasn't her first of the evening. "You poor dear thing. Shall I guess what you're doing?"

"I think it's obvious what I'm doing."

"Well, I guess it is, at that. Using your position in this household to find out why your poor, innocent father left this house in disgrace. Why those heartless Pratts turned him out in the cold and ruined his good name." Prunella stopped on the other side of the desk, placed her wineglass on the edge, and leaned forward. "Dear Olive. I could have saved you the trouble. You won't find it."

"Won't I?"

"Oh, no. My father, you see, was actually quite kind, I think, considering the provocation. He was kind enough not to let the world know the real reason he dismissed Mr. Van Alan without payment. Better the world should just think the man hadn't designed this house to my family's satisfaction."

In the spare glow of the single candle, Prunella's youthful face took on a lurid shadow, and her pink lips and blue eyes lost all color. Olive felt as if something were clawing its way up the back of her head, a premonition of some kind, a warning of impending disaster. *Don't ask,* she thought. *Don't ask.*

"Don't you want to know what it is, Olive? Dear, curious Olive. Don't you want justice for your poor departed father?"

"I already know my father is innocent of anything you might accuse him of."

Prunella giggled. "Oh, my. So you really don't know. Well, I'll give you a hint. It's something to do with that pretty ruby necklace hanging there beneath your dress. A necklace that really belongs to someone else."

Olive's hand went instinctively to her throat. "I don't know what you mean."

"I was wondering where that necklace had gone. It was in my mother's jewel box, you know, and I begged her to let me wear it for my debut. She said I shouldn't, that it was too flashy for a debutante. Too *red.*" Another giggle. "So I took it myself, when her back was turned. And I do believe I was right. That necklace set my white dress off to perfection. It set me apart from the other girls, and Mr. Schuyler asked me to dance three times. Father turned absolutely purple when he noticed, of course, but it was worth it. Really, it's a shame you weren't there. Your father attended, if I recall."

"Yes, I recall." Olive also recalled that her mother hadn't wanted to go. She hadn't anything to wear, she said.

"Such a sociable man, your father. Awfully charming. Well, I can tell you, *he* couldn't take his eyes off my ruby, either. And the next morning, poof! It was gone."

"You can't possibly be suggesting my father stole your necklace."

Prunella leaned forward, so that Olive could smell the excess of wine on her breath. "Well, he stole *some*thing; that's for sure. I'll leave you to decide what it was."

The clawing sensation had turned into a kind of drumbeat, and Olive realized it was her own pulse, knocking in her ears.

Don't ask. Don't ask.

"That won't be necessary. I know my father's character very well."

Prunella sniffed and straightened away from the desk. "As you like. I'd hate to murder your illusions, after all, when you've got so little left to you."

The clock chimed softly. Quarter to midnight.

"That's me, I suppose," said Prunella. "Papa's got the congratulatory toast all ready. Be sure to lock the door when you're finished. We'd hate for anyone to break in and see our private papers, after all." She laughed and turned for the door. The slim bar of light from the hallway illuminated the whiteness of her dress. "And, Olive? You will give your notice and leave this house by daybreak, do you understand? Or else I might be forced to whisper our little secret in an ear or two. Just imagine what my poor brother will say when he finds out the truth. To say nothing of your widowed mother."

"My mother already knows what I'm doing here."

"Oh, I don't mean *that* little thing, Olive. I mean the truth. The real reason my father dismissed the eminent Mr. Van Alan without his fee, and the reason your father didn't object."

Because he couldn't, Olive wanted to scream. *Because he couldn't get another commission if he did.*

But screaming wouldn't help, would it? Screaming wouldn't unsay the words that hung in the air of the study, wouldn't quell the drumbeat at the back of Olive's brain.

Wouldn't wipe the self-satisfied smirk from Prunella Pratt's child-like face.

Olive glanced down at the wineglass at the edge of the desk, and a young woman she didn't know reached out and took that glass by the stem. She blew out the candle and hurried to the door, through which Prunella Pratt had just swept, and she said, in a voice Olive didn't recognize, "Miss Prunella, you forgot your wine."

The noise came up like a physical object from the empty column of the grand stairway: laughter and tinkling glass and violins. Prunella turned, and the brassy young woman who wasn't Olive—whom Olive didn't recognize but rather adored—dashed an arc of red Burgundy across the splendid cream bodice of the Pratt engagement gown, not forgetting the dainty exposed curves of Miss Prunella's bosom, to match the pretty pale pink flowers scattered over the satin.

Olive set down the wineglass on the commode and turned away, toward the stairs to the fifth floor and the small door that led to the attic staircase.

She jumped up the steps two at a time, stumbling once, her breath short and her head swimming. By the time she reached the last landing, she could hardly see the door before her; she hardly noticed that it was not closed but ajar, not dark but gently lit.

"Olive! There you are."

Harry's arms. Harry's shoulder against her forehead.

For an instant, she let herself rest. The black wool was so sleek against her hot skin.

And then she pushed away. "Aren't you going to be missed downstairs?"

"Probably. I don't care. Why, what's wrong?"

"You should go back. There are at least a dozen pretty girls waiting for a kiss. I don't know how you'll choose among them."

"Oh, Olive. Don't be foolish." He reached for her again. "You can't possibly think—"

"Of course I can think. I can think very clearly. All night, I watched you dance with them, while I served the champagne and fended off— fended off—" She was running out of outrage, running out of strength altogether. She just wanted to sleep. She wanted to go to sleep and not wake up, to never have to wake up to the questions hurting the back of her head.

Harry's face grew stern. "Fended off what, Olive? Did someone offend you? Is that what's wrong?"

"No! No, it's just . . ." She touched the filigree chain at her throat and tugged the necklace free, so that the ruby glittered against her black chest. "This necklace. Where did you get it?"

Harry stepped close and cupped his hands around her head. "From my mother, Olive. She gave it to me a year ago, New Year's Day. She said I was to keep it for her and give it, one day, to the lady I loved with all my heart. The love of my life. You, Olive." He bent and kissed her lips. "I kept looking for you tonight, did you know that? Every time they put another doll in my arms to dance with, I looked around for you. I've been miserable."

"You didn't look miserable. You looked delighted with the company you had."

"And do you know how miserable that made me, having to pretend? Having to wear that damned mask, to be the son they expect?" He shook his head. "No more, Olive. Not another day. I've decided. We're not going to wait for June. We're going to leave right now, tomorrow morning. I can't stand another day of this, watching you suffer, helpless to step in and say, *She's mine*. So I'm not going back to college. I'm not going to wait for graduation. I've got a bit of money saved, enough to get us started until the trust comes through. We'll be free, Olive."

She pulled back. "I can't, Harry. My mother. She depends on my wages."

"Why, then we can send for her, too. Or send her money. Please, Olive." He reached for her hand. "Listen to me. There's another thing. I've been a blackguard this past week, head over heels, a careless blackguard who's put you in a very particular sort of danger, and I'm afraid . . . Well, I was thinking that it's possible—I mean, it's not entirely *inconceivable* that . . . or even likely—well, that we can't wait so long as June. Do you understand what I mean?"

Olive stared at the neat line of gold studs marching down Harry's shirt. His words ran past her ears, too much to comprehend, because her mind kept returning to the thing it should not. The thing she dreaded to know. She said softly, "You said your mother gave you the necklace on New Year's Day?"

"Yes. I remember it well." He hesitated. "She and my father had had an argument of some kind, right after the party. She was upset. She said that the necklace had been given to her in love, and that she was passing it on to me in the hope that I should find such a love, one day. And I didn't want to take it, at the time. I thought she was giving it to me on an impulse, because she and my father had had an argument, but she insisted. And she was right." He lifted Olive's hand and kissed each fingertip. "We shall be so much happier than my parents were, darling."

"Why? How do you know that?"

"Because no two people in a million have the kind of connection we have, the connection we both felt from the instant we first saw each other, up on the attic stairs. If we walked away from this house today and went our separate ways, if God led us to marry others and live our lives without ever seeing each other again, I would always know who you were. I would always know you in my heart."

She couldn't speak. Not a word, not a syllable, not a single vowel.

He touched the curve of her ear. "Dearest, practical Olive. Be reckless for once."

"I already have been reckless. I have been very reckless indeed."

"Stay with me tonight, here in our room. In the morning, you can pack up your things. We'll go to your mother's house and explain everything. I'll book us passage on the first ship out. There's nothing to stand in our way."

Nothing and everything, Olive thought. Everything in the world.

"You can't say no. You know all this as well as I do, only you're too practical to say it out loud. So I'll say it for us: We're in love, and we're going to run away together. Do you hear me, Olive? Say it. Say, *I love you, Harry.*"

He was so beautiful. She loved his cheekbones, his jaw, the wave of hair in his forehead, the small bump on the bridge of his nose, his lips, his eyes that gazed down at her in such priceless sincerity. She could see her own reflection in them, the way she looked at Harry. Her adoration, hopeless and eternal.

He bent to her ear. "You can whisper it, if you like."

Well, what was the point in denying it? She had nothing else to give him.

Olive linked her hands at the back of his warm neck and lifted herself on her toes.

"I love you, Harry."

Twenty-four

※※※※※※

JULY 1920

Lucy

He didn't love her.

A heat haze rose from the streets, obscuring Lucy's vision. Or maybe it was the fine mist of tears she refused to shed. What a fool she was! To think herself in love with a man she had known for, what? All of two weeks? Less than that, even. When all along, all he had wanted was to know more about the Pratt family.

There was a certain irony to that, but Lucy wasn't in the mood to appreciate it.

It was before I knew you, he had said, as he followed her to the El, dogging her footsteps, his broad frame casting a dark shadow against the sidewalk in front of her. *You feel it, too, don't you?*

Lucy did. She couldn't deny that she did. That was part of why she'd left him there on the El platform, his words lost in the din of the oncoming train. He'd been gentleman enough not to follow her onto the train.

Whatever you want, he had said. But she didn't know what she wanted, not really. Not anymore.

She had thought, once, that finding Harry Pratt was all she wanted, that being reunited with her real father might fill the hole in her heart left by her father's death. But the more Lucy learned about the Pratts, the less she wanted to know them. She had imagined Harry Pratt as the prince in a fairy tale, golden, shining, the embodiment of all the virtues, separated from her mother only by some cruel tragedy.

So much for high romance. From what she had heard of the Pratts, her father had probably died in a drunken brawl like his brother. And, even if he hadn't, even if he were still alive somewhere, it seemed highly unlikely he would welcome her with open arms, acclaiming her the lost daughter of his heart. The Pratts didn't seem to care for anyone but themselves.

The Pratts had brought her nothing but misery, Lucy thought bitterly. She hated the thought of going back to their house, to that cold marble monument to lost social standing. If any echoes of her parents lurked within those paneled walls, she hadn't found them.

Maybe it was time to throw it all in, Lucy thought wildly. Resign her job at Cromwell, Polk and Moore. She couldn't go back there anyway, not now, not when Philip Schuyler was hiding from her in Philadelphia. He was a partner. She was a secretary. If one of them had to go, it wasn't difficult to guess which.

She couldn't go back to Brooklyn, to the woman she had believed was her grandmother. That life was closed to her now.

And Charleston, that glittering mirage of a future that John Ravenel had held out to her—that was gone now, as swiftly as it had come.

Perhaps they needed good secretaries in California? It was as far away as she could think to go. And why not? There was nothing to hold her to New York.

"Lucy." She was so lost in her own thoughts that she heard his voice before she saw him, Philip Schuyler, sitting on the steps of Stornaway House like a schoolboy playing hooky from school. He rose as she approached, stepping forward to meet her. "Lucy. I need to talk to you."

Lucy's head was spinning with heat and confusion. "How did you know where I live?"

"Your file," said Philip, as though it were the most natural thing in the world to show up on her doorstep. "I need to speak to you."

Lucy glanced nervously at the windows of the house. "Won't it keep until Monday?"

"This isn't a conversation I want to be having in the office."

"But you can't be here." The idea of having a personal discussion in the boardinghouse lounge, with the other girls reading magazines and eavesdropping and Agatha drying her stockings on a rail, made Lucy cringe. "Matron—"

"I'll square it with Matron," said Philip Schuyler, with casual arrogance. "I was in and out of this house long before it was a boardinghouse. But, if it makes you uncomfortable, we can go somewhere else."

"Yes. I think that would be best." Lucy was too rattled to argue. "There's a coffee shop on Lexington."

"Coffee it is," said Philip Schuyler, and offered her his arm.

Lucy hesitated only a moment before taking it, but that moment was a moment too long.

"I won't bite, you know. Not this time," he added wryly.

Lucy grimaced. "I hadn't thought— I'm sorry." She had been so wrapped up in her own worries that she hadn't noticed how tired he looked. His usually impeccably shaved chin glinted with blond stubble.

Like gold flecks, thought Lucy, picking her way across Park Avenue. With the Schuylers, even stubble turned to gold.

Unlike the Pratts, who seemed to be able to turn gold to lead.

"I wish I could say that I was sorry." Philip looked down at her, his eyes serious beneath the brim of his hat. "I ought to be sorry. But I find that I can't be. You may not realize it, but you gave me a great gift."

Something about the way he was looking at her, so serious, so unlike himself, made Lucy nervous. "A hangover?"

"That I gave to myself. And very foolish it was, too." He held open the door for her to precede him into the coffee shop.

Lucy could tell, by the twitch of his nostrils, that he didn't think much of it, of the cracked white pottery sugar bowls and the dingy mats on the tables, but he didn't utter a word of protest. Instead, he ushered Lucy to a table as if they were at the Ritz and she in a long gown and jewels.

"Two coffees, one with milk, two sugars; one with just milk." Philip ordered without waiting for her to speak.

Lucy looked up at him in surprise. "You remember how I take my coffee."

Removing his hat, Philip ran a hand through his blond hair. "Is that so startling?"

Lucy ducked her head. "I didn't think—it's usually the secretary who remembers her employer's preferences, not the other way around."

Philip caught her eye. "I know now that you don't like gin."

Lucy winced. "Must we discuss that? Please, can't we pretend it never happened?"

"Would you pretend the sun never rose or the moon never shone? Forgive me, I'm a bit punchy. It's been a long few days. I had—a lot of thinking to do."

Wouldn't he hurry up and get to the point? Lucy found herself twisting with impatience on the grimy seat of the chair. All she wanted was to get back to the quiet of her stuffy attic room and take off her sweaty stockings and lie on her lumpy bed, where it was dark and quiet and there were no John Ravenels or Philip Schuylers, where she could close her eyes and pretend she was ten again, in her own room decorated with the mural her mother had painted.

Philip Schuyler was still speaking, in his beautiful boarding school voice, the sort of voice that Lucy had thought she wanted to have, that now, after John Ravenel's mellifluous tones, sounded slightly nasal, slightly affected.

Not that it was affected. He spoke that way naturally. He was Philip Schuyler. "I know this is sudden," he was saying, "but . . . marry me."

Whatever fog she had been in, that cleared it with a vengeance. "I'm sorry," Lucy stuttered. "I must have misheard. Did you say—?"

Philip Schuyler leaned forward. "Marry me, Lucy. This week, this year, I don't care when. Just . . . marry me."

Lucy stared at him. He didn't seem drunk, not like last Wednesday, but . . . "Are you under the influence?"

"I'm not under the influence. Not that sort of influence, at any rate." And he wasn't. His eyes were bleary, as if he had been up all night, and his jaw showed a faint and entirely unprecedented sprinkling of gold hairs, but his voice was clear and his hand was steady. Lucy could smell coffee on him, but not the slightest betraying whiff of spirits. "Do you really think I would have to be inebriated to have the good sense to fall in love with you?"

"A penniless secretary? I'm not sure anyone would call that good sense." Or love. How could Philip Schuyler love her? He barely knew her.

Although, Lucy realized with surprise, he knew her a great deal better than John Ravenel did. They had worked together, day by day, hour by hour, for weeks now. He knew how she liked her coffee and that she got cranky if she waited too long for her lunch.

Why was it, then, that when John Ravenel asked her to move to Charleston after three meetings, she had wanted to fling her arms around his neck and shout yes?

Unlike Philip Schuyler, he had never mentioned marriage.

"I've been a fool, Lucy." Philip's gold ring glinted in the sunlight that filtered through the grimy window. "I've known for a while now that I wasn't in love with Didi. I'm not even sure I like her much. I don't know if I've ever liked her. But I thought—I thought that she was the sort of woman I was meant to marry."

"She is the sort of woman you're meant to marry," said Lucy. Her voice felt scraped from the back of her throat. "Someone beautiful, someone accomplished."

"Accomplished in what? Spending her father's money? I saw what my father's marriage was like. Not my mother. I don't remember my mother. Not much." He was silent for a moment, and Lucy, despite herself, felt a pang of pity. How odd, how very odd, to be pitying Philip Schuyler. "But I do remember Prunella. She needed constant compliments, constant attendance, constant gifts. She was the center of the world and everyone was expected to revolve around her."

"Doesn't she still?" said Lucy.

"True. Only now there are fewer left to orbit around her. What I'm trying to say is—she was an ornament, not a partner. I could marry someone because she decorates a ballroom." He looked up at Lucy. "Or I could marry someone like you. Someone strong. Someone sensible."

Lucy wasn't entirely sure that was a compliment. "You make me sound like an old pair of shoes."

"That wasn't what I meant." Philip's eyes crinkled ruefully. "If you'll believe it, I was once accounted rather debonair."

"I believe it." If he was being honest, so could she. "I've been half in love with you."

"Only half?"

Lucy struggled to put her feelings into words. "I think, to be truly in love, there has to be—some measure of understanding."

That was what her parents, for all their virtues, had never had. Her father had admired her mother without ever truly understanding her. And her mother—her mother had relied on her father without appreciating him. There had been a gulf between them that couldn't be bridged by all the goodwill in the world.

Philip put a hand out, not touching her, just near her. "I think we understand each other pretty well. We certainly work well together."

Lucy shook her head. She felt as though she had just tumbled into the wrong story. The prince had proposed to the goose girl, but the goose girl wasn't a princess in disguise; she was an entirely different sort of imposter. "There's a great deal you don't know about me."

Philip turned his cup around on its chipped saucer. "I know that you speak your mind, even when it might be easier to remain silent. I know that you won't let me—oh, sit on a shelf and collect dust like some trophy. You challenge me. You make me a better person. A better lawyer, too." When Lucy didn't respond to his smile with one of her own, he said simply, "I want to be the man you see in me."

Was that how he saw her? Purely as a mirror for his own better self? In that case, he was due to be disappointed when he stopped to look more closely and realized that his mirror was cracked, that she had lied to him, just as John Ravenel had lied to her.

It was time to have it all out, every last bit of it. What more, after all, did she stand to lose?

Taking a deep breath, Lucy said, "I'm afraid you've been deceived in me. I'm—not what I've said I am. I've been lying to you."

"Are you the lost princess of Austrovia? I've always rather fancied myself as prince consort."

He would make a lovely prince consort, all shiny braid and polished buttons. Lucy shook her head. "My ancestral home is a bakery in Brooklyn. My real name isn't Young—it's Jungmann."

She looked defiantly at Philip Schuyler, waiting for the condemnation to follow.

"Is that all?" Philip leaned back in his chair, relief written in his posture. "My maternal grandfather was named Hochstatter. From Hamburg, or thereabouts. He changed it to Howland when he brought the family shipping business over to America. You Anglicized your name. It's been done before."

"There's more." Her name was the least of it. "I wasn't entirely frank about my reasons for wanting employment at Cromwell, Polk and Moore. I wanted access. To the Pratt papers." In a rush, Lucy said, "No one could ever understand why my mother married my father. She was a lady—a Van Alan. And my father was just a greengrocer. But my grandmother said—I think Harry Pratt might be my father."

"Oh." To his credit, after the first stunned moment, Philip took the announcement in stride. His lean face was thoughtful. "Harry . . . He was the younger twin. He disappeared, right before Prunella married my father. There was something of a stink about it. That would have been in 'ninety-three."

"The year I was born," said Lucy quietly. "I was born in November of 1893."

"I see." Philip cocked his head. "That would make you my—what? Stepcousin? I think we can get a dispensation."

He was joking again, always joking. "You don't understand. I lied to you. I came to work for you under false pretenses." She blurted out the worst of it. "When you weren't in the office, I went through your files."

"You're my secretary. It's your job to go through my files." When Lucy didn't crack a smile, Philip leaned forward, taking her hands in his. "I think it's very gallant of you to come clean. But none of this makes a difference. Not to me. It wasn't as though you were trying to embezzle money from the firm. You just wanted to know about your heritage. And who wouldn't?"

Lucy bit her lip, torn by his kindness. "I'm beginning to think I shouldn't. Nothing I hear about the Pratts makes them sound terribly likable."

Philip was still holding her hands, his grip loose, undemanding. "If it helps," he said, "Harry was the best of the lot of them. I was a snotty boy of eight. I can't have been much of a joy to have around. But Harry—he saw me sitting there by myself at the back of the room. I'd been told to sit still and mind my manners. No speaking until spoken to and all that. But he came over to me. He drew a picture for me."

"A picture?" A little shiver ran down Lucy's spine. *A goose walked over my grave,* her mother would say.

A faint, reminiscent smile curved Philip's lips. "I'd nearly forgotten that day. I can't remember quite what he said—something about guessing that I wished I were outside, doing anything but sitting in that room. Because he wished he was anywhere but in that room. And right there, just like that, he whipped out a sketch pad and drew me flying a kite in Central Park. It was a very good likeness, too."

Lucy thought of her mother, of the mural on Lucy's bedroom wall. *Mine is only a secondhand talent.* "He was an artist?"

Philip shrugged. "Artistic, at any rate. His family wasn't the type to encourage that sort of talent. They were . . . grubby. Moneygrubbing," he clarified, with the easy arrogance of generations of inherited wealth. "Old Henry August Pratt didn't approve of anything that didn't translate into dollars and cents. But Harry—he was different." Glancing up at Lucy, he added, "I might still have that sketch somewhere, if you'd like it."

Lucy's throat was tight. She'd lied to Philip Schuyler, she'd deceived him, and here he was, offering her a piece of his past. Of her past. "Thank you. You don't—you don't know anything about what happened to Harry Pratt?"

"No one does." He leaned forward, his eyes intent on hers. "If this matters to you, we can get someone on it. Even after this many years, a good private detective should be able to follow his trail. That is—if you want to know."

He spoke with such easy authority. And Lucy knew, without questioning, that if she were to say yes, within hours the wheels would be put in motion, all of Philip Schuyler's considerable resources placed at her disposal. It was a heady taste of what it would be to be Mrs. Philip Schuyler.

And also terrifying.

"I don't know," Lucy said honestly. "I thought all I wanted in the world was to find my real father. But now . . . I don't know."

"You don't have to make any decisions now," Philip said, and Lucy knew he wasn't just talking about Harry Pratt. "Sleep on it. It's kept for this many years; what's a few days more?"

If I refused you, would you still find my father for me? Lucy wanted to ask. But she already knew the answer. Philip Schuyler might be many things, but he wasn't petty.

Lucy looked at him, at his pale blue eyes and the nose that was just a shade too long and too thin. "Didi Shippen doesn't know what she's losing, does she?"

"From her point of view," said Philip wryly, "an apartment on Park, an Italianate villa on the Hudson, and an allowance of five thousand a year. And a suitably dressed man on her arm for social occasions."

Lucy pushed back her chair, rising to her feet. "Then she didn't deserve you."

Philip tossed some money on the table; the tip, Lucy noticed, was probably twice what their server earned in a week. "And what about you, Lucy?"

It would be so convenient if she were in love with Philip Schuyler, as she had fancied herself two weeks ago. She knew him better now; she liked him better now. But she didn't love him. If liking could make love . . . But, then, that was what her father had hoped, wasn't it? And look how that had turned out.

Lucy fumbled with her gloves. "I have—a great deal of thinking to do."

"All right. I won't push you." Philip grinned a crooked grin. "Or attempt to ply you with gin. But I can't promise I won't ask again."

"You'll think better of it in a week," said Lucy, as they stepped back out into the July sunshine.

"I'm not so fickle as that." With a tip of his hat, he dropped her back at her door. "I'll see you on Monday."

❁

"Who was that?" It was Maud, one of the other women who roomed at Stornaway, on her way out in a new hat and shoes with a strap. "He looked rich."

"Just my boss," said Lucy quickly.

"If my boss looked like that . . . ," said Maud.

Lucy waved to her and quickly let herself in through the front door, into the house where her mother had fallen in love with a man named Harry Pratt.

What should I do, Mama? What happened to you? Why did you choose as you did?

But the marble stones of the old house were silent. There was only the staircase spiraling up, up, up to eternity, around and around, like time, circling and circling, always coming back to the same point.

Lucy's thoughts went around and around in a similar spiral: John and Philip and Philip and John. John had lied to her. Philip had proposed to her.

But it was John whom her heart yearned for, John with whom she felt as though she had found a missing piece of herself. And could she really condemn him for lying to her? She had done the same, and for the same reason. If Philip Schuyler could forgive her, why couldn't she forgive John Ravenel?

When I saw it on you— He had seen her necklace and assumed she was part of Prunella Pratt's scheme, whatever that scheme might be.

But was the necklace on the lady in his father's picture really the same as the one around her neck? And, if so, how had it come to be there?

There was a telephone booth just next to the concierge desk. Fishing in her purse, Lucy put a coin in the slot. "Can you connect me to the Waldorf, please?"

"Just a moment," said the disembodied voice of the operator.

There was a fly buzzing lazily next to the receiver; the sound seemed to blur into the whirr of the wires.

She could put the phone back now. Put the phone back and walk away. John Ravenel would go back to Charleston. And she could marry Philip Schuyler and have beautiful gowns and appear in the society pages.

And wonder, always, if she had made the mistake of her life.

There was a click.

"Your party is on the line," said the operator, as someone else said, rather curtly, "Yes?"

"Hello," Lucy said quickly, before she could think better of it. "Is this the Waldorf? I'd like to leave a message for Mr. John Ravenel. Yes, Ravenel. R-A-V-E-N-E-L. Would you tell him that Miss Young would like to speak to him?"

Twenty-five

AUGUST 1944

Kate

A misty rain slicked the streets as I walked the short blocks from the subway stop. I was vaguely familiar with Brooklyn, having visited my paternal great-grandmother there infrequently as a child. She'd spoken with a heavy German accent and had seemed to barely tolerate my mother. I remembered her mostly by the scent of baking bread that clung to her like a perfume. She must have died before I was ten years old, because I didn't remember the obligatory visits much past then.

The neighborhood I found myself in now wasn't too dissimilar from the one of my memory, with the familiar stench of garbage and the sight of laundry floating like ghosts from lines stretched between buildings. I remembered with a certain fondness the predominant odors of sauerkraut and schnitzel that had always made me feel a part of my mother's life, the part before she met my father and the brackets of disappointment that marked each side of her mouth had become permanent.

I stood across from a three-story brownstone with baby carriages parked out front on the sidewalk, a tired-looking mother jostling a screaming baby on her shoulder, taking turns patting the child's back and flicking ash from a cigarette dangling from her lips, seemingly impervious to the drizzle that dusted everything with a fine mist.

I looked down at the crumpled piece of paper clutched in my gloved hands, double-checking that I was in the right place. Prunella Pratt Schuyler had responded to my request for a meeting with a short note scrawled out in bold script. It had been more of a summons than a response, telling me to be at this address at four o'clock Tuesday next. The expensive stationery was at jarring odds with the street on which I stood, the linen paper more appropriate to an Upper East Side debutante than to this Brooklyn neighborhood of immigrant families and the pungent scents of foreign foods. Remembering what Margie had discovered about Prunella in the society pages, I wondered if that false impression might have been intentional.

I was quite certain this wasn't the same place I'd visited with my parents all those years ago. I had to assume that Prunella's fortunes since my father's death had deteriorated drastically, at least to the point where she'd been forced to move to Brooklyn from the Upper East Side. Which, some might argue, would be a fate worse than death.

I waited for a sputtering milk truck to pass and then crossed the street. The haggard mother barely noticed me as I passed her on the steps and entered through tall double doors into what might have once been an attractive foyer in a single residence. But now the black-and-white marble tiles of the floor were cracked and stained, the plaster ceiling moldings mostly missing or water spotted, the fireplace surround absent, presumably salvaged to grace a more deserving residence.

I almost left the building again to check the address one more time, but stopped myself. I recalled the rest of the information Margie had discovered in the newspaper archives about the demise of the Pratt family fortunes related to bad railroad investments, and then the blow the Schuyler family fortune had sustained during the crash of '29. For a woman like Prunella, who since birth had been brought up and schooled to be nothing more than a society hostess, to end up in a place like this, far away from the familiar world of her youth—it must have been humbling indeed.

The sound of a couple arguing tumbled down the narrow stairs in front of me, the dark green runner of which was threadbare and filthy. A baby cried somewhere in the building, while an out-of-tune piano plunked out a scale behind the door to my right. I looked again at the note in my hand. Apartment 1B. The door opposite the piano, with peeling white paint and only a shadow of where a number one must have once been attached.

I hesitated only a moment before raising my hand and knocking, the sound slightly muted by my glove. I heard a movement inside, like the barest brush of satin against wood, and then nothing. I took off my glove and knocked again with all four knuckles.

This time I heard light but quick footsteps, followed by the sound of several locks being unlatched before the door slowly opened. Two large green eyes beneath a mop of white curly hair peered out at me through the space between the door and frame.

"Mrs. Schuyler? Aunt Prunella? It's Kate. Kate Schuyler. Philip's daughter."

The door widened and the woman stepped back, revealing an old-fashioned and ill-fitting black maid's uniform complete with starched white apron and cap. Her wide smile alone would have been enough to tell me it wasn't my aunt Prunella, but when she opened her mouth and words that danced with an Irish brogue fell from her tongue, I knew for certain.

"Och, no. I'm Mona, the maid." She leaned forward conspiratorially and whispered, "Herself is still abed, too delicate to leave her room in such weather. Between you and me, she's the constitution of a bear and will outlive us all."

She closed the door behind me. "She told me not to offer refreshments, but ye look like ye could use a nice cup of tea. I'll bring some in just a moment." She jerked her head to the left. "Herself is right through that door. Give a knock first, or we'll both be hearing about it."

I watched Mona waddle away toward another door I assumed led to a kitchen, the tight black fabric stretched and shiny across her back. I wondered if she'd once worked for the Pratts and had stayed with Prunella not necessarily out of loyalty, but because she had no other options.

I took a quick assessment of the room around me, familiar only because of the furniture. It seemed bigger here, out of place in the tiny apartment, with china figurines and objects d'art cluttering the heavy dark wood of the oversized pieces. Small paths had been carved between three large sofas and various accent tables and bookcases to allow passage from one room to the next, giving the room the appearance of the ocean's surface after the sinking of a large ship, the debris scattered haphazardly without thought of placement or usefulness.

It struck me as incredibly sad how this was all that remained of a once glamorous and privileged life, the beauty of all these things diminished by the peeling wallpaper and faded draperies of the drab apartment. My father had managed Prunella's finances until his death, which must have precipitated her move across the river. A move she must have loathed, and probably still did. I almost turned away then, to let myself out of the door and into the rain-cleansed air.

"Mona? Who was that? I hope you're not keeping the door open too long—I don't want to catch a draft and be chilled."

The voice hadn't changed in all those years, the same imperious intonations, the perfect finishing-school accent. It reminded me of my father's grimace as he told me that we had to visit Aunt Prunella again.

I'm a grown woman. A doctor *no less,* I reminded myself. I lifted my hand and knocked and, without waiting for a response, pushed the door open.

I didn't see her at first. The small bedroom was the repository of an enormous mahogany four-poster bed and the largest armoire I'd ever seen. An oversized Victorian dresser and settee were crammed into the tiny room, making it easy to miss the diminutive woman propped up against overstuffed pillows in the bed. She was even smaller than I remembered, as if the passing years had pushed out pieces of stuffing.

"Aunt Prunella?"

She squinted at me. "Move closer so I can see you."

I moved two steps closer to the bed.

"Closer. I don't know why you insist on standing across the room."

I bit back a smile, suspecting that vanity was the reason for her lack of eyeglasses. I moved so that my legs pressed against the side of the mattress.

She didn't say anything for a while, her sharp blue eyes examining me closely, as a jeweler might examine various stones to determine their worthiness. Lifting her eyes to mine, she said, "*Kate* did you say? I remember you as a little girl, of course. You have the look of your mother. The same heart-shaped face with that pronounced widow's peak."

It was clear she hadn't meant it as a compliment. "My father used to say that, too, although I wasn't sure I agreed. My mother was a beautiful woman."

"Was?"

I nodded. "She died a few years ago."

If I thought she'd offer condolences, I would have been disappointed. I looked around for a chair, but the settee was across the room, so I remained standing where I was. "I'm afraid you and I lost contact after my father died. I was only recently made aware that you were still alive. As I explained in my letter, I'm a doctor at Stornaway Hospital, in the building I believe was the Pratt mansion where you once lived."

Her lips pressed together so tightly that the blood leached from them, leaving them so pale that her mouth seemed to disappear altogether. "Yes.

I lived there for a short time before my marriage." Her words were cold and clipped, as if to say, *And this is where I live now.*

I forced myself to smile. "I believe I found a gown that once belonged to you. It was in the attic in an armoire. It's exquisite, with tiny pink roses on it, and the tiniest waist. It has your name embroidered inside of it."

Her face softened, allowing me to glimpse the beautiful young girl she must have once been, before the disappointments of her life had overshadowed the good parts. "I wore that gown to my engagement party. My photograph was in all the society pages for weeks afterward." Her lips curved upward in a smile, her thoughts turned inward, making me wonder what it was like to live one's life looking backward.

"I could return it to you, if you'd like to have it back. Although it has a terrible stain on the front. I think it might be wine."

Her eyes snapped, her eyes hard as they regarded me. "Yes. It's wine. A stupid and clumsy maid spilled it on me. Ruined it completely."

Eager to change the subject, I said, "I found some sketches of Harry's, too. Your brother was quite talented."

She gave a quick shake of her head, as if she'd just tasted something bitter. "He was a hobbyist, nothing more. But he somehow got it into his head that he wanted to be an artist. Father set him straight, of course. Pratts did *not* become artists. It just wasn't done."

I shifted on my feet, uncomfortable to be standing next to her bed and having this conversation. She made no offer to find a chair for me, and I was not going to sit on the side of the bed. It seemed as if we were waiting the other out.

I cleared my throat. "I understand that Harry disappeared around the same time as your marriage. Did you ever find out what happened to him?"

She turned toward the window, the dim light reflected in her eyes. "No. He simply . . . left. Never even said good-bye." She paused. "I would have liked to see him again, I think." It might have been a trick of the light, but her eyes appeared to mist, becoming twin pools of shallow blue water. "I did something awful, and I would have liked to tell him how sorry I was. As if that could have changed anything." She paused for a moment before turning her pale eyes on me again, blinking as if suddenly realizing that she had spoken aloud, that she had finally acknowledged her wrongdoing. "You will find, Kate, as I have, that sooner or later everyone leaves you until you are left quite alone with only disappointment and regrets for company."

Mona entered the room, bustling about quickly, as if to deflect her mistress's icy stare. She placed a tray across Prunella's lap and began pouring tea from a silver pot into two mismatched Spode china cups.

"I thought ye might be parched, Miss Prunella," Mona said as she dropped two large teaspoons of sugar and a healthy dribble of cream into a cup and handed it to Prunella. The older woman took it grudgingly and began sipping.

The windows of the room were shut, no doubt to block nuisance noises such as children and traffic as well as the inevitable dirt and dust. But it also made the air stale and stifling, and I found I was indeed in need of refreshment. Mona poured a cup for me and I took it, holding up my hand when she offered cream and sugar. Prunella seemed almost relieved, as if she budgeted her cream and sugar. But not, apparently, her stationery.

I blew on my tea, wondering why I'd come. I'd already known she was related to Harry Pratt, but what else had I hoped to learn? Knowing what had happened to Harry wouldn't have solved the mystery of the miniature or the ruby necklace. They were simply unrelated elements, connected only by my own curiosity. And Cooper's. So why was I there? Maybe I'd come with the hope that once Prunella knew I was alive, we would make a connection based on our mutual loneliness. The war had taught me to treasure life and all the things that connected us as human beings. Prunella and I had no family except for each other.

My gaze panned over the cluttered room as I sipped, taking in the cosmetics on the dressing table and a crumbling bouquet of dried roses that listed languidly in a dome-shaped glass cover on a tall plant stand. *Disappointment and regrets.* I shivered despite the mugginess, and continued my perusal of the room. A low bookcase sat beneath one of the windows, where a large leather-bound volume was squeezed in between much smaller books. I paused with my cup held to my lips, remembering the book from my childhood visits. "Aunt Prunella, is that your scrapbook?"

She saw where I indicated and elicited a bored sigh. "Yes, it is. My mother clipped every article about me from my debutante ball through my wedding. I thought it was quite tiresome, but she insisted." A spark lit her eyes, belying her ennui.

"May I see it?" I asked, already walking toward the bookcase.

"If you must. But do not take too long. I need my rest."

I looked back and saw Mona rolling her eyes. After placing my cup and saucer on top of the bookcase, I slid the thick volume from its place and brought it back to the bed. Mona cleared the tea set before excusing herself for a moment. She returned with a kitchen stool that she placed next to Prunella as I settled the scrapbook against the older woman's scrawny knees.

The glowing young woman in the aged photographs was barely recognizable as the same woman in the bed beside me. I calculated that Prunella would be about seventy years old now, but her air of frailty and helplessness added years to her age. I wondered if disappointment and regret could do that to a person, could etch themselves into the curves and planes of a young girl's face, like time's library stamp.

I let her turn the pages with her still elegant hands, listening to her stories of what it was like for her in the latter part of the last century, to imagine Stornaway Hospital as the glittering mansion it had once been, seeing her handsome brothers in their formal wear dancing with beautiful women at the various balls the Pratt family had hosted in their short stay in the mansion on East Sixty-ninth Street. It made me nostalgic for something I had never known but felt a connection to nevertheless.

I was thinking of an excuse to leave when she turned the page to reveal a large article and photographs that filled facing pages. There was an inset photo of the entire Pratt family in formal attire, posing in front of the familiar circular stairs of the mansion. I pointed to the tall and handsome fair-haired young man standing next to a younger Prunella, his smile full of mischief. "Is this Harry?"

She nodded, her finger gently brushing the clipping. "He was so handsome, wasn't he? Gus was handsome, too," she said, tapping the image of another blond young man, who was still nice to look at yet lacked whatever spark his brother seemed to have. "But Harry . . ." She sighed. "My mother used to say he hung the moon in the sky, and if you'd known him, you might even agree."

I leaned closer, studying his eyes. I examined the curve of his jaw and the way his nose was a little too thin and a little too long but which made it all the more arresting in his otherwise perfect features. "He looks . . . familiar," I said, leaning back to get a better perspective.

"He should," Prunella said indignantly. "We favored each other."

I looked at her and nodded. "Of course," I said, knowing that wasn't it at all.

The larger photo was taken at Prunella's engagement ball. A full orchestra was set up at one end of the ballroom, which was currently being used as examining areas for the patients, with cots running the length of the gilded room. Some of the couples were blurred as they swirled around the floor, smudges of white from ladies' gloves resting on the shoulders of black-frocked gentlemen. I recognized an older version of Prunella, the mother from the smaller photo, holding court near the punch table. I leaned in closely and felt my breath stop.

Standing directly behind Mrs. Pratt was a young woman in a maid's uniform almost identical to the one Mona currently wore. Except this uniform was new and crisp and fit the slender form of the woman who wore it. She had dark hair pinned up beneath a white cap, and her gaze was fixed on the tray of champagne glasses that she gripped with both hands, as if she were unaccustomed to serving.

Despite the pressing heat in the room, I felt a chill dance up my spine and take residence at the nape of my neck. It wasn't that the woman resembled me. It wasn't even that she was a dead ringer for the woman in the miniature portrait that belonged to Cooper and had once been his father's and his father's before him. It was the dark-stoned necklace that hung on the outside of the uniform, the delicate chain tangled in the neck of her dress as if some exertion had coerced it from its hiding place and it had become stuck in the high collar.

It took me a moment to find the words in my dry mouth. "This maid—with the necklace. Do you know who she is?"

Prunella leaned forward and squinted, her eyes then widening in apparent recognition as her expression changed to a scowl. "Her name was something like Olivia or Olivette or something." She shook her hand like she was shooing a fly. "Something *common*."

I forced my voice to remain steady. "And she worked as a maid for your family? At the house on Sixty-ninth Street?"

Her lips formed a single line of disapproval. "She thought she was one of us because her father had been an architect. But blood does tell in the end, doesn't it? My father discovered some horrible things about him and dismissed him, hoping he'd just go away. But the fool killed himself, and his daughter was left to believe that he'd been slighted. The one thing I do know is that she was a thief. She stole that necklace from me. And she disappeared with it before I could get it back."

"The stone, in the necklace. Was it a ruby?"

She gave a small shrug. "I suppose so. It was dark red and had belonged to my mother, so I assume it was a valuable stone like a ruby."

I had been about to show her the ruby that was at that moment hanging around my own neck, had even reached toward the top button of my blouse. But I stopped. I replaced my hands in my lap, watching as they trembled. "What sorts of things was her father accused of?"

"Adultery for one. With a client's wife, no less. Both father and daughter deserved what they got."

I stared at her for a long moment, realizing that she didn't know that Olive was my grandmother or that her own stepson had married the daughter of an apparent thief. A maid. *Was this the reason for my mother's secrets?*

I stood, my knees shaking, desperate to leave. "I should go," I said. "And let you rest. I appreciate you taking the time to see me."

She looked almost disappointed, as if she didn't get visitors very often, and I felt an unwelcome stab of pity for her. *Disappointment and regrets.* Before I could stop myself, I said, "I'll come back, if you'd like. You can show me the rest of the scrapbook."

Her face seemed to brighten, transforming it. "That would be . . . appropriate," she said. "Just please be sure to let us know when you'll be here to ensure it's at a convenient time."

If I hadn't been still reeling from what I'd just learned, I might have laughed. "Of course. Thank you again," I said, then said good-bye to Prunella and her maid.

I nearly stumbled in my haste to get through the outer door, then paused on the outside steps as I sucked in lungfuls of fresh clean air that didn't taste like bitter regret.

❧

I sat at the desk in Dr. Greeley's office behind a pile of paperwork, happy for the distraction. He'd seemed surprised when I'd volunteered to tackle the ever-growing pile, but I knew he'd never guess the reason why I chose to hide in a place in which Cooper Ravenel would never think to look.

I'd been avoiding him since the night we'd spent together. Seeing him walking with Caroline was too painful and would have completely dissipated the fantasy cloud I'd created where it was just Cooper and me, and no war, or fiancées, or futures that didn't involve the other. I found myself dreading his release almost as much as I anticipated it, eager to put the pain behind me. I'd have to take the advice I always gave to my patients, to look forward to each day that took you beyond the pain, that healing would eventually come. I only wished the healing wouldn't hurt so much.

There was a brief knock on the door and Nurse Hathaway stepped inside, closing it softly behind her. "I'm sorry to bother you, Doctor. But I have something for you and I didn't think you'd want anybody else to see."

I sat back in my chair and watched as she placed a small stack of papers on the desk in front of me. "What . . . ?" I stopped, confused for a moment. They were sketches of a woman with dark hair and a heart-shaped face, nude except for the familiar necklace she wore around her neck. I recognized the fireplace in the attic room, and the mullioned windows, and for a moment I thought it was me. Or, I realized for the first time, my mother. Our coloring had been different, but she'd had the same widow's peak, the same shape of the face. As had her mother.

"Captain Ravenel asked me to give them to you. He said he found them in the drawer of the Chinese cabinet in the attic. He wanted you to know that he'd opened the locked drawer, and that he didn't want these to end up in the wrong hands."

Her face remained expressionless, but I thought I saw something in her eyes. "She looks like you," she said.

I felt myself coloring. "Yes. She does. But it's not." I couldn't meet her eyes. It wasn't me in the sketch, but it could have been.

"I know," Nurse Hathaway said. "The artist signed and dated it at the bottom—H. Pratt, 1892."

She must have said something, but I wasn't listening. I was too mesmerized by the single signature, the bold *H* and *P* of the artist on the bottom corner of sketches of a woman who looked like my grandmother, wearing the necklace that had been stolen from Prunella Pratt.

As if she hadn't said anything, I said, "Have you shown these to anybody else?"

"No, Doctor. Of course not. I understand it's a private matter and none of my concern."

I flipped through the sketches, each one more detailed than the last, as if Harry Pratt had spent a lot of time studying his subject. Olive. My grandmother. I sat back in my chair again, regarding the young woman in front of me. "Why are you always so kind to me, Nurse Hathaway? You must know that I'm not a favorite among the nurses or doctors."

She grinned broadly. "Because I want to be you. You're a fine doctor, one of the best I've worked with. You know who you are and what you want, and you never give anybody else permission to treat you like you're less than who you are."

"Thank you," I said as I stood and gathered the sketches. I needed to speak with Cooper, to tell him about the necklace, about how my grandmother had been a maid in this building. Perhaps we would be able to figure out how the miniature came to be in his grandfather's possession. I might even tell him that my grandmother was a thief. But I would not allow him to stand too close, and I could not allow myself to want him to.

I smiled at the nurse. "It's good to hear, even when I'm not so sure if I've made the right choices."

She opened the door. "Well, that's the thing about choices, isn't it? There are always more to make. I've never seen a street where you couldn't cross to the other side."

She smiled again, then headed out into the corridor, her feet tapping briskly against the marble. I'd made it out the door and was shutting it behind me when Dr. Greeley and Cooper emerged from another office down the hall. It was too late to return to the office or run down the stairs. Instead, I held the sketches behind my back and stood where I was while I waited for them to approach, much as I imagined a small woodland animal waited in the middle of a road, staring at oncoming headlights.

I stared at the small cleft in Cooper's chin, unable to meet his, eyes. "Good afternoon, Captain. I hope you're well."

"Very," he said. "Thanks to you."

I felt myself coloring and my gaze jerked up to meet his, and I immediately regretted it. Everything I was feeling—the euphoria, the loss, the regret—was mirrored in his eyes.

Dr. Greeley sounded almost gleeful. "The captain is doing so well that I've just completed his final exam and am pronouncing him fit enough for discharge."

Cooper cleared his throat. "Caroline and I are taking a train to Charleston tomorrow afternoon."

I almost said that it was too soon, that I needed to talk to him about the sketches, and the photo in Prunella's scrapbook, and how I'd suddenly realized why I thought Harry Pratt looked so familiar. But I couldn't, of course. It was too late. I needed to go, needed to get away as quickly as I could before I shattered into so many pieces that I could never put myself together again.

"That's wonderful news," I said to the cleft in his chin, still unable to meet his eyes. *The color of winter grass.* I remembered thinking that the first time I'd seen him, and how now it seemed that I had seen them before, had always known him.

"Good-bye, then," I said, spinning on my heel and racing toward the steps before I made a fool of myself. I headed outside onto the pavement and into the hot sunshine, wanting to feel anything except the sharp sting of regret that filled the cavity in my chest where my heart had once been.

Twenty-six

Olive

All her life, Olive had wanted to stay up until midnight on New Year's Eve and experience the exact instant when the old year turned to the new. When the familiar date passed into history, never to be seen or known or smelled or touched again—like death, she supposed—and those bright exotic numbers that had once belonged to some impossibly distant future—*1893, imagine that!*—became your present reality.

But Olive was an early riser by habit and had never managed to keep her eyes open past eleven o'clock. Since the age of nineteen, when her parents had first let her stay up in the parlor, she had always woken on the settee at two or three o'clock, covered by a kindly blanket and a thick haze of bemused disappointment.

Until tonight. Like the rest of her life, New Year's Eve had now irreparably altered, and Olive lay wide awake as the clock struck midnight and the entire house seemed to shudder with the celebration far below, in the magnificent second-floor drawing room, where everybody else in the world had gathered, except Olive and Harry.

Harry, who lay against her now, the long shanks of his body resting heavily alongside hers, his breath stirring her hair. She thought he was asleep. They had made love swiftly, zealously, reaching a roaring climax within minutes of tumbling through the attic door, and then he had gone mortally quiet, so that she had listened for the thump of his heart to make sure he was still alive.

"Happy New Year," she whispered, into the air that seemed to shiver under the weight of the new numbers, the new future that inhabited the room with them. The skylight soared directly above, each pane reflecting a faint image of their entangled nakedness. A hundred Harrys, a hundred Olives, brought together under the starry new night.

But Harry didn't answer. As she suspected, he had fallen asleep.

❧

The minutes passed; the hours bled away. Harry slept abundantly, a deep and contented unconsciousness for which she envied him. Or did she? Maybe it was better not to sleep. Maybe it was better not to miss a single moment of this, of Harry's warm body united with hers.

She wore nothing at all except the necklace. That was how Harry liked her best, without any clothes at all: not because he was lascivious— or maybe not *only* because he was lascivious—but because he hated to have anything come between his eyes and her skin, between his skin and her skin. Only the necklace, the central stone of which had slipped down the side of her neck and lay now on the cushion beneath, just touching the top of her collar. She imagined it glittering there, priceless and memorable, the token of Harry's love.

Just like the earrings on her mother's ears.

Olive's father had loved her mother—of course he had—but Olive had always known that her father had a boundless capacity for love, a talent for it. His heart was so large and ambitious. And he had been paid a thousand dollars on the first of December, and he had gone to a jeweler and seen a splendid set of rubies—Olive could picture it all, could actually *see* her father glowing with delight at all the beauty laid out before him—and he bought that set on an impulse with those thousand dollars, in the full and infinite optimism of his love.

A pair of ruby earrings for his beloved wife.

A matching necklace for his lover.

His lover. Mrs. Henry August Pratt, the wife of his employer.

The truth. It had been clawing for freedom at the back of Olive's head, as some sensible and logical part of her brain had put all the pieces together, one by one: what she knew of her father, what she knew of the Pratts. The argument after Miss Prunella's debut, one year ago. The necklace that Mrs. Pratt had given tearfully afterward to her favorite son. (It was given to her in love, Harry said, when everyone knew that couples like the Pratts didn't love each other, not really. Love and marriage were two entirely different objects to the Pratts, requiring two entirely different partners.) And then, the day after that, the angry word REFUSED on the final invoice for services rendered.

Prunella's sneering voice: *He stole* something; *that's for sure.*

And now the truth broke free at last, floating magically around Olive's head, bumping up against the sides of her skull.

She hadn't seen her mother since Christmas Day. There was too much to do: readying the great house for the New Year's Eve ball, engaging in a passionate love affair under the noses of her employers. The fairyland she had inhabited this past week did not allow visits to narrow, shabby brownstone houses on the wrong side of the Fourth Avenue railroad tracks.

But Mrs. Van Alan would be expecting her to visit today. She would be expecting Olive to knock on the door in the early afternoon, and she would probably contrive to have that dear, respectable, dependable Mr. Jungmann in the parlor with her. *Just paying a call, Olive. Wasn't that nice of him?*

What would Mrs. Van Alan do if Olive didn't walk through that door, after all? If she received a note instead, explaining that Olive had run off to Italy to live in sin and sunshine with one of the Pratt boys. If, a few days later, Miss Prunella Pratt took her revenge for the whole affair, either by anonymous message or in person, and Mrs. Van Alan would know that her precious earrings were only half of a matched set.

We'll take her with us, Harry had said, but that was ridiculous, a dear and ridiculous fantasy nearly as impossible as loving each other in the first place. Her mother would never agree, for one thing—*run off to Italy with your lover, indeed!*—and for another, how could such a project end in anything else than disaster? Inevitably life would take hold. Inevitably there would be babies and bills and arguments. Inevitably Harry would find out who she really was—Prunella would see to that—and the rosy glow with which he perceived her would sharpen to an ordinary harsh daylight, until she stood before him as she really was, and he would no longer adore her.

And dear Harry, he was so good and true that maybe he wouldn't leave her, not after she had given everything up for him. He would feel some responsibility for the mistress he no longer loved, for the children he had recklessly fathered. But he would regret his youthful impulse, wouldn't he? When she stood exposed before him, the real Olive, in all her human flaws. And she couldn't bear that, *never*, to stand before him and see the disappointment in his eyes. Disappointment, where until now she had seen only love: love of the purest possible distillation.

No. She wanted to remember him like this, exactly as he was now, sated and trustful in her arms.

Oh, but it had been beautiful while it lasted, hadn't it? She lifted her hand and sifted Harry's hair around her fingers, his golden waves that she loved. She stared and stared at the skylight, and the ghostly reflection of the two of them together, enrobed in each other. She had known pleasure, and she had known what it was to be fully and perfectly united with another human being, and surely that was enough to last a lifetime. Surely that was more than most people ever knew.

She was lucky, really.

❧

At some point, the light began to stir below the unseen horizon.

Olive lifted away the heavy arm that draped across her middle and slipped carefully out from under Harry's body. He stirred. "Come back," he said, reaching for her hand.

"I have to go back, Harry. It's almost dawn."

"'S all right." He was still half-asleep. "'S New Year's Day. No one's awake."

"Cook will be awake."

He tugged on her hand. "Come back. Just another moment."

She almost obeyed him. God help her, she almost gave in. But crawling back into Harry's embrace meant making love to him again, as inevitably as light poured from the sun, and she couldn't do that to him. It would be like telling him a lie, and she didn't want to end it with a lie.

She bent down and kissed his forehead instead. "Go back to sleep."

Harry closed his eyes, and his hand fell back into the blankets.

Olive's body was exhausted, aching, but her mind remained painfully alert. She gathered up her scattered garments and put them on again, one by one, struggling a little with the corset, even though it was designed for a woman in service, who had no servant of her own. For women like her. She pinned her hair back in its usual sedate knot, but she shoved her white cap in the pocket of her pinafore apron.

When she was done, when there was not a single excuse for remaining, she stood by the door and allowed her gaze to travel along the brick walls, along the floor stacked with canvases, to the easel, to the drawings and paintings leaning against every possible vertical surface, to the careless bits and pieces of the artist's trade strewn about. (She had tried to tidy it up for him once, but he had only laughed and told her to stop, because he wouldn't be able to find anything if she put it all away.) Her gaze fell at last on the unfinished study for his mural, the one of Saint George, every line of which was sewn into her memory, and for an instant, she saw it as a stranger might: a visitor off the street outside, unfamiliar with the artist and his studio and his work. She thought, in wonder, *My God, he has such an immense talent, such a boundless imagination.* And her chest hurt, because she saw his future spreading out before him, grand and ambitious and full of color, and she had no place in it.

She turned away, without looking at the man sprawled over the cushions near the dressing screen, his beautiful limbs covered by blankets that smelled faintly of turpentine and human love.

The pain in her chest was already too great to bear.

❖

Harry was right: nobody stirred in the great house as she crept down to the nunnery and changed into an ordinary dress, shivering as the chill air of her bedroom struck her bare arms. Outside the small window, Manhattan lay in cold and dirty quadrangles, shrouded in smoke from a million coal fires, so that you couldn't tell who was rich and who was poor. Which block contained a single breathtaking Beaux Arts mansion and which contained a row of cramped and narrow brownstones. Sprawling, striving, charcoal-dusted Manhattan. How she hated it. How she loved it.

She gathered up her petty belongings and put them into the small valise with which she had arrived here, two months ago, on a November morning that now seemed like another lifetime. She settled her threadbare wool coat over her back and wrapped her muffler over the collar, and still she shivered a little. Maybe the cold wasn't on the outside, after all.

As she slipped down the staircase, she caught sight of the handsome Louis Quatorze commode that stood near the study door, and she paused. The empty wineglass had already been removed by some industrious housemaid. *Poor Prunella,* she thought, and the words surprised her. Poor Prunella? But it was true. The fury in Olive's heart last night had ebbed into pity. Poor Prunella, trapped in her pretty gilded body, behind her pretty gilded face, with no way to break free from herself. No possibility of finding happiness, even for a day, even for a single night. No possibility of redemption.

Olive had come to a stop, standing there in the landing, staring at the priceless piece of furniture before her. The rich golden detail was almost invisible in the smoky dawn that filtered from the dome at the top of the staircase. How perfectly silent the house lay! Each chair and beam and tendon, each square of marble and inch of plaster, seemed to hold its breath, as if waiting for some extraordinary turn of destiny.

Another thought came to her through the stillness: that it was in her power, just now, to perform an act of grace.

The study door was closed, but Olive opened it without hesitation. She was surprised to see that the room had not been attended to; each paper lay exactly where she had left it last night. She arranged everything back in its neat leather portfolio and put the portfolio back in its place, and when she was done, and the desk was tidy once more, she opened the topmost drawer with her key and took out a sheet of fine ecru stationery and a black fountain pen.

If a man is wise,
he will sell his assets in the P&R at the earliest opportunity.

From a Well-Wisher

She left the paper on the desk, in the center of the leather blotter.

❊

As Olive opened the small service door in the basement, then climbed up the iron staircase to the street, she heard sounds of life at last. A commotion was taking place on the street outside, a most untoward commotion, involving a delivery wagon and a number of men in a high state of furor. They were carrying something from the back of the wagon, long and thick and wrapped in blankets, and as Olive paused in astonishment next to the small iron gate, a head lolled to the side from one end of the bundle, blond-haired and bloodstained, and she realized that it belonged to Gus Pratt.

"Why, what's happened?" she exclaimed, and one of the men turned and spoke in an Irish lilt.

"Got himself in a wee bit of a brawl, didn't he, poor bugger. Knocked on the old head."

"Is he alive?"

"Only just, miss."

Two of the men began to pound on the great double door, while the others hoisted Gus on their shoulders, in the manner of pallbearers. Olive clutched her valise and stared at Gus's senseless head, and she thought, *So this is what the house was waiting for.*

She stood there until the door opened at last, and a cry sounded from within. The men hustled Gus inside, and the door slammed behind them, echoing down the empty street, into the dawn of the New Year.

Twenty-seven

❦

JULY 1920

Lucy

"Young!"

It was Dottie, one of the other residents, shouting through Lucy's door. The door was closed, but the wood was thin, not like the thick oak of the doors downstairs.

Lucy cracked the door open. "Yes?"

She didn't much like Dottie, who had a rude laugh and a habit of leaving her stockings hanging in the bathroom.

"Gentleman caller to see you," said Dottie. She jerked a thumb toward the stairs. "With Matron."

Lucy started to close the door. "I'll be right down."

"Well, la-di-da," said Dottie, and flounced off in a wave of scent.

With trepidation, Lucy pinned on her collar, straightened her cuffs, anchored the pins that held up her hair in a low knot on the back of her neck. There was something about the way Dottie had said *gentleman* . . . a leer and a hint of envy. Philip had promised to give her time, but Philip was Philip and accustomed to being granted his every whim.

Was that what she was? A whim? Lucy's fingers went automatically to the chain around her throat. Much, she suspected, as her mother had been to Harry Pratt.

Philip had offered her answers, but she wasn't sure, now, that she wanted those answers. Or the price she would have to pay for them.

Lucy shook her head at herself as she started down the narrow back stairs. What a fool she was! Most women wouldn't consider life with Philip Schuyler too high a price to pay; two weeks ago, the very prospect would have made her feel as Cinderella must, when her prince appeared, slipper in hand.

But that was before she had met John Ravenel.

The third floor of Stornaway House was bustling with activity. On a Saturday, the common room was packed with residents and their guests. Some sat waiting for callers, flipping through brightly illustrated papers; others were having a gossip behind the fronds of the large potted palms Matron had brought in, in an attempt to brighten the heavy woodwork of the dark-paneled room. The mural in the narrow hallway leading to the common room, with its knight rampant and cringing dragon, was all but obscured; only the top of the knight's spear and his surprised eyes were visible.

Dottie was there, lounging against the wall. She eyed Lucy assessingly as Lucy walked past, and Lucy heard her murmur, "La-di-da," to her companion, another woman, not a resident, with a too-fussy hat and suspiciously pink cheeks.

Lucy looked for Philip Schuyler's golden head and didn't see it. But Matron was there, standing near one of the potted palms, speaking with a gentleman whose back was to Lucy. Lucy's step slowed as she recognized the curly dark hair, the broad back. Her stomach gave a lurch of excitement, but Dottie was watching, so she made an effort to keep her step steady and a pleasant smile on her face.

"Mr. Ravenel," she said, proud of how even her voice sounded.

"Miss Young." He swung around just a little too quickly, the eagerness of the movement belying the calculated politeness of his voice. His eyes caught hers and Lucy knew, with certainty, that nothing she ever felt for Philip Schuyler would be half the equal of this. It was like magic, the current that leapt between them, that made the rest of the room fall away as if it had never been.

Easily, he said, "I was just telling your good Mrs. Johnston that you were kind enough to invite me to see this architectural gem." In a lower voice, for her ears only, he murmured, "They gave me your message."

Her heart was pounding, her fingers were tingling, but she managed, somehow, to say in a normal voice, "I thought you might enjoy it." To Matron: "Mr. Ravenel is a dealer in art and antiquities."

"So I hear." Did Matron actually dimple? No, that was too much. But she was looking at Mr. Ravenel with what passed for her as unqualified approval. "I have a reproduction of one of the elder Mr. Ravenel's paintings. I had the privilege of seeing the original in the Museum of Art in Philadelphia."

Lucy looked quizzically up at John. She'd had no idea that his father was quite so famous. "We had to let some of the paintings go," he said to her, as if in answer to a question. "I've tried, when possible, to sell to institutions rather than private individuals. My father felt strongly about art being available to everyone, not just the few."

"But one must make a living?" said Matron.

Lucy wasn't sure what magic John had wrought, but they appeared to be on excellent terms. Or maybe, she thought giddily, that was just John. He had a way of setting people at ease, making them comfortable in their own skins.

And he had come here. For her. He placed one hand unobtrusively beneath Lucy's elbow, just a small gesture, not the sort of touch to which Matron could possibly object, but Lucy could feel warmth rushing through her, warmth and the certainty that all would be well, was well.

"This house," Matron was saying, "is very much a testament to that. The carvings are in themselves works of art. It does seem rather . . . out of proportion that all this was intended, at one time, merely for the private use of one family."

"I understand the Pratt family used to live here?" John said, so casually that Lucy wouldn't have known there was anything more to it but for the tightening of his fingers on her elbow.

In the midst of her haze of happiness, she felt a moment's doubt. But no. Just because he was pursuing his own interests didn't mean his feelings for her weren't just as real. She hadn't imagined the way he looked at her, the touch of his fingers on her elbow, the subtle possessiveness in the way he stood, his body shielding hers, claiming her.

"Their loss is our gain," Matron said practically. "Such houses have become unwieldy as private homes, but they serve very well for communal living. We were forced to make some changes, of course, but we have done our best to retain the unique character of the house."

"I was admiring the mural in the hall," said John. "Saint George?"

"A red-cross knight forever kneeled / To a lady on his shield," quoted Matron, unexpectedly and fancifully. Apologetically, she said, "Yes, I believe it is Saint George. But if you want to see the real treasure of Stornaway House . . ."

There was a hullaballoo by the billiards table.

Matron broke off with a tsk of annoyance. "If I have told Miss Brennan once, I have told her a dozen times. If her young man provokes one more altercation . . . Forgive me, Mr. Ravenel. I'm afraid I can't offer you that tour just now. If you would care to return again during visiting hours next weekend . . ."

"Nothing would give me greater pleasure," John assured her. "But I'm afraid I leave for Charleston on Tuesday."

"You have enjoyed your stay in New York?" Matron was frowning over John's shoulder, at the crowd by the billiards table.

"Far more than I ever imagined." The words were for Matron, but John looked at Lucy as he said them. "This visit has been . . . a revelation."

Lucy nodded mutely, not trusting herself to speak. Who knew it was possible to feel this strongly, on such scant acquaintance? She felt as though nerves she had never known she possessed had been awakened; every look, every word, awakened a delightful agony of anticipation.

"Since you are leaving so soon . . ." Beneath the thick spectacles, Matron's blue eyes twinkled. "It is a slight breach of the rules, but for a gentleman involved in the arts . . . Miss Young, would you be so kind as to take Mr. Ravenel up to the seventh floor?"

"There's a seventh floor?" Lucy's voice came out rather more breathless than she would have liked. "That is, I always assumed the attic rooms were at the very top."

Matron looked pleased. "They are usually, but not in Stornaway House. The seventh floor is a well-kept secret."

"A secret?" Lucy felt John's attention being diverted from her. "That sounds intriguing."

"It's nothing so exciting as that, just a rather unusual little room . . . Miss Brennan! If you'll pardon me, Mr. Ravenel, I really must have a word with Miss Brennan's young man." Her voice brisk, Matron said, "The main staircase doesn't reach all the way up, but you'll find the service stairs at the end of the fifth-floor corridor. Be sure to shut the door again when you're done."

Matron didn't mean . . . well. But Lucy felt the color rising in her cheeks all the same. Before, she and John had always been in public, in Delmonico's, in Central Park, in Mrs. Whitney's studio, snatching their moments of privacy in the midst of dozens of uninterested people. But on the seventh floor, they would be well and truly alone.

There were, thought Lucy, feeling a silly giggle rising in her throat, rules about gentlemen in one's room, but this wasn't her room, was it? It was the secret room on the seventh floor. So that was all right, then.

"Thank you," said John Ravenel, snatching Lucy's arm and speaking, for him, quite rapidly. "I surely am grateful for this opportunity."

"You must let me know what you think of our little treasure," said Matron serenely, before turning, and saying in quite another voice altogether, "Miss Brennan!"

John whisked Lucy to the stairs at a gait just short of a run.

"Eager to see what's on the seventh floor?" said Lucy breathlessly, as they rounded the curve of the stair on the fourth floor.

"Eager to see you," said John, pausing so abruptly that Lucy nearly ran into him. "Ever since I received your message, I've been hoping—" One of the bedroom doors opened, and John broke off. "Oh, for the love of— Let's get upstairs. We'll have some privacy there."

"Do you think . . . ," said Lucy, feeling suddenly shy. "Do you think that's what Matron had in mind?"

"An honorable woman like Mrs. Johnston?" said John, his drawl thickening. His voice turned serious as he looked at Lucy. "She just wants to make sure a hidden artistic treasure gets proper appreciation."

"Or improper appreciation?" said Lucy daringly.

"That, too." His dark eyes rested on her lips, moved lower. "Er— where do we go from here?"

The transition was so abrupt that Lucy laughed. "Like Matron said, the main stairs stop on the fifth floor. We'll have to take the servants' stairs. If you don't feel too cheapened by that."

"Nothing to do with you could ever be cheap," said John.

"Then you don't know the cost of this skirt," retorted Lucy, but her hand trembled on the banister. The force of his regard made her feel weak, shaky, as if she were no longer entirely in possession of herself.

From the time she was very small, she had known she had to be strong. Her mother was so withdrawn, her father someone to be protected as much as a protector. With no siblings, her cousins largely estranged, Lucy had kept mostly to herself, a quiet, self-contained child, an anomaly in her father's large, boisterous German family.

For the first time, she contemplated what it would be to let herself go, to relax that stern control. It was both exhilarating and terrifying, the idea of relinquishing her own strength, allowing her to lean on someone else.

There was something so sturdy about John, so reliable.

It didn't take them much time to find the stair to the seventh floor, in an alcove Lucy had always assumed to be a broom closet. The stair itself was narrow and unassuming, the walls painted with the same graying whitewash as the servants' floor, the stairs uncarpeted.

At the top, John paused. "Before we go in— I just wanted you to know that I would be here even if no Pratt had ever set foot in this house. I came for you. Not for them. When they gave me your message—"

Lucy touched a finger to his lips. "Hush," she said firmly.

John hushed.

"Yesterday—I knew as soon as I'd left you that I overreacted. It was just . . ." Lucy struggled for the right words. Her family had never been one for sharing their emotions; this was an uncharted vocabulary. She felt like a toddler, just learning to use language. "I was scared."

"I scared you?" John's face was the picture of remorse. "Lucy, I swear on my father's soul, I never intended . . ."

"No, no," Lucy said quickly. "You didn't scare me. I scared me. The Pratts were just an excuse. I got scared and I ran away. It's just—" She took a deep breath and said, quietly, "I've never felt like this about anyone."

John's arms wrapped around her, folding her close, his cheek resting against the top of her head. "Neither have I," he murmured. "Neither have I."

They stood in the cramped stair, neither of them feeling the heat or minding the musty smell of an enclosed space too long neglected. Lucy leaned the full weight of her body against his, her chest molding to his, her head fitting perfectly into the space between his ear and his neck, and knew that she had, at long last, come home. Wherever John Ravenel was, that was home.

"Do you think," she said, after a very long time, "that we ought to see that room?"

"Most likely," said John, making no effort to move. "We wouldn't want to disappoint Matron."

Lucy thought of the twinkle in Matron's eye. "I don't think she would be disappointed."

John's arms tightened around her. "She's an excellent woman, your Mrs. Johnston."

Lightly, Lucy said, "Shall we invite her to the wedding?"

"Mmm," said John, and with a kiss on the top of her head, reluctantly let her go. "Shall we enter the Bluebeard chamber?"

"You don't think it's full of discarded wives?" Lucy ran ahead of him up the last few stairs. Turning back, she saw a curious expression on John's face. She burst into a laugh. "Oh, really! You don't think we'll find heads on pikes?"

"Was it just the heads?" said John, abstractedly. "I don't remember the story all that well."

"Neither do I," Lucy admitted. The handle resisted her pressure; she had to push before the door gave, creaking all the way. "I just remember—oh."

Light. Sudden, dancing, brilliant light.

Light poured in through long windows that made three sides of the room more glass than wall, making the room seem to float in the sky. But the most brilliant light of all came from the ceiling, refracted through the panes of a miniature dome, the prism-like panels shimmering in the sunlight. Lucy saw rainbows, a miracle of rainbows, glittering across the worn Oriental carpet, dancing across the elaborately incised tin of the ceiling, turning the dusty room into something magical and rare.

"My God," murmured John, behind her, his hands on her shoulders.

Lucy's fingers covered his. "Who would have thought?"

Amazing to think this had been up here all this time, just above her room, and she had never known.

"The proportions—," John was saying.

Lucy let the words wash over her, just taking it all in. On a second view, the signs of neglect were clear. The carpet must have been fine once, but the sunlight had faded it in parts to gray. An old sheepskin rug lay before the cold fireplace, the wool thick with dust, and, Lucy suspected, more than a few moths.

Someone must have removed the furniture that had once been here. All that remained was a faded chaise longue, the upholstery tattered (mice, thought Lucy mechanically), and a squat Chinese cabinet, the once brilliant gold paint filmed with dust.

But even so, even shabby and neglected, the room had a beauty that couldn't be denied. It was a perfect square, the high ceiling with its miniature dome making the room feel cool even in the heat of the July day. There was something magical about it, like walking through a door in a perfectly ordinary house and finding oneself in a piece of the Alhambra.

"Look!" said Lucy, pointing. "Saint George!"

Above the fireplace, three terra-cotta squares had been set into the wall, colored stones creating intricate designs. The two on either side were heraldic shields, vaguely medieval. But in the center square was the saint himself, the same Saint George who had watched over Lucy's childhood bed, shield in one hand, spear in the other.

A red-cross knight, Matron had said. Lucy moved across the room, the worn floorboards creaking beneath her sensible shoes. Despite time and dust, the cross on Saint George's shield was still a brave crimson. Tentatively, Lucy lifted a hand to touch it—and a brick slid out below.

No, not just a brick. A cluster of bricks. Five or six of them, all welded together, and, behind them, a shallow cavity and the pale gleam of paper, sheets of it.

Most likely someone's old laundry list or a pile of bills.

For a moment Lucy hesitated. Matron might have allowed them up here, but that didn't give her the right to rifle through the room's secrets.

And, then, from far away, she heard her mother's voice, faint, gasping. *Harry.*

With sudden resolution, Lucy reached into the hole. It might not be anything to do with her, but if it was . . . she had the right to know; she needed to know.

The sheets of paper had been closely written in an angular hand, the prose tortured and oddly formal.

January 30, 1893

Dear Mr. Pratt,

As per your request, I have discovered the whereabouts of the former Miss Olive Van Alan, once maidservant in your mother's employ. Miss Van Alan married Hans Jungmann in a small ceremony in Brooklyn on January the tenth of this year. The couple currently reside in Mr. Jungmann's mother's home in Brooklyn, where Mr. Jungmann has assumed the partnership in a bakery.

It went on, but Lucy's eyes only skated over the rest, details, as familiar to her as her own hand, of her grandmother's home, her father's family, the grocery in Manhattan he had sold when he married her mother.

Once maidservant in your mother's employ . . .

Her mother, her elegant mother, a maid? The letter was from a Pinkerton agent. Surely, it was a bit extreme to hire a Pinkerton agent to track down an erring member of staff? And why hide the report here, in this forgotten room on the seventh floor? Nothing made sense, nothing at all.

With stiff hands, Lucy turned to the next page. The paper was different, thicker, richer, an embossed monogram at the top, the handwriting fluid, the ink a rich black. The date at the top read January 30, 1893.

My darling Olive, it began. Or had almost begun. The salutation had been crossed out, replaced with a curt, *Mrs. Jungmann—because I can no longer call you dear. But how can I call you anything else? You will always be dear to me, no matter how far you have run, or how you have hurt me. Why? Why, my darling? Didn't you trust me just a little? Didn't you know I knew, almost from the beginning—* The sentence ended there, with a blot.

Knew what? Not about Lucy. He couldn't have known about Lucy from the beginning; there wouldn't have been a Lucy.

These past weeks have been a fever dream, my only hope that I might find you. But I never thought to find you married to another. How could you? How could you leave my bed and—Did you never love me as I love you? Oh, my Olive. . . .

This house has become a prison to me; I see you everywhere, but when I reach for you, I wake, and you are gone. There is nothing for me here without you. I have packed my paints and easel and booked a ticket west. Where I go doesn't matter, not anymore. Perhaps I shall find the lost treasure domes of Kublai Khan. Without you, they will be dim and dull.

Farewell, my love

It wasn't signed. It didn't need to be. Nor was it the only one of its kind. There were three other drafts of the same letter, some crumpled, one torn down the middle, none sent.

Lucy's heart ached for her mother, but also for the man she had always believed to be her father, for Hans Jungmann, who had loved her mother so long and so devotedly, but always from a distance, never quite able to touch her heart.

And now Lucy knew why.

Why had her mother left Harry Pratt? What had he known, almost from the beginning? Why had her mother married Hans Jungmann? How could she have, knowing how she felt about Harry Pratt, particularly if—

January. Lucy's eyes flew to the date, riveted on the numbers, curving and elegant, bold in black ink. She had scarcely noticed the date before, too intent on the content of the letter. But there it was. January.

Lucy had been born in late November. If Harry Pratt had followed through with his resolution, if he had left for parts unknown by the end of January, even if he had seen Lucy's mother again before he left, there was no way he could be Lucy's father.

Lucy felt an unexpected surge of joy, coupled with a weakening rush of tears as a kaleidoscope of memories danced around her, rainbow bright. Her father—truly her father—wiping away her childhood tears, gently painting iodine on a scraped knee, giving her a cookie, reading her a story. The thrill of going for a walk with him, holding carefully to his large hand, the careful courtesy with which he tipped his hat to their neighbors, the joy of being swung up on his large shoulders to pick a peach from the tree in their neighbor's backyard.

Vati, Vati, I miss you so.

She didn't say it aloud, but her throat vibrated with the words. Lucy felt the sunlight through the skylight warm on her head, like her father's hand, like a blessing, and knew that he was there with her, would be always.

With the papers trembling in her hand, Lucy turned away from the fireplace. "John?" Her voice sounded strange in the high-ceilinged room, rusty and hoarse. "I've found something."

"So have I." John was sitting cross-legged on the floor in front of the Chinese cabinet, the bottom drawer open, a pile of yellowing papers on his lap.

"It's—" Lucy didn't know how to begin. Pity for her mother, love for her father, relief and confusion, all warred together. So she just blurted it out, her knuckles white against the yellowing pages. "John— I'm not Harry Pratt's daughter."

"I can't tell you how happy that makes me." John looked up, his eyes meeting Lucy's. His face had a dazed expression, as he said, "Because I'm pretty sure that Harry Pratt was my father."

Twenty-eight

AUGUST 1944

Kate

Danny O'Shea was an older boy in the neighborhood whom I'd grown up with and walked to school with, and I even imagined, when I was very young and didn't know that I wanted to be a doctor, that he and I might marry one day. Danny joined the Army right after Pearl Harbor and had been killed eight months later at Guadalcanal. Before he'd left that last time, he'd given me my first kiss and made silly promises we hadn't meant, for a future when the war would be behind us. He'd told me with the enthusiasm of a child with a new toy what he envisioned his life in the Army would be like, sharing with me how heavy all the gear was that he'd have to march and fight with. It had been inconceivable to me then, how any soldier—any person—could manage to fight battles with such a load on their backs.

But I imagined now, as I navigated through my daily routine, a little of what it must have been like, my knees nearly buckling from the weight of my own burden as I took each step. I kept remembering Danny telling me that a person got used to it. I just had to hope that he was right.

"Kate."

My hand froze on the banister. I'd seen Cooper leave with Caroline an hour before, which was the only reason I'd left the dark privacy of Dr. Greeley's office. Cooper was leaving today, and I didn't want to see him, to offer him a cheerful good-bye while Caroline and Dr. Greeley looked on. I didn't want my mask to crack and reveal my true feelings.

"Kate," Cooper said again.

I braced myself, then turned around to face him, but nothing could prepare me for the way the skin tightened over my bones. He stood on the landing where he'd just exited the elevator, holding his hat and cane, his eyes dark and brooding, and I almost gave in then. But I forced myself to keep hold on the railing, to forbid my feet from taking a step forward.

"Have you been avoiding me?" he asked, his consonants slipping, his accent more prominent since he'd been spending time with Caroline.

"No, of course not," I stammered. "There's just a lot of paperwork . . ." I stopped, watching as he moved to stand directly in front of me.

"We need to talk."

"I'm sorry, but I'm just so busy . . ."

I was interrupted by three burly orderlies approaching the large bookcase behind where Cooper and I were standing. The corner of the oversized piece of furniture had been protruding into the hallway since the first attempt to move it several weeks before. I wasn't sure what had precipitated them being there now, but I was grateful for the interruption.

"Excuse us, Doctor," the largest man said. "We've been instructed to move this piece of furniture down to the lobby."

"It's no problem. We were just finishing up here."

Cooper responded by taking my elbow and moving me back toward the elevator to give the men room. He continued to hold on, as if he were afraid that I would escape, as we watched the men grapple with the bookcase and slowly begin their descent down the stairs. I watched in morbid fascination, glad they were at a hospital with readily available medical help should it be required.

While still listening to the grunts of the men, I looked up at Cooper, determined to shake his hand and give him a brisk good-bye. But his eyes were focused on something behind me, the light in his eyes so strange that I had to turn around to see what it was.

The removal of the bookcase had created a wider hallway, but it had also laid bare the wall behind it. But the wall wasn't bare, exactly. A mural eight to ten feet wide and just as high stretched across the plaster, its brilliant colors not dimmed by time because of its protected spot. But that's not what mesmerized me; not the exquisite artistry of the piece or even the size and scope of it or the fact that the mural had been hidden behind a piece of furniture for decades. *I've seen this before.* Yes, that's what it was, although I couldn't remember exactly *where* I'd seen it. Only that I recalled every detail, from the glimmering metal of the sword to the look of fear in the dragon's eye.

"It's Saint George slaying the dragon," Cooper said, his voice almost reverential.

"Yes," I said. At least I think I spoke aloud. We were both cautiously moving forward, oddly hesitant to approach, as if the dragon were real and could do us harm.

Cooper leaned down to where the artist had scrawled his signature. He stared at it for a long time before standing, his brows knitted together. "I don't understand. I know this artist. The brushstrokes, the use of colors, the . . ." He fought to find the right word. "The movement," he finished. "It's undoubtedly his, but that's not his signature."

I moved to stand next to him and studied the name in the bottom right corner. "H. Pratt." I looked up at Cooper. "Who did you think it was?"

He shook his head. "Does this look familiar to you? Do you recognize the style? It's the same as in the sketches, isn't it? The same artist."

He frowned at the signature. "But I know this artist, and it's not H. Pratt."

I studied the mural for a long time, trying to forget how familiar this particular scene was and focus instead on the artistic style of it. I frowned at the swirl of paint that showed the cerulean sky, and then down toward the way the pigmented light reflected off the dragon's scales. My eyes widened as I remembered. "Yes," I said, recalling all of those art exhibitions my mother had dragged me to when I was a little girl. "Augustus Ravenel." My voice was breathless, as if holding back the two simple words.

"Exactly. Augustus Ravenel." He paused. "My grandfather."

"But . . ." I stopped, my own mind yawning open as I realized where I'd seen it before. "My mother had this exact mural on her bedroom wall that her mother, Olive, painted for her. I never saw it, but this is how she described it to me in such detail. It's almost as if I had actually seen it before." I stared at the mural, at the signature that seemed right and wrong at the same time as all the pieces in the puzzle slowly circled in my brain, each trying to slot itself into the correct space.

Our eyes met in mutual understanding. Cooper put his hand on my arm as if to anchor himself. "It would seem that Harry Pratt and Augustus Ravenel are one and the same."

I recalled Harry Pratt's sketches that Cooper had found in the small chest in the attic, the sketches of Olive wearing the ruby necklace, and the air began to thrum between us. "The woman in those sketches, the woman wearing the ruby necklace. She was my grandmother. Her name was Olive." I paused, wondering how to tell him the rest. "My grandmother . . . ," I began.

"And Harry were lovers." He said it matter-of-factly, as if he'd already figured it out.

I nodded. "But it didn't end well, I don't think. Harry disappeared and Olive married my grandfather, a baker named Hans Jungmann." I touched the spot on my blouse under which the ruby necklace lay. "She never forgot Harry, though. Because she painted this same mural on my mother's nursery room wall. And she kept this necklace." I pulled it out of my blouse. "Harry's sister, Prunella, said my grandmother stole it, but I don't think that's the truth. My grandmother cherished it, gave it to her daughter, Lucy. My mother. And she gave it to me."

He sent me a piercing look. "Lucy? And what did you say her maiden name was?"

"Jungmann. But she changed it to Young when she came to work for my father's law firm. Lucy Young."

He stared at me for a long moment, his cheeks noticeably paler. "On my father's deathbed, he dictated a letter to me to a Lucy Young in New York, to the attention of the law firm of Cromwell, Polk and Moore." He paused, weighing his words. "It was a love letter, telling Lucy that he'd never stopped loving her or wanting her. That she was the love of his life."

"The letter . . . did you send it?"

Slowly, he shook his head. "I planned to mail it right after his funeral. But I left it on my dressing table and my mother found it and destroyed it. I realized how much my father had hurt her, which is why I never tried to find Lucy on his behalf. It would have been a betrayal to my own mother. I never imagined . . ."

He stopped, unable to finish, but he didn't need to. I knew exactly what he was going to say. Something about probabilities and fate, and the vagaries of a chaotic world that had brought us together.

He looked away, seemingly oblivious to the sounds of the orderlies, the ringing phone and chattering nurses. It was all so removed from us and the small cocoon of time his words had created. He took a step forward, staring at something in the top right corner of the mural. It was a small crowd of people wearing medieval clothing, a dark raincloud painted behind them and making the colors of their garments stand out. "Look," he said, pointing toward the middle of the cloud, where swirls of the paintbrush seemed to blend the fog and spectators together.

I leaned forward, too, staring at where he indicated. "What am I supposed to see?" And then I did. Hidden among the group of people and nearly obscured by the gray smokelike fog was a woman. A woman who looked exactly like me, and whose face had been re-created in a small oil miniature and handed down through three generations of men in the same family. I stepped back, my hand pressed against my chest, the solid feel of Cooper behind me.

"Do you see it?" he asked.

"Yes," I said, then stopped, realizing that it wasn't just the woman he was showing me. Cooper's fingers traced over her arm toward her hand. "She's pointing at something."

The background of the mural seemed to shift in front of me like an optical illusion, the leaves of trees in the surrounding forest seemingly transforming themselves into something else entirely. Something that looked astonishingly like a square made of painted bricks, a design that resembled a heraldic coat of arms. A design I was very familiar with.

Without a word Cooper took my arm and propelled me to the elevator, his limp hardly evident. Neither one of us spoke as he slid open the gate and then closed it again before pressing the button for the sixth floor.

"Cooper, really, this isn't a good idea. Whatever happened between our grandparents and parents has nothing to do with us, don't you see?"

He faced me and I realized that he was angry. But there was something else, too, a look of desperation in his eyes that resembled what I saw in my own reflection when I bothered to study it closely enough. Without warning, he leaned forward and kissed me, his mouth hard and demanding, my head pressed against the wall of the elevator. I told myself that I would have pulled away if I'd had somewhere to move, that I didn't want him to touch me, to kiss me. But neither thought stopped me from kissing him back.

The elevator shuddered to a stop, and he lifted his face away from mine, his eyes still dark. He slid open the gate and followed me from the elevator and toward the stairs that led to the seventh floor. I knew without asking that we were headed to the attic room, and I balked, not wanting to be confronted with the memories of the night we'd spent there, of the moonlight mixed with the smell of paint and dust and us.

But I knew, too, that this was where the bricks Olive pointed to in the mural were, and how neither Cooper nor I could leave it alone until we had all the tarnished pieces of Olive and Harry's love affair laid open and exposed before us. The only thing I was unsure of was what we were supposed to do once we had all the answers.

Cooper's bed had been stripped of its sheets, the brown blanket folded neatly at the bottom and matching the other two empty beds. The room appeared to be more of a dormitory now instead of a room forgotten at the top of the old mansion, a room whose walls contained more than just bricks and mortar. I stood by the wall opposite the window, not looking in that direction so I wouldn't remember. As if I could block out that night any more than I could forget the color of my own hair.

Cooper walked toward the bed and placed his hat and cane on top of the blanket. After a quick glance in my direction, he approached the fireplace where three squares had been painted on the bricks in a heraldic design. But the one in the middle was different, displaying Saint George, the red cross over his chest like a beacon marking treasure. Cooper reached out his hand, hesitating only a moment, then gently pressed his fingers against the cross. A cluster of bricks slid out from below the square, revealing a shallow opening.

Looking back at me, he raised an eyebrow. "I feel like Caesar, fixin' to cross the Rubicon."

I almost laughed at his Southernism but found I was trembling too much to do anything else but watch. I didn't come forward, choosing instead to look over his shoulder into the dark space within. At first I thought the hole was empty, hoped it was empty. Because then there would be nothing that would bind us together, nothing that would make our good-bye less than permanent.

But when Cooper reached in and pulled out a stack of paper, I knew that the connection between us that I'd felt the first time I'd seen him was as real and constant as morning following night.

He sat down on the bed and smoothed his hand over the top sheet of paper, staring at the heavily embossed letterhead. "Pinkerton Detective Agency." He looked up at me as if it were my decision for him to proceed. But we both knew that we were already on the far bank of the Rubicon.

I waited quietly while he bent his head to read. When he was done, he slowly raised his head, his eyes troubled.

"What does it say?"

He looked from me to the letter then back again. "Harry hired a detective to find Olive, to make sure she was all right. It says she married Hans Jungmann in 1893. It's dated end of January, the same month you told me that Harry Pratt disappeared. Which, coincidentally, is right before my grandfather, Augustus Ravenel, went to Cuba."

"And changed his name from Harry Pratt." My legs didn't feel strong enough to hold me up anymore, and I moved to the bed and sat down next to Cooper, being careful not to touch him. "I think I know why Olive and Harry were separated."

Cooper turned to me with a lifted brow.

"Prunella," I whispered.

"Prunella, as in Harry's sister. My great-aunt Prunella, apparently."

I nodded. "When I visited her, she told me that she'd always wanted to see Harry again so she could make amends for something horrible she'd done. Maybe she said something or did something that tore them apart. Something they were both powerless to stop."

Cooper nodded slowly. "The timing of it all certainly lends itself to that theory. His sudden disappearance from New York and reappearance in Cuba, and Olive's marriage all in the same year." He gave me an odd look. "When was your mother born?"

I sucked in a quick breath as I found my thoughts wandering down the same dark path. "Not until November of 1893."

"Thank God," he said under his breath.

I glanced at the other letter still folded on his lap. "What's that?"

Laying aside the detective report, he pulled out what appeared to be several attempts at the same letter and then held them between us so we could read them together.

The date at the top read January 30, 1893. *My darling Olive* it began. My eyes read quickly, each word more painful to read than the last, the ink heavier and darker as the author wrote, as if his grief were pouring out onto the paper along with the black ink.

"Farewell, my love," Cooper and I both read out loud as we reached the end, the words soft and sacred.

Cooper carefully placed the letters in the rear of the small stack, leaving another letter, this paper thicker and heavier than the last, the handwriting bolder and crisper, lacking the artistic flourishes of the first writer, and written nearly thirty years later.

Dearest Lucy, it began. My gaze quickly scanned to the bottom of the page. *I love you, Lucy. Always.*

"My father's handwriting," Cooper said softly. "John Ravenel."

I glanced away, not sure I could read it, knowing it was a love letter to my mother from a man who wasn't my father. But I forced myself to read every word of John's plea to convince my mother to move to Charleston and be with him.

"I don't understand why she didn't go with him. There was nothing here for her except for Philip Schuyler, and I know he wasn't her first love."

He let the letters slip from his hands and I looked at the papers scattered around us, the detritus of ill-fated love.

I clasped my fingers together on my lap. "Olive was Harry's muse.

His great love. And even though they both married others and had their own families, a piece of their hearts always belonged to the other."

I stood so I could think clearly. It was too hard with Cooper so close. "And my own mother must have orchestrated her entire relationship with my father so she could somehow claim what she thought was hers, a mistaken belief that she was part of the Pratt legacy because of her mother's love affair with Harry Pratt." I looked up as a thought occurred to me. "She probably even wondered at least at some point if she could be their daughter."

I pressed the heels of my hands against my eyes, as if I could erase the memory of the mural and the necklace. And my mother's constant search for something that could never be hers. "I wonder . . ." I closed my eyes and took a deep breath. "I wonder if my mother ever loved my father. If he ever really knew who she was."

John stood and took my hands. "Were they not happy? Did you never see her laugh?"

"No, I mean, it wasn't like that. My father always made us laugh. He loved us so much, and never stopped trying to make her happy. She must have loved him, in a way. He was just never . . . enough."

He let go of my hands and walked toward the window, his movements agitated and jerky, like a flag in high wind. "Why didn't our parents marry?" He sent me a wry look. "Don't get me wrong—I'm glad they didn't. But why? What happened?" His gaze fell on the black opening behind the bricks. "Maybe we missed something . . ."

His words were forgotten as he walked back toward the fireplace and reached his hand into the dark hole. He screwed his eyes shut for a moment as his hand traveled from corner to corner of the secret compartment, a blind man reading Braille. Then they popped open in surprise as Cooper withdrew something small from the hole behind the bricks.

"What is it?" I asked, but I could tell even from where I stood that it was a black velvet ring box.

Our eyes met as he walked back to the bed and sat down. After a brief hesitation, he lifted the hinged lid. I had already guessed it was a ring, maybe even a valuable one, but I'd never imagined it would be as stunning as the bauble staring up at us from its velvet cushion. The large brilliant-cut diamond nestled in a platinum setting, with tiny diamonds surrounding the larger stone like a queen and her ladies.

"It's at least three carats," Cooper said, his voice almost reverential.

I sat down next to him and reached for the ring. Gently I lifted it from the box, admiring how the designer had made sure that the view from any angle would show off the exquisite artistry of the ring. "There's something inscribed on the inside," I said, bringing it closer to my face, then reading the tiny letters out loud.

To O from H—Always—1-1-93

"He meant to marry her," I said quietly, my heart stretching and pulling inside my chest, an old heartache brought to life again.

"But she married someone else instead, not even two weeks later."

I couldn't look at the ring anymore, a talisman for broken hearts and an *always* that didn't mean what it should. I stuck it back in the box and closed it, then shoved it back into Cooper's hands. "You should take this—it's a family heirloom. You can give it to your fiancée."

He regarded me for a long moment, his eyes narrowed and dark as if I'd just delivered a physical blow.

"So here we are," he said finally. "Back to the place where it all began. It's like fate has brought us together, to find the happy ending our parents and grandparents so desperately sought." He shoved the ring box into his pants pocket, then reached for my hands.

I tried to pull away, but he wouldn't let go.

"Don't you see, Kate? We were meant to be together. From the moment I saw you, I knew. It's always been you." He let go of my hands so he could gently cup my face. "I love you, Kate. And I want us to be together. Come with me to Charleston. You can set up your own medical practice, be the best doctor you can be. And be my wife, the mother of my children. Please, Kate. Let's make all that came before us make sense. Say yes."

How easy it would be to say yes, to give in to everything I'd spent a lifetime fighting. I was an independent woman, my independence hard-won. I knew too much of my grandmother and mother now to believe that love lasted forever, that it would sustain you through an entire lifetime. Wasn't the fact that Cooper and I were here testament to that simple fact?

I pulled away and stood. "And what about Caroline? You are engaged to be married, or have you forgotten? Surely you must have loved her enough at some point to want to marry her. Is she not enough for you now? And how would you know if I'm enough for you? That you won't always be looking beyond me for someone else?"

He stood, too, but stayed where he was. "Kate, I love you. I think I've loved you my whole life. Please. Don't do this. Don't turn your back on something that's taken three generations to make right."

I shook my head, seeing my mother's face as we stood on the sidewalk in front of this same building all those years ago, her expression one of disappointment and regret. *Where had I heard that before?* "No," I said. "I am not Olive or Lucy. I am my own woman who doesn't need a man in her life to survive. I don't want to end up like them. If anything, their mistakes have been the best education for me."

He took a step toward me. "Love isn't a mistake. But I know true love is rare enough that when you find it you fight for it. Marry me, Kate. Come back to Charleston with me and be with me for the rest of our lives."

I began backing up toward the door. "I can't." I shook my head, my eyes blinded with unshed tears.

He didn't follow me, but his words were strong enough to hold me back. "Tell me you don't love me and I will let you go. Just tell me that you don't love me."

I saw him through the haze of tears, imagined I could see his eyes, which were the color of winter grass. And I remembered my mother and her constant sadness. *Disappointment and regret.* I opened my mouth and let the words fall out before I could call them back. "I don't love you."

He didn't move, didn't make a sound. Maybe that was what being struck by a bullet was like, how you didn't know you'd been hit until you began to bleed.

"Good-bye, Cooper."

I didn't run away this time, but walked steadily and purposefully out the door. He didn't follow me, nor did I expect him to. I'd told him what he wanted to hear, what I needed to say so that I could walk away. If only my heart hadn't betrayed me by remaining back in the forgotten room, in that one place where our story had really begun more than fifty years before.

Twenty-nine

꧁꧂

NEW YEAR'S DAY 1894

Olive

For the second time in her life, Olive was awake when the clock chimed midnight on the thirty-first of December, and the old year slid irretrievably into the new.

She hadn't meant to be awake. She had hoped that 1894 would steal in through the window while she slept, silent and unnoticed, but this was the first lesson you learned as a new mother: Small babies have little, if any, regard for the wishes or convenience of their parents.

So Olive cradled Lucy's downy head to her breast and listened to the soft chime of the clock on the mantel, and as each note dinged gently into the air, her eyes began to sting and her fingers to shake. (That was another lesson: In the small hours of the morning, while a baby suckled at your breast, you felt as if you were the only two beings alive in the universe, and this loneliness magnified each emotion—whether joy or sorrow or wonder—into something a hundred times greater than your ordinary feelings.) Before Olive's eyes, the movement of Lucy's urgent little mouth started to blur, and a drop fell on that round cheek, just as the twelfth chime struck, and the room went quiet.

And that was that. Lucy went on nursing, not missing a beat, and the earth presumably continued to spin on its axis. Olive lifted a finger and traced the delicate curve of Lucy's ear, the most beautiful thing in God's creation, and slowly the tremors died away into her middle, deep inside, where no one could see them. As it should be.

Where was Harry at this moment? (She could now ask that question to herself without bursting into tears and perplexing poor Hans.) If she closed her eyes, she could feel him, wherever he was. The other side of the world, perhaps. No one knew where he had gone, and the Pratt house now stood empty of life, waiting for the auction that would empty it of objects, too. That was according to the newspapers, which had also covered, in breathless detail, both the wedding of Miss Prunella Pratt to Mr. Harrison Schuyler in October, and the financial ruin of Mr. Henry August Pratt the following month. Apparently he hadn't taken Olive's advice and divested of those Philadelphia & Reading shares, after all.

Or perhaps he had been too distracted with grief for his sons: one dead and the other missing.

Missing. But Harry wasn't missing, not really. He was right here, wrapping his arms around her, looking down over her shoulder at Lucy's hungry movements. *She's beautiful, just like her mother,* he whispered in Olive's ear, just before he placed a kiss on her temple.

She could actually feel that kiss, warm and soft on her exhausted skin. *You're a wonderful mother. I am so proud of you.*

And then, even more quietly: *I forgive you.*

No, Harry hadn't gone away at all. He was still there, inside her head. Occupying the chambers of her heart.

Lucy's eyelids were drooping now, and the rhythm of her suckling began to slow. The lamp flickered over her skin. She was five weeks old, and just awakening to the extraordinary world around her. She liked the sounds and sights of the bakery. Olive would sometimes nurse her there, because it was so warm, and Hans's face would light up at the sight of his daughter. He would reach out his floury hands and cradle her in the crook of his massive elbow, and she would stare up into his delighted face and brighten, too, just like the Christmas tree that stood in the parlor, decked with candles. Already Lucy adored her father, just as Olive had adored hers.

As if he could read her thoughts, Olive's husband stirred in the bed behind her. The springs creaked under his weight, and his voice emerged from somewhere inside all those blankets, blurry with sleep. *"Meine Frau? Wo bist du?"*

"Right here," she answered. Inevitably, she had picked up a little German over the past several months, just enough to understand her new relatives when they spoke among themselves, though she always addressed them in English. "With Lucy."

"Ah, there she is. *Meine kleine Schönheit.*"

"Your very hungry little beauty. But she's almost finished, I think."

Hans yawned gigantically. "Bring her here, when she is done."

Lucy's mouth dropped away at last, and Olive lifted her carefully to her shoulder. The wind rose at once, thank God. Some nights Olive felt as if she were patting Lucy's tiny back forever, while she staggered with fatigue, mindless, almost falling asleep where she stood. And still patting, patting, the way a snake keeps moving after its head is cut off.

She tucked her breast back into her nightgown and rose from the chair. Hans lifted the blankets, and the warmth of his body seeped out from within, scented with soap. Her husband had clean habits, washing himself with a cloth in the morning and bathing at night before bed. To take away the yeast and the flour, he said, and Olive was grateful for that. She sank into the mattress, and Hans's large hands stole into her arms and lifted Lucy away.

"Ah, *meine kleine Tochter, meine kleine Schönheit,*" he crooned, settling her in his lap. He slid one finger into her tiny fist, and poor Lucy could hardly encompass the thick digit, though she tried her hardest.

Olive smiled and slid under the covers, on her side, facing the two of them. At first, she had been repelled by her husband's giant size, by the heat of his body as they lay together in their marriage bed. On her wedding night, she had felt crushed under his heaving body, and when he had fallen into snoring unconsciousness afterward, one enormous arm thrown across her middle, she had wept so hard and so silently, the tears had rolled down her temples and wet her hair.

But she had grown used to him. They hadn't had a honeymoon, instead plunging right into their busy life above the new bakery in Brooklyn—this tremendous opportunity that could not be delayed—and he was so delighted with his good fortune in marrying her, so kind and attentive, so unexpectedly good-humored (sometimes he brought her to tears with his jokes), that eventually she hadn't minded his heavy, exuberant lovemaking, and his sleeping body had become like a steady and reassuring rock by her side, when she thought she might die inside her abyss of loss. When she told him she was pregnant, he had actually cried with joy.

And now here they were, a little family, nestled in their warm bed this frigid January morning. This was Olive's life, this was reality, and she would make the best of it. Lucy was making little cooing sounds now, looking up into her father's worshipful face in delight, and Olive reached over to tickle her tummy, and that was when it happened: Lucy's little baby lips curved into her very first smile.

"She smiles!" Hans exclaimed.

"She's smiling at *you*," said Olive, and in that moment, because he had made her daughter smile for the first time, Olive loved her husband.

Hans lifted Lucy up in the air, laughing, and Lucy's newborn smile grew even wider. Her lips parted, and for a fragile instant Olive thought she might laugh, too.

"Now, enough of that," Olive said. "She'll never go back to sleep."

"Ah, I am sorry." He lowered Lucy to his lap, clucking and soothing, and Olive thought she heard a familiar voice next to her ear: *He is a good father.*

"Yes, he is," she whispered.

"What's that?" asked Hans, turning to her.

Her husband looked better by lamplight than daylight, even though his face was creased with sleep. The haggard pieces of his face smoothed out, and his pale blue eyes somehow took on a winsome shape. Olive leaned down and kissed his cheek. "Nothing," she said. "Just that you're a wonderful father."

"I am a lucky one. And God willing, we have many more, *meine Frau.* You give me a fine son next, eh? To take the bakery when we are old."

Olive's cheeks warmed. She reached for Lucy and drew the baby back into her arms. "Well, I'll do my best, I suppose. Come now, little angel. Time for sleep."

By the time Lucy was settled in the wooden cradle next to the bed, Hans was back asleep, snoring softly, and the only one left awake was Olive. And she *was* awake now; she was wide-awake, alert to an almost painful sharpness, as restless as a field mouse. She sank into the chair before her dressing table and stared at her harried reflection in the plain wooden mirror, framed by the unadorned white plaster wall behind her. She hadn't had time to think about decorating. Their furniture was brown and simple and secondhand, the draperies hastily sewn and made over from her mother's old things. What a difference from her sumptuous surroundings a year ago, when she had lain with her lover beneath a beautiful wrought-iron skylight, and the rooms beneath her had been full of priceless furniture and exquisite art. When she had been immersed in rich and sinful love.

Where are you now, Harry?

Are you in some other woman's bed? Keeping warm, as I am?

She closed her eyes and pictured this: pictured Harry in bed with another girl, naked and entwined, his body moving, lavishing the same pleasure on this nameless rival that he had once lavished on Olive. The frenetic climax, the tranquil aftermath. And somehow it didn't hurt, this imagined scene, the way it once had. She was almost glad to think that Harry might have found some measure of fleeting joy; that he might, in fact, be finding joy at this exact instant. Harry was made for love; he was made for human happiness.

Olive glanced at the cradle, where Lucy lay fast asleep, her head turned to one side and her mouth slack. Already she was getting so big; she had looked lost in that same cradle a month ago, and now she filled it. Before long she would move into the small room next to theirs, the one Olive was readying as a nursery. One of Hans's sisters had given them a bassinet the other day, and Hans had spent last Sunday afternoon carefully sanding and repainting an ancient chest of drawers he had found at a shop nearby. In the wake of the financial panic last spring, people were losing their jobs and moving on. You could get a good bargain, if you knew where to look.

Olive leaned down and tucked Lucy's swaddling blanket a little more snugly around her. As she bent over, the ruby necklace came free from beneath her nightgown and swung, glittering, into the faint glow of the lamplight.

Olive sat back up and turned to the mirror. She hadn't taken the ruby necklace off, not ever, not even on her wedding day. Not even on her wedding night. She had felt it burn against her skin as she consummated her marriage with her new husband, and she had grasped the stone in her hand when, blinded by the pain of labor, she needed comfort. Now, she hardly noticed it was there. It had become a part of her, taken for granted the way she took her ears for granted.

But now a year had passed since Harry had first fastened the chain around her neck. A year had passed, and Olive was a different person, leading a wholly different life above a bakery in Brooklyn. There was no place for rubies above a shop, was there? There was no last, reckless hope that Harry would walk through the door one day and sweep her away, no hope that she would let him sweep her away in any case. She couldn't leave her husband now, because of Lucy.

And nothing in the world mattered more than Lucy.

Olive gazed at her reflection a moment longer: the ruby bright against the white hollow of her neck, her hair dark and tired on her forehead. No longer a girl, but a wife and mother. Already the tiny maternal lines had sprung into place at the corners of her eyes. She was going to live and die above a Brooklyn bakery instead of inside an Italian villa, and the Olive who had existed for a few precious moments inside the seventh-floor attic of the Pratt mansion was now only a memory, entombed in a few drawings that had not become a glorious mural, after all.

When she was ready, she lifted her arms and reached behind her neck.

The clasp was stiff, but she persevered, until at last the two ends came away in her hands. She opened the small wooden box on the dressing table that held her few pieces of jewelry, and she laid the necklace carefully inside.

When Lucy was older, Olive decided, she would give the ruby to her daughter. She would say it was a legacy from Olive's father, a man whom Lucy would never know.

And in a way, that was the truth.

Thirty

꧁꧂

JULY 1920

Lucy

"Why would you think Harry Pratt was your father?" Lucy looked at John in confusion. "I know you said your father changed his name, but . . ."

But you knew your father, she had almost said. John knew who his father had become; he didn't know who he had been.

Lucy felt like the Red Queen in *Alice's Adventures in Wonderland,* believing five impossible things before breakfast. Harry Pratt, whom she'd believed to be her father, wasn't. Her mother, whom she'd always believed was a lady, had been a servant in this house.

And John, who came from a thoroughly different world, a world away, might be Harry Pratt's son.

"This is his work. I would know it anywhere." Bemusedly, John looked at the sketch in his hands and then up at Lucy. "And they're all signed H. Pratt."

Lucy dropped the detective's report on the top of the Chinese cabinet. "So this is really your house."

"No," said John, shuffling the papers together. "My home is in Charleston. But this does explain why Prunella Pratt was selling my father's paintings."

Lucy looked at him in surprise. "She's your aunt. Do you realize? Prunella Pratt is your aunt."

Not hers. And for that she could be grateful. It meant her father, her warm, loving father, was hers. There was no shadow marring her love for him or his for her.

And if it meant she didn't belong to the contentious, quarreling Pratts, that was even better, no matter how much she might once have believed their world preferable to hers.

John rose gracefully to his feet, the sheaf of drawings in his hands. "No. My father ran away from all that—with reason, I'm guessing. And maybe part of that reason was Prunella."

Lucy bit her lip. "I think I can tell you the reason."

There is nothing for me here without you.

She took a step forward and then stopped, her attention arrested by the drawing John was holding. "That's my necklace. And my mother."

But it was her mother as Lucy had never seen her, never imagined she could look. Her long hair was free, falling down her bare back. Lucy's mother, always so carefully buttoned, boned, and stayed, was naked. Her nudity ought to have been jarring, but it was overshadowed by the expression on her face, an expression of transcendent joy.

"She was beautiful," said John quietly.

Lucy had never realized that before. Her mother was handsome, true, but she had so drawn into herself that it rendered her looks unremarkable, part of the background like a murky wallpaper.

"She was happy," Lucy murmured, and with it came a spark of anger. Why had her mother never looked like that for her?

Because all her happiness had left with Harry Pratt.

"When—" It took Lucy a moment to find her tongue. "When did your father go south?"

"He left New York in January of 1893," said John promptly. "That was part of family legend." His expression turned wry. "I just never imagined him leaving anything quite like this."

"He left because of my mother." Lucy's throat felt very dry. "I found a letter, in the wall. There's a hidey-hole, behind the bricks. He says he can't live here without her."

John set the drawings gently down on top of the cabinet. "Why did she leave him? I take it she did leave him."

"I don't know," said Lucy despairingly. "She never told me."

She wished, now, that they had had that sort of closeness, that she could have asked her mother. Not only asked, but listened, without judgment. At the time—no, Lucy could see why her mother had never told her. She had been too much her father's daughter; she would have been furious to know that her mother had betrayed her father, even in thought.

I'm ready to listen now.

But her mother wasn't there to tell.

"Well," said John, "I, for one, am grateful."

Lucy cast him a startled look. "That my mother broke your father's heart?"

John took Lucy's cold hands in his own. "Without that, I wouldn't be here. And neither would you."

Something about the way he looked at her made the color rise in her cheeks.

"Whatever they may have suffered, whatever wrongs they may have done each other, we're here now. All of this"—John's gesture encompassed the pile of sketches, the tattered chaise longue, the bright sunshine dappling the sheepskin rug—"it brought me to you. And you to me."

There was a dark power in his words, an unmistakable invitation that made Lucy's collar suddenly feel too tight, the fine linen of her blouse heavy against her heated skin.

This, she realized. This was what her mother had felt for Harry Pratt. This irresistible pull. The longing for skin on skin, here, in this quiet room, where the sounds of the city were dull and dim far below, alone in the dusty sunshine, rainbows sparkling around them, the room encasing them like a jewel box.

"What would they say to see us here?" Lucy's voice sounded rusty to her ears.

There was only a foot of space between them, so little space. All it would take would be one step, one movement.

"They would most likely tell us to use our time more wisely than they did," said John raggedly.

But he made no move toward her, just gazed and gazed, with a look of almost painful longing on his face.

"It's at times like this," he said softly, "that I wish I had inherited my father's talent. I would give anything to be able to draw you, there on the hearthrug, like that."

"Like this?" Feeling bold, Lucy undid one of the buttons on her blouse.

John drew in a deep, shuddering breath, his eyes riveted to her fingers on the button. "Just like that."

"And this?" Lucy felt a surge of power as she undid another button and watched him swallow hard, his hands clenched at his sides.

"Lucy." John spoke with difficulty. There were beads of sweat on his forehead. "Lucy, I don't—"

"Want to take advantage of me?"

John nodded, wordlessly.

It was strangely easy to take that step, to bridge the distance between them. Lucy cradled his chin in her hands, feeling the unfamiliar prickle of stubble against her palms, breathing in the smell of soap and leather, good clean smells, John smells.

"I love you," Lucy said quietly. "I never thought I'd say it, but it's true. I can't imagine loving anyone as I love you. I—"

Whatever else she might have said was lost, as, with a low sound deep in his throat, John's arms clamped tight around her, his lips closing over hers with a fervent passion that said more than words just how he felt.

"I love you," he whispered against her ear, her cheek, her jaw. "I love you, I love you."

The world spun dizzily around her, all time reduced to that small, square room, to the space between John's arms, to the feel of his lips on her neck, her breast, his hands in her hair, the muscles in his back moving beneath her palms as she wrenched his shirt free of his trousers, slid her hands up in the space beneath the fabric, skin to skin at last, marveling in the new sensations, the feel of him, the closeness of him. Hers. He was hers and she was his, forever and ever and ever. Lucy knew it as surely as she knew her name, knew the goodness of him, the rightness of what they were doing, a generation delayed.

Whatever her mother and Harry Pratt had lost, she and John had gained, and she would hold on to it, Lucy thought fiercely, digging her fingers into John's back, the pressure of his chest against hers driving the ruby pendant against her breast.

Her blouse fell from her shoulders, her skirt slithered to the floor, leaving only her slip, silky against her legs.

"Lucy," John breathed against her ear, and Lucy wrapped her arms around his neck, determined never to let him go.

Her hip bumped the Chinese chest and papers fluttered to the floor around them like so much confetti: Harry Pratt's letter; her mother with the ruby pendant and little else; the Pinkerton report, all meaningless now, just so much paper.

"Lucy. Lucy." It took Lucy a moment to realize that John's tone had changed. He pulled away from her, his breath coming hard. "Before we go any further—there's something you should know."

His hair was disarranged, his color high, his shirt half-undone, revealing a tanned chest covered with dark hair. He looked, thought Lucy giddily, like a man who had been thoroughly ravished.

"If it's the birds and the bees, Sissy Romich told me all about that in junior high." Lucy put a hand to his chest, feeling his muscles contract beneath her touch, tracing her way up until she could feel the beating of his heart. Daringly, she said, "I could use some help with the practical application, though. I haven't—that is—"

John touched a finger gently to her cheek. "I know," he said, and took a step back, away from her.

"But that doesn't matter. Why wait when—well, you know?" Lucy met his eyes frankly as she said it, even though she could feel herself blushing. Lucy Young, known as the girl who wouldn't. But with John, it felt right. Fumbling for the right words, Lucy rested her hands against his chest. "We're going to be together forever. What's a week more or less? If there are, well, um, consequences . . . well, it won't be that much time for people to count on their fingers."

John pressed his eyes shut, as though he were in pain. "There's something else you need to know—Lucy, when I asked you to come to Charleston with me—well, there's a complication."

His voice sounded so grim. Lucy froze, her hands on his chest. "A complication?"

"It doesn't change how I feel about you," John said quickly. "Or that I want us to be together. Married. Eventually."

"Eventually?" Lucy took a step back to see him better, but his dark face gave nothing away, nothing but a grim resignation that set alarm coursing through her. "Is it your mother? Your sister?"

John gave a brief, unhappy laugh. "I wish it were. No—it's my wife."

"Your wife." Lucy felt like she was falling, tumbling down, down,

down. She reached out a hand to steady herself, the corner of the Chinese chest digging into her palm. "Your *wife*? You're . . . you're married?"

Please, please, let her have misheard, have misunderstood . . .

But John Ravenel was hanging his dark head, his expression somewhere between misery and shame. "Just before the war. Annabelle was one of my sister's friends. We'd gone out a time or two, nothing serious. But when the war came—I was so terrified at the thought of marching off into the unknown that—well, we seized the day, as they say. When Annabelle realized she was expecting, there was only one thing to be done."

The ruby pendant was cold and heavy between Lucy's bare breasts. The flesh on her arms prickled. She felt suddenly cold, cold and very bare.

"You have a child?" Lucy wrapped her arms around herself, feeling as though she were caught in a nightmare, one of those nightmares where you find yourself naked in a public place, hearing horrible and impossible things.

Slowly, John nodded. "A son. Cooper. He's just turned two." Beneath the sheepishness, there was no mistaking the pride in his voice. "He's a bright boy. Smart as a whip. But Annabelle and I—you have to understand, there's nothing there. Just Cooper. We lead separate lives."

Lucy just stared at him, horror freezing her tongue. He was a married man. And he had never told her. He had let her go on believing he was free.

John was still speaking. "It will take a bit to get a divorce, but—"

"You wanted me to be your mistress. You were going to make me your mistress."

As her mother had been Harry Pratt's. From the floor, her mother's youthful face gazed up at her in silent reproach.

"Not my mistress," said John rapidly, reached for her. Lucy yanked away. "My wife. Just as soon as Annabelle agrees—"

"To a divorce." The word was ugly on Lucy's tongue. She was shaking, shaking uncontrollably. One thing to go knowingly into an affair, but it was quite another to be tricked into it, to be made the other woman against one's will. If she had known—Lucy shied away from the thought. She hadn't. John hadn't told her. "Do you really think I would take your son's mother away from him?"

John looked slightly sheepish. "It's not as though you'd be taking her away from him. And Annabelle—Annabelle has a flame of her own. She's been discreet about it, but I don't think she'd be pining over me."

Lucy just shook her head, feeling as though she'd been bludgeoned. "So two wrongs make it right?"

"No." His voice was so warm, so sincere, that Lucy could feel herself weakening, could feel herself leaning toward him, yearning for the comfort of his arms, the press of his lips against the top of her head. For a brief, treacherous moment, she allowed herself the indulgence of letting his hands close around her elbows, sliding up her arms, let herself sway toward him as he said, in his low, deep drawl, "We're right, Lucy. You know that as well as I."

Wordlessly, Lucy shook her head, morality warring with desire. She wanted to believe him, wanted him, more than she had wanted anything. "And what if your Annabelle doesn't want a divorce?"

There was a horrible silence. *But Annabelle does; she told me*; that was all he needed to say.

Her grandmother would disown her; her family would never see her; nice people wouldn't know them, but Lucy didn't care. She would have John and that was all that mattered. And she would do her very best to be the best stepmother to Cooper that anyone could possibly be. She could picture him, a little boy with John's eyes, as smart as a whip.

But John didn't say that. And what she saw in his face frightened her.

"She doesn't, does she?" Lucy whispered. "Your Annabelle—she doesn't want a divorce."

"We'll work something out," said John curtly.

"Work out what?" With jerky fingers, Lucy scooped up her blouse from the floor. "A miserable court battle? Your little boy torn to bits? I won't, John. I won't be party to that. You made your choice." Lucy choked on something between a laugh and a sob. "Till death do you part."

"But that was before I knew you." John reached for her, desperation in every line of his body.

Lucy dodged his hands, her eyes so blurred with tears she could hardly see. "You don't get a do-over." She yanked her blouse up over her shoulders, buttoning it with shaking fingers. "Go back to Charleston, John. Go back to your wife."

"Lucy." She heard his voice from behind her, through a fog. "Lucy, I can't live without you."

Lucy pressed a hand to her lips. Oh, God, what a time to discover each other.

"You're just going to have to, won't you?" she said, and yanked at the door, struggling with the warped boards, the stiff knob.

Ever the gentleman, John reached around her, opening the door for her. It was a good thing he was behind her. The gesture sent a fresh burst of pain through Lucy. Without turning her head, she said, unevenly, "Why didn't you tell me?"

She could see John's arm tremble slightly beneath the weight of the heavy door. Softly, he said, "Because I was afraid I might lose you."

She couldn't look at him. If she did, she would lose all control.

In a strangled voice, Lucy said, "I'm sure Matron will see you out." And then, before she could weaken, "Because I don't want to see you. Ever again."

She bolted down the stairs, her footsteps echoing on the same treads her mother had taken those many years ago, leaving John behind her, a dark shadow in the doorway of the forgotten room.

She made it down to her own room, her back against the flimsy panes of the door before she broke down entirely, sobbing with great, gulping, silent sobs, her entire body wracked with pain. John must have left, she supposed; she didn't know, she didn't want to know. It was easier to hate him, to blame him, when she was away from him. One look, one soft word, and she would be in his arms—and then what?

Maybe what John said was true—maybe there was no love lost between him and his Annabelle— but there was his son, Cooper. How could she do that to the boy? John might think it would all work out in the end, but Lucy knew better. And John—in the fatigue of despair, she knew the truth of it—John would come to hate her in the end, his love weakened by the constant stresses of their situation, being pulled between his lover and his son.

No. Unsteadily, Lucy pushed herself to her feet. Her skirt was crumpled; her hair disarranged. Mechanically, she dragged herself to the rickety chest that passed as a dressing table.

Day had turned to dusk without her being aware; she had to squint to see herself as she pulled a comb through her hair, shoving the ruby pendant away, deep down in the bottom of a drawer. A fresh blouse, a clean skirt. Lucy moved as stiffly as a carousel horse, bobbing up and down on its appointed track.

She knew where she needed to go, what she needed to do.

Her legs felt detached, rubbery, as they covered the few blocks from Stornaway House to the apartment building on Park Avenue. She waited as the doorman buzzed upstairs; time didn't seem to matter. She was wrapped in the cool calm of despair, impervious to the speculative glance of the elevator man as the wood-paneled box lifted her up to a private landing, a marble floor, a large Chinese vase serving as an umbrella stand.

Lucy barely noticed any of this. Her eyes were on the man standing in the doorway. He had shaved since the morning, although his eyes still bore the signs of sleeplessness. After John, he seemed somehow insubstantial, his fair hair too light, his eyes too pale, his body too thin.

But the smile that lit his eyes on seeing her was completely genuine. "Lucy! Dare I hope—that is, would you like to come in?"

Lucy felt a little of the hard knot in her chest begin to dissolve. Just a little.

"Philip," she said, and was surprised at how steady her voice sounded. "Philip, I will marry you."

"Well, then," said Philip Schuyler, the corners of his eyes crinkling as he beamed at her. "You'd better come in, then, hadn't you?"

❁

"Aren't you fancy?" Dottie leaned against the open doorway of the washroom, a pair of damp stockings draped over her arm.

"Thank you." Calmly, Lucy unpinned the veil that sat so smoothly over her dark hair. Valenciennes lace, masses of it. With only one day left before the wedding, it seemed sensible to practice pinning the veil, the mirror in the washroom much larger than the sliver of mirror in Lucy's attic room. "It belonged to my fiancé's stepmother."

Prunella Pratt Schuyler, with much sniffing and disapproval, had eventually lent her countenance—and veil—to the mésalliance between her stepson and his secretary. Not, Lucy was sure, out of any goodness of her heart, but because she had several large bills that needed settling. After a moment of hesitation, Philip had admitted that Prunella's goodwill had been bought with a large check.

"You don't mind wearing her veil, do you?" he'd asked. "She's a viper, but it's good lace."

That, Lucy reminded herself firmly, was part of what she respected about Philip. For all his veneer of flippant charm, when it came down to it, he was as honest as they came. He didn't lie to her.

"I s'pose I'll read about the wedding in the society pages, then?" said Dottie stridently.

Lucy folded the yards of lace neatly over her arm. "I suppose you will," she said equably, and stood, politely expectant, until the other woman reluctantly moved out of her way.

There were, Lucy thought wryly, benefits to being a Schuyler, or almost a Schuyler. Dottie might sneer, but she already treated Lucy differently; they all did.

Lucy's attic room felt empty, her belongings already in boxes, only her wedding dress left to hang in state behind the curtain on the wall, her nightdress lying across the foot of the bed. One more night in Stornaway House, and then she would be gone forever. There would be no more Lucy Young, only Mrs. Philip Schuyler.

Lucy shut the door of her room firmly behind her, shutting out the inquisitive stares of the other residents. She was their Cinderella story, and they were half-envious, half-excited. If Lucy could catch a Schuyler, then surely there was hope for them?

Lucy's lips twisted in a bitter smile. Did Cinderella wake up the next morning to find that the slipper pinched? She was trying hard to fit into Philip's world, to be a credit to him, but it wasn't always easy. She knew people talked and whispered, that everyone knew that she had been his secretary, that she had *stolen him away from Didi, my dear, yes, right under her nose, just like that!* They spied and whispered, and Lucy had to work twice as hard to maintain her serene smile, to pretend that she didn't care.

Panic gripped her. Could she really go through with this? If she loved Philip—

That was the rub, wasn't it? She did love him, just not in the right way. She loved Philip enough to know she didn't love him enough.

But she was too selfish and cowardly to let him go. Without him—

There was a knock on the door. Dottie again, her small eyes avidly scanning the room, feasting on the pile of boxes, hatboxes, dress boxes, the rich tissue paper and glossy boxes so incongruous in the attic room with its peeling paint and grimy windows. Lucy's new wardrobe, for her new life as Mrs. Philip Schuyler.

"This came for you." Dottie thrust the envelope into Lucy's hands. Her eyes rested on a pile of boxes. "Are those from—"

"Thank you." Lucy shut the door in her face, not caring how rude it must seem.

Lucy bolted the door behind her, the paper burning like a brand in her hands. The blurred postmark read CHARLESTON, S.C. The envelope tore as she opened it, her hands too quick, too eager. The letter was thick, pages of it, written in a large, loose hand. A sprawling, easygoing writing, just like his walk, his voice, his movements.

Dearest Lucy, the letter began. Lucy could practically feel John there, in the room with her, standing behind her, his voice warm in her ear.

> *I know I have no right to write you, but when I saw the announcement of your engagement I knew that I couldn't remain silent any longer . . .*

She ought to tear it up, but she hadn't the strength for it; she gulped down the words, greedy for them, dizzy with them.

> *. . . not too late. We can still be together. . . . Love like this doesn't come along more than once in a lifetime.*
>
> *I love you, Lucy. Always.*
>
> *Do you want to make the same mistake our parents made and live the rest of your life living a lie, knowing that love was there, in our grasp, and we threw it away?*

Nights at the opera with Philip, smiling, pretending. Endless dinner parties. Always a little on her guard, even with her own fiancé. Trying, so hard, to pretend to be in love.

Nights with John, curled up together, easy together, never having to try, speaking with touch as well as words, that effortless sense of homecoming, of never having to pretend, of being just what she was, because what she was would always be enough for him.

Philip—Philip would recover, thought Lucy wildly, clinging to the sheets of John's letter, Prunella's veil crumpled, forgotten, on the floor. There would be other women. He was so urbane, so charming. He thought he wanted Lucy; he called her his talisman, his touchstone, but it was nonsense, really. He could find someone from his own world, someone who would adore him as he deserved to be adored.

Train tickets . . . How far to Charleston? When she got there, a hotel, she supposed. John hadn't said anything about where she would stay.

He hadn't said anything about anything.

Lucy fell back to earth with a thump. Slowly, she sat down on the bed and scanned the letter again, looking for the practicalities, the bread and butter of where and how they were to live. There was nothing about a divorce. Nothing about Annabelle. Words of love, beautiful, yes, but utterly insubstantial, like dining on meringues and champagne and rising from the table with a headache and an aching stomach from eating sugar and air.

Come to me, be with me, live with me, love me. Yes, yes, all that, but how?

Lucy pressed her palms to her aching eyes, loving John and hating him all at the same time. Didn't he know that the knight was supposed to ride up and sweep the princess away, not leave her to make her own way out of the castle? The dragons were still there, unslain. Annabelle, Cooper, John's mother, his sister—who was Annabelle's friend.

And then there was Philip. He'd defied his own people for her—whether she had wanted him to or not, thought Lucy shrewishly, and then chided herself for it. She'd run to Philip, had used him as a shield. She was as guilty as he. And, having used him as a shield, she could hardly abandon him now, leave him at the altar to be whispered at by all those carping society matrons, those twittering friends of Didi who would be only too delighted to see him get his comeuppance for daring to choose a secretary over one of their own.

Slowly, Lucy shuffled the pages of the letter back together. Just the touch of the paper felt like a forbidden indulgence, this paper that had touched John's hands and now touched her own, a thin thread tying her to him.

For a moment, Lucy's hands tightened on the pages. She wanted him still, loved him still.

But the cost was too high.

Do you want to make the same mistake our parents made . . . ?

Lucy waited until the sounds of activity had faded from the hallway, everyone tucked away for the night. In the darkness, she felt her way down the hall to the abandoned staircase. It felt different at night, narrower, steeper. The stairs seemed to stretch on forever, the door, without John's strong hand, stuck before releasing with an audible creak.

Moonlight poured through the skylight, turning the studio ebony and silver. There. There John had kissed her. There. There John had told her about his wife.

He must have tidied after she left. The sketches were gone from the floor, the Chinese cabinet closed, the bricks in their place above the mantel.

She half expected the mechanism to fail, but it didn't. When she pushed on the knight's shield, the bricks of the wall swung out as easily and soundlessly as though they had been waiting for her. Inside, she could see the sad remains of her mother's affair with Harry Pratt: the detective's report, his letter.

Before she could think better of it, Lucy thrust John's letter on top of the pile.

"I'm sorry, Mama," she murmured to the empty room. "Sometimes it just doesn't work out, does it?"

Moonlight glinted off the knight's shield, just as it had, in those long-ago evenings, off the mural in her room.

There are consolations. From very far away, Lucy heard her mother's voice, felt her arm around her, sitting with her, late at night, in a small bed a borough away. *Life doesn't always turn out the way you expect, but there are consolations.*

For a moment, Lucy thought she smelled lavender, heard the crinkle of her mother's long, starched skirts, but then it was gone, and the room, once again, was still, its secrets hidden beneath a silver wash of moonlight.

"Good-bye," Lucy said to no one in particular, and, closing the door, went downstairs to face the dawn.

Thirty-one

SEPTEMBER 1944

Kate

"Kate?"

I looked up when I realized that my name had been called more than twice. I blinked, trying to remember where I was and why, and with whom. Not that any of it mattered. Not that anything seemed to matter anymore.

"Kate, would you like another cigarette?"

I blinked again, trying to remember Dr. Greeley's first name, but couldn't. He'd probably be flattered if I called him Doctor even outside the hospital, so I didn't try very hard to recall it. I tapped my fingers on the top of his desk, then took a final drag on my cigarette before stabbing it out in a glass ashtray. "No. Thank you. I should be getting back to my patients."

His hand slid up my arm and I didn't move away. Not that I had any intention of following through with any of his innuendoes, but I simply didn't have the energy to push his hand off me any more than I had the energy to eat or return Margie's calls.

Dr. Greeley leaned toward me with what could only be described as a leer. "It must be nice to have your room all to yourself again."

I thought of the barren room at the top of the stairs, stripped again of its two extra beds and all of the extraneous furniture that had once given it a cozy atmosphere, and suppressed a shudder. Looking straight into his eyes, I said, "I sleep with a surgical knife and I know how to use it."

His hand left my arm, allowing me to step away. His lips pressed together. "I'm a patient man, Kate, but even my patience has its limits."

I opened the office door as I tried to think of something to say, and found myself staring into Nurse Hathaway's raised hand, her knuckles prepared to knock. She smiled brightly. "I was hoping to find you in here. Nobody seemed to know where you'd gone."

I smiled back at her, using my eyes to thank her for rescuing me again. Ever since Cooper had left, she'd been keeping a protective watch over me, which was a good thing since I seemed to be a lost wanderer in the dark, running into walls, unsure of which direction to move. The only thing I could rely on was my medical training, my confidence as a doctor, and my ability to heal and nurture patients. It consoled me, almost reassured me that I'd made the right decision in allowing Cooper out of my life. Almost.

"Nurse Hathaway," I said. "I was just leaving."

"Perfect timing, then. You have a visitor."

I felt something stir in my chest, and she must have seen something in my eyes, because her smile dimmed. "It's Mrs. Prunella Schuyler. She says she's a relative."

I looked at her in surprise. "She's here? At the hospital?"

"Yes. I brought her to the patient consulting office to give you some privacy if you wanted to chat. Should I bring up some tea?"

"That would be lovely . . ."

"She doesn't have time," Dr. Greeley said, looking at his watch. "She has rounds in twenty minutes."

"Thanks for the reminder," I said, turning my back on him as I exited his office and walked down the hall to the same stained glass door of the office in which I'd sat when Margie had come to visit and tell me what she'd learned at the library about the Pratt family.

"She brought her maid," Nurse Hathaway whispered. "So you won't be alone with her."

I nodded my thanks, then pushed open the office door after a brief knock.

Mona had left off her white apron and mobcap, but she was wearing the same black dress of shiny and worn material. She smiled and stood as I entered.

"I told the missus that it would be the polite thing to do to give ye some advance warning, but she'd have none of it."

Prunella scowled at the maid as she plucked off her gloves, finger by finger. "That is enough, Mona. You are excused for the next fifteen minutes."

I held the door open to let the maid pass. "Go downstairs to the lobby. The nurse can show you where the coffee is, and there are some chairs down there, too."

Prunella was dressed all in black, a crow against the crimson red upholstery of the small couch. A fox stole stared at me from its perch around her shoulders. She pressed a starched white linen handkerchief against her nose. "It is an abomination to see all these *people* in my father's mansion. He must be rolling over in his grave." She said the word *people* with the same inflection I imagined she'd use for the word *rubbish*.

"This is a pleasant surprise, Aunt Prunella. I didn't expect to see you again so soon."

She sniffed. "I grew tired of waiting for you to visit me. I might be dead before you made time for me, so I am here instead. And I have something I need to tell you."

"And I, you," I said. "But first would you like a tour around the house to show you how it's all changed since you lived here?"

"Good heavens, no. It is quite enough to simply *smell* the changes from this room."

Without waiting for her to grant me permission, I sat down on a chair opposite. "Aunt Prunella, were you aware of a hidden compartment behind a brick in the attic fireplace?"

Her eyes widened, but she shook her head. "No. Harry used the attic as his studio and never allowed me up there, and certainly never showed me any secret compartment. Of course, I *did* manage to sneak up there from time to time to see what he was up to and saw all of his canvases stacked along the wall. I inherited them, you know. Only because they weren't considered worth anything to auction." She said this last softly, as if musing to herself. Glancing back at me, she said, "Why do you ask?"

"I found some letters hidden there, presumably by Harry. And a letter to my mother, Lucy. Olive's daughter." I looked at her closely, but she never flinched—either from good breeding or because she already knew. *And an engagement ring,* I almost added but didn't. The pain and loss were still too fresh and real to me. I'd tell her one day. Just not today.

"Was there anything in there to tell us what happened to Harry?" she asked, leaning slightly forward.

"Not exactly, but a patient here, Captain Cooper Ravenel, and I stumbled upon some information quite by accident. We discovered that after Olive married my grandfather, Harry changed his name to Augustus Ravenel."

Her eyes brightened with recognition. "Augustus. My father's middle name was August, you know. And my brother—the eldest of the twins—was called Gus."

"What happened to him?" I asked, immediately wishing I hadn't when I saw the color slip from her face.

"He died. In a barroom brawl." She shook her head in distaste. "He died right before Harry left. It was all quite . . . unsavory." She pressed her handkerchief to her lips as if wiping away a stain. "Do you know what happened after Harry left New York?"

"Just the basics, really. After a stint in Cuba, he moved to Charleston, where he became a renowned painter. He even had a few exhibits here in New York that my mother brought me to as a child, although at the time I never realized that Harry and Augustus were the same man." I paused, watching as Prunella clenched and unclenched her fist on top of her cane. "Captain Ravenel is Harry's grandson."

Her eyes glowed with a dim light. "Is Captain Ravenel still here? I would like to meet him. The last remaining Pratt."

I swallowed, pressing back the tears that threatened every time I thought of him. "No. He was discharged last month and went back home to Charleston. He's getting married in November."

She watched me closely, as if I'd given too much away, then relaxed back against the sofa, her face softening. "So Harry married and had children after all."

"Yes. But he never forgot about Olive, nor she him." I pulled the ruby necklace from inside my blouse. "That's how I came to own this. And the small miniature that Harry painted of Olive wearing this necklace was passed down from Harry to his son John and then to Cooper. Cooper showed it to me."

Prunella examined the necklace carefully, then raised her eyes to meet mine. "You look so much like her, you know. And so did your mother. I saw it when Philip brought Lucy to meet me that first time. That's how I knew that Olive hadn't disappeared, too."

She was silent for a moment as I digested her words, understanding that she'd known all along the connection between Lucy and Olive. She continued. "I never could determine how your mother managed to snare my stepson, although I was quite sure it had been deliberate. But

I could never say anything because there was you. You were like the daughter I never had, so sweet and full of joy. I know I never showed it, but I always looked forward to your visits. It was the one bright spot in my rather bleak life." Her lips curled up in a semblance of a smile.

"Olive didn't steal the necklace, did she?"

She looked down at her hands, well tended and soft. "No. I was upset. Vengeful, I suppose. You see, I imagined myself in love with her father."

Her gaze bore into me, but I didn't flinch. I knew she would tell me more if I showed her that I wasn't appalled by her confession. That I wasn't there to judge her.

"But he rejected me for another. Not that I could blame him. I was a spoiled girl, who knew nothing of love. Of course he rejected me. But I was angry, unused to anybody telling me no. And when I saw that necklace on Olive, I couldn't believe that my brother would have given a maid, a *maid*, something so valuable, regardless of where it had come from."

"What do you mean?"

"You don't know that part of the story?"

I shook my head.

"I might not have won the affections of Olive's father, but someone else had. You see, the necklace had been a gift from my mother's lover." She paused. "Olive's father."

I stood, too stunned to continue sitting still. "But why did Olive come to the mansion to work? I assumed she was educated, being an architect's daughter. Surely she had other options than being a maid in the mansion her father had designed and working for his lover."

"Revenge, dear. Simple revenge. She wanted to ruin my father. But I was onto her and her plans. She would never be one of us. Her father was an elevated tradesman, after all."

I began pacing the small room, wishing Cooper were here so I could tell him everything. But he wasn't. He was back in Charleston, planning for his wedding to Caroline in less than two months.

"So you figured out who Olive was and you must have threatened to tell Harry if she didn't leave. That's what you meant when you told me that you wished to see Harry again, to apologize for something awful you'd done to him."

All my energy disappeared as I thought of how such a tiny thing as a lie could be like a pebble tossed in a pond, its ripples felt for decades. I collapsed back into my chair. "Is that what you came to tell me?"

She raised a regal eyebrow. "Partly. You will find, dear Kate, that as one gets older one tends to want to make amends. To fix old wrongs. Admitting my part in the Harry and Olive saga was just one of my sins for which I needed to atone. I am sure I will think of more. But mostly I wanted to pass on a piece of advice I wish somebody had told me when I was your age. It would have saved me quite a bit of heartache. Not that I would have listened, of course. But you're a woman, Kate. Much smarter than I was. Which is why I have hopes that you will take my advice to heart."

To my surprise, she leaned her cane against the wall and reached out for my hands. I hesitated for just a moment before placing mine in hers. Her skin was cool and papery, as brittle as an autumn leaf. "Follow your heart. If you put your heart second and always follow your head, you will end up like me. Disappointment and regret are very lonely bedfellows."

There was a brief tap on the door and Mona popped her head through the opening. "Are we ready yet, Mrs. Schuyler?"

"You took your time, didn't you? I hope you got your fill of coffee and cake, because you're not getting any when we get home."

Mona's smile never dimmed as she picked up the cane and then helped Prunella stand.

I kissed Prunella's cheek. "Thank you," I said. "For everything."

"Yes, well, next time do not make me come all the way out here to see you. You know where I live. And when your captain comes to visit you again, I want to meet him."

I opened my mouth to protest, but she and Mona were already bustling out of the room and toward the elevator. I said good-bye and watched them leave, Prunella staring straight ahead as if she were still the princess of the mansion.

I sat down in my chair again and stared at the wall for a long moment. *Disappointment and regret.* Could it be that in my desperation to avoid both I'd inadvertently embraced them, heading down the same path as Olive and Lucy? And Prunella. Had nobody learned anything?

I closed my eyes as my world shifted beneath my feet and something that felt like hope fluttered in my chest. Standing, I made my way out of the office, my feet confident of their direction for the first time in weeks.

❖

SEPTEMBER 1944

The reception desk nurse scowled at me as she held her hand over the telephone's receiver. "Dr. Schuyler, may I remind you that this phone is not intended for personal use?"

I resisted the urge to grab it from her and instead smiled. "I know, and I do apologize. But it must be an emergency for my friend to be calling me."

"Let's just hope it is. I would hate to report you to Dr. Greeley."

"Yes, let's hope it's an emergency." My sarcasm went unappreciated as the nurse reluctantly handed me the phone, mouthing the words, "Be quick."

"Margie? Is everything all right?"

"Everything's fine. But we're absolutely swamped here and two coworkers are out sick, so I'm it. I can't meet you at the park today for lunch."

I felt more disappointed than I should. Margie had been my champion over the last month. She'd helped me write the first letter to Cooper, telling him I'd had a change of heart. She'd come up with the idea of using hospital stationery so if anyone else found the letter they would think it was official hospital business and not be tempted to open it. I'd written three letters, each one more revealing than the last, each addressed to his family home on Tradd Street where he'd grown up and where he now lived with his widowed mother.

Each week without a reply had left me more and more despondent, and I'd come to rely on Margie to keep my hopes and spirits up. But doubt had begun to splinter my initial resolution, each day seeming to dawn darker and darker. *Disappointment and regret.* At first Prunella's words had been my motivation, but as the weeks dragged on, I began to see them as my destiny.

I tried to put a smile in my voice. "I understand. Maybe Friday?"

"We'll see. But I still think you should go today. It's beautiful outside and the leaves in the park have started to turn. Sit on our usual bench and pretend I'm there. I promise you'll feel better once you get some sun on your face."

"Sure," I said. "Maybe I will."

"Do it," Margie commanded. "Let me play doctor for once."

The nurse tapped her watch with exaggerated movements. "I've got to go. I'll call you . . ." The phone was ripped from my grasp before I could say good-bye.

I retrieved my lunch pail and pulled on a sweater before leaving the building. Margie was right. The weather had shed the heat and humidity of summer, allowing the first hint of autumn in the air, a crisp bite to the breeze that drifted from the park as I crossed Fifth Avenue. I felt marginally better when I found our bench empty and sat down, turning my face toward the sun. For a moment I could even forget the heaviness in my heart. But only for a moment.

From the corner of my eye I saw somebody approaching but didn't turn my head, expecting them to pass by. I closed my eyes, enjoying the warmth of the sun, and didn't open them even as I felt someone sit down on the other end of the bench. I'd grown up in the city and had learned to keep to myself, to not acknowledge strangers, even one sitting on the same bench.

I opened my eyes and focused on undoing the clasps on my lunch pail.

"Growin' up in South Carolina I was told that Yankee women all fell from the ugly tree, hitting each branch on their way down. But then I met you and learned that couldn't possibly be true."

I stared hard at the smooth metal of my pail, wondering if I was dreaming and if I looked at the opposite end of the bench there would be no one there. But there was only one way to find out.

Slowly, I turned my head. Cooper, in civilian clothes, sat back on the bench, one long leg casually crossed over the other, an elbow propped on the bench's back. His fedora was pushed back on his forehead so I could see his eyes. "Hello, Kate."

Forgetting my lunch pail on my lap, I stood, barely noticing the clatter it made as it hit the ground, my apple rolling to my feet. He stood, too, leaving his fedora on the bench so I could see his dark hair, longer now, curling slightly around his ears.

"What are you doing here?" I didn't like the way that sounded, but I couldn't think of anything else to say.

He grinned. "Margie told me you'd be here."

I shook my head. "That's not what I meant. Why are you here, in New York?"

"Because I read your letters. All of them. I would have come sooner but I had business to take care of."

"Caroline?"

He nodded. "It's over. It was over even before I received your first letter. I told her I couldn't marry another woman knowing I loved someone else. Even if that woman said she didn't love me and I thought I'd never see her again."

He paused, allowing his words to sink in.

"I allowed her to end the engagement to save her dignity. She's already seeing someone else."

I took a step forward. "There's so much I need to tell you."

"Not yet," he said, crossing the space between us and wrapping me in his arms. His kiss was new yet familiar, tender yet searching, and as my fingers threaded their way through his hair it was as if the past ceased to exist, the present shimmering at our feet along with the fallen leaves.

He held my head gently in his hands and pressed his forehead against mine. "I love you, Kate. I don't want to live my life without you. We can live here or in Charleston or in Timbuktu; I don't care as long as we're together. You can be a doctor and I can own an art gallery anywhere. Just tell me that you want to be with me."

"Yes," I whispered. Then, "Yes!" I shouted. "I love you, Cooper Ravenel, and I will follow you to the ends of the earth."

An elderly couple walked by, their hands clutched between them. The old man winked as they passed, giving his wife a peck on the cheek.

Cooper's eyes became serious as he studied my face. "I figured out why our parents didn't marry. There was something about that letter from my father to your mother that kept bothering me until I finally realized what it was. The date on the letter. He wrote it in 1920."

I raised my eyebrows, wondering at the significance.

"My parents were married in 1917, and I was born in 1918."

I felt my lips form a perfect *O*. "Well, that certainly explains . . ."

My words stilled in my mouth as Cooper took my left hand and slipped a ring on my third finger. It was the ring bought for my grandmother, Olive, by the love of her life, and then forgotten for more than fifty years, hidden in the dark where no light could reach the heart of the brilliant stone and make it shine. It glittered on my finger in the bright sunshine, filled with promises and possibilities.

Cooper kissed me again as a strong breeze rustled the leaves on the path, tumbling them around our feet and sending more raining down on us from the trees above. I looked up at the scuttling clouds in the autumn sky. "Do you believe in fate?" I asked.

"Maybe. Or perhaps the eternal persistence of love." His lips smiled against mine. "Or maybe it was just Margie. She's very persuasive."

I laughed, then stood on my toes to kiss him this time, my grateful arms holding him tightly. The sounds of the city swarmed around us as life marched on in this corner of the world, where glorious old mansions peered down into the streets, where nothing and everything changed, and where star-crossed lovers had finally found each other in a house on Sixty-ninth Street, in a forgotten room at the top of the stairs.

Epilogue

Harry

To his surprise, the room looked exactly the same. Maybe the auction company hadn't bothered with the worthless scraps of furniture up here; maybe nobody had even ventured up the stairs. There was the Chinese cabinet, probably still filled with his drawings; there was the easel, tilting slightly to one side. The battered chaise longue, still covered in disreputable old velvet; the sheepskin rug, right there in the middle of the floor, scattered with cushions . . . well, he looked away from that. There was only so much nostalgia a fellow could take.

The thing was, he hadn't planned to come up here at all. He was going to let it all lie. If the newspapers were telling the truth, his father had gotten no more than he deserved, losing his fortune after the usual kind of Wall Street skullduggery, in which you tried to cover up your losses and ended up making them worse, dragging down a few thousand innocent middle-class shareholders and a bank or two along with you. Prunella? She could take care of herself, no doubt about that. Gus—poor bastard—Gus was dead.

And Olive was still married; there was nothing an honorable man—and Harry liked to think he had a streak of decency left, despite everything—nothing he could do about that.

She had a daughter. The Pinkerton man had sent him a note last month. The little girl had been born right above the bakery on the day after Thanksgiving, and they had named her Lucy. Harry had read the note and said a prayer for mother and daughter, and he had tossed the paper into the kitchen fire and watched it burn. He had closed his eyes and pictured Olive holding a baby girl to her breast, a baby girl who wasn't his, and his heart had hurt so much, he thought maybe he was having an attack. *Somebody save me.* Maria had come in and asked him what in the name of the holy blessed Virgin he thought he was doing, staring into the fire like that. *Nothing*, he said. She said was there anything she could do, and he didn't say another word, just turned around and took her to bed right then and there, kept her there most of the afternoon, and on Christmas Day she told him she was pregnant, señor. *Feliz Navidad.*

He was on the boat the next morning, heading to Miami and the train for New York.

Now here he was, and nothing had changed, and everything had changed. Nobody lived here anymore; nobody lay with somebody on that sheepskin rug and went to heaven. Nobody danced around the ballroom in silks and jewels; nobody sketched anybody's beautiful pale breasts in the lamplight. Nobody lived and loved and wept. Just furniture, and memories.

God, the memories.

He'd thought it would hurt, coming up here like this, looking around the place and thinking, inevitably, of everything that had happened. And sure enough, the memories had crashed down on him the way the waves hit the beach before a hurricane, one after the other, each one merging foamily into the next. Meeting Olive on the stairs, under the moon. Sketching Olive. Olive in her black dress and white pinafore apron, ducking around a corner. Olive lying like a nymph on the old velvet cushions, Harry kneeling above her, Olive lifting her arms to draw him down, to wrap her legs around him and throw back her head as if she couldn't take any more, and then she did.

Olive's extraordinary face, her huge doe eyes, her spirit and her longing and her striving.

Olive gone.

That terrible morning. Waking up alone, hearing the commotion. Poor stupid Gus, carried half-dead into his room. Looking for Olive, desperate for Olive, more and more desperate. Her room tidy, her trunk gone. *Looks like she's done a flyer,* said the cook, shaking her head, and the housekeeper ran for the cabinet to count the silver.

Painting frantically, waiting for news, because there was nothing else he could do but paint. *Paint,* damn it. Pour his heart out onto that damned wall. And when they found her—this was how he imagined that moment, when she returned to him—he wouldn't say a word of recrimination, not a hint of reproach for breaking his heart. He would take her in his arms and show her the mural he'd made while she was gone. This is for you, Olive. This *is* you, Olive.

This is how much I love you, Olive Van Alan, daughter of my father's architect, the man who used to indulge my interest in drawing by showing me how to draft, and once told me about his brilliant daughter named Olive, the light of his life. Only you wouldn't trust me enough to tell me who you were. I waited and waited, because I wanted you to trust me enough. But you never did.

You ran off instead, and married the first man you met.

Hans Jungmann.

Harry patted his chest, reached into his jacket pocket, and produced that first report the Pinkerton agency had sent him. Jungmann's photograph lay inside. He'd looked at it only once, but it wasn't a face he could forget. Thick, round, smiling idiot head. Shoulders like an ox. Belly like Santa Claus. On the night of the tenth of January, a week and a half after Olive had risen from Harry's bed—well, such as it was— she'd let this fat German bastard roll on top of her and make her his wife. After a little practice—Jungmann looked like the type who needed a little practice—they'd made a baby together.

That single blurred photograph had sent Harry flying down to Cuba and into the arms of so many women he couldn't actually remember them all, until he tired of promiscuity and settled into a kind of habit with beautiful Maria, who was kinder and more faithful than the rest, and also a very good cook. And now they had made a baby, too. *Estoy embarazada, señor.* Merry Christmas, Harry, you're going to be a father.

The old rush-seated chair still rested in its place near the easel. Harry sank down and leaned his forearms on his knees, staring at the folded letter in his hands. It was almost midnight now, and the year would be over. This unexpected year, that had turned out so vitally different from the one he had imagined, as he lay in Olive's arms twelve months ago and drifted into a happy sleep. They were supposed to go to Italy, they were supposed to share a run-down set of rooms in Florence or a shabby little villa in Fiesole, and this baby that Olive held to her breast was supposed to be his. He had actually bought the ring. He had planned it all out. He had meant to ask her to marry him just as the sun rose on the first day of the New Year. What a romantic fellow, the old Harry Pratt.

And this dream, it had been so close! A hairsbreadth away, a few minutes on a clock, an Olive who was perhaps a little less noble, or a little more sleepy, and he would be the father of Olive's child instead of Maria's.

Did Olive think about this, too? Was she awake right now, as he was, in some room above some bakery in Brooklyn? He closed his eyes, and he thought he could almost see her, sitting in a chair with a baby in her arms, and her fat German bastard husband snoring contentedly in the bed behind her.

Except that, for some reason, in this moment, sitting in this room stuffed with memories, while the same eternal moon poured through the skylight to pool on the floor before him, he felt no rancor toward this man. For the first time, he felt no resentment for Hans Jungmann, or for the baby he had made with Olive, the girl who should have been Harry's daughter. His chest still hurt, but it was a warm kind of ache, and as he pictured the baby's tiny face, and Olive's exhausted arms, the ache turned into something else, something fulsome and tender and unending. Forgiveness. Love. The inexplicable certainty that, in a way, this child *did* belong to him. That she and Olive belonged to him, always, carried about in some chamber of his heart that would never close.

Harry opened his eyes. The familiar room assembled again before him. What had happened here was gone, and he couldn't have it back. Maybe he'd just been lucky to have it at all, even for a few weeks.

He turned his head to the wall that contained the fireplace. There was no fire, of course, but the ashes remained in a small and tired heap, hardened by the dampness of a year's neglect. His gaze rose to the mantel, and to the bricks above it.

During that first frantic week of 1893, he had slid the brick out of its place every day, sometimes twice a day, sometimes three times, hoping to find some message there from Olive. But the space remained empty and hopeless, and on that last day, when he had gathered up his paints and drawings, he hadn't even bothered to look. Too mad at her. Too mad at himself. Too mad at God.

Harry rose from his chair and walked toward the mantel. The brick slid out easily in his hand, just as it always had. A few motes of dust and mortar floated out into the air. He stuck his fingers inside and felt something hard and ridged against his fingertips.

For a moment, he closed his eyes and let his hand rest where it was.

The way you might savor a rare glass of wine before taking the first sip, because you didn't want to rush these things. He'd learned that much from Olive, anyway. You didn't want to rush something that happened only once, and was gone.

He drew the object out.

She had wrapped it in a square of old velvet. Harry stuck the envelope under his arm and unfurled the ends, one by one, taking his time. A small folded note lay on top. He opened that first. His fingers shook a little.

Take this, in remembrance of one who will always love you.

And his eyes filled with tears, damn it, so that when he looked down at the miniature itself, he couldn't even see her. Couldn't see the rare and perfect details of her face, the expression in her eyes. But he didn't need to. He knew every brushstroke. He'd painted her himself, exactly as he wanted to remember her. Almost as if he knew he would need it one day.

Through the glass of the doors—or maybe it was the skylight—came a faint roar of delight. *Dong, dong,* sang the bell of a distant church spire. Fashionable St. James', probably, where his sister had married her prey, that tall blond man with the nice kid who always tagged along, hoping someone might give a damn.

Eighteen ninety-four. Time to move on.

Harry draped the velvet square back over the miniature and the folded note, and he placed them carefully into his inside jacket pocket. In the cavity above the mantel, he placed the Pinkerton report, and then, after an instant's hesitation, the scribbled notes he'd written to Olive but never sent. Maybe she would stop by one day and find them. You never knew.

He placed his two hands on the mantel and stood there a moment, contemplating the three terra-cotta squares—the crimson figure of Saint George, sword raised in triumph to the sky—until he couldn't stand it anymore and turned to the corner of the room, a few yards away.

He'd meant to throw it in the fireplace, but his arm had been more forgiving—or more sensible—than his furious head, and the little box had fallen in among the canvases stacked to the right, well away from the danger of the coals. At the time, he had thought about going to retrieve it, but instead he had gathered up his supplies and left the thing where it fell.

Now, as he moved the wooden frames aside, he thought it would be a miracle if the box was still there. He'd spent far more than he should, for a man planning to support a wife and mother-in-law abroad, and how could a small fortune like that remain unmolested, no matter how obscure its location?

But there it was, the little square box that had once contained all his earthly ambitions, wedged between a blank canvas and the plaster wall. He bent down and picked it up and rotated it between his fingers. The velvet was still soft and new.

He didn't open it. He didn't think he could. He carried it to the fireplace and reached inside the cavity below Saint George, until his fingertips brushed against the wall, and he left the box there. At the very back, so you couldn't just see it there. You had to hunt for it. You had to want it badly.

He replaced the brick, which went in a little more stiffly than it came out, and turned to look over the room one last time.

In his haste, he hadn't taken everything. He'd left all his sketches of Olive in the Chinese cabinet, and all of his old painted canvases. Some of his paints and charcoals, too. Well, let them stay. Maybe the new owner would have some use for them.

He walked briskly to the door and hurried down the stairs, refusing to linger over the place where he had seen Olive's face for the first time, or that heavenly spot where he'd taken her against the wall because he, in the impatient lust of new love, couldn't possibly wait another second, and she—equally eager—had just about swallowed him up with her passion. (He remembered resting against her afterward, listening to the beat of her heart, taking her breath into his lungs, and thinking that he was the luckiest man in the world, that you couldn't connect with a human being any more perfectly than that. And sure enough, he'd been right.)

When he came to the fifth-floor landing, he paused.

He had finished the mural in the middle of the night, the day before he'd received the letter from the Pinkerton agency, and he hadn't looked at it since. In fact, he had very nearly taken a bucket of turpentine and erased those naïve and idealistic images from the face of the earth. He had been ashamed of them, ashamed of his own quixotic romanticism, his schoolboy illusions. And what he drew and painted in Cuba bore no resemblance to medieval allegory; he was ruthless now in his realism, unflinching, hard, clear-eyed, a different man. He wanted to show the truth.

But a year had passed, and now he was curious. Had they kept the mural in place, or had somebody painted it over? And if the mural was gone, then was the old Harry gone, too? Was his past erased, and only the present remained?

If this child of his—this new life he had created with Maria in a paroxysm of grieved longing for another woman, and another life—if this child came looking one day for his father's beginnings, would he find nothing at all?

Harry put his hand on the door handle and pushed it open.

He'd forgotten how beautiful it was, this magnificent column of space, soaring upward to the glass dome. Van Alan had shown him the drawings once, while it was all under construction, and the reality was even more breathtaking than he had imagined. The moonlight streamed downward, filling the air with silver, just enough light to see the steps and descend, foot by foot, to the third floor.

The mural was still there, as fresh as the day he had painted it, and smelling familiarly of that peculiar mixture of oil and plaster. He drew a sigh of relief, as if he'd just found proof that he was still alive. For some time he stood there, contemplating the lines, admiring one figure and criticizing another: the use of color, the clever way he'd refracted the light on the dragon's scales, creating a sense of otherworldly luminescence— well, that was a nice touch, at least. His signature, at the bottom: H. Pratt. God, what a boy he'd been, so proud of this pretty thing he'd created.

The light began to fade as the moon moved overhead. Harry ran his finger over Saint George, eternally poised on the brink of murder, and wondered if, one day, his own child would stand here and see what his father had once created. The man his father once was. And he would wonder, wouldn't he, what path had led Harry Pratt from this idealistic dreamworld on Sixty-ninth Street to Cuba, and Maria, and a life he had never expected to live.

After a while, he turned and went back up the stairs, retracing his path to the seventh floor and the room that had lain forgotten for a year, steeping in dust and memories. He collected his remaining paints, his smock, a couple of old brushes that would have to do.

And he went back downstairs and started to work.